I0708969

Whisper of Light

A Novel By
Jennifer DeLucy

OMNIFIC PUBLISHING

DALLAS

Omnific Publishing
P.O. Box 793871, Dallas, TX 75379
www.omnificpublishing.com

First Omnific eBook edition, October 2010
First Omnific trade paperback edition, October 2010

The characters and events in this book are fictitious.
Any similarity to real persons, living or dead,
is coincidental and not intended by the author.

Library of Congress Cataloguing-in-Publication Data

DeLucy, Jennifer.
    Whisper of Light / Jennifer DeLucy – 1st ed.
    ISBN 978-1-936305-41-4
    1. Supernatural—Fiction. 2. Vampires—Fiction.
    3. Spirituality—Fiction. I. Title

10 9 8 7 6 5 4 3 2 1

Cover Design and Interior Book Design by Coreen Montagna

Printed in the United States of America

Prologue

Following the quiet sounds of a sitar, I wound around the house in search of Wendell. He collected the weirdest instruments, but it didn't bother me. I liked them. And he played them all: his wooden Surdo drum set, the autoharp, three guitars, and a mandolin.

But today I wasn't interested in listening to any of them. I was on a mission. I had a really big question, and Wendell would know the answer, because he was a Seer, and Seers could see lots more things than even Sentients could. Plus, maybe, if he wasn't busy, he'd let me tie his hair in a knot. I was the only one he let tie his hair in a knot.

As usual, Wendell was outside on the deck stairs—his favorite place in our big, new house—with his sitar resting against a knee. I didn't want to be rude, so I sat down next to him, as quietly as I could, and didn't say a single word.

He stopped playing immediately. "Hey. Hello there, little bird." He smiled, setting the sitar down.

"Hi, Wendell."

"Whatcha up to?" he asked. "Did you come to sing a song for me?"

"No. I had a question."

"A question, huh? What kind?" he asked, looking me square in the eye. It always made me feel good when he did that, as if I were a grown up.

"Well, I wondered something about my soul."

"Aaaah." he nodded. "I do that, too."

"You wonder about my soul?"

"No," he laughed, ruffling my hair. "I wonder about mine."

"Really?" I puzzled.

"Sure do. All the time."

"Huh," I said, thinking over this new bit of information.

"And what did you want to know about your soul, Nicky?"

"Oh, I just wanted to know if my soul was old."

"Old?"

"Yeah. Like Mommy and Daddy. Their souls are old, right?"

"Yes. This is true."

"So, what if mine's not? What if, when I grow up, I'm not a Sentient like you guys?"

"Everyone's a Sentient, Nicky," he said. "True, some people's souls have been around a longer time, so it shows more. But that doesn't mean they aren't equal."

"But Daddy says a Sentient has a special soul. He says it's more wise, and not everybody gets to be like that."

"Nicole," Wendell soothed, pulling me onto his lap. "Your soul is special. I promise."

"You're sure? As special as Daddy's, even?"

"I'm willing to bet," he began, "that your soul might be so special that some people might not be able to understand it."

"They won't? Well, will you?"

"Yes. I think I will."

"Okay." I nodded, relieved. If Wendell could understand it, then he could explain it to everyone else. "Thanks, Wendell."

"Any time for you, sweetness. Oh, and by the way, there are some men coming over this week with a very big, potentially noisy delivery. And I'd like you to play with it."

"Really? Is it a dog?"

He laughed. "Nope. Not a dog."

What else was big and noisy? "An airplane?"

He laughed even harder. "Creative guess, but I don't think they'd be able to land it on the beach."

I giggled. "What is it then?"

"It's a piano," he said, grinning happily at me.

"A piano?"

"Yup. A nice, big, shiny one."

I frowned. "But I don't know how to play the piano, Wendell."

"Don't you worry about that," he said. "I'll teach you."

"Really? You think I'll be any good?"

He smirked. "Definitely."

"As good as you?"

"Better, little bird. So much better."

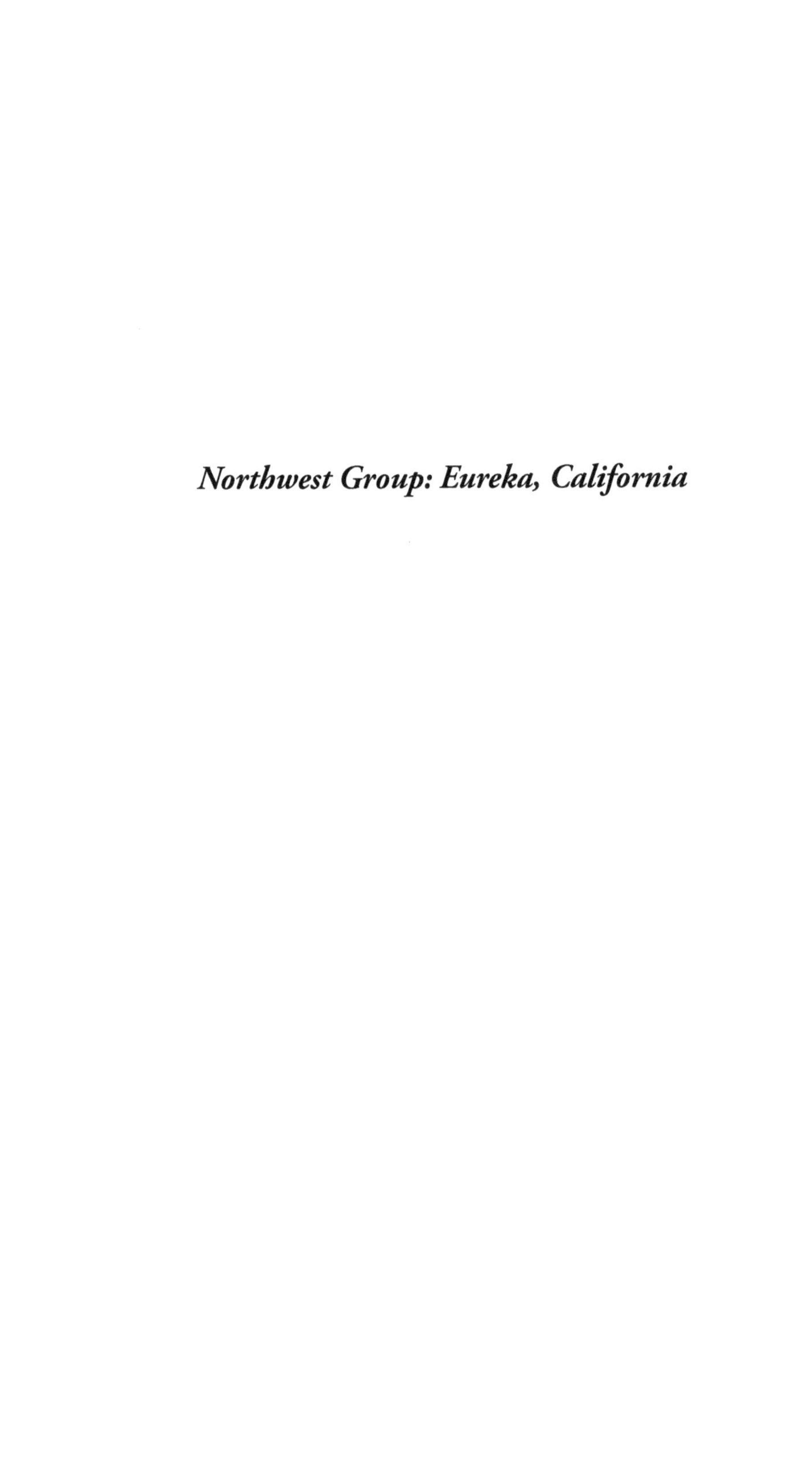

Northwest Group: Eureka, California

Chapter One

"Come on, Nicole! Dance with me!" Gil shouted over Queen's *Somebody to Love*, jumping up from the computer desk to grab my hands.

"Oh, no, no, no." I skirted toward the door, but he caught me around the waist, pulling me into the center of the room. He threw his glasses on the desk and sang loudly, swirling me under his arm.

"You can't dance to this song! Ow, Gil, my foot!" I laughed as he bumped his hip into mine, crooning along with Freddie Mercury.

"It'll heal," he shouted and dipped me low, nearly dropping me in the process.

"Shit," I giggled, flinging my hand to the floor to catch myself. "You are *no* good at this, my friend."

"Somebody tooo…loo-oooo-ooove…" He ignored my comment, swaying me back and forth as the band repeated the phrase.

"Are you out of your mind?" I smiled. "It's one in the morning. You know my dad is Satan when you wake—"

The door to the computer room flew open, crashing loudly against the wall, and my very disgruntled father glared at us, breathing shortly through his nose. He looked older than he should have in his disheveled pajamas, with thick patches of dyed-brown hair sticking out in every direction, but his wide-shouldered build was still intimidating.

"Will you turn off the goddamned music?" he growled. "I have to get some sleep if I'm going to do my job!"

"Sorry, Duncan, my fault," Gil stepped in. "I'm a little wired…all the caffeine." Gil nodded toward his perpetual mug of coffee.

"Just because *some* of you don't have anything better to do" —he looked at me— "doesn't mean the rest of us can slack off. Go to bed, *idiots!*" he roared, slamming the door shut again.

Gil ran to the computer and muted the end of the song, looking at me apologetically.

"Nick, I'm sorry," he started.

I waved his apology away. "Don't. It's okay."

"Fuck that. I hate it when he does shit like that."

"Well, I couldn't care less," I lied. "I'm so used to it by now that it doesn't even register. He's right—it's bedtime. You have to get up early, too, you know."

"Eh. I'd rather stay here with you. Or hey, even better, why don't you tag along?"

"Nah. Uh uh."

"Come on," he pestered, nudging my shoulder. "Why not? Come with. It'll be fun. We can pretend to be those ridiculous TV ghost hunters. I'll let you work the EMF."

"The EMF…you will?"

"Yup."

"Well, in that case, I might consider it. But no confiscation. I get to keep it the whole time."

"Unless you mishandle it," he cautioned.

"I will *not* break the damned EMF meter. When have I ever broken any of your props?" I huffed.

"My voice recorder?" he reminded me.

"That wasn't even my fault. You tripped me."

"Lies!" he barked. "I can't help it if you don't have the presence of mind to anticipate the movement of my feet."

I put a hand on my hip. "Gil, do you want me to come with you tomorrow or not?"

"Yes. Definitely. Fine. The EMF is yours. But these are all mine," he said, fingering a pair of night vision goggles lovingly. "Let the loser with the Intelligence endowment have his toys. I swear, why couldn't I have been a Mind Reader or something?"

"No way in hell do we need another Mind Reader." I shuddered. "Katrina is more than enough."

"What? Wouldn't it be cool if I could hear all the scandalous things your dad was thinking? Then I could call him on them and embarrass *him* for once."

"Let's not talk about my dad, please. I'm tired, and if I need to get up at the butt crack of dawn I'll need some shut eye."

"You're such a slave to sleep patterns," he complained, holding the door open for me.

"Whatever. Not all of us are hooked up to a caffeine IV drip."

"Imagine what you're missing," he whispered. "Nothing compares to the power of pure liquid alertness as it courses through your veins."

"One of these days you're gonna crash and burn, Gilford. I can see it now." I laughed.

"Hey, just have the espresso beans ready."

"G'night, you psycho."

"Night, Mozart."

Nobody looked worse than Gilford Boyd before his coffee in the morning. Nobody was grumpier, either. You didn't dare ask him anything until his second cup was emptied, and even then it was best to keep the words to a minimum.

"Everybody gone?" I asked him, grabbing my purse and setting it on the counter in front of me.

"Yup. You're ridin' with me and the mind freak."

"'Kay."

Once he'd finished his third mug, Gil would be in good shape—for a string bean, anyway. Actually, he was almost handsome, if you liked the techno-geek type. His hair was the funniest thing. It almost passed for blond but clung to its brown with enough determination to muck the whole thing up. I blamed the California sun. And his glasses were a turn-on for some girls, I was sure. He reminded me of a taller, tanner, lankier Harry Potter.

I pulled out some tinted lip gloss which was pointless, because I was average, at best. No amount of makeup would change the fact that I was an introverted twenty-nine-year-old with ghostly pale skin, boring, stick-straight brown hair, thick thighs, and massive daddy issues. A regular catch, that was me.

"Does my dad know I'm coming?" I asked.

Gil shook his head. "Don't think so," he answered. Then he glared at his watch and grumbled before shouting, "Katrina, put a rush on it! We're late!"

Katrina's "Shut *up!*" preceded her clomping down the stairs. She was graceless, that girl, but she was also beautiful, with naturally curly red hair, a creamy complexion covered in freckles, and a long, waifish frame. "What the hell, Gil," she grumbled, slinging her purse onto the counter beside mine. "You haven't even finished your third mug yet."

Gil picked up his coffee cup and tossed back the remnants like a pro. "Done. Let's hit it."

The freeway was busy today, and I gripped the side of my seat to keep from sliding around. Gil stressed me out when he drove. He had no regard for traffic laws, and his temper was absolutely questionable. But his car was far nicer than both mine and Trina's, so we sacrificed safety for luxury. His Saab had been a gift from his parents—wealthy as sin, both of them, and completely absent.

The reason for this was tragic. The Boyds were a respected family in their home town, and Gil simply didn't fit the mold. They never asked about the Sentient business—they didn't want to. All this supernaturally gifted mumbo-jumbo freaked them out. It was all occult nonsense, if you asked them, and as far as their acquaintances were concerned, their son was working a normal nine-to-five in some hipster city with newfangled ideas. That was their story and they were sticking to it, happy to overlook the details. And Gil was happy to let them. Of course, they sent the obligatory birthday and Christmas cards, and they supplied him with a sweet yearly stipend, but that was the extent of their communication.

Like all Seers, Wendell compensated his Sentients with the funds provided by the Worldwide Society, so it was a bit odd that Gil's parents should feel the need to send him money, especially at his age. After all, what self-respecting twenty-five year old man needed an allowance? But even from afar, the Boyds felt they had a reputation to worry about, and the least they could do was make sure their misfit son dressed well and drove a nice car.

"Who's up for a game of I Spy?" Katrina blurted.

Gil nearly choked on his frappuccino. "How would that be fair?"

"What? I won't listen to what you're thinking."

"And if something accidentally 'slips' out of my brain?" He mocked her usual excuse.

"I'll try really hard to shut it out, so help me!" she swore.

"Whatever, freakazoid. I'm not biting."

"You're mean." She crossed her arms and sat back, frowning deeply.

"I am not mean. I just don't trust you where games of the mind are concerned," he explained.

She sighed. "Don't blame me for being remarkable."

"Remarkable at being a cheater!"

"You know," I broke in, "it's a wonder you two haven't killed each other yet."

"But I love my Gilly-bear," Katrina said in a sickeningly sweet voice.

"That's right. She fucking wants my body," Gil said.

Katrina laughed. "Absolutely. You know my weakness for pint-sized dick."

"Take it back!" Gil demanded. "You have no knowledge of my genitalia."

"Oh, don't I?" She smirked.

"Jesus Christ, Katrina!" he bellowed. "Get the hell out of my head!"

"I didn't hear anything, Gil. I was just baiting you," she said.

"June Lake!" I exclaimed, pointing to the exit that Gil had just missed.

He banged on the steering wheel. "*Damn it.*"

"Guys, focus," I said.

"You would be a great Sentient, Nick," Katrina said. "You've got the clear head for it."

"Yeah, well, what will be will be," I said.

I preferred not to think about my little inadequacy—or my monstrous failure as a human being, if you asked my father's opinion. I was not a Sentient. The universe hadn't dubbed my soul advanced enough to warrant a supernatural gift, and every minute I spent among Sentients only drove this point home. I certainly didn't need the verbal reminders.

Gil took the next exit and turned us around again.

"Now, no more talk of my manhood while I'm driving," he ordered. "Unless it's complimentary, in which case, give me time to pull out the voice recorder."

"Fine," Katrina said.

"Hey, how bad is this poltergeist?" I asked. "Should I have brought a suit of armor?"

"Nah," Katrina said. "But it hates Theo's guts. Everything it throws at him just repels backward and smashes to bits."

I burst into giggles. Theo Rush had suffered a major pitfall after he'd come into contact with an entity in Australia. He was telekinetic by nature, and normally he could move anything—from a marble to a car—with little effort and the sheer will of his mind. Now all he could manage to do was toss things around like a lunatic, poor guy.

"I wouldn't worry about him too much," Katrina said. "Wendell swears that his endowment will normalize after a while. Plus, when we go to Abram's, I'll bet they can help him out. That guy always has something up his sleeve. He's a mastermind."

I nodded in agreement. I'd always liked the old East Coast Seer, even if my dad couldn't stand him. Of course, most things my dad disliked were favorites of mine.

"Speaking of Abram, have you thought about whether you're coming out to Georgia with us?" Katrina asked me.

"What would be the point?" I said. "Besides, if I went with you guys, it would just piss my dad off."

"Well, if you're not going, I'm not going," Gil said. "It wouldn't be the same without you."

"Don't be ridiculous. You should totally go. A change of atmosphere is vital. You can take pictures and tell me all about it."

"And *you* couldn't use a change of atmosphere?"

"Gil, there's no way I can break away now. You know I'm working with the Fitzpatrick girl," I said. "I won't just leave right in the middle of our sessions. Not when it's all I can do to get through to her."

Gil shook his head. "You're gonna die of boredom, Nicole."

"Drop it, Gil. You have your job; I have mine."

"And that's all cool," he said quickly. "But again—you don't go, I don't go."

"Suit yourself. But you won't get to meet that pretty new Sentient everybody's talking about."

"Like I care," he said.

"You mean Lily Hunt?" Trina said. "Yeah, Anna told me all about her. Apparently, she's way gifted and has, like, forty-trillion endowments or something. Completely unfair."

"Trina, you should be happy you have any. Some of us aren't so lucky," I said.

The car fell awkwardly silent. Shit, Nicole. Way to make her feel like a schmuck.

"So, how's Anna doing?" I recovered, knowing this would lighten the mood. Trina had always had a thing for the young, British Sentient.

"She's great! Amazing as always," Trina boasted. "Though, I'm gathering that things are a little tense right now between her brother and William Maddox. You know the saga."

"Ah yes," Gil said. "Christian still wants to slice him in half?"

"Apparently."

Katrina smiled. "You wanna know some juicy gossip?"

"Ooh, yeah. Hit us up," Gil said.

"Well—and this doesn't leave the car for now—but, I think William and Lily are a thing."

Gil gawked. "Wait a minute," he started. "The vampire and the new Sentient? They are not!" Gil said, leaning into the conversation like a nosy old woman.

"Yup. But you heard nothing from me, *capisce?* Hardly anyone knows, especially not Christian."

"Woah. Scandalous. But I won't breathe a word," Gil said.

I shook my head. "You know there's going to be some kind of uproar and panties in a bunch when the Society gets wind of it." It was no secret that a large faction of the Sentient world was iffy on the subject of William joining Abram's group. But I could empathize with his plight. It sucked to be the reject.

"All right, hot mammas. We have arrived," Gil announced, weaving down a small neighborhood street. Gil parked in front of a split level, brick-and-siding home with a mint green paint job.

"Looks pretty wholesome," I commented.

"You just wait," Katrina said.

"Duncan's here," Gil said, staring at my father's pickup. My stomach lurched. What would he say when he saw me?

"Family home?" I asked Gil.

"Yep," he said.

"They freaked?"

"Big time."

I nodded, crossing my arms as he knocked on the front door. After a minute, a barely pubescent boy sporting jet-black hair and a Black Sabbath tee shirt let us in.

"Where is everybody, kid?" Gil asked.

"Back," the boy mumbled.

"'Kay. Follow me guys," Katrina said, glancing darkly over her shoulder toward the boy as we passed.

"Black Sabbath?" Gil whispered to me. "That's before *my* time, for God's sake. Doesn't this generation have its own pissed off music to listen to?"

Katrina snickered. "What's old will be new again."

"If you say so. And I don't trust that kid as far as I can throw him," Gil said.

"Me either," she whispered.

"Are you kidding? What is he, like, twelve?" I asked.

"Thirteen," Trina corrected. "And I'm convinced he's the root of all this. His energy is incredibly negative. You should hear his thoughts…that is, if they *are* his thoughts."

"Did you tell Laura?"

"Yes. But she doesn't want to make it look like we're blaming him. She wants to find a way to break it gently, so the family won't kick us out."

"Ah."

"Here they are," Trina said

There was a mini convergence on the sun porch, including Laura Polmieri, our Pathcrosser, whose specialty was posthumous communication, and Elaine Rush and my father, our two Combatants, who were kind of like the bouncers of the supernatural world. There was also a wary-looking priest and a thin, dark-haired woman, likely the mother of the shady kid. All five of them sat awkwardly on flower-covered patio furniture. It was the makings of a convoluted bar joke.

The nervous mother stood up as we entered the room. "Father O'Toole, this is Katrina Winguard, another of the nice people from the local ghost-hunting group. And…uh…"

"I'm Gil," he reminded her.

"Yes, so sorry. Gil."

"No problem, Mrs. Rosencratz. And we aren't actually ghost hunters, remember?"

"Oh, yes, of course not. They're…what are you?" she asked, wringing her hands repeatedly.

"We're an intervention team." Gil smiled at the priest.

"Yes. That's right." Mrs. Rosencratz glanced over at Father O'Toole as he rose from his chair and approached us.

"And you, dear?" Father O'Toole asked me.

"I'm just…I'm Nicole," I began. "I'm here to help with the equipment."

My dad shifted in his seat, his eyes shooting darts through my head. He hated it when I tagged along.

"Mhm. And what do all of you have to offer this family?" the priest asked.

Gil spoke up. "We're sorting through our options, but I think we've pinpointed the problem." His eyes traveled subtly toward the teenage boy sitting at the kitchen counter.

"And that would be?" Father O'Toole persisted.

"Er…" Gil looked at Katrina.

"I'm sorry, Father," Katrina said. "But I doubt you'll be able to help these people. Their problem is out of your league. It might be a good idea if you just left."

"Out of my league?" He laughed. "I highly doubt *that*," he said, then turned his gaze to the elder members of our group. "And this 'entity,' if that's what it is, you feel you have the authority to cast it out?"

"Oh, I wouldn't say cast it out." Laura spoke calmly. "This is pest control, at best. We shouldn't make a bigger deal out of it than necessary."

"And who are you to make that decision?" The priest was losing his patience, now.

Laura smirked. "Oh, it's kind of my thing."

What must Father O'Toole have thought of our free-spirited Path-crosser, wearing her usual billowing skirt and tee shirt with a giant peace sign on the front?

Duncan cleared his throat. "Suffice it to say that we're qualified enough."

"Oh really?" the priest asked.

"That's correct," Duncan said. "And I'd like to ask who invited *you* here?"

"I did," said a booming male voice from behind me, and I turned to see a short, stern-looking man with a sharp nose staring down at me.

"*Mister* Rosencratz?" Katrina said, looking perplexed. "But…you're Jewish."

"This is *my* house and if I want to call a priest, I'll damned well do so," he said. "I've seen *The Exorcist*. I know how this works. And Father O'Toole, I trust that our guests are being respectful?" He eyed us all skeptically.

"Not to worry, Phillip," Father O'Toole said. "I was just inquiring as to what authority they—" He stopped abruptly, jumping forward as the wall phone came unhinged behind him, dangling by a corner screw.

"Huh," Gil pondered. "Look at that."

"What happened?" Father O'Toole asked.

"The phone fell," Gil answered.

"Well, naturally! I'm not blind, young man. I'm asking *how* the phone fell!"

"I blame gravity," Gil offered.

"*Gilford*," Duncan warned, and Gil shrugged, smiling.

"Behave," I mouthed, elbowing him.

Father O'Toole glanced at the displaced phone. "Well, anyway, it's my strong opinion that this situation requires further investi—aah!" He nearly fell over as the phone rang. "It's ringing!"

"It is," my father agreed.

"*Why is it ringing?* It's off the hook!"

"That's not uncommon with a poltergeist," Elaine told him.

"Polter…nonsense! This is likely something more demonic—"

"Stop right there," Laura cut him off. "I can't have you scaring these poor people any further with talk of things you don't understand."

"Don't understand? Look here, I spent seven years in seminary, and if anyone knows how to handle a—"

"Dictionary," Gil interrupted.

Father O'Toole peered at him. "What?"

"Hard bound, above your—" But it was too late. The book dropped with a thud on top of the priest's head and slipped to the floor.

"Saints preserve us!" Father O'Toole squealed, scrambling away from the object. The sound of muffled laughter leaked from the kitchen, and I turned to see the teenage boy smirking shamelessly.

"See?" Father O'Toole continued his verbal consternation. "It knows who I am, and it clearly wants to intimidate me! But I won't be intimidated. I won't be!" He shook his pudgy white fist, only to duck as the phone lifted in the air and rang again.

"You should probably leave, Father," Laura warned. "We're dealing with the manifestation of displaced negative energy here, and you don't want to get caught in the line of fire."

"Displaced energy?" Father O'Toole asked. "Listen, I don't like all this new age business."

"Well, regardless of your opinions, these are the facts." She raised her voice so the boy could hear, saying, "And I think someone here knows precisely what's causing it."

The phone ceased to ring and fell to the floor at once.

"Who?" Mrs. Rosencratz spoke at last, her voice barely above a whisper. "Someone here?"

"Yes," Laura answered. "And I'd like your permission to speak with Justin alone, if it's all right."

"Justin?" Her voice cracked. "What does my son have to do with this?"

Katrina raised an eyebrow toward the kitchen. "You'd be surprised."

"This is ridiculous," Mr. Rosencratz interjected. "There's nothing wrong my boy!"

"I never said there was," Laura soothed. "In fact, I would take this as a sign of impressive psychological aptitude."

Mr. Rosencratz opened his mouth to speak, then closed it again, letting her words sink in.

"Impressive, you think?" he asked.

"I do." Laura smiled. "And it's easy for someone of his age, overwhelmed by hormones and emotions, to unconsciously channel that kind of intelligence in a negative way. We believe that Justin's excess mental energy has simply spun off, taken on a life of its own. It's easy enough to contend with. Elaine?" She turned to our Combatant, who stood up immediately. "Now, before we take any action, a word with your son?"

Mrs. Rosencratz nodded, and her husband—torn between pride and disbelief—allowed Elaine and Laura to pass.

Father O'Toole huffed. "Are you *really* going to allow these shysters to—"

"That'll be all, Father. I'm sorry to waste your time," Mr. Rosencratz said, watching as Laura pulled up a seat next to Justin.

"Hey there," she said to the boy.

He grunted something incomprehensible, his eyes never veering from his hand-held device.

"So," she began. "How long has this thing been under your control?"

His fingers kept moving, but he didn't even flinch.

"Come on, kiddo. We both know what's going on here. Just tell me the truth. I won't think you're crazy."

"You're the crazy one," he said, finally looking up from his game.

"I'm sorry?"

"You think I'm creating some kind of ghost, right? You think that priest lost his balls because of me?"

"Yeah, as a matter of fact, I do. And you might as well quit the act, Justin. I know you're lying—your energy is completely giving you away."

He snorted. "Energy. Whatever, freaks."

She snatched the game from his hands. "Listen, kid…"

"Hey!"

"We can do this the hard way, or you can stop lying and fess up. I know what's been happening, Justin, and I can promise you that it's not something you can handle. Do you understand me? You want to know what freaky is? Freaky is a monster attacking you in your bed because you've let it get so far out of hand that *it* controls *you*. Your alter ego has become its own little person now, hasn't it?" Justin's eyed widened at Laura's question, and she continued. "Justin, its only desire is to eat you and your parents alive from the inside out. In fact, that's already starting to happen, isn't it?" She paused as his face changed from red to white. "He's already keeping you up at night, isn't he, Justin? Already keeping you prisoner in your own room, right? Is it cold in there, buddy? Bet you can see your breath like you were outside."

Justin gulped thickly, saying nothing, and Laura took on a look of concentration. "Answer me, Justin. I know he's trying to intimidate you right now. I know he's twisting your thoughts, but you have to ignore him and answer me."

The boy was sweating bullets, his eyes bugging out, his hands shaking. Whatever was happening internally was obviously a colossal effort. "It was…it wasn't…I mean, I don't know how—"

"Mhm. You probably figured you could control it, but that won't work, Justin. Has it done anything you didn't want it to do?"

Justin looked down at the counter. "It…it goes in my parents' room. I don't tell him to," he said, looking up again. "But he likes it there."

"You know why?"

He shook his head.

"Because your energy isn't enough for him anymore. He'll drain you dry and then move on to someone else."

"Well, what do I do? Just get rid of him!"

"Not that easy. I can finish things off, but you have to bring him out for me."

"I don't know if I can. He doesn't like you guys."

Laura looked over her shoulder at Elaine, who nodded subtly. "Okay, Justin. Take us to your room."

This was the part I loved and hated. It was a privilege to bear witness to a miracle. It was exciting and beautiful to see the relief on people's faces when the weight of some darkness had been lifted from their shoulders. Of course, it was also completely awkward with my father shooting resentful glances in my direction half the time. If there was anything that annoyed him, it was looking out for me on these little excursions. I couldn't, after all, offer any assistance. And I could hardly protect myself, either, so there was a good reason for my rarely tagging along.

Ever careful to avoid eye contact, I focused on the EMF meter, which, in the dark of the room, continued to collect condensation on the tiny screen. My teeth were chattering. Freaking supernatural entities always brought on the cold snaps. Gil noticed and rubbed my arms from behind, but I shook him off. No reason to look even weaker in front of Duncan.

Justin sat beside Laura on the edge of his bed, his arms folded across his chest. "So what if it doesn't work?" he asked her.

"It will," she assured him. "It always works. You just have to do as I say, okay?"

"Okay."

A frightened child, that's what he was. Underneath the eyeliner and greasy hair, he was a scared little boy.

"Now, I want you to think about the very first time he appeared to you, okay? Think about when he first started coming around. Were you really angry?"

"Well," he hesitated, his eyes flitting up to his parents and then back to Laura. "Maybe when my dad rooted through my stuff and took my CDs. I was really pissed that day, ready to break something."

"And you're blaming CDs, huh?"

"Well, yeah. I mean, he had no right to go through my stuff."

"Those CDs were full of inappropriate content," Mr. Rosencratz piped in. "I had every right to take them away. I wouldn't be surprised if they were the cause of all this."

"Oh, I wouldn't go that far," Laura said. "Your son is a teenager, Mr. Rosencratz. His energy is at an all-time high, super-charged, and this is hardly uncommon to see. It could very well have happened to someone who didn't listen to that kind of music at all."

"There, Dad, you see?" Justin said. "I told you—"

"But," Laura interrupted, "it doesn't help, either, because if you're prone to high levels of negative energy to begin with, that kind of anger-enhancing stimulant is only going to add to your problems. Your dad's instincts were right, but his overall conclusion was wrong, because something like this doesn't manifest from a fight over CDs. A human being can't produce an entity unless there's been something acting as a trigger event, so I'm going to ask you to be truthful, Justin—what else happened before this thing started coming around? You need to be honest with me here, honey. What else happened?"

The room became suddenly still, as if everyone knew not to shake the delicate balance between Laura's question and the chance for an answer.

Justin looked at his father, then at Laura. "Does he have to be here?"

"Yes. It's good that he is. He's your father, Justin. He needs to know."

"But I can't say it. Not in front of him."

"Justin, he loves you. Whatever it is, he won't be angry."

"I'm not worried he'll be angry, I'm—"

"Just tell her, son," Mr. Rosencratz added. "Please."

Justin heaved a sigh and dropped his hands to his lap. "It was the end of the day. Sam and I—Sam's my friend—we were on our way home from school. And Sam is, he's this kind of wussy little guy, you know? He isn't big enough to defend himself, and these upperclassmen jerks hassle him every day, so I offered to walk him home, but he was too proud. I mean, who can blame him, right? So, I did what I had to do. I tracked him in secret. I followed him by, like, a half a block behind, so he wouldn't see me. But I lost him after a while. I didn't know where he went, but I knew that he couldn't have gotten that far ahead of me, so I doubled back. And I cut through a yard and was coming around the corner of the old army supply store when I heard him. At least, I was pretty sure it was him, since he wasn't talking, he was just…he was…crying," he said, and his voice cracked. "And

I looked through one of the windows and…shit." His face contorted and his eyes welled up. "I can't. I can't," he muttered, shaking his head.

"Justin, please." Laura rested her hand on his shoulder.

He pulled away, sniffling, and stared at his hands. "The bunch of sick fuckers. They had him on his knees, and one of them was holding Sam's arms behind his back…oh shit…I'm so sorry, Mom, shit…" He shook his head, more tears breaking loose and trailing down his cheeks. Laura rubbed his back, encouraging him to go on. "He was holding Sam's arms behind him," Justin said in a weak voice. "So that he could, they were making him…"

"Jesus," my father's voice tumbled over the confession. "Jesus."

"So, I lost it!" Justin stiffened, trying to control the sobs that were wracking his body. "I lost it. I screamed and broke the fucking door to get in there, and I just started swinging. I just fucking punched them and kicked them until they bled and then it happened. It was like this force just ripped out of me, and I stood there and watched it all happen. And they ran away. They were bleeding really bad, but they must have made up some excuse for what went down, because there was no way they were gonna tell the truth."

Justin stopped, sighing deeply, and then looked at Laura. For a time no one spoke a word, then he said, "I would have killed them. I just know that I would have killed them if they hadn't run."

Laura slipped her hand over his and held it tightly. "I would have reacted the same way," she said. "But this hatred…it's going to make you every bit as evil, every bit as cold as they are. You know that."

He nodded.

"Call it out, Justin," she said. "Call him out and tell him to go to hell."

The boy inhaled deeply, his resolve evident. "I know you're here. Don't bother hiding."

Silence.

"Oh, just come out! They're not gonna leave."

A low groan emitted from behind, in front, beside, but the sound was not in the room. It *was* the room. I looked around anxiously, seeing nothing.

"Come on, asshole. You're wasting everybody's time," Justin goaded, and a tendril of black ascended from one corner of the room, then another, and another. It rose to the ceiling and converged at its center, just above Justin's head, and we all watched it, swirling like a black hole, groaning in surround sound.

"You need me," it whispered.

Justin winced. "I don't need you."

"You're just a child," it said. "You're helpless without me."

"I'm not helpless."

"You are! If it weren't for me, those boys would have—"

"Just shut up!" Justin roared. "I don't need you. I don't want you. Get out!"

"Tell them to leave us alone," it ordered.

"Screw you."

"Justin, I could kill you. I could kill your family."

"No you couldn't, or you would have already. You need us. *You* need me. You wouldn't even exist if I hadn't made you happen."

"Think of what I can still do for you!"

"Just get the hell out!"

At this, the entity began to shrink, the vast whirlpool of black becoming a concentrated, abysmal ball.

"Laura, do you need me for this?" Elaine whispered.

"You know, I don't think I do. I can handle it," she said. I waited for it, and sure enough, as Laura's eyes focused on the unearthly spectacle, a superheated ring of light began to eat away at the edges of the black ball, enveloping the thing until it was a speck. And then nothing.

The room was instantly warm.

"He's gone?" Justin asked.

"More than gone, babe. He's toast." Laura smiled.

"Just like that? I mean, that easy? I thought he'd fight you or something."

"He would have," she put a hand on his face, "if you had. But you wanted him gone. Your fear, your desire to hold on to him, could have fed his strength, but since you denied him, he didn't have a will of his own. This was all dependent on you, Justin. The control was yours."

Laura had an exquisite gift for saying exactly what one needed to hear. And in that moment, Justin Rosencratz needed to know that there was something he could control, that he wasn't helpless, weak, or small.

I knew the feeling well.

Chapter Two

I hated yellow. Whoever thought yellow was a friendly color had no idea what the hell they were talking about. It was loud and mocking and all things unpleasant in my mind. The inside of my mother's room was yellow—a garish, goldenrod hue that reminded me of baby shit. I wondered how she could stand it, all that yellow. I'd have snapped and killed someone if I'd had to spend so much time in there. It was like a story I'd read in college, the one about the horrible wallpaper. Charlotte Perkins Gilman would have known what I was talking about. But my mom loved yellow. It had always been her favorite color, so I sucked it up.

I stood in her doorway with Raj, my childhood friend, and thanked him for keeping an eye on her.

"You know I'm happy to do it," he said. "And Gil has a point, you know. You do need to get out more. It's not healthy for you to spend so much time indoors," he said, the suggestion of a Hindi accent coloring his words.

"Yeah, well, it's awkward going on jobs with you guys. Seclusion may not be the healthiest option, but it's definitely the most comfortable."

"Sure," he said, offering a sympathetic smile. He was looking at me in that way I'd finally grown accustomed to, with those rich-brown probing eyes indicative of wisdom. That was one of his endowments, actually—Discernment. I never had to lie to him, because there was no point. He had a gift for reading between the lines.

Rajeep insisted that my father loved me. He'd always held to that mantra, and I was normally a fervent believer in Raj's mind. I wanted the man to love me, after all. I loved him, though God only knew why. He was harsh and abrasive, unapproachable and hard, basically everything I wasn't, and

I had always irked him—his quiet, mousy daughter, hovering over a piano or closeted away in her room listening to music. But after what happened to Mom, it all fell apart. Where I had only annoyed him before, he wanted nothing to do with me now. I had proven what he'd suspected all along. I truly was useless.

Raj left the room, and I sat on the floor beside Mom's chair, resting my head against her leg. The soft, even movements of her hands ceased, and she let go of the knitting needle to stroke my hair. This was an encouraging sign. She had good days and bad, days when she remembered me and knew who Dad was, and it looked like this would be one of them.

"How's my girl?" she asked.

"Hi, Mom," I sighed.

"You go out today?"

"Mhm. I went with Gil and Katrina."

"Anything interesting happen?"

"Well, they banished a poltergeist."

"Aah. I was always good at banishing things. Maybe your father will let me come along next time."

"Maybe he will," I answered in the same way for the thousandth time in three years. She would never practice sentience again, but we could pretend. We could say what was necessary and then she'd forget, like always.

"Hey, Mom?" I said.

"Mmm?"

"That little girl I was telling you about—Samantha Fitzpatrick, remember?"

"The autistic girl?"

"Uh huh." I smiled. "You remembered."

"Yes. How's it coming along?"

"She reacted, Mom. I was playing a song and she started humming. Just a few notes, but it was definitely happening."

Still playing with my hair, she looked out her bedroom door, thinking intently. "You have a talent for that sort of thing, sweetheart. Music. I always knew you were special. I always told Duncan." Her distant gaze took on a sudden spark of clarity as she turned to look at me. "Is your dad being reasonable, honey?"

"Oh, yeah. Sure," I said.

She sighed, her face softening. "Laura made cobbler."

"She did?"

"Mhm. Apple."

"With a blob of Cool Whip?"

"Mhm."

I smiled, kissing her knee. "She knows you like it that way."

"Yep. She's very nice, that Laura. I'm so glad she's joined us. She's new, isn't she? How long has she been here?"

"Oh, a little while," I said, my heart sinking. Laura was Mom's best friend—had been for twenty years.

"Yes, well, she's very nice, that Laura."

"Yeah. She's great, Mom."

❧

The house was bursting at the seams with anticipation that morning. Most of the group had a long drive ahead of them—cross country, to be exact.

"Has anyone seen my swim goggles?" Wendell Russettman, our Seer, leaned over the kitchen counter, slicing a mango. "My favorite ones? The ones with the beach balls on them?"

"No idea. Sorry, Wendell." Katrina sat on the floor next to her suitcase to pull on a sneaker. "But your rubber ducky ones are in the mudroom."

"Eh, not the same." He sighed, running a pile of spinach and his mango chunks through the juicer, skins and all. "Care for some?" He offered me a glass, pouring himself a muddy-looking helping.

"No, thanks." I grimaced, but he shrugged off the rebuff, drinking the concoction with no hesitation. He said it gave his hair that natural sheen, and Wendell was very serious about his hair. He hadn't gotten it cut in five years, and it hung down, straight and white, to just below his shoulder blades. "Here's hoping they have pools in Atlanta," he said.

"I'm sure they do," Trina said. "But I don't think there's one at their house."

"Huh." He frowned. Wendell swam for an hour every day. He was a fish at heart, and he loved his H_2O. Our proximity to the ocean was evidence of that. Just outside the wide kitchen windows, in fact, was an aquatic panorama. The silver blue of the Pacific lapped at our beach night and day, and Wendell considered the sound nature's perpetual meditation.

He'd fallen in love with the Redwood Coast the moment he laid eyes on it and bought this beach house shortly after. Though they often traveled, his Sentients always returned to this place, thanks to him. It was perfect for me, really. The inspiration in a climate like this never ran out, and I could use the spirit-lifting.

"Aah, this'll get your blood flowing," he said, slapping his emptied glass down, satisfied. "I'm telling you guys, if it's not whole food, it's toxic. You only—"

"Get back what you put in. We know." Katrina smirked. "And this is your last chance, Nick. It's not too late to come with us." She eyed me, grabbing the edge of the glass counter to pull herself up.

"She's right," Wendell added. "Join us for a few weeks, shake the sand from your feet, and follow along."

"Thanks, guys. But me and my sand have a ten-thirty student whose parents would be awfully confused if I wasn't here when they showed up."

"Whiners," Trina said. "But fine. We'll chat on the internet while I'm gone."

"Or, you know, you could *call* me."

She scoffed. "What an antiquated idea."

"Of course it is," I chuckled.

Wendell patted my back. "Take care of my pile of sunshine while I'm gone, okay?"

He loved his Volkswagen bus—loud, proud, and orange as a lava flow, straight off the funk train, tended to and cherished since 1975. Wendell wasn't one to trounce economy. If it could be preserved and reused, it would be.

"No problem. I'll feed her well and whisper sweet nothings into her exhaust pipe," I offered.

"That's my girl," he laughed. "By the way…" He pulled me aside. "You're doing a beautiful job with the Fitzpatrick kid." He looked me deeply in the eyes and grinned. "You're a treasure to this world, you know that?"

"Oh, Wendell." I looked away, embarrassed. "Thanks."

He was always saying stuff like that to me. I never knew how to react, either. At first, I'd tried not to discuss therapy sessions for the sake of patient confidentiality, but Wendell was a Seer in a house full of Sentients—it was understood that often they'd know more than they wouldn't know. What did I expect, really? Plus, most of my referrals came from Wendell, anyway. I guess that was his way of trying to make me feel like part of the whole.

Wendell's style of Seer supervision was about as hands off as you could get. In fact, I'm not sure you could even call it supervision as much as simply being present. This wasn't to suggest that he was indifferent or didn't care. He was always there if you needed him. But like most Seers, Wendell understood the necessity of living your own experience without cheating, without interference, and he was steadfast with that rule. If he knew things ahead of time, which we all assumed he did, he never let on. His job was to assign tasks and keep the peace among his Sentients, not to micromanage their paths.

"Okay, people, ship it out!" he announced.

Theo and Elaine shuffled downstairs, travel bags slung over their shoulders and suitcases waiting at the mudroom door.

"Bye, honey." Elaine smiled, bending in to peck my cheek. "Hopefully we'll see you soon, huh?"

"Yep, knock on wood," I said. Everyone knew the underlying reason for this little trip, and it wasn't so much about travel as it was strategy. Abram Saru, the aged East Coast Seer, faced a vicious cell of vampires gaining in strength on his side of the country. I was sure he could use all the able minds he could get to help figure out a plan of action. While it wasn't out of the ordinary for Abram and Wendell, longtime friends, to pay each other a visit, extended stays often meant trouble brewing. So we were crossing our fingers for a shorter trip.

A sliding sound, followed by a slapping thud, caught me off guard. "Was that—"

"Theo!" Elaine answered from the other room. "Just Theo!"

I peeked around the corner to see his suitcase and its contents splayed across the tile floor of the mudroom. Poor guy. There was never a jollier man than Theo Rush, at least until the spirit messed with him. Theo was a total softie and the polar opposite in physicality to his wife. He was a bit on the husky side, his hair a mop of white, not a speck of color remaining, while Elaine had her youth by the reins. In her early fifties, you could hardly find a gray hair among Elaine's mahogany strands. She was seventy-five percent Navaho, twenty-five percent Irish, and she wore her heritage proudly. And, well, as far as body types went, she put me to shame. The woman was fit as a fiddle, a typical trait of Combatants.

Another trait of Combatants was the tendency to be rough around the edges, which Elaine had definitely been displaying since the onset of Theo's unfortunate symptoms. Now our jinxed Sentient spent all of his time with his arms at his sides and a scowl of painful concentration on his face, trying hard not to destroy anything. Heaven bless them both—they had a really long drive ahead of them.

Laura and her husband, Chris, rushed in to help with the mess, while Elaine placed Theo's dropped duffel carefully over his shoulder again. "There," she sighed. "Just so long as you let me do all the touching we should be all right, babe. Okay?" She looked at him markedly. "Just don't touch a thing. If you need something, ask me for it."

He pouted like a scolded child and followed her forlornly out of the house.

"Nicole, honey, come here," Laura said, holding her arms out to me. The moment I reached her, she wrapped me in an embrace that only a Sentient could deliver, warm and heartening. "We'll call you, okay?

I nodded. I would miss her.

"And let the guys help you out with your mom. Leave the damned house once in a while!" she ordered.

"Okay, I will. I promise."

"Good." She turned to pick up her suitcase. "Love you, sweetheart. Ignore your father," she said over her shoulder. I didn't respond, just in case he was within earshot, though it was doubtful. Duncan had made himself scarce rather than sticking around for the goodbyes. He was still seething over Wendell's continued friendship with Abram, who had seen fit to harbor and protect a "vampire pet." The name William Maddox was not uttered within range of my father. Not if you wanted to keep his head from exploding all over the bright whites of Wendell's beach house.

Cracking my knuckles, I lifted the glossy-black lid of the baby grand. Wendell had tinted the windows in the sunroom so as not to spoil the instrument, and now Samantha Fitzpatrick sat at my side on the piano bench, barely blinking, as always. I began with the same routine, plunking at middle C a few times.

Nothing.

Half a step to a sharp, back down to middle C. *Nada.* I watched her, staring blankly at the Steinway insignia etched into the raised cover. Maybe I wasn't engaging her enough.

Lifting her left hand, I curled her little fingers under, all but the pointer, which I placed over a piano key, pressing down to create a note. Then I let go and waited. Her hand remained poised, finger still resting on the key for an instant, and then it listlessly slipped to her lap.

I sighed. Maybe this one note thing bored her. Reaching for the keys again, I plunked out a simple version of *Mary Had a Little Lamb* and took her hand again, replicating the melody with her finger. Midway through the song, I saw it. Out of the corner of my eye, I could barely make out a growing smile.

That's it, Samantha. Keep it up.

Near the song's end, she beamed brightly and let loose a tiny giggle. I stopped playing and smiled down at her, lifting her face to look at me.

"Oh, Samantha. You laughed!"

Her smile disappeared, replaced again with the empty stare that saddened me and horrified her parents. God, it was torture always feeling like we were so close, only to have some tiny accomplishment vanish, never to be replicated.

"Samantha, hey," I said, and I pressed my forehead to hers, closing my eyes. "Listen. I know you're in there. I heard you laugh. It was beautiful, by the way, and I think you should do it again. Or you could just smile for me! Come on, honey. Just a tiny smile?"

I pulled back to watch for signs of cognition, a glint of life in her violet eyes, but she looked right through me. I could have kicked myself for not speaking with Wendell about her before he'd left, and now I would just have to call him after he'd had time to settle in at Abram's. For the moment, though, I would try one more thing before our session was ended.

Getting up from the piano bench, I grabbed my well-worn Mozart CD and inserted it into the player, setting a moderate volume and turning on the speakers. Track four held a familiar tune—what we now called *Twinkle, Twinkle, Little Star*. Mozart had composed twelve variations of the old French lullaby, but I doubted I could keep Samantha's attention for almost fourteen minutes of classical piano. Perhaps three…

The music began. Harmless really—simple, pleasant melody. Of course, by the third time around, it had taken on a more complex notation. And yet Samantha was unaffected, perched on the bench, tracing the scuff of her loafers again and again and again. I turned the volume up a bit and waited. She rubbed at her shoes harder, but her face did not change. Louder still, not enough to hurt her, but enough to permeate the room. Her lips curled into a grimace an instant before she covered her ears and dropped to the bench, face down and screaming.

I smacked at the power button on the CD player and scooped her up in my arms, trying with all I had to soothe her with words in hushed tones. But she was frantic, dripping tears and mucous across my wrists and hands. I rocked her, pleaded with her to be calm, but nothing was working. Thank God my dad wasn't home. Everyone else knew not to interfere, not to disturb me during these sessions, but occasionally, in instances like these, Duncan would make it a point to pass the room with a bristling glare as if it were my fault. As if I was needlessly causing a ruckus for the hell of it. He had no concept of what was happening here, though Laura had tried to explain it on numerous occasions. This was all just bullshit to him. I was riling up children and playing with noise.

And she was still screaming, clutching fistfuls of black hair so tightly against her ears that I was afraid she would tear some out. What the hell to do? I couldn't play the piano while holding her.

I could sing.

"*Mary had a little lamb, little lamb, little lamb,*" I began slowly. "*Mary had a little lamb; its fleece was white as snow.*" Her screams turned to sobbing. "That's right, Samantha, shh, that's right, baby. *And everywhere that Mary went, Mary went, Mary went, everywhere that Mary went…*" The sobs quieted to whimpers as she unplugged her ears, laying her face against my chest. "*He followed her to school one day, school one day, school one day…*"

I stopped singing. She had stilled, and I knew even before I lifted her face that she was gone again.

Chapter Three

Humboldt County was revered in Northern California for its wealth of scenic beauty. The redwood forests boasted ancient trees, some of which were wide enough to drive a vehicle through, and the coast was nearly unspoiled. You got the feeling of being tucked away in the heart of something larger than you, as if the world hadn't screwed with this place yet. It felt like nature had the upper hand, and I liked that.

It was barely daylight, the sand still cool and moist between my toes. In the heat of summer, the sun would have already beaten down hard enough to turn the sand hot. But it was early autumn now, and I could wrap a shawl around my shoulders, dig my feet in, and enjoy it properly.

No one but Dad would wake at this hour, and as routine, I'd timed things out just right so that he had ample time to himself. I knew that right about now he'd be drinking his coffee (a pot I set brewing half an hour before he rose) and eating his English muffin, just slightly burned with grape jelly on one side and cream cheese on the other, pressed together like a sandwich. Every morning the kitchen smelled like charred bread. I'd tried turning the toaster gauge down, hoping he'd leave it alone, but without fail he would turn it up again. His silent protest. He'd rather eat burned toast than admit I was right about anything. At least he drank my coffee.

The waves were wild this morning with briny spray blowing up-shore, occasionally sprinkling my face and arms and forcing me to turn away from the water. The edge of something mostly buried in the sand caught the sun, and I bent to pick up a pearl nautilus. Simple and uncomplicatedly lovely, a pearl nautilus whispered its beauty. It wasn't showy like a cameo or frog shell, with their twists and nubs and variations. It never competed for attention, but it held and reflected a prism of light that perfectly complimented its surroundings. Someone else may have overlooked a pearl nautilus, but I preferred it.

Wendell and company had been gone for almost a month, and time was crawling without them. In fact, Katrina was talking about staying behind, remaining with Anna's group. The thought saddened me, of course, but who could argue? She had a chance to be with someone she loved, someone who probably loved her on a daily basis. I'd have been angry if she'd turned down such an opportunity.

Were it not for Katrina's incessant updates, I'd actually have had a chance to miss her. The latest report was that dynamite had detonated in Abram's group—the vampire and the gifted Sentient were engaged. In response, Christian had attacked William, and obviously, this didn't sit well with Lily. According to Katrina, "Lily repelled Christian so hard he smashed through a window. It was horrible…and completely fucking awesome!" Christian had taken off and no one had seen him for days. What a mess.

Katrina loved the excitement, but not me. I shunned it with all the strength I could muster. Life was hard enough. Kids were falling apart at the sound of Mozart, for Christ's sake! Who needed drama? What I *needed* was an endowment—just one tiny little gift. Maybe spoon bending or coin levitation. Hell, I'd be a supernatural dog walker if it solved this little issue of mine.

"Nicooooole! Chicken Tikka!!" Rajeep waved his arms like a loon from the deck of the house. My stomach growled. Had he said Chicken Tikka?

"You'd better not be screwing with me, dude!" I jogged through the sand toward him. "Not that I'm complaining, but who has Chicken Tikka Masala for breakfast?" I asked, holding on to the deck rail to catch my breath.

"Not now, crazy woman. For dinner. I'm going out for groceries. Shall I pick up the ingredients?"

"Shall a bear shit in the woods?"

"I'll take that as a yes."

Like I could pass up Raj's cooking. My weakness for Indian food was shamelessly evident to all parties, and I couldn't have cared less. What was one more pound to the extra fifteen I already carried?

I thought a moment. "Sweeten the deal with some *naan* bread and you'll own my first born," I told him.

"Always wanted a little girl," he said.

"Then get baking."

Smirking, he said, "Same to you."

I rolled my eyes. "I'm on it."

Yeah. I'd get right on that.

◦◦

"So what does this mean?" I spoke into my cell phone as I pulled up to the house.

"It means it's happening," Laura answered. "They're going to attempt to take the coven, and the way things are looking, we really need to stick around in case they need us."

"So, you guys have to fight?" I asked, my heart instantly racing.

"Not necessarily, honey. Abram insists we stay in Atlanta while they travel to Pennsylvania, so we'll be here, waiting for word from him."

"How long until they know?" I sighed, compulsively fidgeting with the air vent on the dash. "I miss you guys. And I'm worried now."

"I know, baby. But it shouldn't be more than a few days."

"And Katrina, that traitor," I grumbled jokingly. "Staying behind just because she's found the other half of her soul. Pssh. Whatever."

Laura snickered. "Don't worry, honey. It'll happen for you, too. Just you wait."

"Uuh, yeah. Sure."

"Okay, Wendell is about to take us all out to dinner. Tell the boys I said hi. Give your mom a kiss for me."

"I will."

"'Kay. Oh, and Nicole, stop talking on your cell phone while driving."

"I was being careful!"

"Doesn't matter. Next time pull over."

"She says *after* talking to me for twenty minutes."

"Goodbye, Nicole."

"Goodbye." The phone clicked off and I sighed, staring at the front door. Dad didn't have a job lined up tonight. He would be home and restless, which equaled moody. Ah well, I would take it like a man. I couldn't hide from him *all* the time, after all.

The house smelled like *naan* bread, and a football game blared in the living room. I peeked in to see my father resting with his arms splayed on either side of the sofa back, watching a particularly brutal tackle replayed in slow motion. His roots were showing, but we didn't dare to mention that to him. No one held on to their youth like my father.

Raj had always said to keep trying. He said you win more flies with honey than with vinegar. I bent forward to lay my purse on the seat next to my father. "Hey, Dad," I said quietly, and he jumped sky high.

"Jesus, Nicole!" He gritted his teeth. "You want me to die of a heart attack? What are you doing sneaking around like that?"

"I'm sorry. I was just saying hi," I mumbled.

"And I just missed the whole damned play! Shit." He shook his head.

"I'm sorry," I offered, gingerly taking a seat beside him. He scoffed and turned to the television again. This was mind-numbing. I hated football. Nevertheless, he loved it, so I made sure no one was doing anything on screen before speaking. "Who's playing?" I asked.

He stiffened. "Why are you asking?"

"I'm curious."

"You don't watch football."

"Well, I could start. I just need a little tutorial."

"Then buy yourself a book. Football for dummies, right?" he said, still focused ahead.

I swallowed hard. "I just…thought…"

"Think more quietly, please. I'm missing half the game!"

"I'm sorry."

"Jesus."

I held my breath and fought the ache spreading across my arms and chest. The effort left me trembling, but I would not cry. I would not cry in front of him, at least. An eternal instant later he turned away and leaned forward with his arms on his thighs in dramatic concentration. I stared at his back for a time, wishing I could disappear and sneak away silently. But no need. As it was, he took no notice of me when I stood up to leave.

I'd only been gone for an hour, tops, but I still worried. Raj and Gil were supposed to be keeping an eye on Mom, but it occurred to me now that everything was too quiet. A plate half-full of *naan* sat on the counter, so they'd clearly eaten, but they were nowhere in sight. Grabbing some bread, I ran upstairs to check Mom's room. The door was wide open, but she wasn't there either.

"Mom?" I crossed the bedroom and checked her bathroom. Nothing. Back across the hall I went into everyone else's rooms, including my dad's, but all were empty. "Raj? Where are you guys? Gil? Mom? Shit!" What if she'd had some kind of breakdown and nobody was there to comfort her? Grabbing the cell phone from my pocket, I plugged in Raj's number. His ringer sounded loudly from down the hall in his room. He obviously didn't have his phone with him. Next was Gil, who thankfully picked up on the second ring.

"Hey!" he started, sounding winded. "What's up?"

"What's up? I'm home and yet my mother is missing, as are her keepers for the evening. Where *is* everyone?"

"Beach!"

"What?"

"Beach. We're on the beach. Ugh!" His voice went an octave higher. "Nice toss, Raj. How 'bout you don't aim for that next time, though?"

"Gil, it's cold and dark out there! She's scared of the dark!"

"She's fine. She's sitting on the deck watching me and Raj play Frisbee."

"*You* and Raj?"

"That's right…me. What? You think I have no athletic abilities whatsoever?"

"I think you pulled a muscle trying to reach the coffee creamer." I snorted. "Hang on, I'm coming. This I've got to see for myself." I grabbed a throw blanket as I ran.

"Aaw, now don't go making me all nervous. I don't perform well under pressure."

"Too late!" I called out, waving a hand at my boys as they simultaneously lost their focus and the Frisbee slipped from Raj's grip and into the ocean.

"Oh, damn!" Gil scowled. "Way to break my momentum, Nicole," he shouted over the waves.

"Sorry!" I turned my attention to my mother, smiling. "Hi, Mom."

She watched, mesmerized, as Gil gracelessly fumbled through the freezing cold high tide to fetch the Frisbee. "Hey, Mom," I repeated, more loudly.

She turned to me but not in greeting. Instead, she glanced at me in confusion then cocked her head around as if to search for someone. "What does your mother look like, honey?" she offered kindly.

So, it would be one of *those* nights. "Oh, Mom…" I slumped into a chair beside her and exhaling my frustration. "She looks like the sweetest lady in the world," I began. "Her hair used to be all brown, but now it's mixed with a little silver. And her face is shaped like a heart. And her eyes are gray, and her nose is long and pretty. And her name is Rita Katherine Abbot. Have you heard of her?"

She gave it all she had, her still surprisingly smooth skin wrinkling at the eyes. "No." She shook her head. "No, it's not ringing a bell."

I nodded, trying to smile. "Well," I said, proceeding to wrap the throw blanket around her shoulders. "If…*when*…you see her, tell her Nicole said to come home. Tell her I miss her terribly when she goes away, okay?"

"What a sweet girl you are." She beamed. "If I had a daughter, I would want her to be just like you."

I laughed. "Thanks."

❧

"Another diet?" Gil narrowed his eyes at me. "Why, Nick? You're perfect."

"Shit, Gil, stop it. I own a mirror. I know I'm nothing to write home about."

"You seriously have one fucked up sense of self, you know that? I mean it. Put down the Slim-Fast, Nicole!" He grabbed the can out of my hand. "You're fine. Eat a cookie!"

"Yes, Gil. And Mom, be careful!" I said, dashing to the stove with a second to spare.

"I'm making tea."

"But you can't lean over a flame like that. You'll catch on fire," I said, turning the burner off.

"Fire is bad!" Gil spoke with a cookie between his teeth.

She sighed. "Oh. Well, how will I have tea?"

"I'll make some for you, Mom," I told her, turning on the faucet to fill her kettle with water.

"Nonsense. You don't need to wait on me hand and foot. I know I'm a little forgetful sometimes, but I'm not an old woman, and you fuss over me too much. Why don't you take a nice vacation?"

I laughed and hugged her to me. "I'm good, Mom. Don't you worry about me."

"Okay, then," she said, watching as Gil swallowed his cookie in one bite. "Are you two a couple?"

Gil choked. "What? No, Rita." He shook his head. "A couple of lunatics, maybe."

"Oh. Well, have we met?" she asked him. "I'm sorry, but I can't place you…"

He rounded the counter and looked her in the eyes. "Gilford Boyd, Mrs. Abbot. You used to give me haircuts, remember?"

"Did I?"

"Mhm. And I would pay you fifty cents. And then you'd turn around and give it back to me so I could buy an ice cream sandwich."

She smiled. "Well, that does sound like something I would do." Gil smirked in my direction, shaking his head.

"Come on, Mom," I said. "How about we listen to some Gershwin, huh? Gil, would you mind bringing the tea?"

"Not a problem."

She was getting worse. It was definitely building up to something, and I simply couldn't chance leaving her alone until after it passed. I just didn't trust that anyone else could handle her, even Dad. Scratch that—*especially* Dad. The whole thing was a fitting touch of fate, since it was my fault that she was sick to begin with.

The phone rang just as we'd reached the stairs. "I've got it," Rajeep called to us.

"Thanks!" I called back. "What do you think, Mom? A little Porgy and Bess?"

"Sounds nice."

"Yeah, nothing like a Romantic—" I paused as I caught Raj's tone, so rarely less than happy.

"Oh, Elaine. No. When?" he asked.

Gil and my father crowded around Raj, each in their own state of unease, and I stood with Mom at the stair rail looking down at them.

Raj listened in silence for a moment, and then said, "Yes. I see. Dear God…and William?"

At the vampire's name, my father straightened visibly, looking affronted. Raj lifted his fingers to his eyes and rubbed them while he spoke. "Of course I will. And you'll share our sympathy? Yes, thanks. Come home soon, safe and sound," he added before saying goodbye. He hung up the phone in a daze.

"What is it?" Duncan asked, taking Raj by the shoulder.

"Abram's group has diminished and scattered the coven," he said. "Wendell and the rest are in Pennsylvania."

My father lit up in appreciation. "So they needed us. And?" he urged anxiously.

Rajeep's eyes flitted to my mother, who had made her way back to the banister. I took her hand, just in case.

"They didn't need us. Our people drove out there for the funeral. They've lost the Energy Sensor, Thomas Ward. Thomas is dead."

Chapter Four

"Here, Samantha. Would you like to hold it?" I opened her hand and laid the hermit crab in her palm. Her eyes were fixed on the ocean, far out in the distance. Did she even feel it there?

"I used to be terrified of hermit crabs," I told her, lifting the tiny crustacean so its legs hung below the shell. "They reminded me of spiders." I shivered. I still hated spiders.

The wind blew Samantha's hair in her face, but she barely noticed. I brushed it away, tucking it behind her ears. Spiders…a song popped into my head and I found myself absorbed in the waves, humming a distracted version of *The Itsy Bitsy Spider*. It took me a second to notice that Samantha was staring at me, transfixed. "Oh, hello." I grinned. She dropped her gaze to the little hermit crab, extending its legs and attempting to stand. Her eyes widened as it lost its balance and plopped down again, the soft flesh of her hand a weak launching pad. All the while I held my breath. These moments of awareness had increased in the last several weeks. And almost always in response to…

I hummed again, more deliberately this time, and she turned the crab over, peering up at its under-side. It bicycled its legs in the air, trying to make out which way was straight, and Samantha snorted, then laughed at it, staring from me to the hermit crab in delight.

"Funny little guy, huh?" I giggled.

"Yeah."

Wait. Oh God.

"Samantha, what did you say?" I rested a hand on her face, trying to keep her with me. "Samantha…please."

Waves. Plenty of waves. A stray seagull. But no Samantha. She was looking through the hermit crab now.

Still, I wasn't complaining; I was exuberant! A word! And not just any word. She'd answered me, she'd understood. Samantha was definitely in there. Her parents were going to throw a party when I told them this. They said she'd babbled like a brook when she was a toddler, but she had all but stopped speaking by the time she was four. Now, at six years old, it was as if she was aging in reverse, losing her faculties.

Science strained to explain how seemingly healthy children with all their mental faculties could develop autism, and there were all sorts of treatment theories out there, valid theories, hopeful theories, but not winning theories. Not completely, anyway. One such practice was music therapy—my forte—and even this reported a hair-pulling slowness in outcome. But Samantha, she was proving that idea wrong every day. Each time we met it seemed like she poked her head out of the proverbial groundhog's hole a bit longer, and part of me questioned whether I was dealing with an autistic child at all. But I had to start somewhere.

I would have loved to stay outdoors with her all day, helping her to discover the world one hermit crab at a time, but it was chilly, and she was so small.

"Okay, up we go," I said, brushing the sand from the back of my jeans and lifting Samantha to her feet. I was in a better mood today. Not only because of Samantha's breakthrough, but because Laura and the rest were slated to return this weekend. After learning about the tragedy with Thomas, we all felt an overwhelming desire to get our people home.

Trina's latest report from Georgia said that things had finally settled down between Christian and William, but what a turn of events it had required to make it happen. Raj told us that Christian Wright had been mortally wounded by a vampire during battle. The Combatant was dying if not dead, and William Maddox, being a Healer, had sacrificed his own energy to bring Christian back. Thankfully, Abram had been able to do something to revive William, though the vampire was unconscious for weeks afterwards. All of this touched me deeply, since I'd always empathized with William's situation, but now my respect for him was sealed in stone.

Laura felt the same way as I did about the whole situation, which was typical. I'd never had much in common with women my own age, but Laura and I saw eye to eye on most things. Laura was more of a comfort to me than she probably realized. She was truly the heart of the house. In fact, though Wendell would never admit it, I could tell that he favored her company. Her mind was always opened, and where others would have missed the point, Laura perceived things with an eagle eye.

We had her to thank for the retrieval of a five-year-old Rajeep during her travels through New Delhi. At first, Laura had her sights set on Raj's mother. She had discovered that Mrs. Prabodhan was a Sentient after witnessing the woman cross over a spirit in her yard one day. Laura inquired as to why Mrs. Prabodhan was not practicing with a group, only to learn that her husband had refused to allow it. The woman chose, in accordance with custom, to respect his wishes. However, she'd kept a watchful eye on Rajeep, and the signs were there—her son was gifted. And together she and Laura came up with a plan. They convinced Mr. Prabodhan that if he allowed Rajeep to return with Laura to the U.S., he would receive a topnotch education, all expenses paid. It was an offer he couldn't refuse.

And Gil—neither of his parents had a clue. They certainly weren't Sentients, and they were far too busy to notice that their only son, though lanky, self-conscious and socially inept, was preternaturally brilliant. His grasp of the matter and motion and technicalities of the supernatural world was uncanny. If there was an entity around, he was often the first to know precisely what kind based on the temperature of the room or the particular scent—ozone, sulfur, limestone deposits that often accompanied an energy. Laura had followed a tip that led her to his boarding school, and the first time they met he was reading a quantum physics book in the corner of the school yard. When faced with a miracle like Gilford Boyd, basic science would have labeled him a genius and sent him to MIT. But she knew better. Unearthly intellect was just that—unearthly. Genius was merely one form of sophistication that an evolved soul could take.

Laura saw gifts in a different light than most Sentients. My father, for instance, was cut and dry, black and white. He held an admittedly arrogant view of what a Sentient was, of what a Sentient *should* be, and he had little patience with less-evolved souls outside of his job. To my father, you were either strong or you were weak. There was no middle ground. Wendell had tried, in decreasingly subtle ways, to loosen the iron grip of a superiority complex that wrapped itself around my father's skull and suffocated his brain, but nothing had worked so far. Duncan Abbot had married a Sentient woman and expected to give birth to a Sentient child. It only made sense to him that fate would deem this series of events appropriate.

Not to be. Rather, fate had dealt him a lemon named Nicole. And his dreams of perfection had tumbled downhill from there.

❧

"We're passing by Omaha currently," Laura told me. "We should be there by tomorrow night."

"Yay!" I pressed the volume button on my cell like a mad woman, trying to compensate for the bad reception.

"And…eh…one more thing," she sputtered and paused.

"What?"

"And we have a bit more cargo than when we started."

"Huh? You bringing me presents?" I laughed.

"Well, no." Her voice wavered. "Not per se."

"What do you mean, 'not per se'?"

"*Well,*" she repeated.

"Well what?" I laughed harder. "What is it?"

"Well, what are your feelings on British Combatants?"

❧

"Christian Wright? They're bringing Christian? What the hell?" Gil cursed and dropped the controller for his game system.

"I don't know." I cowered in his doorway. "I guess he just needed a change of atmosphere after everything that went down. I can respect that."

"Well, boo-fucking-hoo." He slung an arm out and grabbed the controller again. "This is a house full of Sentients, not a fucking support group. What's Wendell's angle? As if we weren't already buried under the weight of your father's asshole. Ugh!" He flung the controller again.

I shrugged. "Sorry, Gil. But I don't see the big deal. If he's half as conceited as you think he is, then he'd barely notice me enough to bother me. And you're an established Sentient in this house. You have a sort of seniority, so to speak. So chill out. You're making me nervous."

"Gimmi a break, Nick. I am not a Combatant and I'm not a Pathcrosser. My status in the Society is already a running joke. This whole thing is bullshit," he argued.

"Calm down, Gil. You're being…damn it." I recognized those footsteps.

Duncan stood in the doorway and narrowed his eyes at Gil. "Is there a reason you're throwing a tantrum in the middle of my day off?"

"Don't mind me," Gil settled down. "Just blowing off some steam."

"What the hell is the problem? You lose your Rubik's Cube?"

"Hilarious, Duncan. And no. My problem is that it's about to get a little crowded in here," Gil said.

"How so?"

"Wendell's got a tagalong. He's bringing Christian Wright."

Dad raised an eyebrow and cracked a smile. "Christian Wright, huh? Well now. I always liked that kid. I fought with his dad a few times," he said. "Christian Wright. That's not so bad at all." He beamed. "He could teach *you* a few things, boy."

Gil scowled. "*He* could teach *me* a few things?"

"Gilford." I spoke up in an uncharacteristically firm voice. He looked at me, and I pleaded with him wordlessly. The last thing we needed was the new Combastard *and* my angry father making our lives a living hell.

"Fine," Gil backed down. "But I'm not taking on a roommate."

"There's plenty of room around here. Lots of room," my father repeated, turning to leave. "Christian Wright," he mused as he walked away.

Gil exhaled loudly. "Of course your father is okay with it. He's about to get himself a Mini-Me."

"Knock it off, Gil. Seriously. I don't want to talk about this anymore, okay?" I begged him. Things were hard enough without Gil painting apocalyptic pictures.

"Yeah. Fine. I'm sorry, Nicky," he offered, standing up. "Come here."

I smirked and weaved my way across the mass of splattered game cases to his open arms.

"I'm overreacting," he said, squeezing me tight. "It'll all be cool."

"Yeah," I whispered.

Task at hand—examine the room soon to be Christian's. No one had ever slept in the guest room, though it was pleasant, I guess, in a very astringent sort of way. White bed, white carpet, white walls. Good God. I was going to go blind in here. Laura had asked me to see if I could warm it up a bit before they arrived, and I was beginning to think I needed a blow torch to manage that.

I'd gone to the Sears in Eureka and bought a chocolate brown bed spread and pillow cases, even picked up a few chunky candles that a guy might not be embarrassed by. The walls were barren, so I chose some black and white prints of local redwoods and hung a few around. Could this stuff honestly make a difference to someone who'd suffered devastating loss, a broken heart, and a near death experience? Doubtful. But the candles smelled fantastic.

Raj was busy making Indian for dinner. Laura informed us all that lamb *korma* was Mr. Wright's favorite, and Raj had been on the phone three times with his mother trying to solidify the recipe. It was questionable, in my opinion, that anyone who loved Indian cuisine as much as I did could be that bad, but it was better not to get my hopes up.

My dad, he'd been floating around on a cloud since yesterday, muttering excitedly about the virtues of a good, strong Combatant, regaling Rajeep with stories of his adventures with Christian's father, Daniel.

"The only thing I could fault Daniel with was being too damned soft with people. In fact, I bet he'd still be alive today if he'd listened to me once in a while," Duncan announced over his newspaper. "There's no room for bleeding hearts in battle. But everyone has their vices, right? And Christian, that poor kid. Who could blame him for going off on that son of a bitch of a leech? I don't care how many times that vampire saves his life, when you whittle it down to the facts, Maddox is a goddamned freak, soul or no soul, and I hope Christian remembers that."

Raj and I exchanged doleful looks. We both hated it when Duncan brought this up. In our minds it was akin to a kind of racism, and listening to him prattle on with ever-increasing vulgarity sent both our blood pressures soaring. Plus, Mom was sitting beside him, and she never took it well when Dad cursed. Every time he swore, she flinched.

"Mom, let's go pick out a nice outfit for you before they get here," I said, inventing an opportunity to get her away from Duncan. As precarious a state as she'd been in lately, the less harmful stimuli the better.

By six o'clock we were all chomping at the bit, trying to find ways to occupy ourselves. Gil was deafening himself with rap music, his iPod embedded purposefully in his ears, while I tried reading a psychological journal article on the merits of sound therapy techniques in the treatment of trauma victims. Duncan, of course, was attempting to look busy and unaffected, with his Blackberry in hand and a list of possible hauntings in Washington State. Still, every time a car drove down the freeway he'd subtly perk up and then glance at his watch. The only one of us who seemed truly unaffected was Rajeep, who stirred the contents of his *korma* calmly, humming something lovely all the while. He had a beautiful voice.

By six thirty-seven, Duncan was ready to make a phone call. "Hate for a meal to go to waste, after all," he said to Rajeep, "even if it's all that exotic stuff. I'll give them fifteen more minutes to show and then we're eating."

Only five minutes of my father's fifteen minute allowance were necessary. Just as Raj was taking the *naan* from the burner, a car pulled up in back of the house—then another and another. They had arrived.

I shifted on the couch, contemplating the odd sensation in my gut, before I realized that my stomach was in knots. Sociality wasn't my specialty. In fact, it often took me a few days to readjust to my own group if they'd been gone for any prolonged period of time. Now, enter Christian Wright, practically a total stranger. In fact, when I really gave it some thought, I couldn't even picture his face. Oh God, it would be okay, right? He probably wouldn't even see me there. I would smile politely and keep my words to a minimum, and I'd eat my *korma* from underneath the table.

"Here we go. Stir the curry for me, will you, Nicky?" Raj called, darting for the mudroom door and opening it wide.

I blew air out in a puff and ran for the refuge of the kitchen, catching my sweater on a chair.

"Shit." I looked at the pulled spot and determined that it wasn't so noticeable, but the occurrence had me second guessing my choice of attire. Maybe I should have gone with a lighter sweater. It would have been more slimming. And maybe I should have pulled my hair up. Damn it. Too late all around. Excited greetings and the sound of luggage being dropped filled the living room, while I stirred Raj's sauce distractedly. *How long should I keep this up?* I wondered. I didn't want to look antisocial.

"Nicky! Where's my girl?" The loveliest voice on earth called my name, and I dropped Raj's ladle.

"In here," I called weakly, and Laura waltzed into the kitchen at full speed. I couldn't even re-lid the pot before she had me in a spleen-bursting hug.

"You…look…beautiful, as usual," she remarked, leaning back to smile at me. "But a little pale." She placed the back of her hand against my forehead. "You feeling okay?"

"Oh, great. Fine," I said, a hefty storm still swirling in my stomach. "And incredibly happy to see you."

"Right back at you, babe. You coming out to greet everyone?"

"Course," I said in an ill-executed effort to sound casual.

"Well, come on, then!" She motioned with her arm, waiting for me to take the lead.

I forced a closed-mouthed smile and left the safety of the kitchen, Laura on my heels. The first face I saw was Theo's, and he was wearing the happiest expression he'd worn in months. Something had changed. I wondered briefly if Abram had managed to help him with his destructive tendencies.

When he noticed me approaching, Theo smiled in greeting and nudged Elaine, who was deep in conversation. She smacked at his arm, clueless to his intentions, and he shrugged in defeat as I settled into a fairly hidden hovering spot behind Gil. Everyone else was gathered around the new Combatant, and I couldn't see him properly.

"Nick!" Wendell called, dislodging himself from the crowd. An unfamiliar head turned in response, and my immediate reaction was to cease breathing. The man I could only marginally recognize as Christian—golden-blond hair, turquoise eyes, the strongest jaw line I had ever seen—was staring right at me. It may have only lasted a few seconds, but for the love of God, I swear to you on my life that time stopped.

Hadn't people been chattering away just a moment earlier? Where had the sound gone? Was I suffering from a freak onset of deafness? Panic! This was bad. This was a *nightmare*. What kind of expression was I wearing? Was I smiling? Was I gawking like a fish? I couldn't feel my face but for the intense burning in my cheeks. And why was my throat so dry? Oh, Christ—this was the worst case scenario, wasn't it? He was the most beautiful man I'd ever laid eyes on, and even in my bewilderment, even as Wendell dragged me—legs trembling—over to meet him, I knew without question that I was completely, royally screwed.

Chapter Five

"Christian, this is Nicole…Duncan's daughter, if you remember," Wendell said in introduction. "I talked about her."

Christian smiled politely, and that small gesture made him look even more stunning. "Yes. The miracle worker, right?" He extended his hand. "Good to see you, Nicole."

What the hell sort of bullshit exaggerations had Wendell been feeding him?

"I'm…" I laughed, nervously. "I'm not…nice to meet you, too," I said. "I mean, I meant…that it's *nice* to meet you, but I'm not a miracle worker." Oh, *God!*

He chuckled at my rambling, and my face burned again. Ugh! Close your mouth, Nicole! You may never speak words again for as long as you live!

"Well, then, thanks for the clarification. And I hate to be so forward, but is that *korma* I smell?"

"It is!" Laura chimed in. "You're in for such a treat. Rajeep isn't lacking where cooking skills are concerned."

"Rajeep, I am your slave for life," Christian kidded, still smiling brilliantly at my friend.

"Offer accepted," Raj answered. "Now let's get through with dinner so I can start compiling my request list."

They all rushed the kitchen, but I stayed behind, contemplating a very serious concern. How was I going to navigate this dinner without making a joke of myself? It only took a second to recall the value in my earlier solution. *No habla ingles.*

So, I put my strategy to work, inwardly contemplating the miracle of condensation on a water glass, crafting my napkin so that it resembled something close to a triangle but just short of a pyramid, and thoroughly sopping up every spare inch of *korma* with my *naan* bread. After all, butterflies or no butterflies, this *was* Indian food.

Long after the meal was over, the conversation continued.

"You'll note that Theo has not sentenced a single object to oblivion." Elaine smiled proudly.

"Hey, that's right!" Gil said. "Theo, you've gone a whole meal without smacking me with a fork!"

"Thanks to Abram," Theo said. "He had William working with me the whole time."

I could clearly make out the blood-red splotches seeping across my father's face, but Theo paid no attention, continuing with his spiel. "The kid's a Healer, all right," Theo continued. "William's okay."

Uh oh.

"Are you out of your mind?" Duncan barked. My mother jumped in her seat, and I took her hand. "You let him screw with you? There's not a damned thing that's 'okay' about a vampire! You know my feelings!"

"Yeah, yeah, we all know your feelings, Duncan," Wendell said. "But they're *your* feelings. And I think we should choose a more relaxing conversation topic than this, don't you?"

Good luck with that, Wendell. My dad was seething, of this I was certain. The thick vein in his neck was throbbing.

"Nicole?" Mom turned to me. "Why is he yelling at that nice man?" she asked, everyone's eyes falling on her.

"Damn it, Rita, it's Theo, remember?" Duncan growled. "He's Theo! Christ's sake, you've only know him for twelve years. And I'm not yelling!" he yelled.

She shrunk a little at the sound of his voice, and I tightened my grasp on her hand. "It's fine," I whispered to her. "Just ignore him."

Christian sat perfectly still, his face unreadable, obviously waiting for the storm to pass.

"Oh, by the way," Elaine piped up, saving the evening. "Katrina sends her love."

Wendell nodded. "Yep. It seemed a fair trade-off, a Mind Reader for a Combatant."

Duncan shook his head at the idea. "Only one Combatant now?" he questioned. "Abram better have plans to get a replacement soon. No group should function on less than two." He turned to Christian, clapping him behind the neck. "Not that we aren't happy as hell to have you, son. It's a fine thing to have another soldier in the house."

I expected Christian to glow in light of my father's approval and watched for the reaction. There was none. Where was the obnoxious egotism? Surely it would have leaked through by now.

"How do you like California so far?" Rajeep asked him.

"Oh, it's quite nice. Very scenic," Christian said.

"You should see it when there's leaves…on…things…" I heard myself say. *Uhm, what?* Leaves on things? Duncan rolled his eyes. *No, Nicole! You broke the word rule! No words!*

But Christian seemed amused, chuckling at me. "Yes. I look forward to leaves on things," he said. I gripped my napkin in my lap until my fingers turned white.

"We have possible vengeful entities in Seattle and Orange County," Duncan redirected the conversation. "Interested in helping out on either of those?"

"Of course," Christian said. Oddly, I didn't note any real enthusiasm there.

"Great. We'll take Laura or Raj along for the crossover, and then maybe we can hit a few bars, huh?"

Christian smiled. "Sure. But I'll admit I'm kind of a light weight."

"Ah, that won't last long." Duncan laughed.

Beautiful. My dad wanted to relive his glory days and recruit a drinking buddy. Oddly, I felt a sudden rush of protectiveness toward Christian. There was something just under the surface of his outward collectedness that was painful to watch. He had come here to escape, and Duncan couldn't wait a few hours to suffocate him with an agenda.

"You must be tired." Again, the words slipped from me without my permission.

Christian looked at me, a bit heavy lidded and more than a little striking. "I am," he said simply.

"Long trip," I continued. Was I *still* talking?

"Very. I'm exhausted, actually."

"Well," Laura began, "your room is upstairs, fourth room on the right, ready to go. It just needs someone to break in the bed."

"Happy to volunteer." He grinned.

"Yup. Sounds like a fine idea." Theo stretched his arms and yawned. "Think we could all use some shut eye."

"Agreed." Rajeep stood up, reaching for his plate.

"Leave it," I insisted. "You've been slaving over a feast all day. I've got the dishes."

"If you insist," Raj said.

As usual, I stayed behind with Mom, waiting for the room to empty, and then collected plates from around the table. I smiled when I reached Christian's seat. He had eaten two helpings of Raj's food whereas my father hadn't even bothered to finish his first. Christian obviously had a hearty appetite…and good taste.

Half an hour later the dishwasher whooshed away and the pots had been scrubbed. Mom worked a word-find puzzle book from the table, and I noticed she'd circled some things that were clearly not found in the Oxford English Dictionary.

"Mom? I'm not sure that 'J-U-O-R-T-F' is a word," I said, sitting down next to her.

"What? Oh," she giggled. "No, it isn't. Not too sure what I was think-ing," she trailed off.

Something clonked loudly from inside the dishwasher, and she peered at it distrustfully. "It's too loud, Nicky," she said, frowning.

"I'm sorry. Maybe we should leave the kitchen and go to your room. It's much quieter there."

"But what *is* that thing?" she asked of the machine, her eyes wide in slowly mounting panic.

"It's just a dishwasher. It's nothing to be scared of." I got up and opened the door, and steam billowed out. "See? It's just a loose Tupperware container," I explained, reaching my hand under the deluge of dripping water to adjust the object. "It won't be so noisy now."

I started the machine again and sure enough, it whirred more content-edly. Mom sat back, relaxing her shoulders. "Oh. Yes. That *is* better."

"Mhm," I agreed, taking a seat again and wrapping an arm around her shoulders. "Hey, look—I found a word. Present, see?" I touched my finger to the page. "P-R-E-S—Oh," I stopped spelling and turned to face Christian, who stood beside us patiently waiting for me to finish my grammar lesson.

Mom laughed at me. "Silly. There's no 'O' in present."

"I know, Mom." I forced back laugher and greeted Christian. "Hi."

"Hello," he said. "Forgive me for interrupting your present spelling, but Laura mentioned that you're the force behind the masterpiece that is my bedroom. I just wanted to thank you before I collapsed."

"You're welcome," I said. "I'm glad you like it." There. A sensible, non-humiliating reply.

Mom took him in, blinking thoughtfully. "Dear, has anyone ever mentioned how handsome you are? What was your name again?"

Christian's face lit up in a smile. Yes, he clearly understood he was handsome, and he knew how to use it, too. "It's Christian," he reminded her.

"Ah, yes. Well, you told me that, didn't you?" Mom clucked at herself. "You'll have to forgive me. I forget a lot of things lately."

"It's quite all right," he said, his gaze falling on my arm, still wrapped protectively around her shoulder. "And I do like the room, Nicole. It's very relaxing."

"Good. Kind of the point of bedrooms…relaxing," I said.

He nodded. "Absolutely," he said. "Well, I'll be going to bed, then."

"Okay. Good night."

"That's right," Mom said. "Good night, young man, erm, Christian." She grinned, pleased with her recollection.

My personal philosophy dictated that I should never take on more than one serious client at a time. It didn't seem fair to divide my feelings, observations, and insights among more than one child. They were too individually precious to lump together in a mass of overlapping ideas. But while Samantha was my current case study, I needed to supplement my income somehow. That was where my piano students came in.

"Your fingers will get longer," I assured the little boy at my side, his tongue jutting determinately between his lips while he struggled to widen the span of his hand.

"But what if I miss one of the notes in a chord?" he asked, looking eerily tense for an eleven-year-old.

"Then you miss a note here and there," I laughed. "It's not the end of the world. Just remember your finger stretching exercises. It'll get easier, I swear."

"Ugh." He dropped his elbow to the piano keys and laid his head in his hand. "I'm gonna look like an idiot at my school recital, aren't I?"

"No way! Peter, relax," I said. "Don't get yourself all riled up again. Did you remember your inhaler today?"

"Uh huh," he said, patting the pocket of his pants for reassurance.

"Then no problem, right? Now, why don't you practice those key chords one more time?"

Peter was neurotic. It was hilarious, really, how someone with so little life experience could be coiled as tightly as a stockbroker. Nevertheless, his mom and dad had obviously done a hell of a number on him. At this point in my existence, I was convinced that anyone who believed a parent did not directly have a hand in the way their child turned out was either high or guilty of being a really bad parent themselves.

After a few more laborious chords and the fear that poor Peter might suffer an aneurism, I called it a day and sent him home, hoisted my music books and CDs under an arm, and headed for the kitchen.

Gil bounded down the stairs ahead of Christian and my dad, slinging a jacket over his shoulders.

"You coming with us?" he asked me.

"Uhm…to the Lopez thing?"

"Mhm." He pulled an arm into a sleeve. "The possession. I figured you'd be interested in this one, you know, since it's a kid and all. And before you say anything, I've already talked to Wendell. He'll stay with your mom."

I shifted my stack of books to a counter. "Well…"

"She's not coming," Duncan stated, buttoning his coat up to the collar.

"I believe my question was directed toward her," Gil bit back.

"Too damned bad. She'd either get in the way or get herself killed. And I don't have the patience for either."

"Dad," I attempted to reason with him, "it might actually be beneficial for me to—"

"Beneficial?"

"It's just that there are all kinds of reasons behind behavioral problems in chil—"

"Save it. These cleansings are not fodder for your little hobbies."

"Her *job*, Duncan," Gil defended. "Her motherfucking career, Duncan!"

"Gil." Christian spoke evenly. "Perhaps Duncan has a point. Possessions are dangerous."

"Are they? No kidding?" Gil feigned surprise. "Well, lucky for me you came along and clued me in since I'm not a big strong Combatant and I obviously have no idea what—"

"I wasn't suggesting you were incapable," Christian added quickly.

"You'd better not."

"Gil, don't," I implored.

He'd promised to keep his cool, and I wasn't going to let him forget it. Though he looked to be chewing on nails, he held it together. "Nicole's got impeccable judgment. She's better with children than anyone I've ever met, and she's not stupid. She knows to lay low. Plus, Laura will be there."

"Fine!" Duncan snapped. "Let her pal along. In fact, why not invite a few wingless birds and an amputee while you're at it! I could give a shit at this point."

Christian frowned. "Duncan, she's your daughter…"

"I'll drive. Let's move it," Dad growled, grabbing his keys.

Christian hesitated, watching Duncan exit the house, and then said, "I suppose I'd better not keep him waiting. See you there?"

"That's right," Gil said.

I held my breath, and the moment Christian was gone I rounded on my friend. "Gil, what is wrong with you? You don't have to be so rude to him. And why did you make such a big deal out of this? I *don't* belong there. Shit, if it weren't for Mom, do you think I would even be *here?* They're right. I have no business participating in any of this."

"You do if Wendell says so, and he's always wanted you here."

"Because he's Wendell! He wouldn't turn away an axe-wielding giant!"

"Bullshit, Nicole! Just because he isn't loose lipped with all his secrets and doesn't say exactly what your purpose is here, that doesn't mean you don't have a place with us. And let's be realistic. Even if you left it all behind you, it would still be in your head. You're the child of Sentients. Knowing what you know, what better place for you than here? This Society is developing a fucking silver spoon complex, Nicky. It needs some perspective, and I'm sick of Duncan shutting you out of everything. Now put this on!" He held out my coat.

"Gil, no," I pleaded.

"*Coat*," he repeated, holding it out to me. He wasn't yelling anymore. He'd tired of yelling and was now utilizing unbending will. Once Gil reached this stage there was no refusing him. Had I tried, he would have thrown another fit, and I only had the energy to deal with one of those today.

I held out my arms in surrender.

Mateo Lopez was a family man, though his family was considerably smaller than what you'd expect. It consisted of a gray and white border collie named Rey and a teenage daughter—Adalia—the reason he woke up in the morning, and as of late, the reason he lost sleep at night.

In the past month, Adalia had suffered violent illness, vomiting so profusely that she became dehydrated, and if someone didn't do something fast, well, things were looking awfully grim in the Lopez household.

Gil, my father, and Christian stood around Mateo, asking the usual line of questions.

"I took her to the ER," Mr. Lopez told Gil. "They told me there was nothing seriously wrong, that she had a virus and I shouldn't worry. They gave her two rounds of IV fluids, kept her overnight for observation, and sent her home the next day."

"And then what happened?" Gil inquired.

"Then…*Madre de Dios*," he began, running his fingers through his hair before speaking. "She went crazy! She lost her mind!"

"How?" Duncan asked, ever impatient.

"Oh, Jesus. She started pulling her hair out in patches. Her scalp was actually bleeding," he said, breaking down in tears. "She was…she was having accidents, soiling herself. And now she only stares. She won't answer me anymore."

Gil exhaled, his eyes narrowing. I was sure he was working the near empty equation over already. "Did anything out of the ordinary happen before all this began?"

"No. Everything was fine. We were happy. She had nice friends, she made good grades. She was fine. We were fine," he repeated, taking hold of another chunk of his hair and crying a little harder. "God help her, my poor baby."

"So, no changes in habits? Where has she been lately, can you remember? Away on vacation? On a field trip, maybe?"

"No. I…I don't think so. No. Not in the last month."

"And you've been living here long?"

"Five years."

"Nothing odd has ever happened in your time here?"

"No. This is our home. We painted these walls." He waved his hand around. "In fact, the texture—Adalia made it with a sponge, see? She was so proud," he sobbed.

Christian placed a hand on Mateo's shoulder. "We'll find a way to fix this, I promise you," he said, his voice sure but gentle. "We will *not* allow your daughter to suffer any longer than necessary. And I know this must be killing you. I'm sorry."

I observed how Mr. Lopez lightened under the promise, the way Christian still clutched the man's shoulder, obviously comfortable with the physicality. Never once in his line of questioning or reassurances did Christian break eye contact with Mateo. My chest ached with a sensation so potent it filled my lungs, shortened my breaths. I wanted to look away, wanted to distract myself, but no matter how I tried, my will faltered and my gaze would fall on him again—absorbed in his gestures, the way his evident kindness stood in stark contrast to the things I'd heard. Had they gotten him all wrong, or had something changed him? Maybe both. But either way, I needed to avoid thinking about it, since it didn't matter how I felt about Christian Wright. He was positioned so far above me in the chain of favor that I was amazed he even remembered my name.

"We'll have a look at her now." Duncan's gruff voice shook me back to reality.

My father was the first in her room. The rest of us lined up behind him, with me—appropriately—in last place. The room filled, and I hung back, standing just outside her door with Gil at my side.

Her skin was so off-color. Where it should have been the rich tan of her father, it was gray and cast the light in a green glow. She was sitting up in bed, her back pressed to the headboard, staring at the blanket with little interest. I guessed she couldn't have been much older than fourteen.

"Addy." Her father addressed her with caution from beside the bed. "*Querida*, these are nice people…good people here to see you." He reached out to touch her, and then changed his mind. Poor man was afraid of his own daughter. "Adalia, please," he urged.

Laura stepped forward, stopping at the foot of the girl's bed. "Adalia, look at me."

The girl shivered in a wave that traveled from her feet to her shoulders, but she did not look up.

"Fine," Laura began, "then we'll do this my way." She breathed out, working whatever magic she molded with her energy, and the girl's head jerked forward, meeting Laura eye to eye.

"*Amo mi hija*," the girl said.

I fought the gag complex and held my breath as the stench of infection clouded the air.

Laura grimaced and breathed through her mouth. "What did you say?"

"*Amo…mi…hija*," she repeated.

"What did she say, Mateo?" Laura asked, still staring Adalia down.

"She said…" He swallowed. "She said 'I love my daughter.'"

Laura peered harder at Adalia's face. "Your eyes are older. You're not a child. What's your name?"

"*No tuve la culpa*," she cried. "*No tuve la culpa. Amo mi hija.*"

Laura chanced a quick look in Mateo's direction. "What…what is she saying now?"

"She said it wasn't her fault. And she loves her daughter."

"What wasn't your fault?!" Laura demanded. "What's your name?"

"*Me…me llamo es Isabel*," she choked, crying.

Mr. Lopez gasped, clutching Christian's arm for support.

"What is it, Mateo? Who's Isabel?" Laura asked him.

"No, no. No, no." He shook his head, repeatedly muttering prayers in Spanish.

"Mateo, please," Laura said. "Who is Isabel?"

"*Soy Isabel.*" The girl lurched forward and grabbed Laura by the chin. "*Por favor! Mi hija!*"

"What about your daughter!?" Laura insisted. "Who is your daughter?"

"Adalia!"

"Oh, shit," Gil muttered.

Laura gawked. "You're Adalia's mother?"

"*Si*," she answered.

Mateo collapsed and Christian bent to bear his weight.

"Why have you taken over Adalia?" Laura asked Isabel.

The possessed girl promptly shook her head, speaking Spanish too fluently to be absorbed.

"Mateo, you have to help us here," Laura said finally. "I know this is traumatic for you, but please, for your daughter. What did she just say?"

He sobbed a few times against Christian's sleeve before composing himself. "There's a book," he heaved in labored breaths, "under her mattress, there's some kind of book." He wept.

Duncan bent and felt around for the item, pulling out a leather bound book with worn writing across its cover. "I can't read this. What's it say?"

Gil approached him and examined the script. "It's Latin," he said, reading the scroll. "Huh. A book of Wiccan spells."

"Interesting," Laura said. "Someone's been busy. Gil, open up and check where she has it bookmarked. See the Kleenex hanging out? Right there," she directed him.

Gil flipped through pages and stopped somewhere near the end. "The spells are in English. Hmph. Figures—Beckoning the Dead," he said, tapping on the article before handing it to Laura. "So this shit actually works?"

"Well, now, that's the thing," Laura said. "Not literally. The spells in these books are nothing more than Bloody Mary games. But belief combined with giftedness can do wonders. And there's only one nature of person who can merge with a soul." She looked at Mateo.

"Wha…what is it?" he sputtered.

"Your daughter is a Sentient," Laura said, smirking.

Christian nodded in agreement. "And I'm assuming she's missed her mum so much that she found a way to summon her. Apparently, it backfired."

"*Si, si!*" Isabel nodded, her voice entreating. "*Por favor, ayudame!*"

"She wants help," Gil went on. "She's trapped. And two souls in one body? No wonder she's failing. It'll kill Adalia to stay this way much longer."

Gil's announcement thrust Mateo into a fresh round of hysterics, and Christian stooped over him, taking the man's face in his hands. "Mateo, calm down!" He shook him. "I promised it would be okay, and I meant it! Now, pull it together. You'll need to be calm for this to work, okay? Laura will need to concentrate. Otherwise, we'll have to take you out of the room."

Mateo sniffled back tears, nodding and composing himself while Laura sat beside the inhabitant of Adalia's body. "All right, Isabel. Time to go home."

I waited for it…and there it was, the hint of a golden glow that my eyes could barely fathom. To most Sentients, Laura's light would appear brilliant and cast a radiant heat, but I would never know that wonder. Not in this lifetime, anyway.

All was peaceful silence for a moment, and then Adalia's body began to seize, her eyes rolling back in her head. Mateo jumped up, prepared to interfere, but Christian held him firmly in place. "This is good, Mr. Lopez. Just breathe. This is what we want."

The troubled father looked unconvinced but obeyed, and his faith paid off. Adalia collapsed in Laura's arms, taking in a few ragged breaths before opening her eyes.

"Papi?" She pulled away from Laura, scanning the room for her father. "Who are these people?"

Christian released Mateo, who grabbed his daughter up in a massive hug.

"*Ai, querida*. I love you, baby," he wept, rocking her.

*

I raised an eyebrow at the pallet-sized crate of oranges in Wendell's already teetering shopping cart. Damned Costco. You may have arrived with the idea of buying a pack of toilet paper, but after all was said and done you were going home with an eight pound bag of frozen peas and a year's supply of Fig Newtons.

"I really hesitate to uproot the girl," Wendell told my dad, grabbing a two-pack of red wine as we walked. "Her abilities haven't peaked, and right now what she needs most is her father."

"Well, supposing she's a Combatant?" Dad argued. "That's years wasted that could be spent sharpening her skills."

"She has plenty of time. I'm not worried," Wendell resolved. "And I doubt that combatance is her particular endowment, Duncan."

Adalia Lopez had been the matter at hand all day, and opinions among the group varied, but generally it was agreed that Adalia's family had been through enough. Wendell would not be retrieving the poor girl anytime soon. I was glad to hear it.

"Kids," Duncan grumbled. "It's like an epidemic. Seems like all we ever deal with nowadays. Don't ghosts haunt the over twenty-one crowd anymore? No real threats or malicious spirits, no leeches. I haven't broken a goddamned neck in ages. Bet you're chomping at the bit too, huh boy?" My father beamed at Christian, smacking him on the back.

Christian's face tightened. "I could do without the heavier stuff for a while."

Wendell nodded. "That's right, Duncan. Uneventful is a *good* thing," he reminded him. "Believe me. After what happened in Pennsylvania, I wouldn't wish for it."

"Yeah, well, it's what I was made for," Duncan said, lifting a massive jar of deli style pickles.

"You were made for peace," Wendell stressed, stopping abruptly to face my father. "So much so, that fate saw fit to equip you with the means to preserve it. Remember that."

Dad grunted and put the pickle jar back. Evidently he'd changed his mind.

Wendell turned to me. "Nick, would you mind picking up the rest of the raw stuff?"

"No. Sure," I said, happy to ditch the sunshine and flowers of my father's disposition. "What would you like?"

"The usual. Tomatoes, mangos, bananas…uuh…potatoes, strawb—"

The look on my face must have clued him in to the fact that I'd only been born with two arms and *he* had the cart.

"Uh, sorry, *chica*. Christian? You mind helping her out?"

"Of course I will," Christian said. "Nick? Care to lead the way? I'm better at locating people than produce." His smile was charmingly boyish.

Anything you want. "Sure," I said.

❦

"So how can you tell if it's ripe? I mean, green is bad, right?" Christian asked, pressing a finger into his mango.

"Yeah, green is bad. So is yellow in some cases…like with limes. But not in others, like with bananas." *Oh God. I was doing it again.*

"Okay, so, yellow limes bad, yellow bananas good." He picked up a tomato and peered at it. "This is green. That can't be good."

"Actually it is," I said. "They're supposed to be green. Because they're, well, they're green tomatoes."

He frowned. "Sounds like circular thinking to me."

"I'm sorry," I laughed. "God, are these potatoes or boulders?" I puffed, struggling to lift an enormous netted sack.

"Here, let me get that," he said, walking up to take the bag from me. He offered a warm smile, and heat rose to the surface of my skin. It was baffling how his face was so contoured and strong while still youthful. And the way his smile extended to his eyes…

"Uhm…thank you," I said, remembering myself.

"You're welcome. I'm told you're magnificent on the piano, and I'd hate for you to injure something before I've had a chance to really hear you perform."

I smirked. "Wendell. He likes to spread rumors."

"Yes, but not lies. Will you play for me sometime? I realize you do it for a living, but for some reason the most I seem to catch are fragmented versions of nursery songs."

"Yeah," I chuckled, looking down. "Not much demand for Chopin from five year olds."

"Well, then. I demand it," he continued. "Tonight."

"Okay. Though, I'll admit I don't usually play for the sake of entertaining. I mean, I play by myself, but…well, my dad doesn't, you know, he thinks it's distracting and noisy. But okay, yeah." I nodded, forbidding myself from uttering another syllable.

"I look forward to it," he said, hoisting the bag of potatoes over his shoulder.

Chapter Six

"How are those mums shaping up?"

"Oh, they're almost ready for showing off," Laura's husband, Chris, whispered over the television, wary of my sleeping father on the chair beside him. "Thanks again for the seeds. It was a good batch."

"You're welcome. Can't wait to see them," I said.

Chris Polmieri was, by far, the quietest member of the house, even when compared to me. But he was also blessed with an endowment far too amazing to be real. Granted he was not a Pathcrosser; he could not speak with the dead, nor could he understand them. He was not a Combatant, and though his energy was invaluable in battles with vampires, his abilities had nothing to do with strangle holds or cracked heads. No, Chris's soul was so in tune with nature that he could—to some degree—control earthly elements. This came in handy when you wanted a plant to grow more quickly or forgot to bring your bug spray on a camping trip, but his gift extended beyond that still. Chris Polmieri could manipulate the will of nearly anyone he desired so long as they were within close range.

Of course, this hardly meant he *did* so, but his endowment was yet another miracle of unconventional sentience that Wendell had the foresight to appreciate. It had come in handy during many vampire encounters, and poor Chris had been specifically targeted by the creatures for turning on repeated occasions. Everyone wanted Chris, and yet he avoided the world. Botany was his one and only love, aside from Laura. He fondly tended his boxed herb gardens and relished the greenhouse Wendell had set up for him. He grew anything and everything he could get his hands on, and no one ever wondered where Chris was. We all knew that if we needed him, he'd be hunched over a barrel of potting soil or watering his hosta plants, looking every bit like someone's favorite teacher.

Chris was incredibly aware of the world around him, but most people wouldn't know it because he didn't say much. Still, he noticed everything, and I could say this with a certain degree of confidence because I was the same way.

He and Laura had met and married barely five years ago, and he was incredibly content now. But this happiness came only after having suffered the overzealous attentions of some federal agents who'd gotten wind of his abnormal abilities. Once Wendell learned of a Sentient under scrutiny, he jumped in to save the man, and it took every vital contact that Wendell had to engineer the situation, convincing the agents that it was a fluke, that they'd been mistaken, that the eyewitness reports of Chris saving a group of kids by throwing his arm in the air and somehow stopping a tree from falling were false—mass misconception. So, Chris joined our group and was eternally grateful to Wendell for his intervention.

Being so aware, it did not escape Chris's attention that something was off about my father. To be honest, Duncan's treatment of me disturbed Chris to such a degree that it drove him to contemplate the breaking of his own vow—that he would never manipulate the mind of a human being outside of self-defense. Vows aside, our favorite green thumb had offered to take some proverbial pliers to my father's brain and attempt a repair job. I turned him down—though for a quick moment, it tempted me. But the idea that Duncan might love me or treat me with respect because he was wired to do so, not because he *wished* to, was somehow more disturbing to me than enduring his ill temper. In my heart, I had hoped he'd come around on his own, that he'd forgive me for my inferiority and carelessness.

Instead, every day that Mom's condition worsened, so did Duncan's. I knew it pained him to see her this way, and my continued presence made things worse, reminding him of everything that had gone wrong and why. Regardless, I couldn't just leave. Mom didn't take well to many people—my father included, though that was mainly his fault. Her reactions infuriated and humiliated him, but I imagined they must have crushed him as well. Mom was the one person who had ever behaved fearlessly around my father. She was never intimidated by his mood swings, never disinclined to show him affection, and in turn, he had been gentle with her, even warm. But now, he had no one. And in spite of his coldness, my heart went out to him, because I knew the feeling of being alone.

"I'm about to hit the hay," Chris said. "Night, honey."

"Night."

It was dark outside. It had been for several hours. Mom was in bed while Duncan snored like a tractor in his recliner chair. I couldn't help but think that it was a good thing my parents didn't still share a bedroom, or Mom would never sleep again.

The whole house was still, and everyone but my dad had finally retired to their rooms for the evening. This was one of those nights I felt the powerful urge to play the piano, alone and uninterrupted, with the ocean as my only audience. But there was an obstacle. Earlier in the day, Christian had asked that I play for him. Even with the French doors closed, he might hear me playing and feel obligated to show some interest. I'd never thought I deserved his attention, and I didn't want him to think I did. It was a twisted form of pride rooted in self-loathing, but I couldn't help it. Kind of a Catch-22. *I want you to notice me, but I don't want you to notice me wanting you to notice me.*

Coming off as needy or eager was not an option. No way in hell was I delusional enough to believe that I had any chance with Christian Wright. In fact, I wasn't going to think about it anymore. I over-thought everything, and it only depressed me. I just wanted to crawl into a hole in the ground and hide from my pretense of a life or—a saner alternative—go to sleep.

Getting up from the couch, I gave my drooling father one last look and headed toward the stairs. Then I froze at once, my guts leaping into my throat to see Christian heading down the steps, phone in hand. Obviously, he had plans for the evening. Attempting to pull off casual, I forced myself to smile in passing.

"Evening," he said. "Wait—you're going to bed?"

"I'd thought about it. Kind of dead around here."

"But it's only nine o'clock. And you promised you'd entertain me!" He smiled. "You owe me a song."

"A song? But right now, though?"

"Why not?"

"I might disturb somebody."

"They're all awake up there."

"Oh, but, aren't you making a phone call?"

"I was. I was talking to my mum, but I'm done now. Come on, Nick, just one little song." He arched an eyebrow. "Are you that shy about performing for people?"

I looked at him guiltily. "Always. Isn't that obvious?"

"But you have to play for your students, don't you?"

"It's not the same."

He nodded, laughing quietly. "Well, I suppose it isn't. So I'll just have to bring you out a bit, won't I? Because shy is not in my repertoire."

I grinned. "Thanks for the warning," I said, following him back downstairs toward the sunroom.

"Embrace your fear. It will only make you stronger," he joked.

"Right."

The moon was near to full and hung above the ocean like an ornament. It was a stirring backdrop to a private concert, and yet Christian gave it a run for its money, reclining on the wicker loveseat in front of the window. His hair was looking a bit disheveled this evening, a deviation from its usual perfection, but I liked it all messed up this way. If only he wasn't so distracting. If only his arms and shoulders weren't so completely perfect, somehow treading the line between muscular and lean. And if only he didn't keep smiling like that, his expression of anticipation causing me record levels of performance anxiety.

Why the hell hadn't I played more for people, gotten used to the stage fright? I was a jittery mess.

"Can't…" I swallowed, laughing self-consciously. "Can't seem to concentrate."

He chuckled. "Take a deep breath, Nicole. And do keep in mind that I have absolutely no musical skill whatsoever. In fact, were I to sing for you right now I'm confident that you'd be irreversibly ruined for life. So, even if you play half as well as a green tomato, I'll enjoy it."

I hadn't meant to, but I giggled openly at his comment. The way he pronounced "tomato" with a British inflection was positively adorable. Sighing, I stared at the instrument with resolve, reminding myself that the keys were my friends, that this piano had been the keeper of my emotion, my heartache, my desires for years, and in turn, I had made it sing. Surely it would not desert me now, in my hour of need.

"Okay. Do you have a request?" I asked him.

"Me? No. No, no, no. I hardly know anything about music, er, good music that is," he specified. "Surprise me."

Surprise him. *Okay*. What did I know by heart? I knew a lot of things by heart, but there was definitely one piece that tumbled most comfortably from my fingers.

"'Kay. I've got one. But it's kind of long," I warned him.

"Good! The longer the better."

This was it. Beethoven, don't fail me now. Hands to the ivories, I closed my eyes for a discreet moment and swallowed the lump in my throat.

Then I began.

Beethoven's *Pathetique Sonata* started in a slow, bittersweet sort of way, as if he had written this part to mourn a memory. The usual swell of emotions clouded my vision, but I pushed away the impending tears. *Can't play if you can't see, idiot*, I scolded myself. *And don't look up!* One glance at Christian's face was sure to kill my flow. Though I could tell, from the corner of my eye, that he had moved and was hunched forward, watching my hands.

Thankfully, there always came a point where the song carried me along in its current, where thoughts of technique and measure would cease because it was engrained, it was natural. My fingers had memorized the movements and my heart took over, lulling me into a sort of melodic sleep. My eyes fluttered closed and only opened once I'd reached the adagio movement. It was impossible to remain entranced through this section. The notes built to a quick, more intense purpose in the minor key, creating an involuntary adrenaline rush.

It occurred to me, in those moments when every ounce of self-conscious thought, every insecurity and biological manifestation of fear was gone, that as long as I kept playing, as long as I rested my head on the shoulder of this gift, that I did not dread what Christian thought, what *anyone* thought. I knew little short of the overflow of feeling between the music and myself. It desired me. It embraced me. It adored me. When it ended, I would be lonely again—but for now…

Back to the grave allegro of Beethoven's mind I went, back to the reverie of its melancholy and soft, entreating arms. Right now, my soul understood its purpose here. It was content and fulfilled. And as I played, something—and I would contemplate this with much frustration afterwards—whispered on the edge of my understanding.

The final notes slowed my heart rate, and I dropped their low chords for the finish. The world came back into focus, first the air around my ears, then the waves outside.

"God…"

I turned my head, still heavy with the solemnity of the moment, to face Christian. Casting him a tired smile, I breathed deeply for the first time in over seven minutes. His eyes were glassy, as if he'd been crying, but that wasn't possible, was it?

"Nicole." Duncan's put-out voice preceded his arrival. He shuffled into the sunroom, rubbing his eyes. "Why do you always play this shit so late when people are trying to…uh, hey, kid," he addressed Christian.

"*I* asked her to play for me," Christian remarked, a harder edge to his voice than I'd heard him use before. "In fact, I forced her to. She didn't want to, really. I can't believe you don't have her playing night and day, for Christ's sake. She's bloody well brilliant, isn't she?"

Duncan glanced at me indifferently for a few seconds before speaking. "It's late."

"Dad…"

"Show some consideration. I said it's late!"

An angry mix of pain and embarrassment glued my eyes to his face. Could he even see what he did to me? Did he even care? And what could I say? He'd already made enough of a scene for everyone.

"Fine. Good night," I said stiffly and stood up from the piano bench, my whole body shaking with the familiar effort of beating back tears. I hadn't wanted to see Christian's face, didn't want to see whatever pity was probably there, but it was unavoidable if I was going to get the hell out of here.

Passing the two men, I was surprised to find that Christian wasn't looking at me at all. He was looking at my father, his expression one of disbelief and something else, but I didn't stay to analyze. Rather, I kept going without looking back, straight up the stairs and down the hall to my bedroom, barely getting the door closed before the stupid tears sprang loose and washed down my face with a vengeance. I dropped where I stood and curled up against the floor, holding my breath.

"Damn it," I cried quietly, drying my face with my palms.

It was super early on a Saturday morning and I had no clients, so this was the perfect day for Elaine and me to take Mom on a little expedition, maybe to the redwoods. That would guarantee as little interaction with people as possible. After last night, I didn't think I could face Christian ever again, and I was itching to disappear as quickly as possible. My embarrassment had not faded much with sleep.

"So, how do you feel about going to Fern Canyon today?" I grabbed a napkin from the island's blue glass countertop to wipe away some cream of wheat from Mom's cheek. "We haven't been there in a while."

She mulled the idea over. "Have I ever seen it?" she asked.

"Yes. And you love it."

"Really?" She seemed convinced. "But I thought we were going to see the trees."

"We are." I refilled her glass of orange juice. "Fern Canyon is part of the redwood forest, Mom. Don't worry, there will be trees everywhere."

For some reason, my mother had an inexhaustible love for the redwoods. And even more bizarrely, they were the one thing that stuck with her. She forgot her way from the front of the house to the back, but she always remembered the redwoods.

"Have you eaten breakfast yet?" she questioned with a look of motherly concern.

"I did. I ate while you ate. Here." I showed her my empty bowl. "Remember?"

"Oh. I ate too, huh?"

"Yes," I giggled. "Look at your bowl. Don't you feel full?"

"Well, yes, I do." She laughed as well.

"Oh, Mom." I sighed, a sudden wash of sadness threatening to crack my smile in half. Leaning in, I kissed her forehead. "I love you, you know that?"

"Thank you, dear. You're so good to me. When are we—" She stopped, focusing on my face.

"When are we what? What's wrong?" I frowned.

She didn't respond, only pushed away from the table and stood cautiously, looking around the kitchen. "I'm lost," she said, wide-eyed with panic.

"No, Mom." I got up quickly and approached her. "You're not lost. You're exactly where you belong. This is home. You're not lost."

"I'm home?" She scanned the room again.

"Yes. You are. You're in your home, with me and Dad and Wendell, and we're going to see the redwood trees today, okay?"

"Oh." She released a breath. "I love the trees."

I nodded.

"And you're a sweetheart." She patted my cheek. "Erm, can I ask your name just one more time?"

"Mom, I'm Nicole. Please don't forget me." I could barely get the words out, my throat was aching so badly.

"Aah. No, of course not, honey." She smiled. "Definitely not."

"Okay. Then finish your juice and we'll get going, huh?"

She nodded, glancing over my shoulder. "Oh, good morning! Would you like some juice, too?"

"Good morning," Christian answered. "I bought donuts." He held up a paper bag that looked like it had just barely survived a bout of hand-to-hand combat. "And I'd love some juice, thank you."

"You're up early," I said.

"So are you." He set the donuts down on the counter and got himself a glass. "Is it the kind with pulp in it?" he asked.

"I think." I turned the carton over to examine the label. "Yep. Pulp."

"Fantastic. My favorite." He sat down, pouring himself some juice. "I like beverages with bits of things in it," he explained, smiling at his admission. "Don't know why."

I laughed a little. "You're in the right house, then. Wendell does, too."

"Smart man, that Wendell," he said, downing the juice in a few enormous gulps. He licked the excess pulp from his lips and my legs went limp. "So, you ladies have any plans for the day?"

"We're going to see the redwoods!" Mom said excitedly before I could answer. "They're wonderful! Have you ever seen them?"

"No. No, as a matter of fact I have never been to the redwoods," he admitted.

"Oh, what a shame! You should come with us!" She beamed as if this was the greatest idea ever contrived, and I thought I might throw up. Surely he had better things to do.

"Mom, he probably—"

"I'd love to," Christian said. "Sounds brilliant. Nicole? Do you mind a third wheel?"

Oh, God. He was doing this out of pity, wasn't he? He felt sorry for me.

"Of course not," I began. "I mean, usually Elaine comes with us, because Dad doesn't think it's safe to take Mom to the forest alone, but if you come we wouldn't need her. We could be gone for quite a while, though…if you had anything else planned." I offered him an out.

"Nope. Whole day's clear. I'm quite excited about this, to be honest…" He sounded sincere enough. "I could use an excursion."

"Okay, well, grab a water bottle." I nodded toward the fridge, and then cringed. Shit. He wasn't a little boy. He didn't need me to tell him what to do. And yet, he hopped up from his chair, obediently opening the refrigerator door. Retrieving an Aquafina, he considered the bottle carefully, his eyes scrunching together thoughtfully.

"Hmm. Maybe I ought to bring two?" He sounded torn.

My heart melted. "Maybe." I smiled, wanting to cry. *Or you could have mine*, I thought. *Or you could have everything.*

⌇

Fern Canyon was splendid; few would disagree—especially in autumn. But should you be the least bit claustrophobic, its beauty quickly faded to the back burner. Canyon walls, nearly fifty feet high at most points and covered in moss and fern, pressed against either side of the forest floor. The redwood trees, towering like gods in the background, were evergreens, and they'd retain their color throughout the year, but the floor of the forest was coated thickly in vermillion-colored needles—the giant sequoia's idea of falling leaves. It was early November, and the fern was yellowed now, the air steeped in the aroma of dead leaves, moss and sodden wood. Fall's perfume, Wendell called it.

"Do you need my scarf?" I asked my mother for the second time in half an hour.

"No. I feel fine," she insisted. "Really."

"Nick, you've buried her beneath a sweater, a hooded jacket, and a winter coat. I'm quite certain she's maintaining a healthy body temperature," Christian said.

"I just don't want her to get chilly," I said, shivering myself. Typically, it wasn't quite as cold as this in our area. The climate was pretty moderate, hovering around sixty degrees or so this time of year. But today it was only in the forties, so I'd given my mother half my wardrobe since we began walking, and I was starting to feel the chill myself.

Christian frowned at me. "You're starting to resemble a corpse," he said and shrugged out of his coat. "Here."

"No! No, it's okay. I don't need it." I crossed my arms.

"You do, too." He laughed at me. "I'm not blind, Nicole. I remember our little produce lesson. Eggplants and plums should be purple. Lips should not." He wrapped his coat around me, and the warmth sunk into my body immediately. I smiled to myself, realizing that it smelled like him.

"What cologne do you wear?" *No! Why had I asked that?*

"It's called Woods, ironically. Abercrombie, I believe. My sister picked it out for me since she didn't like the one I was wearing." He snorted a little.

I nodded. "Your sister has good taste."

"She'd agree with you on that one," he said with a smirk. "Glad you don't despise it, since you'll probably smell like it for the rest of the day."

"No. It's nice," I said, breathing deeply. No way would I have a problem with that.

"So, do you bring her here a lot?"

"Well, *here* here, like, Fern Canyon? Or to see the redwoods in general?"

"Just in general," he clarified.

"Often enough, I guess. She really likes it."

"Hm." He nodded thoughtfully. "Well, perhaps Elaine wouldn't feel too put out if I de-posted her from the position of Redwood Excursion Combatant. I'm quite taken with these woods. Do you mind?"

"You…oh…okay," I stuttered. I was blushing, wasn't I? *Son of a bitch.*

He chuckled. "Anyway, I have to tell you how incredible you were on that piano. I mean really, truly amazing. It's pretty intimidating."

"Uh," I laughed. "I don't know about intimidating."

"Yes, intimidating," he persisted. "I mean, the thought of trying to plunk out *Chopsticks* makes my nose bleed, and there you are, with your bloody eyes closed like some kind of musical goddess, making these incredible things happen with a giant wooden box and some metal strings!" He rolled his eyes. "Intimidating," he reiterated.

I smiled in spite of myself. "Thank you. But anybody can learn," I said. "Honestly. It just takes practice."

"And no small modicum of giftedness," he added. "Yes, anyone could play. But I doubt they could do what you do."

What in the blazes? How was I even supposed to respond to something like that?

"Hey, Mom, remember the pink flower petals you collected last spring?" I changed the subject.

"From the ground?" She glanced at the dirt around her feet. "The rhododendrons?"

"Mhm. You still have those, remember? They're pressed into a book."

"I do? How nice."

"Yep. I'll show you when we get home."

"All right."

Christian looked to his left, at the canyon wall. "What about these?" he asked, plucking some yellow fern. "Can you press these?" he asked me. "It seems like something my mother would like."

"Sure you can," I said, trying to hide my astonishment. "I'll show you how." What kind of a Combatant *was* he? Gushing over piano technique? Collecting leaves? Surely he was breaking some kind of masculinity rule. My father would be appalled.

"You know, now that you mention *teaching*," Christian started, looking a bit sheepish as he ran his fingers through his hair. "I don't suppose I can impose upon you to…well…"

I lifted an eyebrow, waiting.

"That is, do you suppose you could possibly teach me how to play piano? I mean, even just one song," he said quickly. "It sort of, I don't know. It seems very calming somehow."

Jesus. "Okay. Yeah, we can start with one song and decide where to go from there," I said.

"Right. Good." He smiled again, that youthful, glorious expression that would have been blissful had there not been something broken behind it. I could guess what that look was about. He still loved her, Lily, I was sure of it, and he was trying to find a way to console himself. But that was fine. I would gladly help him.

Chapter Seven

Nessun Dorma was one of my favorites. It had been performed by all the greats: Placido Domingo, Jose Carreras, Mario Del Monaco. But no one sang it like Pavarotti, and so he serenaded me from my laptop while I checked e-mails. The Brocksmiths were querying again. I had told them nearly a month ago that I was already with a client, apologized profusely, and recommended a few local therapists. But thanks to Wendell's ridiculous pimping of me to everyone he'd ever met who might remotely suggest they needed an alternative therapist for their child, I was turning people down left and right, and it killed me. But I was adamant about my one client rule. I knew I couldn't completely fix these kids. I knew some of them would never get better, and I might as well have been beating my head against a brick wall. The universe hadn't intended for everyone to experience this life from the same perspective, and I could accept that—so long as we tried anyway, just in case.

I gave it six months. Six months and I knew. If improvement was made, I could teach the parents how to continue therapy at home. If nothing more could be done, then I would recommend they take a different route. After that, I would seek Wendell's guidance in choosing another client, just as I had always done. If this meant I was a piano teacher a majority of the time, so be it.

I wrote the Brocksmiths back again, pressed send, and an instant message window popped up on my screen.

TrinaWin81: I miss you! How's your mom?

AbbotN: Katrina! Miss you, too! She's not doing too well. She's getting worse.

TrinaWin81: Oh no, Nicky! Do you think she'll have another episode?

AbbotN: I hope not, but this always happens. She'll probably be better afterwards.

TrinaWin81: Is your dad helping at all?

AbbotN: What do you think?

TrinaWin81: Grrr. I'm sorry, babe. I wish you'd let me beat some sense into him. I'd enjoy that.

AbbotN: Thanks, lol.

TrinaWin81: And how's Christian working out? He being an ass?

AbbotN: No, actually. He's really nice. The way Gil talked I expected him to come in and take over. He's asked me to teach him to play piano.

TrinaWin81: Uhm…what?????

AbbotN: *shrug* Yeah, I don't know.

TrinaWin81: Shut the fuck up. Huh. You know what they say. Music tames the savage beast.

AbbotN: It's breast, Trina. Music tames the savage breast. And he doesn't really seem all that savage to me. Honestly.

TrinaWin81: You sure about the breast thing? And okay, hopefully he's gotten it all out of his system, but he's been pretty fucked up, Nick. Just be careful.

AbbotN: I'm positive. And okay, I will. But I'm not worried. Really and truly.

TrinaWin81: Good. Hey, how's Samantha?

AbbotN: She's been making progress. But she's missed the last few sessions, so I hope it doesn't set us back. She's coming over today.

TrinaWin81: Good luck! Hope she improves by leaps and bounds!

AbbotN: That makes two of us.

TrinaWin81: Anna says hi, btw.

AbbotN: Hi, Anna! Okay, I have to go and get ready. I love you!

TrinaWin81: Love you, too! I'll call you this week!

AbbotN: Kay. Bye

TrinaWin81: Bye, Nick.

I shut the computer off and gathered my thoughts. What did I know about Samantha so far? We'd been together for nearly two months, and in that time she had smiled, laughed, reacted badly to Mozart, and spoken her first word in three years. Definitely improvements. But her parents had been trying things at home—playing music, even bought a keyboard in hopes of rousing her interest, and Samantha would not respond. In fact, they were skeptical of my reports altogether until I proved it to them, made the little girl giggle one day by singing a theatrical rendition of *Wheels on the Bus*.

As I understood Mondays, they were usually thought unpleasant, and people wanted nothing to do with them. But I welcomed Mondays. They meant that Duncan would probably be out and about, finding things to pummel, and I could do my job in peace—even better if he worked a job that required he leave for several days. He liked to stay busy, my father.

This was one such Monday, and my father wasn't due back until tomorrow. On days like these the house was lighter, everyone laughed louder, stayed up later. I wondered if Duncan knew the effect he had on the people who were, in the best sense, his family. No one wanted to be around him any more than they wanted to be around a hungry lion—and even those you could appease with some road kill.

It was eleven o'clock on the dot, and the doorbell was already ringing.

"I'll get it!" I heard Christian's voice from downstairs, so I slowed my descent.

By the time I'd reached the door, Christian had already let Mrs. Fitzpatrick in and was holding Samantha by the hand, leading her into the kitchen. "There she is." He smiled when he saw me.

"Morning, Carol," I greeted Samantha's mother. "You've met Christian, I see."

She grinned. "I have! And good morning! You have no idea how eager I am to get her back on track. After she left you last, she smiled at least three times in twenty-four hours! But, because I haven't been able to bring her lately, well…" She frowned at her daughter. "It shows."

I nodded. "Well, you know, I can always bring a session to your house if we have to," I said.

"Oh, could you?" she gushed. "Gosh, that would be so fantastic. I mean, it wouldn't happen often, but when my customers run over their scheduled times…"

"I'd be happy to do it," I assured her. "Now, hello, sweetheart." I leaned down to look at Samantha. "I missed you. I found a song you might like. Do you want to hear it today?"

She lifted her face a little, focused her eyes.

Carol laughed, delighted. "That's unbelievable, Nicole," she said. "How do you do that?"

I shook my head, smiling. In truth, I was just as surprised as her mother to evoke such a quick response, but I took it as a good sign and squeezed Samantha against me. "Okay. Let's get started," I said.

"Pick her up at one, right?" Carol asked.

"One o'clock," I agreed.

"Thank you so much, Nicole! Nice to meet you, Christian. I'll see you all later." She kissed Samantha on the top of the head and left us to our session.

"Well." Christian bent to her height. "It was very nice to meet you, Samantha," he said. "I'll just leave you two alone," he finished, cutting across the kitchen toward the living room.

Samantha blinked and shot her head around. "Christian."

I gasped as Christian stopped dead in his tracks, turning slowly.

"Oh my God," I breathed. "Christian, come back," I whispered, still watching Samantha.

He came toward us again, warily, stopping in front of Samantha and questioning me with his eyes.

"Samantha," I began. "Where's Christian? Can you show me?"

Her breaths picked up just slightly, like the act required exhaustive effort, and she lifted a hand to his cheek, holding it there. Her tiny fingers rested so tenderly against his face, as if in a gesture of comfort, and Christian's expression read pure bewilderment.

"He…hello again." He barely spoke, smiling ever so slightly at the child. I thought I would cry when she smiled back, but I wasn't prepared for what happened next.

"Hello," she answered.

I covered my mouth, muffling the urge to squeal. Nearly everyone in the house had met Samantha, but she hadn't responded to any of them. What kind of a miracle was this?

"Christian," I composed myself. "I don't know what else you had planned for the next two hours, but I'm going to have to ask you to cancel it. I'm not letting you go anywhere."

He chuckled distractedly, still mesmerized by Samantha's contact. "Consider me your prisoner then."

"It has to be your energy," I said, contemplating Samantha seated contentedly in Christian's lap. "She won't let anyone else near her but me and now you. She won't even let her parents hold her for this long."

He smiled down at the child, clasping her hands in his. "I don't…I don't know much about children," he admitted. "I mean, I've always wanted them, but I haven't had much experience. We have a little girl back in Abram's group, Ginny, her name is. You remember her?"

"I think so. Vaguely," I said.

"Yes. Well, I never paid that much attention to her, to be honest. I suppose I didn't pay that much attention to anything short of myself," he said, frowning. "And you know, this isn't so bad, really." He motioned to Samantha.

No. It wasn't so bad, watching him—strong and soft at the same time. It wasn't so bad knowing that the core of him was so warm and approachable that this unapproachable child was sitting there, fidgeting with his fingers, looking positively at ease for the first time since I'd met her. But the mystery of it would make me crazy, keep me up at night, until I understood. What was it about him that appealed to her so? What could she sense?

"I'm going to try humming while you hold her, okay?"

"Okay."

This had been the typical daily routine for Samantha and me, adding a few new songs every session. *London Bridge is Falling Down* seemed an appropriate starting place today, and worked nicely in combination with Christian. Samantha proceeded to hum with me for half the song, losing interest only during the second section. Then it was on to *Mary Had a Little Lamb*, one of her favorites. I stopped humming midway through, but she kept going, humming the song to its end, and then looked up at me.

"Aah, I know, I know. New song." I giggled at her impatience. "What haven't I sung to you before?"

A thought popped into my head. I wondered how she'd react to a vocal version of the dreaded *Twinkle, Twinkle, Little Star*. It had been a disaster when we listened to it on the CD player, but maybe she just hated surround sound. Plus, Christian was here.

"*Twinkle, twinkle, little star*," I sang. "*How I wonder what you are.*" She stopped fidgeting in Christian's lap and went rigid. "*Up above the world so high, like a diamond in the sky.*" Samantha whimpered, flinging herself around to bury her face in Christian's chest, clinging to his arms so tightly her fingernails dug into his shirt. Christian wrapped his arms around her and I stopped singing.

"What's happened?" he asked me, looking just as frightened as she was. I scooted across the floor to rub her back.

"It's the song," I said, confounded. "What is it about this song?" I pleaded. "What is it, Samantha?"

She ignored me, only easing her terrified grasp once I laid my face against the back of her head and hummed something benign. We must have stayed like this, the three of us, for a good five minutes until Samantha was back to normal—well, normal for *her* anyway.

"Thanks for doing this," I said to Christian.

"You're welcome. I'm glad I could help you. Though it seems you're at even more of an impasse than you were before."

I sighed deeply. "Yeah, I know. But one thing seems certain," I added, smiling at the little figure of Samantha molded into Christian's arms.

"Hmm?"

"You're some kind of key for her, Christian. Maybe we should talk to Wendell."

"You think?"

"I do."

"Yes, well. That might be wise, then," he agreed, pausing to watch as I straightened Samantha's now disheveled hair. "And Nicole…"

"Hmm?"

"Your father is an idiot."

☙

In college, I used to teach piano students for free as field work. It amazed me how rude the students could be, how ungrateful and demanding despite the fact that they were getting something for free. Or maybe it was *because* they were getting something for free. Perhaps people inherently distrusted something they didn't have to pay for. That aside, Christian was the epitome of gratitude.

"So this is a staff," he reviewed.

"Mhm."

"And these are the notes on the staff."

"Right."

"And this…" He squinted, pouting at the music in front of him. "Er…I've forgotten this one."

"It's a measure," I reminded him.

"Oh! Yes, measure. Right, sorry." He scratched his head.

"It's okay!" I laughed. "There's so much to remember here. Do you want to go over notes again?"

"Okay. Sure. Uuh…C is here."

"Yep."

"Then D, E, F, G, A, B, and C again."

"That's right. Remember: Every good boy does fine. E-G-B-D-F." I touched the notes as we went. "And all cows eat grass. A-C-E-G. Hmm?"

"Right. It's so easy now, but God help me the moment I'm stuck alone with this jumble. I wouldn't remember a bloody thing."

I laughed. "You will. I'm quite certain."

"Well, at least one of us is." He rolled his eyes. "How the hell do you go from *this*" —he flicked the simple tutorial song I'd set before him earlier— "to this!" He nodded at my stack of classical piano pieces.

"Patience."

He sighed. "Well, let's try that up and down the chord thing again, shall we? At least it almost *sounds* like I'm playing something."

"Okay," I giggled. "Start here at middle C."

He fumbled once, twice, knitted his brows together endearingly, and fumbled again. "Bugger," he grumbled.

I snorted. "Okay. Part of the problem is your finger placement. Here." I took hold of his hand, positioning his fingers properly and ignoring the fact that my heart was beating inexcusably quickly in response. "It'll be a lot easier for you this way. Try again."

Sure enough, he made it through the first three scales without an error.

"See? Told you!"

"Hmm. Show me once more," he said. "This way?"

"No, your pointer finger goes here, your thumb goes here…and…" I paused, noting that Christian's eyes were no longer on the piano, but rather his face was turned toward mine, and there was the edge of a smile on his lips.

"And?" he whispered.

I jerked my hand away. "And…then you…play stuff."

His half-grin turned full-fledged, and he laughed at me. "Right. Stuff." He nodded. "Is that relatively close to *things*? As in, what leaves grow on?"

My jaw dropped, and he continued to chuckle, spreading his fingers across the keys for a new round of chords.

Chapter Eight

I sifted through all of my memories, trying to identify what it was I had been feeling lately, and with some effort I settled on hope. This wasn't something I was used to having, so it had concealed its identity from me as long as possible. But I was dragging it from its lair anyway, kicking and screaming, and leashing it to my life.

Christian had attended the last few of Samantha's sessions, and she continued to react well. She still wouldn't speak much more than his name, but her tendency to mimic our activities and awareness of his presence continued to grow. What a shame that Christian couldn't join us today. Samantha would miss him. I would miss him. But he did have an actual job, and I didn't want to provoke my father's wrath by monopolizing the son he never had. Still, Duncan couldn't stop me from moping on the inside.

In the meantime, I needed to find Gil. The house would fall apart around us if it weren't for him. Pausing outside of the bathroom, I tried to discern what manner of sound was issuing forth from inside. It was almost human, but shrill.

"Gil." I smirked, opening the door. He didn't hear me, just kept straining for notes in the most hilariously awful way. "Gil, good Lord," I giggled over the sound of water running and more hideous vocal contortions. "Gil?" I rolled my eyes.

Oblivious.

"Gil!" I shouted.

"Oh, shit! Hey! Jesus, Nick, turn around!"

"I can't see you, you lunatic. The door's all fogged up. And what the hell are you singing?"

"Kanye West!" he said. "It's *Gold Digger*." How could you possibly not know this song?"

"I've heard the song, Gil. I just can't identify the noise you were making as anything close to it."

He heaved an impatient sigh. "Is there something I can help you with this morning—other than serving as the butt of your jokes? Shit, I swear you're channeling Katrina or something."

"There is, as a matter of fact. I need you to have a look at the icemaker before you leave. It's making unnatural noises, and Theo is convinced that it's possessed."

He snorted. "Fine, sure. You know, I'd like to know when I became the Sentient repairman."

"That would be when everyone realized there wasn't a thing on this planet you couldn't fix."

"Whoopty-doo." He turned off the water, sticking his hand over the top of the shower door. "If you don't mind…towel? Please?"

"Uuh, sure," I said, handing one over. "So, I'll see you in the kitchen."

"Right. Hey, wait. Nick?"

"Huh?"

"What's up with Christian and the kid? Laura said he went all Mr. Mom at your session the other day."

"Yeah. Samantha took to him immediately."

"Well, I guess she's too young to know better."

"Gilford Boyd."

"What?"

"Quit saying stuff like that, okay?"

"Why?' he laughed. "What, are you guys friends now or something?"

"I dunno…yeah," I said.

The shower door opened a bit, and Gil craned his head around to look at me, water dripping down his face. "You and Christian—friends?"

I shrugged. "He's a human being, Gil, who just happens to be a Combatant."

"Yeah, well, you of all people should know that Combatants have a short fuse, Nick. He could go off at any time, and I don't like the idea that you'd be around to catch some of the fallout."

"He's harmless."

"He attacked William," he reminded me.

I stared at him. "I'm sure he regrets that."

"And what makes you think that?"

I considered his question before answering. "You guys aren't the only ones who can sense things, okay? Now hurry up and get your soggy ass downstairs. The icemaker's waiting."

"Check yourself, Mozart. I have to leave for a job, and I don't know if I'll be able to fix it yet."

"Fine," I sighed. "And how long will you be gone?"

"Might be a day, might be a few days."

"Helpful. Is Wendell going?"

"Think so."

Crap. I'd have to track Wendell down immediately. I really wanted to talk to him about Samantha before he left, and if there was anything I'd learned in my years with Sentients, it was the merit in grabbing a word while you had the chance. They could be out the door at the drop of a hat.

"Can I have some privacy now?" Gil asked, shivering behind the shower door. "I'm freezing to death. Seriously, we're talking major shrinkage."

"I'm out!" I backed away, blocking my ears at the word shrinkage. "Need to talk to Wendell anyway."

"Well, you know where he is," Gil called after me.

Yep. I sure did. It was nine o'clock on a Wednesday morning, which meant that Wendell was on the beach, tearing up the sand.

The Seer had been practicing tae kwon do for longer than I'd been alive, and at this stage, he'd stopped caring about his rank, though Chris, who knew a thing or two about martial arts, guessed that Wendell was probably at least a *Sahyun,* if not a Grand Master. And that was all fine and good, but I was only sure of one thing: that I couldn't even think about moving the way Wendell did, because if I tried, it was likely that the bones and muscles in my body would simultaneously rip in half, and I'd be left writhing on the ground like a dying jelly fish.

Wendell's hair was in a ponytail today—typical for him when he practiced—and the casualness of his sweats was in direct conflict with the grace and ritualism of his movements. Of course, no one would give two shakes, because he was mesmerizing to watch, balanced so perfectly still for the moment, then switching from one stance to another, from Zen to deadly and back again.

I wasn't about to take any chances with my life, so I waited until he was quite finished before approaching, clearing my throat to get his attention.

"Hey there, peaches!" he said, barely out of breath. "What are you doing out here in the cold morning air?"

"Watching you fight invisible Ninjas."

"Hah!" he laughed. "And did I win?"

"You *so* won."

"Excellent."

"So, while you glory in your victory, can I have a word with you about Samantha?"

"Of course. Speak to me," he said, bending to grab a towel from the sand.

"Well, something crazy happened a few days ago."

"With Christian?"

"Well, yes, actually. Laura told you?"

"Naturally."

"Naturally. And I don't know what to make of it. I was hoping you'd have an idea of why she'd reacted so well to him."

He wiped off his face and neck, slinging his towel over his shoulder. "Well," he started, "would you believe me if I told you I had no idea?"

I frowned, raising an eyebrow in demonstration of my incredulousness. "No, I wouldn't, since you tend to say you don't know things, when, in fact, you know a hell of a lot."

He snickered. "I'm not so sure about that, either, but I can say that, for whatever reason, the universe doesn't want me to know this one. I haven't the foggiest, Nick. It's all a blank."

A blank, my ass. "Come on, Wendell, seriously?" I pleaded.

"Very seriously," he said. "All I can advise is to keep it up. You'll figure it out when you're supposed to."

"Ugh, fine," I groaned, moping more than ever. That would teach me to hit Wendell up for information right after he'd tae kwon do'd himself into a metaphysical nirvana. I would just have to believe him—or at least pretend to—and keep on trucking with Samantha in the dark, which figured, since that was my perpetual state of existence, anyway.

"I'll need to take the whole thing out," Gil complained, his head still in the freezer.

"So long as it stops making that damned noise," Theo said.

"I'll pick up what I need before I come home." Gil stood up straight, closing the freezer door. "It'll be fixed by the end of the week at the latest. But for now, you'll have to suffer a warm can of Mendota. Sorry, buddy."

"T'sokay. I'll just put it in the fridge, thanks," Theo said. "So where are you guys headed today?"

"I don't know. Something about the spirit of an old lady."

"It might be a hag entity." Duncan entered the kitchen with Christian behind him. "But we're not sure if it's human or not," he said, stopping to fill his thermos with coffee.

Gil shuddered. "Creepy as hell, if you ask me."

"Nothing we can't handle, right, son?" Duncan smiled at Christian. "By the way, how about a round of beers after?"

"Sure." Christian nodded politely.

"Great!" Dad's buttons nearly popped off his shirt. "Well, grab yourself some grub, kid, and let's get this show on the road."

Christian snatched a couple of pieces of toast from the table, holding one in his mouth while he shoved the other in his pocket.

"Would you like a Ziploc bag for that?" I chuckled at him.

"Oh." He glanced at his pocket. "Yes, actually. I really do like this coat. Hate to get crumbs in it."

Still smiling, I grabbed a bag from a drawer and handed it to him before returning to my seat.

"Thanks," he said.

"Mhm."

"By the way. Tell Samantha I said hi. Sorry I can't be at today's session."

Duncan stopped buttering his toast and glared at me. "Don't waste his time on a bunch of senseless crap, Nicole."

"Duncan, I don't mind," Christian told him. "I like doing it."

"You don't have to patronize the girl!" Duncan laughed. "You're not obligated to keep her company."

"No. I am *not* obligated. I *enjoy* her company," Christian said.

Duncan peered at me again, then at Christian, then at his toast, shaking his head. "There's *important* work to be done, son. Don't let yourself get distracted."

Christian gawked. "I'm…I'm *not*," he asserted. Meanwhile, the sick, rippling pain was back, but I ignored it. Tears were the enemy. Tears would only prove my weakness to a man who already thought me feeble in mind and body.

Escape. Escape! "Good luck with the old hag," I said, manufacturing a smile, and then grabbed my toast and headed off to check on Mom. I would engross myself in coming up with various projects to keep her busy while I saw my students. Then it would be time for Samantha.

❧

"How 'bout we bang on a drum today, honey?" I lifted up a little set of bongos and a spoon, with Samantha on my lap. "Okay. Here we go."

Sixty seconds of this was more than enough, and it wasn't getting me anywhere.

I put the spoon down on the piano. "No drums. How about maracas? I've got maracas." She barely blinked, and I touched my face to her apple-scented hair. "Samaaanthaaa," I sang. "Where is my responsive girl today, huh?" I sighed. "I wish Christian was here."

She lifted her head and looked to my right, toward the door.

I smiled. "Who are you looking for, Sam?"

She took a few quick breaths, her little lips parting. "Christian."

"You're looking for Christian," I laughed.

The tiniest smile, hardly noticeable to someone who hadn't spent hours every day memorizing her face, lifted the corners of her mouth.

"I don't blame you. You know, just between you and me, I kind of like him, too. Maybe we can lasso him for the next session, if my dad will let him. Of course, now that I've got your attention…"

I banged on the drums again, and she jumped, snapping her head around to look at the spoon. "You wanna do it?" I asked, opening her fingers and placing the spoon in her hand. She didn't drop it—a good sign. "Come on, you. Give it a try, you know you want to." I took hold of her wrist, and we banged it together a few times before I let go. At first she did nothing. Then she lifted the spoon and hit the drum…and again…and again. My eyes prickled. This was good. This was so good.

"We need to show Christian!" I squeezed her tight.

She stopped beating the drum. "Christian."

"Yes!" I laughed loudly. "Exactly!"

In my mind, I was compiling a whole slew of things I wanted to try with Samantha when Christian was around. Maybe I could get her to sing, maybe even teach her to play a few notes on the piano. But I was getting ahead of myself. It probably wasn't wise to start planning her debut at the Met when she had yet to speak a complete sentence in front of me. Still, this little occurrence had me on pins and needles all day, waiting for Christian to get home so I could tell him what had happened. On the other hand, I felt pathetic and presumptuous, thinking that he'd be as concerned with Samantha's case as I was. After all, Dad had a point. Christian had his own work to do. And killing evil monsters *did* kind of qualify as a priority engagement.

I wasn't the early-to-bed type, but once the clock read eleven-thirty I gave up waiting and headed upstairs. This was stupid, waiting for him. What was I thinking? It was a blessing, really, that they had yet to come home. It saved me from making a fool of myself.

The night was unseasonably warm, so I pulled my hair up in a ponytail even knowing that it wouldn't stay there. Its baby fine texture often meant the hair tie would slip out before night's end. Then I dressed for bed—a tee shirt and shorts seemed like appropriate sleeping attire, since I couldn't sleep when I was too hot.

It was amazing how a routine could keep my mind off the fact that I was alone. Little comforting things, like watching TV in bed or reading whatever I could get my hands on. These served to keep the sadness at bay most of the time. But lately, since Christian's arrival anyway, those routines weren't hacking it.

I grabbed a bottle of lotion from my night stand and got into bed, prepared to moisturize. One look at my legs, though, and I wondered why I bothered. The calves were shapely, I supposed, but I could never get my thighs to look the way I wanted them to. Not that I hadn't tried. I'd been dieting for years. I'd been through workout tapes, DVDs, gym memberships. I'd taken up walking, swimming, and even had a short tryst with Pilates. But the stubborn extra pounds always came back, and I didn't have the willpower to starve myself. I just liked food too much. I liked to cook it, I liked to experiment with it, and I liked to eat it, plain and simple.

Fine. Once again I would embrace sleep and hope to dream about something worthwhile, something completely out of the realm of possibility, but beautiful nonetheless. And if Christian just happened to play into said dream, so be it. I tossed the lotion on the floor, fluffed my pillow and lay down.

Sleep had almost found me, my mind drifting into a state of half-awareness, but someone was talking loudly, and the deep haze rushed away. I opened my eyes, and though I couldn't make out a word they were saying, my first thoughts were of my mother, who had always been a light sleeper. Surely this would wake her up.

Throwing the blanket off, I got up and listened at my door. It was Duncan, a very boorish and, from the sounds of it, very inebriated Duncan. Shit. The last time he'd been drunk was nearly a year ago—a violent rage-filled episode that led Wendell to contemplate asking him to leave.

I took a deep breath. Nothing short of Mom could drag me out to witness this, but I knew she'd be up by now, and I prayed she hadn't left her bedroom. I steeled my nerves and opened the door. Without the walls of my room to mute it, Duncan's voice was near to shouting. He was close to the bottom of the stairs from the sound of it, and Wendell, Gil, and Christian were trying to calm him down. What was more, Mom had left her room and was sitting on the top step, coiled in a frightened ball.

"Just get the fuck off! I can get my own goddamned self upstairs!" Duncan slurred. "Don't need your goddamned help!"

Wendell said, "Duncan, you can't even stand up straight. Either you sleep on the couch or you let us help you to your room."

"Mom," I said as loudly as I thought was safe, but she couldn't hear me. "*Mom*, come here," I said a little louder, but her attention was rapt.

I had no choice but to go and get her.

Walking at a near creep, I approached her and dropped on one knee, taking hold of her shoulder. "Mom," I whispered, refusing to glance downstairs. "Come with me."

"Nicole!" she blurted just loud enough for everyone to hear. "He's yelling!" she said, and then she started crying.

"It's okay, Mom. Don't do that. Just come with me. It'll be fine. I'll stay with you tonight, all right?"

"What the fuck is she crying about?" Duncan pulled out of Wendell's grip and leaned against the stair-post.

"Dad, she's just scared," I said. "Come on, Mom. *Please.*"

"No," she sobbed. "No. I can't stand up! My legs are shaking. I'm afraid."

"Don't be scared. I'll help you wa—"

"That's right!" Duncan mocked. "She's scared. Because her fucking brain is shot to hell! Because my goddamned offspring destroyed my wife! Did I ever tell you…" He turned to Christian. "Did I ever tell you why my wife is a fucking mental case? It's a…it's a great story!" he said, half-slouching. "Because Nicole, as everyone knows, is fucking defective! And her mom—"

"Don't do this." Wendell spoke warningly, but my father ignored him.

"Her mom coddled her, tried to make her feel like she was actually worth a shit!"

Christian stiffened. "Duncan, you need to stop."

"But she's *weak*! And common, so fucking useless. My wife" —he pointed a shaking arm at my mother— "my wife was destroyed trying to protect her from a fucking dark astral!"

Wendell grabbed my father by the shoulders. "There's no one to blame, Duncan! Things happen!"

"Fuck that!" He turned to me. "If you'd had one ounce of decency, you would have stayed behind…you would have stayed invisible…exactly where you fucking belong. You're a cross, Nicole. You're my fucking cross."

My mother, now a wailing mess, shook with her face pressed into my chest. I knew my expression betrayed nothing. I could feel the numbness there. My survival instinct had kicked in. If I'd allowed myself to feel even a small portion of what was threatening to swallow me up, I was certain I would have been crushed under its weight.

And so I stood up, my mother's arms slipping from my waist, and took her hand.

"Mom. You have to come with me now," I said.

Miraculously, whether it was by her will or because the detachment in my demeanor suggested everything was well again, she stood up and let me lead her down the hall to her room.

I lay with her for nearly an hour, until the commotion had finally died down, and everyone—Duncan included—was silent. When her breaths became shallow and slow, I left her, making my way to my own room.

Everything looked different, surreal, though I'd just been here and knew the room like the back of my hand. Duncan had finally said it. He'd finally copped to everything he'd *nearly* said in the last few years. And even if he didn't remember in the morning, everyone else would. We would all have a breathtaking image to go with the common knowledge. Duncan Abbot hated his defective daughter. No—he despised her. And he wished she'd never been born.

I doubted I'd sleep tonight.

Sitting cross-legged in the center of my bed, I stared at my feet for a while. My toes and fingers were frozen—a common reaction to trauma—while my face and neck were super-heated. In the back of my mind I wondered if I could sit like this forever: silent, motionless, staring catatonically at nothing, blocking out every thought. But I never had the chance to test that theory.

My door cracked open, and I was mildly aware that a figure had entered my room. Then, he closed the door behind him and crossed to my bed.

"Nick." Christian sat down beside me, placing a hand on my back.

I considered saying hello. I even considered—though dimly—that it was rather unconventional to enter someone's room without knocking. But I was still frozen, my head and my heart disjointed.

"Nicole," he whispered again, running his hand up to my face. It was warm. I shivered. "Nicky, I'm so sorry."

I felt myself breathing and concentrated on that, trying to collect the clarity to respond. "It's okay," I said, finally. "It's nothing."

"Nothing? Nicole…" He turned himself to look at me, taking my face in his hands. Immediately, my feet became compelling again. I couldn't meet his gaze.

"Nicole, it's a big deal. Family…they lift each other up. They care for each other, they don't judge, they don't belittle." He brushed my cheek with his thumb. "My mom…she would love you. You're a lot like her, you know—kind, gentle. You take care of people so well. And you never complain, even though—God knows—you really should."

Somewhere, far away, his words echoed and resonated, but all I could make out were bits and pieces. His hands were so warm. I closed my eyes.

"Hey." He brushed my cheek again. "How about if you just say one thing, huh? Maybe just 'Take a hike, Christian' or something."

Say something? But there was only one thing in my head right now. It was a flash of images. "I'd been gone away to college," I said calmly. "And Mom was so excited to have me home. She didn't want to be away from me for one minute. It seemed like a routine thing, you know? Just another cleansing. But it wasn't. There was a black entity that had spun off a whole group of people. It was ridiculously strong. And it was smart.

"She was wrapped up in watching my back, but that left her vulnerable, and the entity knew it. It must have been some kind of energy drainer, because it sucked her dry of everything she had. She couldn't walk." A trickle of feeling was returning and my throat felt tight. "She couldn't see, she couldn't hear or speak for months. And then when she could…she didn't know me. She couldn't remember us." I pictured her face, empty of light and reason. "And I tried so hard to *make* her remember. I showed her everything she'd ever loved. I taught her how to tie her shoes again and how to brush her teeth, and I took her to see the redwoods…and…"

Christian gathered me up in his arms, pulling me against him so hard I thought he'd suffocate me. "I'm so sorry. I'm so sorry, Nicole," he repeated. "It'll be okay."

"No. It won't." I pulled away from him. "It will never be okay. I can't fix this. She loved me, she knew me. It might have been the only gift this life allowed in spite of what I lack. And now, she can hardly remember my name! And Dad, I can't make him love me. I've tried. But I represent everything he hates. I could never do anything good enough, because it's not what I do, it's what I *am*."

"Nicole. I've seen what you are, and it's better than Duncan can ever hope to be."

"Christian, cut the after-school special bullshit."

"Listen to me!" he insisted angrily. "I know a thing or two about guilt, Nick! About feeling helpless!"

I shook my head. "It's fine. This is just how it is. It's fine."

"You aren't fine! Shit. You're allowed to get upset. You're allowed to bloody well *feel* something!"

"Well, good, because I feel like a fool!"

"*Damn it*," he said, burying his fingers in his hair. Then his eyes intensified, and I could tell he'd decided something serious. I couldn't conjure the desire to ask what, but it didn't matter because there was no time to. In the quickest instant, he'd slid his fingers behind my head and was kissing me, his lips moving over mine in a fury.

At first, I sat there, unresponsive and empty. But then, oh, God…

I hooked my hand behind his neck, trembling and sealing myself to him, and his body pressed into mine, lowering me to the bed.

"Wait," I breathed. "Wait."

He lifted his head, looking at me. "Too fast?"

I nodded. "I'm sorry."

"It's okay," he said, sighing. Then he smiled weakly and rolled to the side.

We lay there for a second in silence, and then he said, "Shall I stay with you awhile?" Not waiting for an answer, he pulled me against him and tucked my head under his chin. "This makes a good hiding place," he said. "Here." He lifted the cover over our heads. "No one can find us now. We're invisible."

I nodded, my eyes watering, and laid my head on his chest, wondering what he knew of helplessness. He was strong, he was admired, he was able. Considering his past, that he'd been forced to kill his own father to save him from transitioning into a vampire, one could easily ascertain that helplessness was not something Christian Wright fell victim to.

He probably thought I was sleeping when he finally slipped from the bed. Lying perfectly still, I let him go without a word.

Chapter Nine

Mom was perched before the television in the living room, eating French toast and watching *Gone with the Wind* again, captivated by the period dress. And I paced the back deck repeatedly. *Where was my nine-thirty student?* I'd been counting on Mr. Kempf to keep me out of the line of fire this morning. Reginald-but-you-can-call-me-Reg Kempf, who was always at least five minutes early for every lesson, who couldn't keep his stinking hands to himself and embraced my tutelage a little *too* enthusiastically, had chosen this, of all mornings, to stand me up. Ugh. But I was being ridiculous. I couldn't sneak around the house like a mouse forever.

Now that morning had come and I had a clearer head, it was all too easy to beat myself up for my own naivety. What in the hell had happened last night? Surely it meant more to me than it did Christian—and thank God I'd stopped it when I did. This morning would be awkward enough as it was, minus a walk of shame scenario.

But who could have helped it? I mean, his accent alone made me crazy, but honestly, there was no competing with that level of handsome. From up close his eyes were crystal blue, like water, and even before he'd kissed me, I knew those lips would be soft. The only shocking aspect was the power behind them—there was too much feeling in his kiss, and no way was all of that intended for me.

I left the deck and headed for the sunroom, checking my watch again. Jesus! I was going to lose my mind if I didn't just *do* something! I would have to face him like an adult. It was now or never.

Several folks gathered in the kitchen, drinking stimulants and downing carbohydrates before their various tasks sent them scattering in different directions. I shifted my eyes, subtly as I could, to see Christian sitting at the counter beside the fridge—which was now noise-free and ice-filled thanks to Gil—and sipping a glass of pulpy orange juice while he worked a crossword puzzle. As inconceivably uncomfortable as I was, Christian still took my breath away. He was always so well put together, and this morning was no different. In jeans and a slate blue sweater, the contrast of his eyes and the gold in his hair was doing nothing to calm my nerves.

I edged my way around the island inconspicuously…or so I thought, but the moment Laura noticed I was there, she brightened. Then, peering at me perplexedly, she donned a look of astonishment.

My heart stopped. *She knew.*

Goddamn it! Not possible. It was just a kiss! It wasn't like we'd…you know. Most even remotely empathic Sentients could tell if you'd just had sex, and it was a common source of teasing that anyone in the Sentient community learned to live with. They could see light energy, after all, and it would have been mind-numbingly evident to everyone else had Christian and I slept together, but we hadn't! So, why was Chris giving Laura a sideward smirk? God, maybe I was just being paranoid.

In fact, I'd have effectively convinced myself that nothing was awry if it weren't for the sudden wink that Laura shot in my direction. Son of a bitch. She was making assumptions that went way beyond the facts, I was sure of it, and I considered running off like Cinderella at midnight, but that would have only attracted more attention. So I held it together, gulping back my embarrassment, and thanked the stars that my dad had yet to come down to breakfast. He would probably be hung over for days.

Through all of this, I hadn't sincerely looked at Christian once yet.

Chancing a quick peripheral glance, I noted that he was, indeed, not looking at me, but the corner of his mouth was turned up. He knew what she knew, and I knew what she knew, and…*Oooh God!* Had he told her? Had she wheedled it out of him? What the hell was going on? *Just grab a muffin and run, Nicole!*

"Good morning," Christian said, smiling at his crossword puzzle. "Hungry?"

"Uh…I'll, I'll—no," I lied.

My stomach growled, and he snickered, shaking his head. "Liar. Here. Want to finish my eggs?"

Wait—he was sharing food now? What the hell? But no. It was fine. If he could do this, I could do this.

"Sure. Thanks." I sat down, slid his plate in front of me and stared at his fork. He had eaten with that fork. Would they notice that we were sharing a fork? What would it mean that we were sharing a fork? Nothing! It would mean nothing. Because he'd acted out of kindness, out of pity, and that was that. So why was I eating his eggs?

Well, it was too late to stop now. Everyone was watching, and it would be rude to just turn my nose up at his generosity. Maybe I could get a new fork…but wouldn't that insult him?

Why hadn't I just taken a muffin when I had the chance? Oh my dear God get me out of this nightmare!

"Juice?" he offered, nodding at his glass. I gawked at him. Now he was just doing this on purpose. He knew I was squirming, and he was enjoying every minute of it. The cocky Combatant side had come out to play.

I sighed. Why fight against a prevailing wind? Grabbing his glass of juice, I threw back the contents, and Christian's jaw dropped. What? Was it really so unusual for me to show some spunk that five seconds of confidence threw people off?

Christian set his pencil down, smiled broadly, and took the glass to refill it. Okay, so Mr. Wright was being nice. His mother had taught him well. Now, if only I knew what to do next. Where did we stand? Had the kiss been a spur of the moment, meaningless thing, or did he have some other idea? Shit, I missed Katrina so badly. This situation called for a Mind Reader. No, screw a Mind Reader. I needed a Man Translator. Why hadn't I dated more—wait, his *hand* was on my *knee*? I dropped the fork, the metal clanking loudly against the plate, and laughed nervously.

"Oops," I muttered.

Elaine snorted over her coffee. "Slippery fingers there this morning?"

"Actually, I…have a student coming and…thanks for the eggs." I barely looked at Christian before ducking out of the kitchen, comforted only by the dawning knowledge that, should my dignity be lost forever, I could always just drown myself in the ocean.

I laid my head in my hand, massaging my forehead with my fingers as Mr. Kempf painstakingly butchered *Fur Elise*. Typically, I was a patient sort of person. You had to possess steady nerves to teach, since ninety percent of your work was spent on repeated stops and starts. But Reginald had me close to drumming my fingers.

"Reginal, er, Reg, have you been practicing?" I asked, knowing full well what the answer was.

"Sure, sure, yeah. Every day," he claimed, poking at an E-flat like he was testing a roast.

"Right. And by 'every day' do you mean 'hardly at all'?"

"Uh, I might have missed a few times, here and there, you know."

"Mhm. Well, take it back to measure five and let's go over—"

I stopped mid-sentence. Something had hissed from the direction of the living room. Narrowing my eyes, I strained to hear over the return of Reginald's clumsy racket, but the odd sound had already stopped. Shaking it off, I focused again on the task at hand.

There it was again! Someone was clearly *psst*-ing at me.

"Uhm, Regin, ah, Reg, will you excuse me for a moment? Just keep playing."

"Yeah, sure, honey," he said. "Take your time."

I stood up, trying to ignore the mis-keyed note indicative of Mr. Kempf's eyes on my behind, and left to investigate. Rounding the corner, I crashed into the source of the interruption, gasped, and jumped back a few feet.

Christian chuckled. "It worked."

"What worked?"

"I was creating a distraction." He beamed proudly.

"Well done," I laughed.

"Are you distracted?" He stepped closer to me.

"I'm...I'm something. Maybe more like flat-lined."

"Aah." He flashed an absurdly perfect grin and closed the remaining space between us. "I can save you, though." He barely spoke above a whisper. "I know CPR."

I swallowed, reddening like mad, and dropped my eyes.

"Nicole, Nicole," he said, placing a feather light kiss on my cheek. "That wasn't a very friendly greeting this morning," he continued, drawing his lips around to my ear. "I feel scandalized," he whispered.

I shivered. "Sorry. But everyone was s-staring."

"So?" he breathed, the bass of his voice rippling against my skin. "We're okay, aren't we?"

"Yes. I mean...yeah?"

"Of course."

"But it's just, I guess I figured that…you know, I didn't assume."

"What?" He smiled, watching me intently.

"Like…that there was anything. I mean, it was just a kiss."

"Hmm." He pulled back a little and stared at me. "I don't make it a habit of kissing just anyone, you know."

"Well, no. I hadn't meant that you did."

"Certainly not."

"No. So…"

"So?" He smiled again.

"I don't know."

He bent and touched his nose to mine. "Shall we try this again?" he asked.

Holy shit. I couldn't even answer. The sounds were caught in my throat—no words *aqui!* Then, as my reeling senses processed the action in slow motion, he bent and kissed me deeply in that same kind of unbroken, intensely emotional connection that was starting to define him. My mind failed, my flesh ignited, my limbs melted, and somewhere in the smallest recesses of my brain it occurred to me that Mr. Kempf had finished playing and that perhaps I should act on this knowledge. But this would have required that I break away, that I part with the taste of Christian's tongue, the feel of his teeth, the scent of his breath. I didn't have the strength to do that, but mercifully, he did.

"Nicky, I think your ward needs you," he said, nudging me down from my place in the clouds.

"Who?"

"Your student?"

"My…oh. Yeah." I laughed quietly.

"Will you be seeing Samantha today?"

"Yes."

"Shall I join you?"

"Sure. She'll be thrilled."

"Of course she will. She is positively smitten with me, after all—not that I blame her," he said, grinning.

I smirked.

"Fine," he went on. "I'll stop interrupting you. You seem quite revived now."

"Thanks."

I was still shaky as I took my seat next to Mr. Kempf. "All right…*Reg*," I said, suddenly smiling so hard my face hurt. "Let's go over those chord dynamics, huh?"

❧

Christian sat at the piano with Samantha in his lap.

"Play what you learned for her," I told him, and his eyes widened in alarm. "Just the melody," I added quickly, "with one finger."

He nodded, his dread fading, and began to play a one handed version of *Nearer My God to Thee*. Samantha studied his hand, following the movements of his fingers like they were dancing. I was so proud of him. He'd made it through more than half of the song without a single noticeable error and all from memory. It was better than I could say for some of my students, all bias aside.

On his way down a scale, Samantha touched the piano, and Christian stopped, looking to me for direction.

"Keep going," I mouthed, and he continued with the next line of melody, playing his way back to the refrain when Samantha's finger moved, striking an identical key to Christian's, but down an octave. He paused, his eyes fixing on her hand, and then began once more. Again, she mimicked his playing in near unison. Should he falter, she faltered; when he played well, so did she.

How was this happening? Was she some kind of savant? If Wendell were here, he probably would have touted the Seer's adage about universal balance, about the granting of exceptional gifts when something else had been taken away. But Wendell *wasn't* here, so this was all conjecture.

Christian played the song all the way through, and she followed right along. When he was finished, she held her hand in place, waiting for him to continue. When he didn't, she turned her head to look at him.

"Christian."

He laughed. "What, honey? You don't want to stop?"

She took hold of his hand and laid it on the piano again. There was his answer.

"You're the boss," he chuckled, and began the song again. Over and over they played, and had it not been for her mother's arrival, Samantha probably would have continued until she'd exhausted herself. Christian, on the other hand, had never been better practiced.

Carol Fitzpatrick, rendered stunned and tearful at the image of her daughter's sudden awareness, could not rave enough about the changes in her. "She smiles so much now," Carol glowed. "And she only cries at night. Sometimes we have to go to her room and calm her down, but otherwise, she's so different!"

"Fantastic!" I agreed. "Just what we want to hear."

"And Christian," she added, "she always asks for you before she goes to bed."

He cocked an eyebrow at me. "You see? Smitten."

"If she keeps improving at this rate, can you imagine the progress at the end of the six months?" Carol squealed. "Oh, I am so happy I could just kiss you both! In fact…" She grabbed Christian's head and pulled it down to kiss his cheek, then bounced over to me to do the same. "You two are a blessing, you know that? A blessing in our lives."

Her declaration filled me with satisfaction. What she believed was so far removed from Duncan's idea of me—a curse, a burden. I could be a blessing. And there it was again. Hope.

❧

"So what is this supposed to mean, Nicole?" Gil quizzed me as we pushed an overburdened shopping cart through the parking lot.

"It means we're…I don't know. We're just…I don't know!" I grabbed the frozen turkey, tossing it into the trunk.

"How is that an answer!" he demanded. "If it's no big deal then why are you being so secretive?"

"Because you haven't shut up about it since we got here! And you obviously aren't happy with it, so what can I say? God, I'm sorry I ever told you."

"Well, I'm not! Nick, this is a huge mistake, you and him."

"Gil, tomorrow is Thanksgiving, and probably one of the first I've had in a long time where I felt even remotely happy, so please don't wreck this for me, okay?"

"Yeah, fine," he said. "But let me tell you, Nick. There's something about his energy. It's like he hides the darker parts, like he's holding something in," he said. "One of these days he's going to run out of places to bury that shit, and what do you think is going to happen then? You think you can handle another Duncan? Because God the fuck knows I can't! None of us can."

"That wouldn't happen!"

"You don't know that!" he argued. "And when your dad realizes what's happening?"

"He doesn't need to know," I said.

"And how long will that last? You can't keep this from him, Nicole. He's a Sentient. He probably knows already, anyway, and he may not be able to control Christian, but he'd find a way to make you suffer. He always does."

"Ugh, stop! I'm not discussing this anymore!"

"Nicky, don't be stupid! Have more respect for yourself than that. Has it not occurred to you that this guy might just be…"

I glared at him. "Might be what, Gil? Say it."

He straightened up. "Well, somebody needs to! That he might just be using you to get over his little slump?"

My face burned. Of course Gil would think that. Likely they all would. Hell, I did. My eyes burned, and I dropped my gaze to the groceries beside me. "Thanks," I whispered.

Gil sighed. "Aw, Nicky. I'm sorry. That was harsh. I'm jus—"

"Forget it. You're right." I threw the last bag of groceries in the trunk and slammed it as hard as I could. Gil winced. "Let's go home."

❧

"Why do *you* get to sample the food?" Christian moped at my turkey, an image of golden perfection on a platter of harvest vegetables.

"Because I cooked it. Christian, do you ever get full or are you just perpetually hungry?"

"As a matter of fact, I am," he admitted. "I'm quite ravenous a good majority of the time, and you cook really, *really* well. So what do you expect?" He nabbed a blob of pumpkin pie filling with his finger.

"Flattery will get you nowhere," I grinned, thrilled with the compliment.

"I disagree," he said. "Flattery will get you everywhere. It's like an American Express card. For instance, if I were to tell you that this pie is exquisitely rich and perfectly spiced, what would you say?"

"I know."

He broke into a laugh. "Good answer. You must have tasted it already."

"No, actually, I haven't."

"No?" He slipped an arm around my waist and pulled me against his chest. "Care to?"

Breathe. Was anyone looking?

"No one's looking." He grinned, reading my mind.

"Okay," I squeaked.

He leaned in and traced my lips with his tongue. "So," he whispered, "what do you think?"

I bit back a groan. "Uuh." *Breathing…more breathing.* "Don't know."

"Well, I didn't mean to be stingy. Do you need a more substantial sample? Here," he offered, dipping his tongue into my mouth and swirling it around. The next thing I knew he had me pressed into the counter, and all thoughts of pie tasting were lost to the gods. Oh, what a sight we must have been when Raj cleared his throat from the kitchen door.

"Eh hem. Sorry to interrupt." He pursed his lips in a restrained smile. "But I have to check on my squash, and Duncan is coming," he added, nodding over his shoulder. Christian held onto me firmly, but I squirmed away.

"Not in front of my father," I whispered.

He frowned at me, obviously irritated, but said nothing, and just as Raj had warned, Duncan entered the kitchen seconds later, a bottle of eggnog in hand. He set it down on the counter and looked at Christian.

"You care for a drink, son?"

"No, thank you. I'll pass," Christian said. After what had happened the week before, we'd all been turned off alcohol for a while. As predicted, Duncan hadn't remembered a damned thing he'd done while drunk. In fact, he'd spent the following two days so hung over he could hardly open his eyes. This was ideal. In my mind, he didn't suspect a thing.

"Spirit," Wendell began, and we all bowed our heads. "We're grateful for the food here, of course, but more so for the hands that prepared it. We're grateful for the wealth of heart at this table, for the depth of love and empathy. Thank you for the life-giving energy that connects us all, the same light that moves from one to another in equal portion. We're grateful for the power to create and encourage good in the world. Thank you for the eyes to see, the ears to hear, the flesh to feel, and the wisdom to know their purpose. Amen."

"Amen," we repeated. Oh, Wendell. Always trying to enlighten us. But if Dad had grasped a word of his prayer he didn't let on as he dug into the mashed potatoes enthusiastically with two spoons.

So be it. Duncan had started shutting me out by the time I was twenty-five, and his resentment had been forged in stone by my twenty-eighth birthday. Now nearing thirty, I'd passed the defining years without even a hint of Sentient abilities, so it was extremely unlikely I was one.

Depressing as these thoughts should have been, Mr. Wright was doing wonders to boost my morale, and I was being lulled into a state of not caring as much what my father thought anymore. If someone like Christian could embrace my presence so enthusiastically, I'd find the strength to be happy without guilt.

"So, Nicole…Tell us about Samantha," Wendell began. "What wonders have you produced as of late?"

I smiled. "Well, she's improving every day, especially with Christian around. The other day she actually played—"

"You're still dragging Christian into this?" Duncan interrupted, forking a piece of turkey. "He's a busy man, Nicole, and he doesn't have time for games. What's the difference this week? Did she smile twice in an hour? Blink at the floor five times instead of four?"

Ignore him. Ignore him. It'll pass. Busy yourself. Cut something.

Wendell sighed. "Duncan, I wasn't talking to you. I asked your daughter a question, and I trust you can remain silent long enough for her to answer it."

Duncan scoffed, chewing loudly, and shook his head. "Go ahead, Wendell. Keep mollycoddling her," he said, turning to me. "You know, Nicole, it's not too late to go to medical school. Maybe you could take up something a bit more redeeming than *Name That Tune* with mental cases. And for Christ's sake, enough with the goddamned food! You're going to look like a cow by winter's end."

I froze, knife in hand, eyes glued blindly to the table cloth.

Laura gawked. "Jesus, Duncan, what the—"

"Stop, Laura." I lifted my hand. "Don't," I choked out. My face was on fire, my throat was burning, but there would be no tears. *Not now and not here. Not in front of everyone. Not like this.* "I forgot something. Excuse me," I muttered the first thing I could think of. Dropping my napkin on the table, I left the room, fighting the urge to throw up. If I could make it to the kitchen without crying, maybe no one would follow. Maybe they'd pretend that nothing had happened. I only made it halfway to my destination.

"Nick, wait."

Damn it. I squeezed my eyes shut and composed myself before turning to face Christian.

"Wine glasses," I said, lifelessly. "I forgot them. I won't be long."

He frowned and laid his hands on my shoulders. "You didn't buy any wine."

Ah well. I had no face left to save, anyway. I was thoroughly disgraced. "I know," I said.

"Oh, Nicole." He wrapped his arms around me, pulled me close, but I held stiff, ashamed to hold him back. If I had strived to be something more impressive, something more heroic, if I had been thinner, been prettier, if I had worked harder to compensate and stayed out of his way, maybe I could have pleased my father. Maybe I *had* wasted my life on weak, childish, sub-standard, simpleton mediocrity. And now I was imposing that same mediocrity on Christian, letting him console me when he should have been out there enjoying himself with his peers.

"All right," I pulled away. "Enough of this. I'm fine."

"Nick, you don't have to lie to me."

"I'm not lying. And I'm not ruining everyone's Thanksgiving. Let's go, Christian."

He stopped my exit, stepping in front of me to block my path. "Nicole, I have really been keeping my cool around that man, but I warn you, I am this close to ripping him a new one."

I cracked a smile. "I'd buy tickets to that show."

"Never mind that. I'm pulling you on stage," he promised.

No one liked to wash dishes. Aside from scrubbing toilets, it was the pox on the chore list, the black sheep of house cleaning. But for me, the custom was a welcome thing. I could hide elbow deep in an easily replenished supply of warm, citrus-scented water and lose all sense of time. And considering my unnatural love for the act, no event offered more mental repose than post-Thanksgiving cleanup. It was just me and a box of steel wool at midnight, scouring away the world, while Christian napped contentedly on the sofa, full of dressing and tranquilized with tryptophan.

Deep in thought—some good, some not—I stared out the window at a squall of snow flurries that stubbornly refused to stick to the ground but rather seemed to melt into thin air. I wished for snow every year, but we rarely got any. Though we had an abundance of precipitation, it was rare that things got cold enough to allow for snow. I would just have to savor the flurries. They were hypnotizing, dancing in midair like icy ballerinas, and so I hadn't heard him arrive, only noted his presence from the smell. My father had worn the same aftershave for decades.

"You and Christian," he began, dumping a dessert plate into my dishwater. "You're spending a lot of time together lately."

My blood turned cold and the metal shreds of my Brillo pad cut into my skin. "I guess."

"Uh huh. Well, I'm curious, Nicole. What exactly do you expect to come of it?"

I scrubbed at the turkey tray with enough elbow grease to move a tanker. "What do you mean?"

He laid a hand on the counter next to the sink, leaning in so only I could hear him. "I *mean*…at what point did you begin to believe that you would be enough for him? That a Combatant could reasonably be expected to settle, in the long run, for someone who would suck his energy, his attention away from his job, his whole purpose in this world?"

How had he known? I'd been so meticulous! "Don't do this."

He shook his head. "Do you want him to resent you? To hate you? You're not strong enough for him, Nicole. And maybe not now, maybe not tomorrow, but inevitably, one way or the other, you'd drag him down. That is, if it even lasted that long."

"Dad, I can't—"

"Open your eyes!" he fumed. "A Sentient needs an equal in strength—especially a Combatant. He doesn't need to be a babysitter, to constantly have to look over his shoulder, watch someone else's back instead of his own. Look what happened to your mother. Do you want to see that repeated? Are you *trying* to destroy him?"

"No." The scrubbing pad slipped from my fingers and sunk to the bottom of the sink. "Never."

"Then you know what you have to do," he said simply. "End whatever nonsense you've got going on. It's a mistake, Nicole, and you know it." I looked at him, and whatever expression I wore must have made him uncomfortable. He averted his eyes and went on. "I suppose you think you love him. But that's all sentimental bullshit. Love means sacrifice, Nicole. He's grieving, and he's bothering with you out of pity and convenience. Show some dignity," he said, finally meeting my gaze again. "You were a rebound. Acknowledge your situation and do the right thing."

My chest was caving in. I was going to be crushed into a frigid pulp. Surely he wanted me to answer him, but if I'd tried to, I would have started crying for certain. My father must have taken that as a sign of defiance, and he grabbed my elbow. "Nicole, listen to me," he said, attempting, in a fouled up way, to sound comforting. "If you've ever wanted the chance to gain my respect, this is it. Let him go."

Let him go. Like he'd ever really been mine to begin with.

I nodded stiffly, and he released my elbow.

"Thank you," he muttered.

I looked out the window again, hoping he'd take the hint and leave me alone. He did, and once he was out of earshot, I allowed the tears come, wiping them away with the back of my greasy, sudsy hand. Duncan had found the loophole in my hope clause. My life for my mother's. So this was how the universe would find its balance.

Chapter Ten

"Mom, your shoes are on the wrong feet." I sighed, kneeling down in front of her. "We put letters under the tongue so you'd remember, see?" I lifted a flap. "L for left, R for right."

"Oh. That's right. I'm sorry. I'd forgotten again."

"That's okay. Here. I'll switch them."

Laura came around the corner, her skirt bustling. "Hello, sexy ladies," she said. "You going out?"

"Black Friday. We're going shopping."

"Aah. Fun! I wish I could come with you," she lamented. "But I've got to drive to Red Bluff with the hubs and Elaine. We think there's a vampire hanging around an RV park in the area, and those sons of bitches don't wait until the sales are over to feed."

"No. I guess not," I agreed. "And you're wearing a skirt to a vampire hunt?"

"What?" She shrugged. "There's no reason to be unfeminine."

I chuckled, slipping Mom's shoe onto the correct foot. "You are unique among the masses, Laura Polmieri."

"Coming from you, I'll take that as a compliment." She smiled and leaned down to hug me from behind, kissing my cheek enthusiastically. "Love you, baby. See you later."

"Thanks. Be careful!"

"Always."

Christian passed Laura as she made her exit. "Where's she going today? Surely a ghost can wait 'til after the holidays?"

Oh God. How could I find the strength to do this? How was it possible to do this? "Vampire harassing a campsite."

"Ah," he nodded. "Never mind then. And what about you?"

"Shopping."

"That's right, Black Friday," he said. "Mind if I join you?"

"You can if you want to," I said, finishing with Mom's shoes and standing up.

He chuckled. "If I *want* to?"

"It will probably bore you."

"It won't bore me if I'm with you," he said, reaching for me.

I pressed my hands into his chest, stopping him. I could do this. "Christian, don't."

"Don't?" He laughed again. "Nick, no one is around. You're PDA safe," he teased, brushing his hand against my cheek.

"Let's sit down," I said. "I really have to talk to you."

His smile disappeared, quickly replaced by a look of concern. "What's wrong?"

I turned to my mother. "Mom, we need gloves and scarves. Would you mind getting them for me? They're in the closet."

"Sure, honey." She deliberated on choice of directions, then settled on the correct one and shuffled off. I took a seat on the couch, and Christian sat beside me.

"Christian. This isn't going to work." I heard the cliché leave my mouth and then kicked myself. *Smooth. Really smooth. Jesus.*

He raised an eyebrow. "What isn't?"

"This. Whatever it is we're doing. This thing…us. It's a bad idea."

"Wait," he said, taking me by the shoulders. "Stop. Just stop. You don't mean this."

"You need to listen to me—"

"No. No way. What did he say to you? What the fuck did he do? And don't lie to me."

"He has nothing to do with it." I steadied my voice. "And please, please don't start anything with him. *Please*, Christian. This is for me."

"I need you!" he blurted.

I stared at him, my heart falling further at his words. Sure, he needed me, but would he ever *want* me? "You're not over that girl."

"Stop it!" he ordered, still holding onto me. "You don't know what you're talking about."

"Let go of me, Christian."

"No." He shook his head, clutching even harder.

"Damn it, let me go!" I pulled free of him. "You've got your own issues, and I don't need another Duncan in my life!"

Christian's expression turned hard, and he turned away from me, speaking in low voice. "I'll never be like him. Don't ever say that again."

My stomach pitched. This was hell. He was shocked and hurt, but even more, I'd insulted his character. It was a slap in the face, my bringing this up. Why had I chosen *this* as an argument? Was Gil's reasoning the best I could come up with? This was unforgivable—but, then, that was the idea, wasn't it?

"I'm sorry. But haven't you ever considered that it's not me you actually want? That I was just convenient and there?"

"How could you—"

"I won't be a detriment to your life or your job, Christian. My mind is made up."

He glared at me. "I see. And I don't get any say in any of this, is that right?"

"I'm sorry."

"Stop saying that!"

"I don't know what else to—"

Mom interrupted, calling from the coat closet, "I can't find a match! The gloves are all jumbled. Can I use mittens?"

"That's okay, Mom," I answered, still looking at Christian. "I have to go," I told him, knowing that if I didn't get up this very minute and walk away, didn't pretend not to notice his shaking, the broken look on his face, I'd end up throwing myself at him and never letting go.

So I got up and gathered my mother and the scarves and the coats and the stupid, fucking mittens, leaving the house and my sanity behind.

Black Friday. How despicably accurate.

❦

"Hi, Carol? It's Nicole."

"Nicole! Hi! Uh oh, are you still sick?"

"Yes."

"Oh, no! You poor thing. And Samantha's not doing well with the lengthy separation."

"I'm so sorry, Carol," I apologized.

"It's okay, girl. Can't help getting sick, right? I hope you feel better soon."

"I'll try."

"Okay. I won't keep you. Take care."

"Thanks. Bye."

"Bye bye, Nicole."

Day five of my sham of an illness was upon me. I'd cancelled all my piano students for the week, and I completely avoided the idea of Samantha. She would have asked for Christian, and then I'd have fallen apart.

Obviously, it was wrong for me to make her suffer just because I couldn't deal with my own decisions, but I couldn't make myself care at the moment. It was hardly unexpected, what had happened. On a very real level, I'd known it was coming. I was only surprised that I'd been the one to end the whole thing. Yet with the preservation of that small bit of pride, I'd lost my hope for something better, something more than what I had. I felt like the world's most foolish idiot for believing it could be otherwise, and I just didn't have the strength to face people yet.

You know, if you stared at a wall long enough, all kinds of things appeared. The shadows on the outsides of your eyes swirled and took shape, hopped around and flitted in and out of view. I found that I could stare at the wall in my room for hours, with just my face poking out from under the covers. In fact, that's what I'd been doing for days. I'd been staring at the wall with my door locked.

I was a therapist, and when it came to depression, I knew all the symptoms well. I was in trouble, for sure, but the mere idea of getting up—of giving a shit—was utterly exhausting. The dark and quiet took nothing from me. Sleep was easy. I had no desire to move from this place. Not even a little. Even the question of who was taking care of my mother didn't stir me at all. The world could fall away and leave me here in a dim, unwashed, droopy-eyed mass, and that would have been fine. Besides, I could always dream. In fact, I'd been doing just that when—

"Get up, Nicole!"

I was jerked from sleep at the feel of my blanket being ripped off me. I scrambled down the bed after it, but Laura had it in hand and was already at my window, pulling the shades wide open.

"What are you doing?" I said, taken aback by the scratchiness of my voice. "I locked that door!"

"Well, I unlocked it! Get up, Nicole. Face the music."

"Go away, Laura. I'm sick." I slumped on the bed again.

"You are not sick, Nicole! Get the hell up and take a shower and eat something and get a grip before I slap your ass."

I ignored her, squinting away from the sudden brightness and burying my face in a pillow.

She sighed deeply, and then I felt her weight settle onto the bed beside me. She laid her hand on my arm. "Sweetheart, you have to get up. You have to live your life."

"I have no life."

"You have a life, Nicky. It sucks right now, and partly because of *you*, I might add, but you have one."

"Please, don't start."

"Well, just explain to me—if this was the right decision, why in the hell is Christian such a mess? He's a total wreck all over again. It's not pretty."

"He'll get over it."

"That's not my point. My point is that he cares about you."

"Laura, so help me God, I am *not* talking about this. *Not. Talking.*"

"Suit yourself. But I'm through with only seeing your face when you grab a breakfast bar or pee. And look at your hair! You look like someone's dragged you along an electric fence! This has got to stop. I won't leave this room until you swear to pull yourself together."

"Oh my God, fine!" I sat up again, scowling intensely at Laura. "How did you get in here?"

"I picked the lock."

"What the—"

"That's right."

"Why? Since when can you pick locks?"

"It was time, and Wendell showed me how. Now, I'll give you the rest of the week to finish weeping around and then it's back to living. You understand me? Mourning over."

I frowned. There was no way I could win this. Not with Mrs. Life-Coach *and* Wendell plotting together. "Right," I said blankly.

"Thank you." Laura got up from the bed and headed for the door. "I'll see you at dinner tonight."

"I don't—"

"And you're coming with me on a little trip this weekend."

"Laura!"

"The end!" she finished.

I groaned and tossed my pillow at the door just as it closed behind her.

If anyone was looking for the location of the most uncomfortable dinner ever, they'd only have to type that criteria into their GPS, and they'd be directed to 77 Riley Cliff Drive, Eureka, California.

Laura insisted on sitting beside me, which was highly inconvenient, because that meant she felt compelled to try and talk to me as well, and I didn't feel like talking. I felt like taking my plate of garlic pasta, and possibly a roll, into the closet and eating in the dark. But could I do that? No. I couldn't, because not only would Laura be pissed, but she'd probably break into the closet in no time. That's right, folks. There was a new menace in town. No lock was safe.

To further my bliss, I got to watch Christian jab at his cherry tomatoes with murderous intensity while my father prattled on and on in his ear about his favorite aspects of vampire extermination.

"What I like best is when I catch 'em before they know I'm there, that way the neck is all limp and it snaps like a bread stick!" Duncan said. "And that look in their eyes right before they—"

"Honestly," Wendell intervened. "We should pick a more appetizing topic."

"What? It's not bothering anybody, is it?" Duncan looked at Theo and Chris.

"It's not my favorite subject," Chris admitted.

"Bah, that's because they're not Combatants, right, boy?" He chuckled at Christian. "You get it, don't ya? That satisfying *crack*—"

The sound of Christian's knife clattering against his plate interrupted Duncan's excitement. "I'm sorry," Christian said. "I'm not feeling well tonight. I think I'm finished."

Duncan frowned. "You kidding me? Boy, you need to bulk up, not slim down. You need to eat. Need to keep yourself in—"

"*Stop* calling me boy, Duncan." Christian threw his napkin on the table and stood up. "And I said I'm finished."

Duncan watched, stunned, as Christian left the table. "Don't know what's wrong with that boy lately," he muttered, shifting in his seat when he was gone.

Wendell raised an eyebrow. "Don't you?"

Duncan didn't answer, just stuffed some bread in his mouth and chewed away.

"What did I tell you," Laura mumbled to me. "He's a basket case."

I stiffened. "Not now."

"Well, you have to admit he's—"

"I'm warning you…"

"Christ, Nicole," she raised her voice. "Who gives a shit what Dun—"

"I'm finished, too," I said, standing abruptly.

On my way out I heard Theo say, "Oh, for crying out loud," but I couldn't make out Wendell's response because I was halfway upstairs by then.

It would appear that I'd successfully escaped, but I knew these people better than that. In fact, I could count on it. Five, four, three, two…

"Okay, so it was a start!" Laura said from a few steps behind me. "Even if the meal was a disaster."

"Back off, Laura."

"Nicole…"

"What?" I halted to face her. "What? So he's miserable. Of course he is! He's in *love* with her, Laura!" I said quietly. "And he's confused, and he's pissed at me, and I get it! But if I'd been selfish and dragged things out, it would have been worse for both of us once he realized that he'd been substituting a name brand with a generic."

"You're wrong, babe."

"No. I'm not. And he's been through enough. Let it die! Let it go."

"Nicky." She stopped herself and was turning all kinds of colors, fighting to hold her tongue, but I knew full well that silence from Laura Polmieri was more to be feared than anything else. And that expression—shit—that mix of pissed and dogged—it meant trouble. She may have shut up, but she wasn't giving up. Not by a long shot.

Laura had always been blatant and unapologetic in her tactics, and normally I liked that about her, but this was different. This was personal. This was a raw wound, and she was prodding at it like a salted brand.

"Laura," I began, backing up the stairs. "*I* am going to my room," I continued cautiously. "And *you* are not."

"Fine," she said.

"And I swear to God if you pick my lock again I will freeze all your panties while you sleep."

She snorted. "Right. And pack a weekend bag, Nicole. We leave in the morning."

"Wait—where are we going? For the job? And what about Mom?"

"She'll be fine. You know, Nicole, you're not the only one capable of caring for your mother."

"Laura, where are we going?"

"It's a surprise."

"A surprise."

"Yep."

I sighed, shaking my head and feeling the obligation to argue. But after a moment, I realized that getting the heck away from this place was exactly what I wanted to do. "And you won't harass me? You swear to God?"

"I promise. I swear."

I didn't trust the woman as far as I could throw her, but I'd take my chances. There was a decided lack of space to breathe in my life, and the chances to run away came few and far between.

"Okay."

Chapter Eleven

Since night vision had always been an issue for me, the headlights on the highway were making me nuts. So I put my reading glasses on in hopes that the glare would lessen. It worked, but only a little. Ah well. I wasn't driving anyway—Laura wouldn't let me. The bitch. Even Elaine was keeping mum.

"I'm going to find out eventually," I grumbled.

"Sooner than you think," Laura said.

"Hope so. I don't feel like driving around forever."

"You?" Elaine laughed. "You've been moping. *I've* been driving."

"So?" I ignored her comment. "Do you think I haven't noticed that we're headed in the direction of the airport? And why isn't Chris coming with us, Laura?"

"It's a girl thing."

"Are you serious?"

"Mhm."

"Then at least tell me where we're going."

"You'll find out when we get there."

"Oh come on. Now you're just being dramatic!"

"Absolutely," she smiled.

So, Mrs. Breaking and Entering was going to drag this out, was she? "You know I hate surprises."

"Sure do. Don't care. Not telling."

Right. So be it. We were rolling up to the little airport entrance in no time, anyway, and Elaine idled the car outside. "Okay, ladies. See you on Monday!"

"Wait…you're not coming?" I said.

"Nope. Just dropping you off."

"I see. So, you're leaving me alone with her all weekend."

"Suck it up," Laura said, jetting out of the car to open my door. "And we won't be alone. Now, be a good girl and grab your bag."

The Arcata airport, or ACV as locals called it, was so small that you barely had to step through the door and you were checked in. Of course, the flip-side to this was the tiny commuter plane that we'd have to tolerate before the required transfers.

"Where are we going?" I pestered Laura again as we passed through security and headed for the ticket counter.

"Give it a minute," Laura complained.

I did my best to be patient, standing in line behind a very large man with too many suitcases. Naturally, he'd have to check every bag excruciatingly slowly. And looky here—he'd forgotten to put a tag on one. How convenient.

Laura stared straight ahead, smirking through my sighs and fidgets, and when it was finally our turn I scurried ahead as she stepped up to the desk and handed the gentleman our tickets.

He tore off one half and handed them back to Laura. "To Philadelphia, layovers in Sacramento and Chicago," he confirmed.

Philadelphia…

I smiled as Laura handed me my boarding pass and we sat down in the waiting area.

"Jeez, Laura," I laughed. "Why didn't you just say we were going to see Trina? And by the way, this had to be so expensive! You've got to let me pay you back."

"Not a snowflake's chance in hell."

"Why not?"

"Because, it's a gift. And if you bring it up again, I'll pick every lock you ever own."

"Hmm. Well, when you put it that way, fine. And thank you," I said, still grinning.

❧

I'd never been to Pennsylvania before. In fact, though I was pretty well traveled for a pathetic loser with no life, I'd never been this far east. Traveling was more of a necessity than a desire for me. I had covered a lot of territory with our group as a kid, simply because I had no choice. I went where my parents went. But after Mom's accident, we all kind of understood how lucky we were that Wendell had bought a home.

There was an unspoken understanding among the group that there should be at least a few Sentients around to help me with Mom. She could still attract a dangerous energy, and I certainly couldn't protect her—yet another example of how I'd seriously put a drag on the whole group. They'd all had to alter their lives because of me.

I found it ironic that I'd managed to be so much of a nuisance when all I'd ever really wanted was to fit in, to blend into the same world as everyone else in my life. I just wanted to be like them. And even though I was happy that I'd get to see Katrina again, I would also be seeing a bunch of other Sentients. And these weren't even the regular kind. No. These were *Abram Saru's* Sentients—all of whom were highly gifted and renowned for their rebellious streak.

They were all loyal as hell, too. Abram's people had chosen to remain with him and support his wish that William join their group, even after the Worldwide Society made it very clear that they disapproved of this decision. The Society held that William should have been kept under isolated observation for some years before he was allowed to practice Sentience again. But Abram believed he'd suffered enough, and his Sentients stood behind him. That kind of system-bucking took guts, and I'd always admired them because of it.

And now they had Lily.

No offense intended, but I was really kind of thankful that she'd ended up an East Coast Sentient. If Wendell had adopted her into our group, I think I'd have absolutely shriveled up and died. She'd have been one more person for my father to compare me to—and God knows I didn't need that.

I was definitely nervous about meeting her, too. A part of me wanted to—but the truth was, I was just plain intimidated by the whole idea, mainly based on the things I'd heard and the fact that Christian had been so hung up on her. I was convinced that seeing her in the flesh would only drive home how much I paled in comparison.

Thankfully, I didn't have a chance to dwell on these thoughts for long—I was too busy going deaf. In all of science, I doubted that anyone had invented an instrument to measure the pitch of Katrina's shrieking when she saw us at the flight gate. Surely a few planes went down after the decibel level messed with their engines.

"You came, you came, you came!" she squealed, hugging me as she hopped.

"I did," I laughed.

"And how did you manage to drag her ass away, Laura?"

"Oh, I bullied her into it," Laura said.

Trina nodded her approval. "Good deal."

A lovely blonde cleared her throat beside us, prompting an, "Oh!" from Katrina as she remembered her manners. "Nicky, you remember Anna, yes? Christian's sister? Daniel and Clara's daughter?"

Shit—Christian's sister—of course. "I do. Hi," I said, smiling as sincerely as possible, though I was sure they could smell the fear on me. And in spite of her bright smile and hearty hug, the concentration with which she looked at me could only mean one thing. She was sizing me up. Oh, God. What had Laura been telling them? I had specifically asked her not to mention anything to Katrina, since the entire universe would then be alerted via satellite blast to the heavens. Now Anna knew that I'd made her brother miserable again, and she probably wanted to rip my hair out. Why the hell—

"She didn't mean to," Trina broke my train of thought.

"Huh?"

"Laura didn't mean to say anything, Nick. We were talking on the phone and she just…"

Laura intervened. "I hadn't intended to say anything. It just accidentally came out, and then I *had* to tell her the whole thing. You know she'd never let me rest otherwise."

"Nicole, it's okay," Anna chuckled. "I quite like you," she pronounced, wrapping an arm around my shoulder as we walked.

"You do?" I gulped. "How is that possible? I mean, you don't even know me."

"Of course I do!" She laughed. "That is, I know what Katrina's told me, and I can feel your energy. You're adorable, actually. I'd rather like to wrap you up and protect you," she finished, suddenly taking on a serious frown. "I must ask you, though, how long has it been since you've had any fun? I mean, you're more tightly wound than my brother. And that's saying something."

Well, now. Walk amongst Sentients and face the consequences.

"Eh…" I laughed a little, and then sighed deeply. "A very, very long time," I admitted.

"I can vouch for that," Laura piped up.

I rolled my eyes. "You would."

❧

"What's the difference between a split Victorian and a regular Victorian?" I pondered, searching the stately old neighborhood for something resembling half a house.

Trina laughed. "It's a whole Victorian, but we only live in half."

"How's that even possible? Did someone make a duplex out of it? That's hideous."

"Rather tragic," Anna said. "But it's still quite lovely."

"Do you get both halves?"

"Thankfully, yes. So there's more than enough room."

"How'd you determine who gets which side?"

"Well, the younger among us like to stay up later and make more noise, so we've taken the left. The stuffy crowd gets the right," Anna explained.

Laura cocked an eyebrow. "Would that include me?"

"Heavens, no," Anna said. "You're no fuddy-duddy. You may sleep on whichever side you wish."

"Why, thank you." Laura grinned.

When they said split Victorian, they meant it. The house, though it was still charming with white scalloping along the rim of the roof and a lovely front porch, had clearly been divided at some point, and there were two front doors with a banister between them.

"Welcome to Casa de Abram," Trina said, opening her arms to the house. "At least, for now, anyway."

"It's really lovely," Laura said. "And freezing. Can we go inside?"

"Absolutely."

As we trudged up the steps, I felt the sudden urge to vomit. Thankfully, Anna didn't appear to want to hold my head under water, but I had yet to meet Lillian Hunt, and I feared that once I did, I'd be tempted to do it myself.

"Where is everybody?" Laura peered into the empty great room.

"Other side. Mom cooked," Anna said.

"Aah. I'm surprised we can't smell it from here."

"Me, too."

"Clara's food is legend," Laura told me. "If she cooks it, you want it in your mouth."

"So true," Trina agreed.

Hm. Now *this* I could appreciate.

"Up the stairs." Trina pointed to the steep staircase. "The two rooms at the very end of the hall are up for grabs. Take your pick."

"Go ahead, girl." Laura nodded me on. "You get dibs."

"Thanks," I laughed, heading upward.

My word. This place was so different from the beach house. It was much darker, much warmer. The walls were all painted in various tans or jewel tones, and it almost felt like I was stepping into another era. The renovated design had been very true to the house's prime, even if they did split the poor thing down the middle.

My eye was immediately drawn to the very end of the hall, to the room with the tan walls and white curtains. "Do you mind?" I said of the brighter room, and Laura shook her head.

"Not at all. It's yours," she said.

So I set my things down at the foot of the bed and then checked myself in the mirror. You know, for having airport hopped and flown around for nine hours, I almost felt pretty today. There was a glow in my cheeks—probably due to the crisp air—and my hair was a bit fuller, resting nicely around my face for once.

Being this far away from my dad was clearly a good thing.

"Let's eat, people!" A male voice shouted from downstairs. "I'm starving, and I can't wait anymore!"

Katrina laughed and yelled, "Chill out, Paul! We're coming. Give us a minute."

I giggled to myself. I remembered Paul. Who in the hell could forget Paul? That much booming testosterone combined with the Brooklyn accent was a real stand out.

"Will all females please convene on the main floor and escort me to dinner?" he badgered, his voice muffled in what sounded like an impression of a megaphone. "I repeat, will all—"

"Keep it up, DePrimo!" Trina threatened.

"Or what? You'll read my mind to death?"

"That's it." She stood at the top of the stairs and made two fists. "You want the hospital or the cemetery?

"All right now, Katrina, show him some mercy. We're coming." Laura emerged from the room beside me, and we headed downstairs.

"Thank you," he said, stepping aside to let us pass. "Do you have any idea what Clara's made? It's lasagna, Laura. The woman has made lasagna."

"Oh, my God. Kill me dead," Laura moaned.

"I know. And hey, Nicole." Paul grinned at me. "Still growin' 'em pretty out there in Cali, I see."

I glanced at my feet and smiled, blushing at the compliment. "Thanks."

As we exited our quarters and paraded outside, I was hit over the head with the richest, most drool-inducing scent that I had ever experienced. My stomach was utterly confused and knotted up, because while I was starving by now, my nervousness had not abated. On second thought, *was* it nervousness? The idea briefly flitted through my mind that maybe it was more resentment than anything else.

"Clara! They're here. Let's eat!" Paul announced once we were inside. This half of the house was almost identical to the other, except that everything was reversed, and it was crammed with milling Sentients.

"Fantastic!" Clara Wright left the kitchen wiping her hands on an apron. She was simply lovely, soft-featured with gray-streaked blond hair that touched her shoulders. "Hello, loves! I hope you're hungry. I've made too much food, and we'll be eating leftover lasagna all weekend."

"Sounds good to me," Laura chuckled happily, hugging Clara close.

When they parted, Clara turned to me. "And you, my dear," she said. "Let me have a look at you." Then, just like Anna had, Clara stood in front of me and stared me right in the eye, and I had to lock my knees to keep from passing out. What was she looking for? Ugh, did these people not believe in quick, impersonal greetings? And why wasn't she saying anything?

"Welcome, Nicole," she said finally and bent to kiss my forehead. "I'm glad you came."

"Thank you." For some reason, I suddenly felt extremely calm. It was almost like…oh, hell. She was doing something to me, wasn't she? She was using some Sentiently hocus pocus to ease my nerves.

"Dinner is served." She cupped my cheek quickly before heading back into the kitchen. I stood alone and stared after her, thinking that it might be polite to join everyone else in the kitchen, but all I could do was sigh dreamily.

"I always feel kind of guilty when she does that to people."

Turning to see who'd spoken to me, I was met with a pair of blue eyes set against creamy skin with long, wavy black hair as a backdrop. "I'm Lily, by the way," she said, grinning.

Oh my *God*, of *course* she was Lily—and she was sickeningly beautiful. Suddenly, I was even more nauseous than usual. I was going to vomit all over myself and be dubbed hurl-girl for the rest of eternity. I was going to throw up all over Lillian Hunt.

You need to react, Nicole. Don't just stand there, you stupid moron! React! Just…not in a barfy way!

Lily stepped forward. "I'm glad to finally meet you," she said, and then she reached out and hugged my unmoving form against her without reservation.

I can report that I did not throw up on Lillian Hunt. Instead, I did much, much worse.

I started crying.

❧

After a hasty trip to a side room and a few attempts to compose myself, I whispered my apologies.

"Don't apologize," Lily insisted. "It's okay."

It was *not* okay. It was humiliating! Why had this happened? I'd become an expert at sucking back tears a long time ago. "I don't know what's wrong with me. Please don't say anything to Laura."

"I won't. And I'm the one who needs to apologize, Nicole. This Empath thing…it's complicated. Stuff like this is pretty common, actually."

I nodded, sniffling, and blotted my eyes with my sleeves. "But still. I've been around Empaths before, for God's sake. I'm so sorry." This had never happened around another Sentient. How powerful *was* she?

"Well, if it's any comfort," Lily offered, "this only seems to happen when people are doing some major repressing.

I frowned. "Not sure how I feel about that," I said. "But I'm okay. Really, I'm sorry about this."

"Nicole, you apologize too much."

"Oh. Okay. I'm sorry. I mean—shit!" *No more words for you!*

She started laughing. "How about we erase this from our memories and go drown our sorrows in lasagna. What do you say?"

"Uhm. Yeah. Sounds good." Lasagna was great! You couldn't say much with a mouthful of food.

"And Nicole?" She looked at me, smirking.

"Yeah?"

"Thanks for not throwing up on me."

Right. Of course.

Chapter Twelve

So, the night had started out well. Ten seconds in and I'd blubbered all over Lily, she'd pitied me, and I felt like a colossal idiot. Life as usual, really.

Thankfully, this group liked to talk…a lot. Hell, Katrina and Anna blabbed enough for the whole house. And I appreciated that, not only because I was thoroughly enjoying Clara's lasagna, but because I didn't deserve any more of anyone's attention for the evening.

On top of all that, the potential for people watching was fabulous in this house. I'd always been an observer, always liked to take people in, absorb their conversations and ideas without the obligation to chime in with something interesting. Contemplation was more fun anyway.

I considered my tablemates for the evening. There was an older couple, Demetre and Ophelia. Demetre was rough around the edges, tall and loud with a bit of a country accent, but he had a friendly way of speaking. Ophelia reminded me of Mrs. Claus. I'd almost forgotten that Ophelia wasn't a Sentient, but seeing her again had reminded me that she and I shared that trait.

Then there was Clara. She had Christian's eyes and his laugh. The realization made it hard for me to watch her for too long without feeling horrible all over again, so I watched Lily instead. The way she spoke—with a teasing smile and natural confidence—I could guess why Christian was attracted to her. Hell, I was attracted to her.

Perhaps the most endearing dinner guest was Demetre and Ophelia's seven-year-old granddaughter, Ginny. And like Anna and Katrina, she had plenty to say.

"Did you show Lily your new worry stones?" Ophelia asked the little girl.

"Oh no, not yet! Lily, I got a whole bag of them at Harry's."

"How cool! You'll have to show me after supper," Lily said.

"Yeah!" Ginny beamed. It was obvious that she thought the world of Lily. "Uh, Grandma? May I please be excused? I have to feed Umbrella."

"Sure, honey. Go ahead."

I watched Ginny leave the table. "Umbrella?"

"Her hamster," Ophelia explained.

"She named her hamster Umbrella?" I asked.

"Yep," Ophelia said. "It was either that or Cracker Barrel."

I giggled. "Wow. She's got an amazing imagination," I said.

"Thank you," Ophelia said. "Coming from you, I take that as a high compliment. Laura has told me about your work with children."

I shook my head, looking down at my plate. "Has she now?"

"Well, of course I have," Laura said. "Next to music, children are your gift. I'm very proud of you, Nicole."

"A double endowment," Abram Saru added kindly.

I smiled. Abram was so warm, and even though he was a Seer, I felt the least intimidated by him. He was warm, his voice was tired, and his eyes were gentle. The creases in his deep brown skin ran from ear to ear.

I'd only been with Abram's group for an hour, but already I felt great relief. There was a different kind of dynamic with these people. Not that Wendell's Sentients weren't good and kind, but with my father around, all the compassion in the world couldn't make up for his oppressive, dark presence.

"You know, Clara, I think this is the finest lasagna I have ever eaten," said Abram, patting his stomach.

Clara laughed. "You say that about everything, Abram. The finest roast you've ever eaten, the finest bread you've ever eaten."

"Do I?" Abram laughed. "Well, I must truly mean it."

"You must," Clara answered, laughing.

Glancing across the table at Lily again, I remembered something I'd meant to say earlier. "Lily, I wanted to extend my best wishes…about your engagement? I think it's wonderful."

Her face lit up and flushed faintly. "Thanks."

I nodded. "Do you have a date picked out?"

"We…no," she said, her smile fading. "Not yet."

"Oh."

Anna peered at the door. "I'm surprised William's not back yet."

"So am I," Lily answered. "He was supposed to have been here a few hours ago."

"Where is he?" Laura asked.

"He's driving back from Cambridge," Lily said.

"Oh," Laura said. "Everything okay?"

"Yeah." Lily smiled. "Just, there was a Society member there, and he wanted to talk to William while he was stateside."

Laura frowned. "I see."

"That reminds me," Demtre said. "Any word from Hyde Ballinger yet, kid?"

"No," Lily said. "But they did say it could take several months."

What in the world was *this* about? A Society member meeting with William? And what could take several months? I refrained from asking for fear of being nosy, but I didn't like the sound of any of it. Hopefully I was just reading too much into the conversation.

❧

"Hah! You've met your match at last," Anna taunted Lily as I set the game controller down, shaking some circulation back into my hand.

Lily nodded. "I have to give it to you, Nicole. You are freakishly good with the hand-eye coordination."

"Well, I've lived with a techno-geek, rocket-scientist genius for years," I explained. "Bear in mind that I haven't beat him yet. But I keep trying."

"And she plays the piano like fucking Chopin," Trina added.

"I see." Lily smirked. "So this was a set up?"

"Precisely." Anna smiled broadly. "Well assessed."

Lily laughed and then sighed, slumping a little. "I'm going to call him if he's not back in the next ten minutes," she said, obviously referring to William.

"Save those minutes, Lily," said a voice from behind us. I swiveled around to see a tall, pale, and very handsome man with dark hair wearing a wry smile. I had never actually met William Maddox. It had been several years since I'd been in the company of Abram's group, and William wasn't with them at the time. But it was quite obvious who I was looking at—especially with Lily catapulting from the couch and into his arms. That was kind of a giveaway.

I should have completely averted my eyes, given them a moment, by I couldn't help peeking just a little. They were holding each other so tightly; it was the most passionate hug I had ever witnessed, and I felt a pang of both jealously and pity. Obviously, I'd have sold a kidney to hold Christian that way, but I also worried for them. That kind of greeting wasn't the typical, everyday hug. It was the kind of embrace you see when two people are relieved to see each other. I could envy their affection, but not their circumstance. God only knew how hard it must have been for them, especially when I suspected that the Society was starting to wig about the whole engagement thing.

"I missed you," Lily whispered.

William kissed her cheek. "I'm here now. No more missing me while I'm here. It's demeaning to my actual presence."

I suppressed laughter, and Lily remembered we were in the room.

"Oh, William, this is Nicole Abbot," she introduced me. "She and Laura came together."

He smiled at me. "Nicole. Very nice to meet you."

"You, too," I said.

"Ladies, would it be rude if I stole Lily for the evening?" he asked.

"Nope," Trina said. "You kids go have fun."

"Appreciated." He smirked. "Nicole," he said, nodding at me. Lily smiled at us and then they made a hasty retreat. Somehow I doubted they'd be sleeping much tonight.

"And then there were three," Trina said.

"They're sweet," I said, smiling.

"They really are," Anna said. "Though honestly, she was really tough on him when she first joined us."

"She was?"

"Good Lord, yes. She didn't trust him, mainly because of my brother."

"Oh, I see."

Katrina cleared her throat. "Speaking of which, let's talk about Christian, shall we?"

My cheeks ignited, and I glanced away. "Shall we not?"

"Nicky," she said in a scolding tone. "Come on. You didn't think you'd get through this weekend without telling us what happened, did you?"

"Trina, no," I pleaded. "I really, *really* don't want to talk about it."

"Well, no shit, Nicole. You loathe talking about anything. But get over it. This is important."

I looked past Katrina at Anna. Might as well just say it. "You must think I'm an awful person." I spoke my fear aloud.

Anna cocked her head quizzically. "Now, why on earth would I think that?"

"Well, what did Trina tell you?" I asked.

"That you and my brother were involved for about twenty seconds."

"Oh."

"And that you broke up with him."

Oh, God. "I didn't want to, Anna. It wasn—"

"Nicole, it's okay. Truth be told, I think you did the right thing."

Hold the phone. She did? Well, of course she did. He was too good for me, wasn't he? Ugh. I tried not to react, but my expression must have given me away, and Anna sighed.

"Nicole, it's not that I don't think you're good for him."

"No, it's all right, please don't say—"

"Eh hem, I wasn't finished."

"Oh, sorry."

"As I was saying, it's not that I don't think you'd be good for him—on the contrary, you seem like the very sort of person that could put up with Christian, but from what Trina has told me, you're extremely vulnerable. I know about your mum, Nicole. And I know about your father, too. And while my brother is dealing with his own issues, I wouldn't recommend getting involved with him unless he's good and moved on from them."

"Anna, don't worry," I said. "I'm not delusional. It was dead on arrival."

Trina laid a hand on my back. "Sweetie, we're not trying to tell you what to do, and I'm not saying to rule him out. I just want you to protect yourself first. And start with Duncan. When he behaves like an ass, I want you to start sticking up for yourself. You need to develop that backbone."

"Definitely," Anna added. "And around my brother, as well."

I raised an eyebrow. "Are you calling your brother an ass?"

"Well?" she snickered.

"He's not an ass, Anna. He's sweet," I defended him, more bravely than I'd expected. "And he's kind. And he's never given me a reason to have to defend myself."

Anna grinned. "I'm glad to hear that. And he has a good heart. But he's also incredibly protective and absolutely insecure."

"Insecure?"

"Terribly."

"That makes no sense."

"It makes perfect sense, Nicole. He feels like an enormous git, you know. He blames himself for my father's death, and he thinks he's failed our whole family."

"He said that?"

"Absolutely not!" she laughed. "He won't talk about it. He won't even bring it up. But I know my brother. Family has always meant so much to him. What happened with my dad…it was more than he could take, and he's dealt with it horribly."

"Oh."

I didn't dare ask about the gory details of her father's death, but I knew enough already. A lot of our Sentients had been there when it happened. The Vancouver battle wasn't one to be forgotten anytime soon. Hell, it's not like my dad would have let us, anyway. Duncan enjoyed recounting the tale with a kind of macabre excitement.

"Daniel was turning," Duncan would say. "He'd been attacked by vampires, and if the Wright boy hadn't killed him, well, he was as good as one of them."

I could understand Christian's issues all too well. He probably felt like he had irreversibly screwed up everyone's life and he needed to be doubly strong now. He probably went to bed hating himself every night, and when he woke up, he probably spent every minute of the day wishing he could turn back the hands of time and fix the whole mess.

There were definitely some eerie parallels between Christian's life and mine.

❧

"I rather thought I'd enjoyed playing in leaf piles," Anna said, turning her head toward me. "But it's not quite the same now as when I was five. And I'm definitely not keen on these little thorny bits." She winced, sucking on her finger.

"Oh, don't be a wuss," Katrina soothed her, rolling over the heap of leaves to kiss Anna's malady.

Man, late autumn in Philadelphia was brisk. Don't get me wrong—Northern California could get chilly enough, but this was different. It felt sharper, fresher. The smells in the air were so strong you could literally taste them. I liked it.

The lot behind the old Victorian was rather small, since houses were closer together around here. And I hadn't been in Philadelphia one full day, but three of the neighbors had already waved at me. People were a little more aloof in California. I supposed it had something to do with being spread apart. There was no need to get too personable when your closest neighbor lived a block away.

I squinted at the sky from my place on the ground, while trickles of laughter carried from the back porch where Lily and Ginny were sorting through worry stones. Ginny had laid them all in a line across the side railing and was deeply concentrated upon the task. Every once in a while she'd knock one down and then hurry to put it back in its proper spot again. The idea that the stones might be safer in a more contained area didn't seem to faze the little girl. She was enjoying having them all out there for the world to see.

Ginny glanced at me and waved, and I smiled, returning the gesture. She resumed looking over her stones for a moment before engaging Lily in what looked like an intense conversation. Then Ginny grabbed one of her stones and bounded across the yard toward me.

"Hey, Nicole? You like worry stones?" Ginny shouted as she ran.

Lily laughed from the porch landing. "You're about to be inaugurated."

I was about to be…huh?

"These," Ginny said, breathless, and fell to her knees beside me. She opened her hand to show me the stone, and I sat up, plucking a leaf from my hair.

"I love it," I said.

"Really?"

"Yeah. Definitely."

Lily shouted, "You should feel privileged! She only gives those out on very special occasions!"

I laughed. "Oh. Well, this is awesome, Ginny."

"You really like it? The red swirly part is pretty."

"It is."

"Yay! Here!" She held the stone out to me. "Try not to lose it. It's extra smooth, so it's my favorite!"

"Your favorite? Why are you giving me your favorite, honey?"

"Cuz. There's more love in this one, and I don't wanna give you one that doesn't have enough love in it yet."

I stared at her, my eyes prickling against the cold air. "Thank you, Ginny."

"You're welcome. Hey, you know how it got that smooth?"

"How?"

"Well, cuz it's really super old. And water ran over it and over it, and it used to be all rough and sharp, but now it's not. The guy at the store said it takes a long time. Like *hundreds* of years," she stressed.

"I see. That's a long time."

"Yeah. But it had to take that long, so now you can hold it and it won't hurt your hand."

"Ah. I see. You're very clever, Ginny."

"Thanks!" She rocked on her heels. "So, I'm going back to the porch!"

"Okay," I chuckled after her, flipping the stone over in my hand. It was so smooth, and the red flowed and ebbed and swirled and mixed into the charcoal gray so naturally that the two colors seemed born for each other.

I smiled to myself. Smart kid.

℮

"So, this is it?" I didn't know what I'd been expecting, but all disillusionment aside, the Liberty Bell was considerably less massive than I'd anticipated.

"Yep. Kinda smallish, isn't it?" Trina pondered.

"Mhm."

"Still bellish, though," I offered.

"Yep."

"But it absolutely smacks of liberty," Anna added. "I can feel the independence wafting from it in waves. We Brits never stood a chance."

Trina cocked an eyebrow. "Annalise Wright, are you making fun of our wafting independence?"

"Certainly not."

"Well, all right then."

"And by the way, our visitor has returned."

I swung around fast to inspect the area behind us, but couldn't see anything unusual. Grumbling inwardly, I crossed my arms against the cold and sighed. I really enjoyed tourism, or at least, I wanted to really enjoy tourism. But it never seemed to fail that any time we'd travel the halls or cabins or galleys of one particular historical landmark or another, someone would spot something that needed banishing or crossing over. It was the hazard of traveling with these people.

Take today, for instance. Apparently, something had been tailing us through Independence Hall, and Anna was getting pretty damned perturbed with it. In fact, according to Anna anyway, he'd followed us through the majority of the Constitutional Walking Tour, straight across to The Liberty Bell Center—quite the modern building.

It was disappointing that I couldn't see him myself. It seemed that some ghosts I could make out, while others were just too concealed for my weak senses to perceive. And it was too bad, since they really didn't scare me much. I'd learned a long time ago not to fear most human spirits. They weren't like dark astrals. Their presence was no more frightening to me than any fleshy human's would be. But they didn't suck up half the energy from their environment that dark entities did, so they were often too weak for my detection.

"Let's go and find Laura," Anna said. "She'll kick his Revolutionary ass into the light and be done with it."

"A fabulous idea, as usual," Trina said.

Both Laura and Ophelia had joined us for sightseeing, while the rest of Abram's group had gone to cleanse an animal shelter. I vaguely recalled them mentioning something about a ghostly Rottweiler.

We spotted the two women studying a plaque replica of the Declaration of Independence.

"Laura, he keeps following us," Trina whined, laying her head on Laura's shoulder and jutting out her bottom lip. "Banish him?" She batted her eyes.

Laura laughed, kissing Katrina on the forehead. "Okay, sweetheart. It shall be done. But let's lure him out of the main area, okay? Get him where there aren't so many people around."

"Consider it done!" Trina grinned, walking deliberately toward a side hall with Anna.

Laura turned to me and Ophelia. "Mind staying behind, ladies? We don't want to spook him." She paused, staring at us expectantly. "Get it? Spook him?"

Ophelia giggled. "Cute, Laura. And we're just fine here, aren't we, Nicole?"

"Yep."

"Fabulous. We'll be back in a blink." And off she went to contend with her ghost.

Ophelia really was a sweet looking woman—chubby-cheeked and crinkly-eyed, and she was wearing her hair the usual way, in a neat bun atop her head. I wondered if the rest of Abram's group saw her as a tagalong or if she was accepted as one of them. How had she managed to get by in such a gifted group without an endowment?

"We'll just have to entertain each other for a bit," Ophelia said. "Care to have a seat? These old dogs are barking."

"Sure."

It cracked me up to think that the spirit of some old-school American soldier was traipsing about a building as new as this. The Liberty Bell Center was bright and clean and modern and, as usual, nothing like where you'd expect to find a ghost. But it didn't matter if you were cleansing a castle or drying your hands in the bathroom at Yankee Stadium—if you were some kind of path-crossing Sentient, they'd find you. I guess there *was* a down side to being gifted.

"My lands, this has been a long day," Ophelia said, settling into a plastic orange chair.

I nodded my agreement and shifted around, trying to get comfortable, but it was no use.

"It's sure been nice to have you ladies with us this weekend. Shame you have to leave tomorrow."

"Yeah," I said. I really was kind of sad to be going back. It felt different to be here—everything about it, from the smell in the air to the feel of the people, was pleasant to me. It was great. But there was one thing that drew my mind away from this place. Christian. Even though I knew that I had no real right to miss him, I couldn't help it.

"You'll just have to come back and see us again soon," Ophelia said, patting my knee.

"Really?"

"Certainly. It's been a pleasure, Nicole. And truth be told, it's kind of nice knowing someone else in this whole crazy ruckus who doesn't chase specters all over the globe."

Her statement made me laugh. "Ophelia, I don't know how you've done it for so long, living with Sentients, marrying a Sentient, without losing your mind. Don't you ever feel…" I paused, shrugging a shoulder.

"Feel how, honey?"

"Well, I don't know."

"You mean inferior? Or in the dark? Or undervalued?" She smiled a little, her eyes soft with understanding. "Of course I do. At least, I used to. But, I s'pose not so much now."

"No?"

"Nah. Here's how I see it—these folks, they have their heads stuck up in the clouds all day long, which is fine, 'cause that's their job to have their mind halfway between heaven and earth. But somebody's got to remind them that the rest of us are still down here trying to catch up, you know? We're walking on the same road they are; we just started the marathon a little later, is all. And besides, this life's not just about chasin' ghosts all over town and strangling vampires, anyway."

"No?"

"Nah."

"Okay. So, why do you think we're with them, Ophelia? I mean, honestly."

Her brow furrowed. "Well, now. We know that the universe doesn't put you anywhere you're not supposed to be, right? And it sure doesn't leave you there unless you've got a job to do."

I nodded. "Wendell's told me that. So, if I can ask, what do you think your job is?"

"Oh, Lordy. Mine?" She sighed and took on a kind of distant look, like she was watching a movie only she could see. "After all these years, I'd say it's to love what I can't fully understand and take what comes with it."

Chapter Thirteen

I watched the patchwork earth miles below my airplane window and imagined what a freefall would feel like. In my mind, I was floating blissfully above it all, free and disconnected, and my body was weightless. I was absolutely flying. I was a bird…in my mind.

In my body, I was sitting in a cramped airplane seat, my head and my ears throbbing, and staring through a watery plastic cup of ginger ale. This weekend had been a wonderful escape. I'd enjoyed almost every minute of it—with the exception of my first meeting with Lily. That part I could have done without. Now, I was heading home to more than I knew how to handle. And what was worse, this trip, short as it was, had left me questioning my tolerance of the current circumstances and pining for a change. But with my mother vulnerable as she was, I knew the idea was preposterous. It wasn't like I could go away with her—she was still my father's wife, after all. Besides, and this was the more important factor, she still needed the protection of other Sentients. That much I couldn't deny.

"You got enough leg room there, toots? I can move that bag under my seat if it helps," Laura offered.

"Nah. It's okay."

"'Kay. Lemme know if you change your mind."

"I will."

She grabbed the band of her seat-belt and released the clasp. "Can't stand these stupid things. They make me feel like some kind of a prisoner."

"Seatbelts save lives, Laura."

"Yeah, I know, thank you, Mother. But I'm going to take my chances without it for a few."

"Don't jinx us, Laura."

"We'll be fine."

"Mhm."

She sighed, laying her head back against the headrest. "So, you have a good time?"

"I really did. Thank you for doing this."

"You're more than welcome, my love. It was fun seeing them again. Trina looks so happy."

"Yeah, she does."

"And Lily…" She turned to look at me. "What did you think? You like her?"

"Lily? Actually, yeah. I did. And she's beautiful. I can see why Chri—"

Oh, damn it. I'd cut myself off as soon as I could, but it was too late. Laura was hanging on every syllable, waiting for me to continue. But I wasn't in the mood to bite. I didn't want to discuss Christian just yet. She'd let me have a whole weekend in peace, and I wasn't about to incite a conversation about him if I could help it.

"See why Christian what?" she pestered.

Figured. "Why he loves her. That's all."

"Hmm." Laura narrowed her eyes at me. "You should've talked to Lily more. I think she could have shed some light on that subject."

"Yeah, I don't think so. That would have been both awkward and none of my business."

"Suit yourself. It's too late now, anyway. But since I've finally got you in a position where you're completely stuck with me, I'm going to give you my take on that little situation."

"Of course you are."

"Of course I am. Now, I'll make this brief, so spare me the evil eye, but I happen to have a very strong opinion—"

"Of course you do."

"Shush. I happen to have a very strong, and I wouldn't say unfounded, opinion on the matter."

"And what's that, Laura?" I asked.

"That he was never in love with Lily to begin with, and he sure as hell isn't now."

I held my breath, peering straight ahead at the chair in front of me. "Fine. Is that it?"

"What do you think?"

"Yeah, go on."

"Uh huh, well, I've had more than a few conversations with Clara Wright and enough of them with Anna, as well. And from what I've observed, Christian was pretty obsessed with the notion of what *should* be done. He held on tight to those ideas for a while—probably because he felt like his world was spinning out of control. And when Lily came along, I'll bet it just seemed like he should have loved her. The notion fell into a reasonable, safe line, you understand?"

"Sure, Laura."

"Nicole…"

"Hey, I heard what you had to say. Now, what if I tell you how I feel?"

She closed her mouth, looking surprised, then said, "Please do."

"Thank you. So, regardless of whether or not Christian is or isn't still in love with her, I'm not selfish enough to think I'm enough for him. And also, it was too quick. It was just all too quick to be real, you know? He was rebounding, and I was sucked in there for a moment, but I know better now—and *that's* how I feel."

"So you're going to shut him out?"

"Maybe, if I have to." Two seconds into the idea and my stomach turned. "No," I sighed. "If he needs a friend, I'll be there."

She seemed satisfied with this, relaxing in her seat again. "Promise?"

I couldn't help smiling. Dear God, she was impossible. "Only if you swear not to pester me about this anymore."

"Deal."

Rajeep was a quiet presence. He could reasonably compete with me for the house corner-hugger, and his uncomplicated nature made it a comfort to have him in the same room. Everyone else had an opinion to give. Everyone else had a bone to pick. But not Rajeep. Being with him didn't take any energy out of me.

I watched him light some incense, the heady, sweet fragrance wafting through the air and seeping into my pores. Raj was an early riser. And after he'd showered and dressed, he would head to the small altar he'd set up in the kitchen and intone a prayer—his *Karaagre Vasate*—an invocation to God for the day's blessings. For some reason, I always kind of felt like I was praying along with him, like I was invoking some grace by proxy.

I needed grace today. I was feeling incredibly empty. The distraction of our trip to Philadelphia was gone, and now I had to find a way to face this house, to face Christian. Hiding in my room was out. Laura and my bank account saw to that. Starting today, I was determined to be back in business, or at least *back*, and the idea was daunting. It would take some considerable effort to make myself care.

When Raj was finished with his prayers, he padded across the tile floor in his bare feet and stopped at the counter, pouring himself a cup of coffee. "Could I talk you into coming with me to dinner this week? At my parents'?" he asked. "If I tell Mom I'm bringing you, she'll make *gulab jamen*."

"Ah, Raj. Your favorite."

"Mmm. But she only makes it for special occasions. So I need to bring a guest or it will be *kheer* again."

"What's wrong with that?" I frowned. "I love your mom's rice pudding."

"Nothing at all." He smiled. "But will you come?"

"Sure. Of course I will."

"Great. I'll call Mom right away. You know if I don't give her a day to prepare she'll have a nervous breakdown."

Listening to Raj talk to his mother was intoxicating. He spoke mainly Hindi with her, a colorful and expressive language, but interspersed in their conversation were English words that flew right into the rest with no hesitation. England's past colonization of India had caused the adaptation of the language, and as was common in the culture now, everyone in Raj's family was bilingual. Still, it had been a goal of mine to learn at least one new Hindi phrase before each time I'd go to visit them, and his father was always immensely pleased with the effort.

When I was a teenager, Raj bought me sheet music for the Indian National Anthem, and I had played it on the piano for his family as a gift for their hospitality. His father had loved me ever since. Mr. Prabodhan had softened considerably over the years. When I'd first met him, he was an imposing figure, stoic and serious-faced, who governed the household with an iron fist. He adhered to traditional ideas of class and societal place despite the relaxing of the caste system in his native country years earlier. But his wife had a tremendous spirit, a huge heart, and she was able to bring out the best in her husband, even convincing him to move to the U.S. to be closer to his son. This was good for Raj, since he was so much like his mother and not at all like his father, and it took nothing short of a huge feat to help the relationship along. Because of our similar circumstances, Rajeep and I had clicked early on. Both of our fathers struggled to accept us, but while Mr. Prabodhan had come around, the most my father could offer was a grunt of appreciation for what I'd done to Christian.

So dinner plans would be made, and this event would be the beginning of an imperative practice for me. This week, it was *gulab jamen* at the Prabodhan's, and I'd take whatever I could get after that to keep my mind off my own life. Anything and everything to soothe the ache and pit of sickness in my heart, the pathetic urge to break down in spite of my better judgment and beg Christian to have me.

❧

"Nicole! Welcome, *sanam*, welcome!" Rajeep's mother lifted her hands to my face, and I bent to touch her foot, a sign of respect that I'd seen Raj perform countless times before.

"Hello, Uzma," I smiled. "Your house smells incredible, as usual."

She blushed and laughed, giving my cheek a squeeze. "I hope so! This son of mine had me slaving away all day!" she joked, swatting Raj behind the head.

Raj laughed. "Sorry, Mamma. But you know I can't resist."

"Mm. Of course you can't. Who could resist my cooking, eh? Now, into the dining room. I've made far too much food, and your father is fat enough for the both of us."

Uzma's sari was especially beautiful today, a deep midnight blue with gold trim around the edges. She reminded me of a Virgin Mary statue, and I admired it as she buzzed around, laying out an apparently never ending supply of platters, each one smelling more fantastic than the next.

The menu for the evening was varied and delectable. Uzma didn't normally cook for people outside of her husband, so she'd gone all out. Lamb curry, vegetable *korma*, *papadum* and *naan* with mint chutney graced the table, and I swear I wanted to drown myself in her Chai.

While I reveled in her *korma*, I dismissed the thought of how much Christian would enjoy this meal the moment tears began to cloud my eyes.

"Too spicy?" Uzma noted, watching me.

"Oh, no. Perfect," I said, popping a purposeful mouthful.

She observed me with a look of skepticism before refilling my glass of water.

"So, Rajeep tells me that you have a new Combatant," Mr. Prabodhan commented, chewing happily on a mouthful of curry covered rice. "He is a Combatant, right?"

"Uh, yes, he is." I nodded, reaching for another piece of *naan*.

"Mm. Men are better suited to the task, I am certain. It is very dangerous, your work. I would not have given Rajeep my blessing had he been a girl."

Rajeep cleared his throat, dabbing at his lips with a napkin.

"You should consider yourself lucky you weren't born Sentient, Nicole," Mr. Prabodhan continued. "It is a danger. I'll never forget the first time I woke to find the ghost of Uzma's father leaning over my bed. It nearly gave me a heart attack! No, it is best that you did not practice, Uzma." He nodded at his wife, taking a sip of water. "Believe me."

"Of course, Sanjiv," Uzma said, lifting the water jar to refill her son's glass. We all knew the truth—Raj, Uzma, and I—that there was no way to circumvent the practice once you were a Sentient. Even if you chose not to embrace a group, entities still found you, they still sensed you and sought your help, and Uzma had been dealing with this all her life, crossing spirits over on the sly, destroying harmful ones. She had been the quiet protector of Mr. Prabodhan's home for as long as they'd been married.

Raj supposed that his father did not endorse his wife's involvement with sentience because it made him feel, if not inferior, then useless to his family. In Sanjiv's mind, he should have been the protector; he should have been able to provide whatever they needed, not the other way around. And so, instead of taking Duncan's route, judging sentience as a gift and those who had not achieved it as unfortunate, Sanjiv saw the whole business as a dangerous occupation, a risky business he'd much rather Raj not have become involved with.

After we'd finished eating, which was no easy task, Raj's parents ushered me into their family room for a private recital. Sanjiv was an avid fan of all kinds of music and had a particular weakness for opera. He already had a few pieces laid out for me, ready to be played, and so I accommodated him, as always. By the time I'd finished, Sanjiv was snoring away on his sofa, lulled to sleep by a ballad from *Tristan and Isolde*.

"We should probably get back," Raj suggested to his mother, quietly.

"Yes, you should. But Nicole, could I speak with you for a few moments before you leave, *sanam*?"

"Sure." I got up from the piano and followed her into the kitchen. "Are you sure I can't help you to clean this up, Uzma? This will take you all week!"

"Ah, nonsense!" She waved her hand. "It's nothing. Besides, I wanted to ask you something."

"What's that?"

"What has happened to your lightline, baby? Why is it faded?"

Of course. *Of course* she'd noticed. This was ridiculous. I couldn't go anywhere.

I sighed. "It's complicated."

She put her hand on her hip. "Try me, eh?"

Ugh!

I sat down on a nearby chair, resigned to the fact that I'd have to find a cave and develop a love of grubs if I wanted to avoid nosy Sentient interference. Once Uzma had made herself comfortable beside me, I lay my face on my hand and pondered where to begin.

"Is it Duncan?" she guessed.

I laughed quietly. "Again complicated. Yes and no."

She tapped her fingernails on the table, waiting for me to continue.

"It's Christian. The new Combatant."

"What about him? Is he giving you trouble?" she asked.

"No. He's just…I don't know. Never mind. It's fine."

"Is it now?" She narrowed an eye. "And your father? Is he still behaving like a buffoon?"

"Dad? He's…I don't know. He's been nicer to me lately. I think. Kind of."

"Hm. Well, I'm glad of that."

Maybe she was glad of it, but was I? The reasons behind my father's subtle shift in mood left me feeling somewhat dirty. But Duncan did make a valid point. My mom had tried to protect me, and it had ended up wrecking her life, wrecking my father's life. I couldn't let that happen with anyone else.

"Would you like to take home some leftovers?" Uzma asked, not waiting for me to answer before she was gathering up Tupperware containers and grocery bags.

❧

He was eating alone tonight—some pitiful excuse for a meal that looked an awful lot like a Hot Pocket. God, he was beautiful. Honestly. Even stern-faced and emo, Christian Wright was sickeningly handsome. I just wanted to touch him. I just wanted to…wait…*Nicole Alexandra Abbot, knock it the hell off!*

But he was so sad looking. The kind of sad that compelled you to cook everything in the fridge for him and then tuck him into bed. I wondered, did I look the same way?

Every little contact took courage now—walking through the same room as him, passing him in the hall. It was all awkward, wordless scowls. But something about his state tonight drove me to exhibit a molecule of bravery.

"That doesn't look very appetizing," I said, setting the leftover Indian food on the counter. Christian ignored me, taking another bite of his processed sandwich replica.

I sighed, guilt and discomfort causing the skin on my arms and face to prickle. Well, no one could stop me from being kind. Even if he hadn't said a single word to me since I'd gotten back, my desire to be nice to him had not gone away. Pulling out a plate from the cupboard, I loaded it with rice and curry, then stuck it in the microwave and put the remaining food away while it heated.

When the plate was finished, I grabbed a fork and laid everything down next to his hand. "Compliments of Raj's mom," I said, not daring to wait for a response. He'd probably dump it down the garbage disposal once I'd left the room.

No matter. After I'd left him, I lay in bed, considering the Combatant's melancholy state, and it occurred to me that he needed kindness badly, that I hated the idea of his feeling so unhappy, and that I cared about him so much that I would be his friend, if he would allow it. Besides, Christian in a platonic capacity was better than no Christian at all. And though the notion was admittedly pathetic on my part, it offered a bit of comfort, poking a hole in my screw-this life-raft, nonetheless.

Chapter Fourteen

Samantha and I were back to square one. It had been a little while since she'd last seen me, but it was ridiculous that she could regress so far in such a short amount of time. The idea was extremely disheartening. After all, if she couldn't retain the improvements made in my presence over the long run, how could I hope to send her off with her parents for good? Most of the kids I'd worked with had maintained their development. But not Samantha.

Thankfully, she hadn't asked for Christian once, but on the flip side, she wasn't reacting at all.

"Sam, are you even hearing this?" I rapped on the piano top in another attempt to get her attention. "Come on, baby. It's been an hour. Where's my girl?"

Stubborn, unresponsive child. "Sam, please? Smile or speak or…here." I fingered the melody that she and Christian had played just a handful of weeks earlier. She turned to look at my fingers.

"That's good! Good girl." I kept playing, and though she was nowhere near replicating the events that had unfolded when Christian was here, at least I knew how to capture her interest, even if it did tear me up to hear the song again. Getting Samantha to recognize the melody was only a small recapturing of our previous advances, but I was grateful for it. I'd have to get over my own personal discomfort. She'd been my favorite client, after all, albeit the most frustrating.

When I'd first met Samantha, she was a frightening sight to behold. Her eyes were dead. She simply wasn't there. Her body functioned, her reflexes worked, but her mind, everything that constituted life in a human being was gone. Reaching far enough into the secret recesses of her mind to whatever place the real Samantha hid and played and thought and understood had been my obsession—before Christian came along, anyway.

It was time I got my priorities back in order.

After our session had ended and Samantha was gone, I gathered up the ammunition from today's battle—my bongo drums, a pair of maracas, and a toy xylophone, all of which had been dreadfully ineffective.

I had planned on getting some notes done before my students started showing up, but the sight of the piano paired with an empty house was too tempting to ignore. Dropping my armload of musical paraphernalia, I sat down in front of the instrument and pressed on a key. Christian had touched this key. If I played the song that he'd learned, it would almost be like I was touching him. Yes, I knew the idea was stupid and pitiable, but I proceeded anyway and allowed myself to get every bit as lost in the music as I could. No one was home. It didn't matter how ridiculous I looked.

I let the notes have me, let them share the heavy burden of feeling, while warmth and wet trickled from the corners of my eyes. What harm could it do, really, crying alone? It was good therapy. It was cleansing.

Before I was ready to stop, the song was over, and I stared at the keys like they were withholding some kind of secret.

"I could practice for the rest of my life and I'd still be nowhere as good as you." Christian was standing in the doorway.

I didn't look at first, just sat, frozen with surprise. He'd talked to me—a whole sentence, even. "I thought you guys would be gone a lot longer."

"It was easier than we expected. The astral wasn't a spirit at all. It was a broken heating system."

"Oh." I smiled. "I see."

I endured a few seconds of awkward silence before he asked, "How's it going with Samantha?"

"Not so well. She seems to have lost a lot of ground since…well, I haven't seen her in a while," I muttered.

He sighed. "Do you think she remembers me?"

"Yes, I'm pretty convinced she does."

"Would…do you think it would help her at all if I was at the next session?"

My heart was beating so quickly I could hear it in my ears. "Probably. Yes."

He nodded, and I rubbed at the ebony gloss on a B flat, trying to control my reaction. "Okay," I said.

"We'll be in Seattle the day after next, so I can't this week."

"Oh. That's all right."

"But when I come back, yes?"

"Sure." Thank God. "That would be great."

Damned coastal weather. If Gil hadn't stayed behind, I'd be all alone with my increasingly frightened mom in this big, empty house while the storm of the century raged outside. Okay, maybe it wasn't the storm of the century, but it was a heck of a squall, and the waves were thrashing up the beach something vicious. It would probably be a mess out there when it was finally over.

The news had said the storm would last through the night, so Laura kept calling us every few hours to make sure we were okay. I was praying that the weather person had gotten the forecast wrong, because Mom was terrified of noises, and if the wind kept howling the way it was she was going to break down for sure.

Gil snoozed on the loveseat while Mom and I huddled on the couch, sharing a throw blanket. We were watching *The Sound of Music,* and she'd always loved the part where the boat flips over in the lake, drenching the von Trapp children and their famous *fraulein,* so I rewound the scene a few times to distract her from the rattling windows. It was working well, and she chuckled at their repeated misfortune.

"Mom, you feel like popcorn?"

"Okay, honey."

"And some cocoa?"

Gil popped his head up, half-asleep, and mumbled, "Mmph. Yum."

"I take it you want some, too?" I laughed.

"Mmph."

"All right. I shall return."

After inspecting the kitchen cabinet, the same one that housed Gil's world famous coffee collection, I realized two things. Number one, Gil had a horrible addiction that needed rehab badly (good thing we lived in California), and two, we were nearly out of cocoa.

"Gil, we only have two cocoas left!" I called from the kitchen. "Don't suppose I can interest you in tea?"

"Aaw! Not cool!"

I sighed. "Fine. The cocoa is yours. I'll drink the tea."

"I love you!"

"Uh huh."

Setting the water to boil, I dumped the last two packets of cocoa into mugs and crumpled the empty wrappers in my hand, barely registering the sound over a particularly loud crack of lightening. Then the lights went off.

"Nicole!" Mom shouted through the sudden darkness.

"It's okay, Mom. I'm coming." I maneuvered my way across the kitchen, smacking my hip into the corner of the counter and wincing through the pain as I went.

Gil passed me on my way. "I'll get us some candles," he said.

"Thanks."

I felt for the couch and slipped beside my mother, pulling her close and wrapping the blanket tightly around us both. "Well, this is an adventure, huh?"

"Nicole, what's happening?"

"Oh, we just lost power for a little bit, Mom. It'll come back on soon. And Gil is getting some candles. It'll be like camping. You remember when we used to go camping? At the lake?"

"No."

Not surprising. This was yet another precious memory she'd lost, but I hadn't.

"One of the times, when I was probably, oh, seven or eight maybe, Dad had built up a huge bonfire for us to roast marshmallows. Remember Wendell liked to play his twelve-string?"

"No."

"Hmm. Well, he did. And you would always make him sing *Let It Be*. You remember that?"

"I remember the song, but I can't remember Wendell playing it. Have I known him for a long time?"

"Yeah. You have."

"Oh."

"So, anyway, Wendell was playing *Let It Be*, and we were roasting marshmallows, and one of the sparks got out of hand. It flew up and landed on my arm and burned me."

"Oh, no."

The image of that night was so vivid that I could still smell the wood smoke. I'd been crying inconsolably until my father came to the rescue. He'd picked me up and sat me on his knee and blew on it. And then he said, "Don't cry, Nicole. You're a brave girl, and brave girls don't cry."

His intent had been good, I'm sure. He was trying to make me strong for what he'd hoped would be my impressive future as a Sentient, and so I'd stopped crying, all right. In fact, I'd tried never to cry in front of him again.

Yep. I was one massive hypocrite. I knew that emotions were healthy, that expression was good. I promoted these things in my professional life. But how could I possibly apply these principles to my own life while sharing quarters with some of the most gifted people on the planet? I was the exception to my own principles, to the rules I enforced with my kids. And yeah, I was ashamed of that, but shame was my middle name.

Someday, maybe I could do what Trina had demanded and say how I truly felt. Maybe I'd speak up; I'd dare to question my father's character. But for now, I had a very unstable Rita to worry about, and the last thing she needed was a sudden outburst by the only person she could count on to bring her peace.

"Gil? Candles!" I yelled through the house. What was taking him so long, anyway?

After a momentary scuffling sound, a beanpole of a figure jumped through the doorway, hands on his hips. "*Mortals!* I bring you sun!" Gil pronounced, and I was blinded as he flipped on a flood light, aiming it directly at us.

"That's great! Now stop trying to light us on fire," I said, shielding my eyes with my arm.

"Oh." He turned it away. "Sorry."

"Gil…*what* in the heck are you wearing?"

He glanced at his shoulder. "It's a cape. I'm a superhero."

"It's a towel. And you're a crackhead."

"Same thing."

"Where did you find that flashlight?"

"It was in the garage."

"Nice. Now I just wish we had one for the rest of the house."

"Well, what if we all spend the night down here," he suggested. "Would be kinda fun—like camping."

"You hate camping."

"I like indoor camping. No bugs."

"I see. But, you realize when you're not outside, it's not exactly camping, right?"

"Whatever. Don't go using logic on me. Won't work."

"Gil, you have an Intelligence endowment."

"A cruel trick of nature. I am one hundred percent clueless and intend to stay that way for the rest of my life. Hey, is someone knocking?" He dropped the fog light onto the coffee table and darted for the front door, towel-cape still draping from his shoulders. Chuckling, I made a mental note to start dispensing his caffeine per prescription only.

"Gil, it was probably just the wind," I said, watching as he opened the door. "You're going to let the rain—"

Wait…what the…

I stood up quickly, crossing the room to join him at the door. If there was anything I wasn't expecting to see on a stormy night at a Sentient beach house, it was this.

"Adalia?" I asked, slack-jawed.

It had only been a few months since Laura had exorcised the possessed girl, and I hadn't expected to see Adalia Lopez again this soon. In fact, Wendell had determined to wait until she was at least eighteen before beginning the teenager's Sentient training. But here she stood, her hair matted to her head, sopping wet and shivering wildly. Everything on her was soaked, from her jeans to her flannel shirt.

"I need to talk to that lady. The one who came to my house."

"Laura?" I said, gathering my senses. "You mean Laura? Yeah, Adalia, come in here!" I pulled her out of the rain, snatching the towel from Gil's shoulders to wrap it around hers. "Are you alone? How did you get here?"

"No. My dad's in the car."

"Outside?"

"Yeah."

"Well, I'll tell him to come in."

"No!" She rushed to the door ahead of me and closed it quickly.

"Why not?"

"He's having a nervous breakdown. I made him promise to stay in the car. I can't talk to Laura with him around."

"Why? What's going on?"

"It's…something's wrong. Something is *totally* wrong. I mean, like, at first I was fine after Laura came over. But now I'm just freaking out!" she said, teetering on the verge of tears.

"Okay. Okay, deep breaths. First, here, can we take this flannel shirt off? It's drenched. Just keep your tee shirt on and let's dry your hair, okay? Gil, will you make her some tea?"

"I'm on it," he said, grabbing the flood light and heading for the kitchen.

"Mom, do you think you'll be okay in here? Maybe you can take a nap?"

"Sure. You four enjoy your tea."

"Thanks, Mom."

She'd miscounted. There were only three of us, but I'd have to stress over her loss of mathematical faculties later. At the moment, I urged Adalia into the kitchen and hung her shirt on the back of a stool, pulling it out for her to have a seat. "All right," I said, massaging her hair with the towel. "Now, first bit of bad news—Laura's out of town."

"What?" She pulled away from me, staring wide-eyed.

"She's in Seattle, Adalia. I'm sorry."

"Oh, God," she moaned, dropping her arms to the counter and laying her head over them.

"Honey, what is it?" I sat down beside her.

"I'm some kind of a freak. I'm crazy or cursed or something. And you guys talked to my dad. You told him I was different. So you tell *me* what it is!"

"I'll try, but it would help if you'd explain what's going on," I said.

She sat up to look at me, and I observed how lovely she was. In spite of her ragged, shaken up appearance, she was quite a beautiful girl. With deep brown hair, eyes to match and skin a perfect, natural tan, the only thing wrong was the tiredness of her eyes. She looked like she hadn't slept in days.

She took a shaky breath, and said, "They sit on the foot of my bed and touch my feet. They shake me awake. They whisper in my ear when I'm alone." Her eyes welled up and she wiped them with the pads of her hands. "They follow me."

From the stove, Gil said, "One followed you here, didn't it?"

Adalia nodded. "Yeah. She was in your living room a second ago." She pointed to where my mom was.

Panicked, I grabbed the flashlight and ran in to check on Mom, but she was fine. Better than fine, in fact. She'd fallen asleep on the couch, just as

I'd asked her to. Still, I was smarter than that. Everything may have looked normal, but I realized that it didn't matter how it looked to me. Adalia was clearly the one with the spirit problem.

"Guys, how about we bring the conversation in here, huh?" I suggested.

"Sure," Gil answered. "But the tea…"

"It'll whistle when it's ready."

"'Kay." Gil and Adalia came as directed, sitting on the loveseat where Gil had been napping.

"Why didn't you tell me you saw something come in with her?" I asked Gil.

"I didn't. I sensed something, though. I don't always see ghosts like Laura does," he said, sounding a little bitter. It had always bothered Gil that he didn't have a Pathcrosser's gift.

"Well, I think my mom may have," I said.

"Rita? Why do you say that?"

"She addressed us as 'you four' just a bit ago. Don't you remember?"

"Four? Huh. I wasn't even paying attention."

"Yep. Adalia, do you see anyone now?" I asked her.

She looked around, peering reluctantly into the darker areas of the house. "No," she said.

"Okay, good. Now, Gil, you want to talk to her about this?"

"Me?" He looked appalled. "Why me?"

"You're the Sentient."

"Uuh, yeah, no thank you. I don't do teenagers, no offense, kid," he acknowledged Adalia. "Just…I leave the heart-to-hearts to Nick. That's her forte."

"Thanks." I narrowed my eyes at him before returning to Adalia. "You know, I'm not sure why this is happening to you. It's really odd, because Sentients—that's what you are—don't usually start seeing things like this until they're much older than you."

"Like, how much older?" she asked.

"Well, how old are you?"

"I'm fifteen."

"Okay, then, you should have about ten more years to go."

"Oh." She looked utterly downtrodden, and I had no idea how to fix it. They hadn't offered courses on how to deal with adolescent Sentients—let alone early bloomers—in any of my college classes. We needed Laura and Wendell.

"Laura won't be back 'til the end of the week," I explained. "And we can't have your dad sitting in the car all night, can we?"

She frowned, shaking her head.

"So." I sighed. "What if you go home and I call Laura to see if she can—"

"No! No, I can't go home! I can't. You have no idea. I mean, Dad knows stuff is happening, he knows I'm freaking out, but I can't tell him why. I'm trying to keep him calm, you know, after what happened before, and I'm *so* scared and he can't help me. Please, can't I stay here with you?"

"Stay here? You want to stay here?"

"Yeah. Please. At least 'til that lady…'til Laura gets back."

I looked at Gil, who shrugged, then nodded.

"Well, I guess if it's okay with your dad. But we should really let him in the house, Adalia."

"Fine," she grumbled.

About an hour and a Valium later, we'd convinced Mr. Lopez to let his daughter stay with us and to call her school and report that she was sick until Laura's return. It was no easy task, either. The man was a basket case, every bit as nervous as I'd remembered him, but he obviously adored his daughter and wanted what was best for her. Now we just needed to figure out what the hell to do with a terrified fifteen-year-old for three more days.

On the bright side, at least our power was back on, and that was a relief. There would be a lot of TV watching and video game playing in the next couple of days. I hoped these would help divert Adalia's attention from her perplexing circumstance.

"No way, Nick! Come on," Gil argued in a whisper as we stood at the living room door, watching Adalia and my mother sleeping in the living room. We'd ended up camping inside after all.

"Gil, I have to do my job. And this situation is part of yours. The kid is scared shitless, okay? And she doesn't want to be alone, but I can't have her with me while I'm working with Samantha."

"Why not? You had Christian with you."

"That's different."

"How?"

"I'd gotten permission from Samantha's parents to use him as a part of her therapy. That isn't the case with Adalia. One disturbed child doesn't benefit another."

"Oh? Then, again, explain your use of Christian."

"Gil!"

"Nicole, this sucks."

"Why? What's so hard about hanging out with a fifteen year old? Shit, you *are* a fifteen year old."

He scowled. "You owe me."

"I owe you? Why is that?"

"Because…because, you were the one who turned into little Miss Rescue Ranger and let the kid in and got her all dry and 'Oh, Gil, make her tea. Oh, Gil, let her stay.'"

"Uhm, would you stop talking about her like she's a stray dog? And you agreed to this, too."

"I don't remember that."

"Well, you did. So suck it up, Gilford, or I'll toss all your toys in the ocean."

He peered at me and then broke into a smile. "You know, if you talked to your father like this, I don't think he'd even recognize you."

Well…the point was worth considering. In fact, *I'd* hardly recognized myself. And I kind of liked it.

❧

Just as I'd expected, the beach was a shambles. Kelp was everywhere, stretching all the way down to where the rock cliffs began. I picked up pieces of it with my foot as we walked, kicking the slimy, smelly, sand-encrusted weeds to the side.

Samantha's hair blew every which way, blocking her eyes, but as usual, she didn't make a move to push it aside. Instead, she trudged along the beach, holding my hand and staring ahead at everything—and nothing.

For any other child, this beach would have been a wonder and a play-ground. There were shells and stones of every imaginable kind in the sand today, although sadly, there was also a lot of man-made debris. The winds had blown all kinds of junk onto our beach from the surrounding area, so I carried a bag in hand and gathered the trash as I went along.

"Let's go this way, honey." I pulled Samantha away from the water and bent to pick up a takeout container. It said Mr. Chen's House of Chow on the box, though the rain and sand had worn enough of the letters away that it looked like Mr. Chen's House of Ch.

I grimaced at our remaining strip of shoreline. The whole mess saddened me. When I thought about how much of this stuff was probably clogging up the rest of the beaches around here, collecting below the rims of rocks and screwing with the wildlife, it made my stomach turn.

Growing up in this area had taught me a lot, but traveling away from it had taught me more. It was easy to take a place as beautiful as this for granted, but I tried not to be immune. Seers would tell you that human beings, while early in their journey, often misconstrued their place and purpose on the planet. For ages, people were convinced that they held some kind of monarchy over everything else. They assumed, simply because they could, that they *should* do as they pleased, have what they pleased, take what they pleased, and manipulate their surroundings as they pleased. And they were wrong, obviously, but Wendell felt that slowly, surely, people were finally starting to comprehend this. I hoped he was right.

Wendell said that our race was still developing its human mind in accordance with its soul. We were still learning. And as Sentient wisdom went, humanity evolved in stages. Some of us perceived the larger picture of things, while others saw the same world but through a narrower telescope.

Sentients were human, too, and they had their faults. One of them, in my humble opinion, was the tendency to feel superior when faced with so much ignorance. I knew a few who were like this, my father included. After all, ego was still an infuriatingly stubborn human vice that even some Seers fell prey to. But though I struggled with my own non-sentience, even I knew better. There was no point in thinking yourself any greater than anybody else, because, in the end, we'd all end up in the same glow of unbreakably connected light.

The correlation between spirit and psychology had always fascinated me. It was the whole reason I'd gone into the field to begin with. But despite its trial and error, one thing was certain about the evolution of a soul—you were supposed to change for the better. So what had happened with Duncan? His soul had been around a long time. As a Combatant, he was endowed with a psychic ability so strong that it extended to the physical, and yet, when I contemplated him further, I realized that he was clearly not using the entire scope of his vision. I mean, if he believed what he'd been taught in Sentient circles—that there was a very precise reason for everything—then what excuse could he use for ignoring these teachings and being disgusted by me? I couldn't understand my father, and it left me paranoid. It left me fearing that he saw something awful in me that no one else could see.

I was so conflicted, torn between anger and shame, and I hated it with all my heart. And more than that, I was alarmed by the fact that I couldn't count on my own father. He wanted nothing real to do with me, and it seemed more and more he felt the same way about his wife. That left the cheese standing alone, and I didn't know if I could bear the pain of Mom's decline by myself.

Chapter Fifteen

"Hey, you're not playing fair!" Gil's angry accusation traveled down the stairs and into the music room.

"Uhm, Gabby, just keep playing…*loudly*," I directed my three-o'clock student.

"But Ms. Abbot, this song is pianissimo."

"Uh, well, pretend it's not, okay? Be right back."

I took off upstairs to hear Adalia arguing vehemently. "I am *not* cheating. You're slow!"

Swinging around Gil's doorway, I spoke in a hushed voice. "I've got a student downstairs. What's the problem here?"

Gil pointed at the TV screen. "She's cheating! She keeps killing me!"

"Do not!" said Adalia. "You're just slow getting to the next level!"

"I was going slow for *you*," he claimed.

"Hah! You were not and you know it. You just can't deal with the fact that a kid is beating you."

"Oh, you know what?" Gil got up and stomped toward the door. "I think it's time to call it quits, little girl. I'm getting some food. Play time's over!" he announced, pausing as he passed me to mumble, "I was letting her win."

Adalia perked up. "Hey! I heard that!" she said, then returned her concentration to the game.

Lord have mercy, they'd been at it all day, arguing like siblings and demanding just as much parental supervision. I shook my head, rolling my eyes at the whole thing before entering Gil's room fully to sit on the arm of the chair where Adalia was sitting. "So," I began, smiling at our house guest.

"Yeah?"

"Go easy on him, will you, Adalia? He's not used to losing."

"Well? Sucks for him. He's the elder. He needs to man up."

I pursed my lips, suppressing a laugh. "Uh, yeah." That wasn't likely to happen in several lifetimes. "You hungry? You want to come and get something to eat? Maybe we can order a pizza."

She nodded. "Okay. I like pizza."

"Good. Then I'm going back to finish with my student. You come down when you're ready, okay?"

She dropped the game piece like a rock and shot up from the chair. "I'm ready. I don't wanna be up here alone," she said, eyeing the hallway behind us.

"Oh. Okay."

She was still scared to death, but I had no idea how to make her feel better other than to keep vigil at her side until Laura came back. Only one more day of this, and I was counting the hours. Gil was no help. In fact, he seemed to make the situation worse. I'd never really noticed how much attention he required, but I could see it now. Despite her youth, Adalia was forcing him to act his age, and he didn't care for that very much.

I counted my charges. Mom, Gil, my students, and now Adalia. What in the world was the universe trying to tell me? That I should start an orphanage?

On the way back to my music lesson I stopped by the kitchen. "You might want to put the cold-cuts back," I told Gil.

"Mrwhy?" he asked through a mouthful of turkey.

"Because we're ordering a pizza. Well, specifically, *you* are. Please?"

"Oh. Okay. I like pizza."

That sounded familiar. No wonder he didn't get along with Adalia. They were two peas in a pod.

Returning to the sunroom, I stood beside my student and cringed as she played with all her might. "Okay, hon. You can quiet it down now."

She didn't answer.

"Gabby?"

Oblivious.

"Gabby!" I practically shouted over the piano.

"Oh! Hi, Ms. Abbot. Did you want me to go back to pianissimo?"

I smiled. "No, that's all right. I think we can call it quits for today, huh?"

"Sure."

By seven, everyone was fully sated with cheesy, saucy food, so I decided to add to the sedative effect and issue another movie night for the household. This evening's pickings would steer clear of anything even remotely scary. A family film would work just fine—preferably something with animated characters.

"Real people do not even look like that," Adalia complained.

I examined the screen. "You don't think?"

"No way," Gil added. "Look at how disproportionate her head is when compared to the rest of her body."

"Hm." I supposed they were right, but honestly, who cared? It was a cartoon.

"Yeah," Adalia agreed. "I mean, the pixilation is amazing, their expressions and everything, very realistic. So why mess up on the rest?"

Gil nodded his agreement. Talk about spoilsports. The fact that the characters were flying around in sky boats after being sprinkled with moon dust was perfectly believable. But their inaccurate body proportion was absolutely unacceptable.

In spite of the entertainment, every so often I'd catch Adalia peeking out of the room. She was trying to be subtle about it, trying not show her paranoia, but I caught on readily enough. The girl was on edge, more so at night than during the day.

"Everything okay, Adalia?" I asked her at last.

Her eyes flickered back to the screen when she realized I'd been watching her. "Yeah, just, I think she's watching us."

"Huh? Who?"

"That spirit that followed me here the other night," she mumbled.

"Oh." Surprisingly, her comment alarmed me, and I felt goose bumps forming on my arms. Normally ghosts didn't bother me at all, but then again, I was always around path-crossing Sentients when astrals were present, and though I suspected that Adalia was destined to be a Pathcrosser, she was nowhere near that status right now. Laura wasn't here to give our invading spirit the what-for, so that was troubling. Gil could repel it if he needed to, using the energy of his aura to scare the ghost by throwing it around a little, but he couldn't cross the spirit over if it was human, and he sure as hell couldn't banish it if it wasn't.

"What makes you think she's still here?" I asked. "Let alone watching us?"

"Because I keep catching glimpses of her eyes," she said, almost whispering. She had a habit of doing that when she was scared.

"Just her eyes?"

"Well, that's what's left by the time I look at her," she explained. "The rest fades away too fast."

By now, Gil had muted the TV and was actually paying attention. "What kind of eyes?" he asked.

"They were green, kind of bloodshot. They're gross."

He squinted in thought. "What else you got, Adalia? What else?"

"She has long hair. She stares…looks mad."

Gil froze. "Does she smile?"

"Yeah, but she still looks angry."

His eyes widened before he put on a poker face and looked at me. "Nick, can we alk-tay in the itchen-kay for a second?"

Adalia snorted. "Pig Latin? Are you serious? Jeez, Gil, I'm fifteen, not four."

"Whatever," he said. "So, Nick? You coming?"

I got up and followed him, watching as he turned on the living room light as we left.

Once we were out of earshot, I asked, "Why'd you turn on the lights?"

"Because you don't want to leave a kid and a feeble-minded woman alone in the dark with an old hag. That's why."

"What? Here?"

"Yeah. Here."

"Well, what do we do?"

"Call Laura," he said, in the most sober, adult voice I'd heard him use in days.

I knew about hags. They were one of a very few things, aside from vampires, that freaked a Sentient out. A hag wasn't a spirit to screw with. It was a once female, human astral that had been reborn in, warped by, and perverted with anger for some great wrong endured during life. The spirit of a hag was ancient, sometimes called a banshee in European cultures, and it was single-minded. It wanted revenge, even if the victim had done it no wrong. Hags were typically ugly as sin, their appearance a reflection of deep hatred, and they liked to make themselves known—usually through a tremendous stench, screaming, moaning, or other such creepy-assed noises, so they were the one type of ghost that humans could almost always detect, Sentient or not. But this one was obviously being sneaky—and that freaked me out more than anything else.

"Get her on the phone," I said. "And pull out an air mattress. We're all sleeping in the living room again."

❧

"Yeah, I know," Gil spoke into his cell, pacing the kitchen like a madman. "So what, we should sleep in shifts?"

I watched him as I poured some mugs of strong black coffee, half-tempted to swap Gil's out for decaf, but I'd have to break his addiction some other time—this was going to be a long night.

"Okay," he went on. "Okay. So, we'll see you tomorrow night."

I hated the fact that we had to spend another night without Laura and the rest of our group here to deal with things. They could have banished a hag in no time. It sucked being so helpless.

Gil hung up the phone and slipped onto a stool, pulling his coffee over to take a drink.

"Game plan?" I asked.

"We take turns sleeping, just in case. And the lights stay on."

"Will that really help?"

"It can't hurt. They prefer the dark. Hey, should we mention any of this to the kid?"

"No! No way. She's already freaking out. She doesn't need to know the details."

"Well, maybe she wants to know the details."

"Doubtful, and even if she did, the answer is no. Not now. Not this time."

"You don't think you're being too protective?"

"Absolutely not," I said.

"So what do we tell her?"

"It's a ghost and we're being extra careful. End of story."

"Okay.

Nothing makes you look over your shoulder more than talk of a hag in your house. The laundry room, the piano room, any space that would normally be dark at night would stay fully lit this evening. It would be hard to fall asleep with all the lights on, but honestly, it wasn't not like we'd be all that relaxed anyway.

Adalia was no slouch. She suspected more was happening than we'd let on. She only had to look at the facts. We'd known something had followed her here from the very first night she'd arrived, yet *now* we were sounding the alarms?

"How come we can't turn the lights off?" Adalia observed, staring at the floor lamp in the corner.

"We're just playing it safe, honey. Just in case," I said.

"In case what?"

I sighed. This kid was persistent. "In case our visitor is feeling mischievous."

"Like how? Are we talking blanket stealing mischievous? Cuz I've had that happen already."

"Well, let's not worry about it too much. Just try and get some sleep, okay?"

"Okay." She rolled over on the couch, pulling the blanket closer around her.

I looked at Gil, and he shared my worried expression. We'd already spent two nights with a hag in the house and she hadn't done anything yet, but she'd decided to show herself to Adalia tonight, so she'd probably been biding time, maybe to feel out the competition.

We took turns nodding off, me two hours, Gil two hours, and after Gil woke me from my first round of sleep, I dragged myself up from the air mattress and blinked blearily. The DVD player read 2:46 a.m.

"I need to use the bathroom," I said. "Spot me two minutes?"

"No prob."

Shuffling across the kitchen and into the laundry room, I rounded the corner to the half-bath and shut the door behind me. There was a poorly insulated window to the right of the toilet, and the room's position in the house always made it so damned cold compared to the rest of the down-stairs—especially the toilet seat. Pleasant.

After I'd completed the task, I glared at the mirror on the wall. Any time you watched a movie with ghosts in it, they always appeared in a mirror, and that wasn't so far from the truth. Ghosts did love mirrors, but not because of the added dramatic effect. Actually, Laura said that spirits were attracted to reflective surfaces, mainly because they couldn't see themselves in it, and the phenomenon fascinated them. Humans could sometimes spot a spirit in glass or water, but the spirit itself could not, because the very definition of a lingering astral meant that they never fully acknowledged what they were.

So I approached the mirror with some trepidation, half-scolding myself for being a sissy.

Standing bravely in front of it, I was met with the most horrific vision mankind could ever behold—myself. My hair was insane, my eyes were droopy, my skin washed out. Good grief, I needed to start using facial cream, pronto. But other than that and the window behind me, the coast was clear.

I snorted, turning around to leave, and was immediately nailed to the floor in frigid shock at the sight of a face—the menacing, nearly lunatic expression of a haggard old woman smiling at me from outside the window. My words caught in my throat as I tried to call for Gil. The look of her was grotesque, with absolutely corpse-like skin, deep gray, sunken flesh beneath her eyes, filthy teeth. The worst were those eyes. They glowed a putrid green, with tendrils of red that spidered along their whites. As I stood there she laughed, low and sinister, and though she was outside of the window, I knew she could be beside me, before me, behind me, at any moment she wished.

Finally, I said the first thing that came to me. "Get the hell away from us, you bitch!"

Redirecting one's feelings into anger wasn't always a healthy way to deal with fear, but it worked just dandy this time, thank you very much. I had no idea if the tactic had made the tiniest difference to the hag, but it had given me the clarity to run the hell out of the bathroom and call for Gil. I was grateful that I'd been breathless with fear when I did, since the sound wasn't likely to wake the others while still getting Gil's attention.

Flying into the kitchen, he caught me as my knees gave way. "Hey, Nicky. What the hell?"

"She was outside the bathroom," I said, still unable to control the full body trembling. "She was outside the window. The bathroom…"

"Jesus." He pulled a chair out from the table and led me to it, then darted off to the bathroom to have a look. I steadied my breaths, still fast in tandem with the beating of my heart. I was more terrified than I'd been in years. I'd never seen anything so creepy before, and I was praying to every deity known to man that I'd never see it again.

"Guys!" I jerked around at the sound of Adalia's cry and without blinking threw the chair away and ran into the living room to find her sitting up, her eyes fixed on the foot of my mother's air mattress. "She's here."

"I can't see her," I said, my voice shaking. "Gil!"

At this point, my mother was sitting up as well, staring back and forth between Adalia and me. It seemed the hag wasn't visible to her this time, which was probably for the best.

"She looks different," Adalia said, calmer than was rational. "She's…she was younger last time, prettier. She looks so ugly and mean now."

"She was hiding her true form," Gil said, appearing at my side.

"Can you see her?" I asked him.

"I can see her shadow, and I can smell her," he said, making a face.

"Can you repel her?"

"Let's find out."

He raised his hand a little, palms forward, and took on an expression of great concentration. Before too long, Adalia gasped and whipped her head around to stare at Gil, wide-eyed.

"Holy shit!" she said.

My mom looked horrified. "Oh, sweetheart, you shouldn't be using language like that!"

"Oh, sorry, Mrs. Abbot! It's just, holy shit!" she repeated. "That was the coolest thing I've ever seen! Like, ever!" She smiled at Gil with a look that bordered on worship.

"Thanks," he grinned.

I sighed. Man, what I wouldn't have given to see that old hag get repelled. "What happened?" I asked. "Did she slam into the wall?"

"No, she slammed *through* the wall!" Adalia clarified. "Holy shit!"

Gil laughed. "You know, you'll be able to do that, too, Adalia."

"I will?"

"Oh yeah, man. And lots more, too. If you're a Pathcrosser, which I'm venturing a guess that you are, it'll be a regular part of the job description."

"Awesome," she said.

"So, this Sentient thing, it's not so bad, eh?" he added.

"Maybe not," Adalia said, losing some of her gusto as she examined the wall where the hag had been served. "Only, she's gonna come back, isn't she?"

Gil shrugged. "She might, but I'll just keep tossing her on her ass if she does. And then when Laura gets here, she's toast."

"Yeah?"

"Yeah. Wait 'til you see *that*."

Adalia smiled at him again, and I could tell that their dynamic had taken quite the turn. There would be peace in the valley after all.

Chapter Sixteen

We couldn't keep Mateo out forever. And though he'd promised to let Adalia have her space until Laura came back, he'd called several times every day. So I was more than happy to hear everyone's vehicles crunching up the gravel driveway. Only problem was, I was nervous, too. Again. Always. That tug in my gut when I thought about Christian was going to be there for the long haul.

The more I tried to block the anticipation, the jumbling, tumbling emotion of seeing his face, the worse it was. The second Laura trudged into the house with her duffel, I panicked. I needed to build up to seeing his face—maybe start with the sound of his voice first.

"Welcome back," I muttered to Laura, then grabbed her bag and pulled it into the laundry room like a lunatic. It would be full of dirty clothes, after all. The cover made sense.

Laura trailed behind me. "Hey, thanks," she laughed, watching as I set the bag on top of the washer, busying myself further by unzipping the sides. "Uhm, you wanna stop rifling through my skivvies and give me a hug, though?"

I dropped a sock. "Yeah," I said, and let her have a proper greeting. "Where is everyone else?"

"Should be arriving any minute. How you guys holding up?" she asked. "She show her ugly face again?"

"No! Thank God. Gil repelled her last night, and she didn't show up again after that."

Laura drew back. "Oh, Nicky, she's still around. It stinks like a corpse out there," she informed me. "She's hiding."

"What? Great. Just great," I said, frowning.

"Nah. Don't worry. I'll take care of her. She's definitely stalking the wrong house!"

I smiled and then tensed as my dad entered the adjacent room, hardly breaking his heavy gait as he headed for the stairs with his things. Now would have been a good time to tear my eyes from the entryway, but the muscles controlling my head and neck were apparently independent of my will, and against all better judgment I watched until Christian came in, his bag slung over his shoulder. It must have been packed full, tugging at his right side the way it did, and the idea of stress injuries gave me the fleeting urge to run over and take it from him, Donna Reed style. Smacking the thought away, I scolded myself. *No entertaining delusions, Nicole! You masochist.*

He glimpsed up as he passed, then smiled tiredly, nodding a greeting. I exchanged the expression briefly before returning to Laura.

"How was the job?"

"Boring." She slung an arm around my waist, leading us out of the room. "Boring as hell. Not nearly as exciting as the time you had, I can promise you that."

"Well, after this week, I'm ready for some boring, please."

"No problemo," she said. "And oh, the beach is looking pretty clean! I was expecting a bigger mess."

"Samantha and I spent some quality time with a trash bag."

"Aah. That's my girl. But you should have asked Gil and the kid to do it. Would have been good for them."

"I don't know…leaving them alone with a giant plastic strangulation device might have ended badly."

"Aw, come on. Seriously?"

I raised an eyebrow.

"Details?"

"They fought like teenagers, Laura. And that's fine for Adalia, considering that she *is* a teenager. But Gil? Not so much."

"What did you expect? Really, Nicole. You made him share his toys."

"True."

"Are they still at it?"

"No. Nope. They seemed to have reached some sort of treaty. Adalia was all kinds of smitten with Gil's repelling," I said, smirking.

"That'll do it." Laura released me and stopped in the living room, dead center. "Get Adalia, will you? I want her to see this."

"Right now? You've only been home for five minutes."

"Why waste time?"

"Well, if you insist," I said, turning to call upstairs. "Adalia! She's back!"

After a moment, both Gil and Adalia appeared at the top landing, peering down the stairs with a look of alarm.

"Oops! Sorry, guys," I said, realizing my error. "I meant Laura! Not the ghost."

"Oh!" Gil said, snorting.

"Hello, again, missy," Laura addressed Adalia. "Come on down here, will you?"

Adalia descended the stairs with no hesitation and stopped just short of running into us. In Laura's typically warm fashion, she pulled Adalia close to her side and smiled at her. "Okay. Ready for something fantastic?"

"What?"

"I'm going cross over our hag."

"Cross over?"

"Mhm. I'm going to send her on her way."

"Oh! Good!" She was definitely paying attention now.

"So, first thing's first. We need to find her."

"Follow the smell," Gil complained, wrinkling his nose.

"Have you noticed where it's strongest?" Laura asked.

"It changes. Last night it was everywhere, and then it faded after I repelled her. Now it's mainly in the living room."

Laura nodded and still holding onto Adalia, headed in the direction Gil had indicated, stopping to note the rolled up air mattresses on the floor. "Bless your hearts. You guys had a tough week."

"It sucked," Adalia agreed.

"Well, we'll take care of that." Laura released Adalia and cleared her throat, taking in a deep breath and moving to another part of the room. She breathed again, then made a perplexed face and walked over to the couch, sitting down and feeling the cushion beside her.

"Hmm." She stood again, staring at the windows as she walked over to touch their curtains. Then in a dramatic sweep, she pulled them open quickly and Adalia gasped, grabbing me by the arm. I stared at the window and after a moment, the hag materialized, glowering at Laura.

Laura responded by waving her hand in front of her nose and grimacing. "You've been smelling up the whole house," she said.

The hag opened her cracked, diseased lips and screamed maniacally, her eyes bulging in anger. The sound was so frightening that Adalia buried her face in my side, crying. Then, just as my ear drums threatened to burst and my stomach turned with the unholy tone of the hag's voice, Christian ran into the room and she fell silent, her eyes filling with venom.

"You don't like men," Laura said, calmly. "We know that. But whatever some offending male did to you however many years ago, it's time you let it go."

The ghost dropped her head and shoulders to a hunch at the sound of our Pathcrosser's voice. She was pissed.

"Do you talk?" Laura asked. "Or just scream and smell?"

The hag growled. "Why aren't you afraid?"

I shrunk, surprised at the sound of the hag's words. How could I hear her speaking? Hags really were exhibitionists. And what a horrid sound her voice made. The femininity was gone, and the noise coming out of the ghost seemed to me like several rattling, wheezing voices at once.

Laura stared the hag down, standing completely tall. It was important to give the appearance of strength when faced with dark or angry astrals, because like bullies, they often lost courage when faced with a strong opponent.

"We can do this the easy way or the hard way," Laura explained. "I can heal you and cross you over normally, or I can force you over as you are, and that will not be pleasant, I promise you."

"You come with the light?" The hag spoke in understanding, backing away apprehensively. "Keep it away from me!"

"Calm down," Laura demanded. "It's not going to appear unless I show it to you." She turned to Adalia. "She's afraid of being crossed over. You'll find this sometimes, because human spirits that have turned malicious are notoriously fearful of light. Occasionally, the universe offers it to them in hopes of moving them on. But they often refuse, thinking it's come as punishment." She turned to the hag again. "How many years have you been running from the light?"

The hag looked suddenly worried. "Many."

"It won't hurt you. It won't judge you. It'll simply take you out of your current torment and into understanding."

The hag was having trouble processing Laura's words. "Keep it away from me," she repeated, backing up to the window.

"Don't try to leave," Laura said. "I told you—I'll force things if I have to. And unless you've gone into this willingly, it'll hurt."

"Why?" Adalia spoke up. "Why will it hurt her?"

"Because she'll be resisting pure light energy, Adalia. She needs to completely give herself over, needs to merge with the light with abandon, molecule by molecule. If she's fighting the process the whole time, it'll feel like being ripped apart."

Adalia's looked at the hag. "Don't you want to be happy?" she asked.

The old ghost stared at the girl, confused, and Adalia let go of me, taking a few steps toward the hag. I reached for her, but Laura stopped me.

"It's okay. Let her go," she told me, and I nodded, watching as the hag glared at Adalia. She seemed horribly confused by the girl's bravery.

"Why are you so mean and angry all the time?" Adalia asked her. "Why do you want to scare people? What's the point?"

The hag's angry grin returned. "They deserve it."

Adalia shrank a little at the sight, but she didn't move. "Why?"

"Because. They're evil. They're callous. They're selfish. They lie. They kill. They deserve it."

"I've never killed anyone. I don't like to lie. I'm not even sure what callous *means*. And I know I'm not evil. So you're not being fair," Adalia said, suddenly angry. "It sounds like you have issues. Didn't they have therapists when you were a human?"

I smiled a little. This kid was going to be one awesome Pathcrosser.

The hag sneered at Adalia. "You're a child. You'll change."

"No, I won't. I choose to be good for the rest of my life, and that's that. And you know what? It really seems like you're the one who's evil and selfish and whatever that other word was. Why don't you just get over yourself?"

The hag stood tall and opened her mouth, screaming again, and Laura rushed to Adalia's side, covering her ears. "Eh hem," Laura cleared her throat when the hag had finally quieted. "Well, that was just excessive."

"Do you think he still loved me when he *stabbed me through*?" the hag screamed, viciously angry. "Did he feel remorse when he *burned* me, not even dead yet, to hide what he'd done? And all so he could be with her? You can drag me to hell! But not" —she disappeared and then reformed in front of Christian— "before I share the pain!" she finished, and before we could comprehend, she'd made a motion in the air with her hand, and Christian winced, grabbing his chest. I noted two rips in his shirt where she'd scratched him deeply, and crimson crept through the holes.

Laura released Adalia and wasted no time. Taking the Pathcrosser's stance with her palms forward and opened, she gathered her energy to capture the hag. Almost instantly, the spirit froze, eyes wide, arms splayed. She screeched in agony, over and over, convulsing wildly, but I couldn't see the light that caused her pain. I could only see her deteriorating in front of me, particles flying outward, upward, everywhere. Then, when she was fully gone, the echo of her cries reduced to a whisper and soon nothing. She was gone.

I looked at Christian. "You're bleeding."

"It's okay.

Adalia, dazed and shaken, sat down on the couch and blinked at Laura. "So, what happened to her?"

Laura sat down beside her. "She's one with the Source now," she said. "She'll understand what she's done, she'll feel remorse, she'll judge her own actions and go from there."

"Is that what happens to all of us?"

"Yes. But typically when we die, we don't fight the light—it feels good and compelling to us. But people can carry their fears, their anger, their confusion straight over to the afterlife with them, and that can cloud our ability to perceive even the most obvious things. And sometimes, just like they did during life, these things hold us back from moving on."

Adalia sighed. "You do this stuff all the time? This is your job?"

"It's my life," Laura corrected her. "And it's going to be yours, too."

Mateo Lopez was not going to be happy. Actually, we broached this event with the presumption that he would freak out when he grasped what Wendell was suggesting. How did you tell a parent that they're child was no longer safe in their care?

Wendell had politely excluded my father from the conversation. He didn't trust what he'd say. Duncan had spent half a day bragging to Wendell that he just *knew* Adalia needed to be with us. He'd said so, after all. He'd called it. But who could have predicted Adalia's sudden rush to the finish line? She'd surprised everyone.

In this house, we served tea with every possibly traumatic conversation. It had been Wendell's tradition, originally, but we all practiced it now, and in the last week, we'd been drinking up a storm. Laura poured Mateo a cup and sat down next to her husband. Chris's seldom heard perspective would be important if Wendell was going to earn Mateo's cooperation.

Gil and I were rather close to Adalia now, so Wendell had asked that we join them while Adalia played video games upstairs alone, finally convinced it was okay to unhinge herself from our sides—for now, anyway.

Mateo looked like a hot mess, and rightly so. He had no idea what was truly going on in his daughter's life. In fact, we were all pretty thrown by her coming of age so early. We'd never met a Sentient that evidenced their abilities this young.

"Mateo," Wendell started, "before we discuss anything, I just want you to know that we all have Adalia's best interests at heart. We care about her, we want her safe, we want what's best for her. I hope you believe that."

The man nodded, cupping his tea and staring at the liquid blankly. "You're going to ask me to let her stay here, aren't you?"

Laura and Wendell exchanged surprised looks. They hadn't expected him to cut to the chase so readily.

"I'm sorry, Mr. Lopez. I know you feel like your family has been torn apart," she soothed Mateo as he blinked back tears. "We're so sorry to take her out of your house." She placed her hand over his. "But, she can't live with you now. Something has happened, something has given way, and whatever abilities I told you about when last we met—those abilities that would require Adalia to join this kind of group someday—those abilities have prematurely manifested themselves."

"No offense," Mateo said to Laura, looking disgruntled. "But is it possible this is *your* fault?"

Laura let go of his hand. "Why would you think that?"

"Well, whatever you did to her to…to make her better—is this some kinda side effect?"

Laura frowned. "Look, your daughter was a Sentient long before I came along. She was born that way, which is what caused your problems to begin with. Now it's possible that when I merged with her energy, it may have opened things up sooner than the ideal, but this was unavoidable, Mateo. This would have happened, regardless. And it's nothing to be afraid of or ashamed of. Your daughter's soul is advanced, and she displays that advancement very prominently."

"So what, she's like a superhero or something?"

Laura nodded. "Kind of, yeah."

"That's right," Gil piped in. "She's like an adolescent Wonder Woman."

"Huh." Mateo smiled a little, taking a sip of his tea. "So, what do we do? When can I see her?"

"Every day if you want to," Wendell said. "Our home is your home. She can even go to regular school if she can handle keeping this a secret. But that's one of the crucial points here. This life, people like us, we live privately for a reason. There's a select group who are not Sentients that know about us. And you're one of them now, which means that we're placing a huge amount of trust in you. Please understand that Adalia's well-being depends upon your secrecy."

"What happens if someone finds out?" Mateo asked the magic question.

"Chris?" Wendell addressed our most reserved Sentient.

Chris made a thoughtful face, rubbing the slight stubble that shadowed his jaw. "Mateo, seven years ago, someone with the Federal Bureau of Investigation found out that I had the ability to manipulate living matter. Now, I didn't know I was Sentient at the time, I'd never heard of Sentients, so I'd been making some pretty stupid mistakes for years, thinking that something was wrong with me. Heck, it was probably sheer luck that I hadn't been discovered earlier. And the scientists assigned to me, they didn't know the half of what I could do, but they poked and prodded and bullied and interrogated. There were plans for a surgery, Mr. Lopez. They wanted to know what I was, and I believe they would have destroyed me in the process."

Mateo looked horrified. "Is my baby in danger?"

"Not as long as she's with us," Wendell stressed. "But out there, trying to manage this on her own? The results would be disastrous. Should anyone suspect anything, they'd be all over her. That's what people tend to do when they don't understand something. They want to experiment, pick it apart. But the system isn't equipped to understand us. They're not able, they're not ready, because they don't believe. You see what I'm saying?"

"Yeah, sure. I guess."

"Plus," Wendell said, "there's something else. Being followed around by dangerous spirits or curious scientists, those aren't the only threats we face. There are others—and because of them, your life would be at risk so long as she was living with you."

"How?"

I was curious how far Wendell would take this. Was he actually going to mention vampires? Surely not. He knew the Society's rules.

"There are some lethal creatures living on this planet that are drawn to a Sentient just like Adalia. And you can't protect her from these. Plain and simple."

"What kind of creatures?"

"I'm sorry, Mateo, but this is one point that our Society keeps to itself. It's a rule that we're sworn to follow, and I've already said more than I should."

Mateo sighed. "This is all too much to take. Too much."

"Understandable," Wendell said. "I'm sorry, Mateo."

"But what else can I do? I only want what's best for her. I just want her to be okay."

"She will be," Wendell promised. "Better than that, in fact."

I crossed the kitchen to the laundry room and tossed an armful of dark clothes into the machine. As I poured detergent into the bottle cap, I heard paper ripping and then a hiss. Following the sound's source to the bathroom, I found Christian standing at the mirror, bandages in hand, antiseptic gel spread across his fingers. He was wearing flannel pajama pants but his shirt was off. I gawked at the sight of his bare back, strong, toned and smooth, the muscles flexing as he tried to shake the excess gauze from his hand. Then I noted a scar about two inches long and still somewhat pink. The injury had to be fairly recent. Where had he gotten that? The answer occurred to me just as Christian cursed at his bandage predicament.

"Having issues?" I asked, stepping into view.

He saw me in the mirror first. "This could...this could probably use a woman's touch, yes." He sighed and turned around.

"Oh, ugh."

He grimaced. "Yes, it is rather unpleasant," he said of the two deep gouges across his sternum. "I cleaned and bandaged it quite well this morning, but now it's all a mess and I seem to be sticking to everything...or everything seems to be sticking to *me*."

Who could blame things for sticking to him? Lucky bandages. "Honestly, have you considered having it stitched up? I mean, they're deep."

"No worries. I'm fine. Besides, scars are sexy," he said, a slight smirk playing at his lips.

"Have a seat and I'll help," I said.

He sat on the edge of the sink, staring at his hands forlornly.

"Well, these are a lost cause," I said, pulling the wrecked gauze from his palms and using it to wipe up the excess gel. "Supplies?"

He reached around to grab the Neosporin and the box of gauze, pulling out several pieces and handing them to me. I spread them open wide, layering the squares together before squeezing some gel onto the whole thing.

Lifting the bandage to his chest, I rested my hand there, letting the gel warm and smooth to his skin. Suddenly, the bathroom was stiflingly hot and I could hardly breathe. The heat from his body, the freshly showered smell of him, his skin still damp—it was overwhelming, and I needed to finish up before I did something stupid. Avoiding eye contact, I bent to grab the tape, and as I did, Christian rested his hand on my wrist, a tender, intimate act that threw me utterly off guard. I struggled for composure.

"Chri—"

"Nick—"

I yanked my hand away more forcefully than I'd intended and rushed to tear off pieces of tape to secure his bandage, sure not to look him in the eye again.

"There. You're good," I said, still concentrating on the bandage.

"Right. Thanks."

"I'm just…okay." I fumbled over the words, rushing out of the bathroom, ignoring the dirty laundry and stopping only when I'd reached the living room. I pressed my back against the wall, practically hyperventilating. God help me. I couldn't get that close to him again or I was sunk. I was just absolutely sunk.

Chapter Seventeen

"I think that we might have a special guest today," I whispered in Samantha's ear. "But I can't say who, just in case it falls through."

She laid her head against my chest, staring into her own personal void. Christian had seen Samantha come in, but I didn't say anything to him about joining us. That was his call.

"I wonder if he remembers his song," I mused, but not for too long. That train of thought was a step in the wrong direction after the previous night. I'd been so resolved about this man. I'd made up my mind. It was friendship all the way. I wasn't strong enough to be with him. So why did I have to keep reminding myself of this, over and over, like some kind of drug addict in rehab?

Footsteps. Someone was coming.

Christian paused in the doorway. "Morning."

I fought hard not to smile and said, "Hey, Sam, look who's here."

Not even her breathing faltered. She had no clue.

Christian approached the piano and knelt down in front of her. "Hello, Samantha." He bent his head to look up at her face. "You know me, darling. I'm the love of your life, remember?"

My entire body melted, and gelatinous Nicole spilled over the piano bench and seeped into the floor boards. *Oh, hell! Stop it this instant!* "Samantha? Look, it's Christian."

Her head perked up. "That's right, sweetheart," I said.

Her eyes lightened and watered, and she lifted her hand to touch his face, just as she had the first time they'd met.

"Samantha. Say my name," Christian said kindly. "Come on, honey. Who am I?"

Her tiny body began to tremble, and she threw herself into his arms, crying.

"Woah…my God. Okay." He gathered himself. "Okay. It's all right," he soothed her, pulling her close. "I've got you."

I couldn't see anything; tears were skewing my vision so badly. I could completely relate to Samantha's plight. There wasn't a day gone by when I didn't fight the agonizing desire to react the exact same way.

"Hey, what's wrong?" he asked, peeling her arms from around his neck so he could look at her properly. "Samantha?"

She stopped crying.

"What's the matter?" he asked her.

Her expression was dumbfounded, as if she was only now realizing he was there.

"What?" he asked, brushing the moisture from her cheeks. "Would you like to play a song with me? Come on." He stood up and took her hand. "May I?" he asked before ousting me from the piano bench.

"No problem." I would just have to put my ego aside for now, even if it did appear that a Sentient could do my job better than I could. And to add to the injustice, why in the hell did he have to be so damned good with children? Wasn't it monstrous enough trying to scoop him out of my heart with a razor blade *sans* the potentially incredible father act? What to make of this. There they were, two of my greatest mysteries, side by side again.

Christian led her hand to the piano keys but met with a similar result as I had earlier. She seemed more fixated on the wooden Buddha in the corner of the room than anything the Steinway had to offer.

"I'll try playing," he told me and began a basic chord exercise only to mis-key halfway up the scale. "Sorry." He cringed. "Rusty. But regardless, she isn't even flinching, is she? I mean, what do you suppose happened to all our progress?"

I shook my head. "I don't know. But it's enough that she reacts to you the way she does. I can't be certain what's happening in that brain of hers, but God, something about you just…" I stopped short, deciding that perhaps I'd rather not finish my thought.

"What?" he asked. "What were you going to say?"

"That something about you calls out her fears. I mean, that's not to say you scare her," I corrected as he sat up straight. "But that you probably…probably appear to her as something…" Ugh, where was I going with this?

"Yes?"

"Something safe. I mean, you *are* a Combatant."

He joined Samantha in studying the Buddha figurine. "So are your dad and Elaine. And she's met them both."

"Yeah, I know. But maybe something about you makes her feel more protected than them."

He made a sound, almost a laugh, but not quite. "Well, then why won't she really let me in?"

"I don't know. I wish I knew. Hopefully she'll show us if we just keep at it."

He tilted his head slowly to look at me. "It so happens that I'm quite pigheaded. I hardly ever give up. I'm as bloody immovable as a boulder, really. Believe me—I'll keep at it."

Wait…what were we talking about here?

There was something very intentional about the way his eyes held mine. And I knew it was wrong of me, another proof of my weakness, but my heart launched out of my chest and was pounding on my head to surrender. I told myself not to let him persist with this, to be adamant that he should forget about whatever it was he planned to "keep at," but goddamn it if I could. So I did the next best thing. No one was better at a change of subject than me.

"I'm thinking we should try some percussion instruments."

☙

Adalia hated lying to her friends about her life change, but as long as she wanted to finish her high school career in a public way there would have to be some deception involved. We'd settled on a version of the truth. That she was undergoing medical treatments and counseling after her illness, that she'd never recovered from the death of her mother, and she was living in a kind of alternative youth therapy house.

The tale wasn't the most flattering for poor Adalia or her father, but it would explain who we were to her friends, should they visit, and to family should they get too nosy.

I had to give it to the kid. Adalia was eager to learn. Actually, she seemed desperate to take in everything Laura had to offer after the old hag incident.

In the time she'd been with us, she'd been a real straight-A student, even if Laura had left her behind on the last few jobs, deciding Adalia could use a little less drama in her life for a while. So Laura had been teaching Adalia the basics from the safety of home while promising to let her attend the next job.

Christmas came and went, and it was an especially frustrating season for me. Between Samantha's stubborn, mysterious behavior and my mother's more frequent incidents of panic and confusion, I could have used a merry season. Christian left us to spend the holiday in Philadelphia for a few weeks, and though I'd wallowed, feeling more alone than ever before, it also helped me to detach from him.

Most irritating of all, I still couldn't pull myself completely out of depression, though I was giving it all I had. Thankfully, the problem seemed to subside a bit when I threw myself into work, so my current dedication to Samantha was helping a lot. Christian had been attending as many sessions as he could since he'd returned to us, even though all of our painstaking progress seemed to undo itself over the weekend. It left me wondering if maybe there was more to Samantha's home life than met the eye, if there was some traumatic trigger there. I made a mental note to do a possible home session, scope out the situation.

Sessions with Samantha had reminded Christian of his piano lessons. Only once had he mentioned the possibility of beginning them again, but I'd skirted the issue effectively, and I was relieved that he didn't press the matter. There was no way I could chance being around him in that way. I had too much on my plate to deal with the addition of fending off terrible temptation.

It was early on a Monday morning, and Adalia observed Gil as he stirred a third heaping teaspoon of sugar into his coffee. She made a deeply disapproving face and then said, "Wasn't the triple shot of espresso enough?"

Gil ignored her.

"She has a point," I defended her. "Any minute now you're going to keel over, your heart beating at the rhythm of a bird's. And you'll probably be reaching for your coffee the whole time."

"Damn straight," he boasted. "By the way, Nick, how do you feel about haunted theaters?" He picked up his mug and swung around to face me at the island counter.

"Noncommittal. Why?"

"I just thought this gig might interest you, what with the musical history there and all."

"Where? What theater?"

"Richard Sweasy."

"Oh. That place is nice. They have a ghost?"

"Mhm. This is a good old fashioned haunting, nothing hazardous. You want to come along?"

"What about me?" Adalia interrupted. "I want to come along!"

"Ask Laura," he said.

"Laura!" Adalia shouted and Gil cringed. He wasn't quite awake enough for yelling yet.

"Yes, dearest?" Laura answered on her way in from the sunroom. She'd been reading her newspaper there.

"Can I go with you guys to Richard Weazy's theater?"

"Richard Sweasy," Gil corrected.

"Whatevs. Can I go?"

Laura hedged. "I don't know, Ad—"

"Come on. Please? I'm so tired of staying home," she complained, moping and crossing her arms.

"Fine," Laura said. "You can come."

"Yes!"

Gil rounded on me. "And you?"

"I don't think so. I have lessons today and Samantha."

"We're not going out there 'til tonight. So now what's your excuse?"

I rolled my eyes. "I'm not making excuses. But fine, I'll go."

"Beautiful," Gil said. "Get out. Get some air. I'd hate to see you turn into a Kaczynski brother. Christ, you're even paler than I am. And you're looking kind of peaked. Here, have some candy." He pulled a bowl of sweets over to tempt me.

I smirked and sighed, picking out a Snickers bar. Gil picked up a lollipop and hesitated, frowning at it. "Nah, can't do it," he said, changing his mind and putting it back.

"What the heck?" I peered at him.

"Lollipops. They take commitment."

"What?"

"Commitment. You don't enter into their consumption lightly unless you're dedicated to finishing. It could take hours to eat this thing."

"You could always bite it."

"No way! That would ruin the experience."

"Okay, so wrap it up and save the rest for later?"

"Uhm…no. It's one thing for me to swallow my own spit when it's fresh, quite another to suck on it when it's days old."

"My God, you're weird."

"Nowadays it's called unique, Nicole," he defended himself.

"My God, you're unique."

"That's better."

Mr. Gingrich was a distinguished looking man, the kind of guy who wore suits every day of the work week, even when surrounded by a younger staffer whose idea of professional attire was a polo shirt and khakis. It made me feel like he really knew something about something—like I could ask him any historical question about the Richard Sweasey Theatre, and by darn it, he'd know the answer.

"I'll show you some other hot spots later, but most of the reports we get concern this room." Mr. Gingrich opened the dressing room door to let us in.

The space was long, with mirrors, counters, and chairs lining every wall. There were columns of side lights flanking each mirror that robed everything in a dim yellow glow, and it certainly did look eerie, but who could really say in the Sentient world? Things you thought should be haunted—cemeteries, for instance—were clear of human entities, because ghosts didn't want to hang around a gravesite any more than you did. On the other hand, I'd seen haunted pre-schools, football fields, laundromats, veterinarians' offices and automated teller machines. There was no telling what a specter would choose to attach itself to.

Wendell said that, more often than not, spirits seemed to favor what they loved most in life, taking up unearthly tenancy wherever their hearts felt at home. The idea made sense, and statistically, it was valid. But on this particular occasion, I had to wonder why anyone would haunt a theater unless they were a total show boat in life and the stage was their idea of paradise. Ah well, my work focused on the neuroses of the living, not the dead, and so I would observe from afar and enjoy the show.

"So tell us about this building," Gil said to Mr. Gingrich. "How old is it?"

"Well, it was built around nineteen twenty—was a theater back then, too. Vaudeville, you know? Changed hands to new owners, then the whole interior burned down in nineteen twenty-nine, just sat there 'til nineteen seventy-three. Then the Dalys turned it into a department store. It stayed that way until ninety-eight, and then it was back to the theater again."

"Any reports of hauntings by the store owners?" Laura asked.

"Nope, not that I can say. But I haven't seen anything myself, so who knows? The only reason we're even pursuing your assistance is because he keeps spooking the actors! People are actually hesitating to book with us now. They say it's bad luck to see a ghost before the show. Old theater myth, you know?"

"Sure," Laura continued. "So he drops in here a lot, huh?"

"Yes. Here and the green room."

"And how do people describe him? What does he look like?"

"Older and dressed like a hobo. Maybe he played one in an act or something."

"Does he interact? Does he say anything?"

"No. In fact, here's the odd thing. The actors say that he seems more afraid of them than the other way around. He just takes off like he's been caught doing something wrong."

Christian snorted. "I would say spying on people while they dress qualifies as something wrong."

Mr. Gingrich laughed. "True."

"So, shall we have a look at the green room, then?" Christian suggested.

"Sure," Mr. Gingrich said. "Follow me."

The green room was yet another example of the last place on earth you'd ever think to find a ghost. It was obviously set up to accommodate the big names, the important members of the cast, with leather furniture and sharp, vibrant artwork set against a mellow, olive-tan wall color.

"Nice," Gil said, examining a painting of a cello player.

"I'm glad you think so," Mr. Gingrich said. "Well, here it is. You want me to leave you all to do your business?"

"If you wouldn't mind," Laura said.

"That's no problem. You have my office number. Call me if you need me."

After Mr. Gingrich had left, Laura scanned the room, her hands on her hips. "Okay, guys, who's going with whom?"

"Do you have any preferences?" Christian asked.

"I have no preferences. We can do rock, paper, scissors if we have to."

"No need," Gil interjected. "So we should just split up, huh?"

"Yep."

"Okay, Nick—"

"I'll take Nicole," Christian interrupted him.

"What? Why?" Gil narrowed his eyes. "There's nothing to protect her from. It's just an old man."

"We *think* it's just an old man," Christian stressed. "But doesn't it seem logical to you, considering she's more vulnerable, that she should remain with a Combatant?"

"It seems *logical* to me that she should pair up with whoever has the presence of mind to know a threat from Casper the Ghost!"

Laura sighed. "All right, cowboys. You both lose. She stays with me."

Gil gawked at her, clearly pissed off with her decision.

"Watch yourself, kid," she said. "Don't be giving me any flack. Now, you and Christian stay here, and Nick and Addy and I will check out the dressing room."

"Sorry," Gil grumbled. "I think I'll fly it solo. The mezzanine is calling my name," he said, heading out of the room.

"I'll go with you!" Adalia offered, following him.

He paused. "Great," he muttered, and they both took off down the corridor.

I grinned at Laura. "It seems she's a little attached to him."

"It seems," she said, chuckling. "Okay. Let's get kicking."

"Wait." Christian stopped Laura before we could leave. "Call me up if anything happens."

"Of course we will," she said, still walking.

"Wait," he caught her arm. "Is the volume up on your two-way?"

Laura laughed. "Nick…" She threw a hand out for me to give over my walkie-talkie, turning the sound up all the way in plain sight of Christian's anxious stare. "There. Feel better?"

"Yes. Thank you."

"Welcome. Come on, Nick!" She ushered me down the hall before Christian could come up with any more points in the safety check.

"Good God, he worries like a mother," she said as we rounded the corner to the elevators. "And he's still got it bad for you, missy."

I winced. "Laura Polmieri. Don't you dare. You promised."

"Yes, but that was a long time ago! Can't I say even one little thing yet?"

"No."

"Even though—"

"He's protective, Laura. It's his job to protect the unarmed."

"Bull-fucking-shit," she laughed, holding the elevator door open for me. "Now, it's true I normally heed your masochistic request and keep my mouth shut with regard to your father, but I think it's bordering on cruel for you to ban me from vocalizing an opinion on Mr. Wright."

"Laura, all it'll do is confuse me!" I whined.

"Good! You need to be confused, need to be shaken up a bit. Give me thirty seconds to say my piece, baby—you can even time me if you want, okay?"

"Fine," I groaned, darting out of the elevator the moment it opened.

"Okay," Laura began, tailing me as I sped along. "He's loving, Nicole, and he's loyal as a fucking puppy dog, and he's crazy about you! Honey, stop." She jumped in front of me. "He's a god-damned super model, too. You notice that?"

I half-smiled at her.

"Nick, he's not like your dad. He displays his affection so openly, and he loves deeply. I've *seen* it, Nicole."

"Then that's all the more reason for him to be with someone stronger who won't be so susceptible to danger," I argued.

"You think you're not strong? Nicole, that's the most ridiculous thing I've ever heard, you know that? Seriously. Do you realize that someone else in your set of circumstances would have lost their damned mind by now? You take all this shit from your dad, you care for your mom with such patience, you deal with her decline with composure. You ask for nothing in return. You've got your own kind of strength, Nicky! It's quiet, it's unassuming. But it's amazing!"

Strong. I was strong?

Maybe I was.

But that didn't solve the bigger issue. "I'm still a drag on his sentience. And I don't want to be the fallback girl, either. It would kill me. I *love* him—"

Laura raised her hand to cover her mouth, and I shut my trap. Oh, God. Had I said that I loved him? I *had*.

"Oh, Nicky," she said. "You're in love with him?"

"Thirty seconds is up," I said, shooting around her and heading toward the dressing room.

"Nicole," she ran up behind me. "You want to marry him." She laughed. "You want to bring him slippers in the morning and sit on his lap and have his babies! Admit it! Tell the truth!"

I stopped, half-incensed, half-worn out. "The truth?" I narrowed my eyes. "The truth is that he's galaxies out of my league, Laura. It doesn't matter if I love him, because he's…he's the top of the Empire State Building and I'm the subway! The Christian Wrights of this world want something special. They don't want me. Not for the long haul. I'm plain and unevolved and—"

"Aah, I see." She shook her head. "This isn't just about protecting him, is it? You're afraid of getting hurt."

"No shit! I can't…" I blinked back tears. "Just…look at Duncan. No matter what he thinks about me, I still can't help loving him. He's my dad! It's kind of the rule that he's supposed to love me back, right? Yet I'm useless to him. I make him sick."

"No, baby." She shook her head. "It's true he's an enormous prick, but your father *does* love you!"

I couldn't help laughing. "Have you lost your mind?"

"He does! And he makes fucked up calls and says fucked up shit, but underneath all that, I know it's because he thinks he's doing the best thing. And he won't admit to loving anyone at this point. Don't you remember when you were little? He doted on you, Nicole."

"Sure he did! I had all the potential to be something important then. But once he figured out that I wasn't what I was supposed to be, all that changed."

"Nick—"

"And it's only a matter of time before Christian feels that way, too."

Laura glared at me. "Oh, Nicky." She spoke gravely. "Your dad has played a number on your head. But fuck all that! Hate his guts if you have to. But you've got to trust someone sometime."

"I trust myself."

"Do you? Because right now you're completely rejecting what your soul is telling you to do."

There was no arguing with Laura. She had an answer for everything. "Can we just do the ghost thing? Please?"

She sighed. "Let's go."

The dressing room was darker than when we'd left it. Mr. Gingrich had obviously turned off some mirror lights.

"Looks like our spook likes to mess with the electrical," Laura said.

"Huh? Ooh. I get it."

"Okay. Let me know if you notice any cold spots, otherwise I'm just going to walk around the room and try and draw him out," she instructed.

"'Kay."

This was anything but glamorous, shuffling around, studying the walls, and waiting for someone to pop out of the woodwork. In fact, there were so many mirrors that I didn't have to do a speck of work, anyway. The second a spirit appeared, I would see it about thirty times.

"Beside you," Laura nodded.

"What?" I jumped and skittered over behind her, then turned around to look at what she'd seen. "That's him?" I whispered.

"Yes," she giggled at me.

Our astral was a hunched over, disheveled gentleman who could easily have been mistaken for an old man, but upon further examination of his face, I realized that it wasn't so much age that marred his appearance as dirt and lines of worry.

"What's your name?" Laura asked him gently.

I hated this part—just standing there, listening to a one sided conversation. But normal human spirits could only be heard by Pathcrossers. In fact, there were plenty of Sentients who couldn't understand what a ghost was saying, simply because they weren't endowed with a gift like Laura's.

The spirit must have answered her question, because Laura took to calling him Charlie.

"Why are you here, Charlie?" she asked.

In response, the figure dissipated and reformed just in front of her. As icy air shot across my face, I consoled myself with the thought that only a Pathcrosser could get used to this.

"I realize my energy is tempting to you," Laura said. "Do you want to come closer?"

The spirit lifted his arm as if to touch her, then faded, and in the same moment, Laura began to choke and wheeze, her head rolling back to expose her neck.

"Laura! Shit," I reached around my belt for the damned walkie-talkie and grabbed the device, just as she took a deep, loud breath and lifted her head to look at me.

"Are you okay?" I asked her.

"Look, lady, it's awful cold out there," she said in a voice that was not in any way similar to Laura's. In fact, she sounded an awful lot like a man. My skin crawled. Son of a bitch. He was inhabiting her.

"Get out of her right now!" I demanded.

"I ain't got no place else to go!" he pleaded. "Mr. Orntz lets me stay here. Ask him! He'll tell ya. He'll vouch for me."

"Who's…who's Mr. Orntz?"

"The guard outside the theater."

Pounding footsteps indicated that, thankfully, Christian and Gil were entering the dressing room.

"Why did you curse? What's happening?" Christian looked at me.

"How did you know I cursed?"

"Focus, Nicole. Laura?" He turned to our Pathcrosser.

"She's been inhabited," I said. "Charlie, tell them what you were just telling me, about Mr. Orntz."

"Mr. Orntz, yeah! He's the guy who lets me stay here at night! It's mighty cold out there, mister," he repeated. "I ain't got nothin' or no one. I lost everything. Please, don't call no police."

"Woah. Cool." Adalia listened excitedly to our possessed Pathcrosser.

"Charlie," Christian began. "We're not calling the police, okay? But who is Mr. Orntz?"

"I already told ya! The night guard outside the theater."

"They don't have a night guard," Gil stated. "I mean, I think they used to, back in the Vaudeville days, but—"

"Charlie," Christian interrupted. "What year is it?"

"Year? Look, buddy, I ain't crazy, I just lost my house! The banks shut me out, and I lost everything. I'm just having some trouble getting by, is all."

"What year is it, Charlie?" Christian insisted. "Please."

"It's…it's nineteen twenty-nine, ain't it? I told ya I wasn't no loony."

Gil nodded. "That's the year the fire hit."

Christian furrowed his brow, deep in thought. "The Depression."

"That's right," Laura, a.k.a. Charlie, nodded. "I ain't had my life back since twenty-nine."

Christian sighed. "So you were sleeping here when the building caught on fire."

"Fire?" the ghost questioned.

"Charlie," Christian began, "I'm going to have to ask you to leave my friend's body. I know it's probably very comfortable there, but I would imagine she isn't terribly thrilled with you right now."

"What body?" he asked.

"Charlie. You're a ghost…a spirit. And the year isn't nineteen twenty-nine. It's two thousand eight. You died in a fire here nearly eighty years ago."

"Oh, you think that's a real laugh, don't ya, mister? Pokin' fun at me cuz you can. But I ain't movin'! I ain't budging 'til Mr. Orntz tells me to *himself*." Charlie crossed Laura's arms.

"Just look in a blazing mirror!" Christian laughed. "Turn around, Charlie. Have a look for yourself."

Charlie scoffed, but eased his head around to look in a nearby mirror.

"Jumpin' Jehosaphat!" He tumbled backwards. "I got a bosom!"

Giggling loudly, Adalia shut her mouth, stifling her laugh so that her cheeks bulged out.

"So, will you leave her now?" Christian pleaded.

"Well," Charlie turned from side to side, examining Laura. "I don't know. I kinda like it."

Christian sighed regretfully. "I'm sorry, Laura. I'll be gentle as I can," he said, before reaching his arm out and grasping at thin air.

I'd seen my father do this countless times. It was his forte. The Combatants' main form of non-physical contact was to channel their energy through a natural route—their hand being the logical one—and use it to dominate an opponent without ever actually getting close enough to be in harm's way. This was ideal when facing a vampire, as the threat of enthrallment, or being held hypnotically hostage, was greatest when they touched you.

Presently, however, Christian was not seeking a simple flesh and bones grip. He was using a more complex form of his sentience, one that required him to determine the difference between the spirit of Laura and the spirit of Charlie.

"Hey! What the hell are you doing to me, mister!" Charlie bellowed as Christian found his mark. "I can't breathe! You…you…tryin' to…tryin' to…"

"Get out of her, Charlie." Christian spoke calmly. "Get out and I'll let you go."

"No! I…I don't know…what the…lemme…" he choked and sputtered.

"If you don't get out of her, I'll be forced to rip you out. And though I cannot kill you, I can continue to make the rest of your immortal existence excruciatingly painful."

"Fine!" Charlie wailed, and Laura fell backward at the loss of his soul.

I ran over to her while Christian held the spirit—who was now looking very much like Charlie again—in place for a few seconds more.

"You said…you'd…let me…go!" the ghost complained.

"Ah, yes, sorry." Christian smiled politely.

Laura wretched and dry heaved, trying to clear the feel of Charlie from her system. Then when she'd recovered, she grabbed my hand and stood up.

"Damn it, Charlie!" she blasted him. "When I said come closer, I did *not mean that!*"

We all watched, absorbed again in Laura's end of the conversation, and gathered from her responses that Charlie had never known there was a fire. He had probably died in his sleep from smoke inhalation before anything else—a peaceful but disorienting way to go. And so Laura, in the unfathomable, interior practice of all Pathcrossers, saw Charlie to the other side—with a good amount of coaxing. It would be very warm there, she told him. He'd be able to continue on his journey, she told him. The usual facts of the afterlife.

The mirror lights that had malfunctioned earlier turned on, and we knew that was the end of it.

"Everybody okay?" Laura took a poll.

"Yeah, fine," Gil said and Christian nodded.

"That was awesome!" Adalia squealed. "I can't wait to do it myself."

Laura laughed, patting her on the back. "Pretty soon, darlin'."

"You okay?" Christian questioned me.

"Sure."

"Were you even going to call us on your hand-held?" He peered at me.

"I was going to, but he started talking to me and…wait. How *did* you know to come?"

Christian hesitated, his eyes flitting to Laura.

"What?" I said.

"Eh, you left your radio on," he said.

"I…what?"

"Your radio. You left it on. I could hear it all for myself."

Wait. "How long was it on?" I asked, daring to peek at Christian again.

"Long enough," he said.

No. She *couldn't* have. She wouldn't have let me carry on the way I had about my father, about Christian, knowing that he would hear everything. I turned to Laura, and she countered my scathing expression with a look of innocent ignorance.

Oh God, where were the blunt objects with which to bludgeon myself? Or a balcony! People threw themselves off balconies all the time. Why the hell didn't this building have a balcony?

"I'll meet you in the car," I said, pushing past a bewildered Gil.

Chapter Eighteen

Gil had a fantastic collection of old school games—Operation, Don't Break the Ice, Hungry Hungry Hippos. He'd kept them since childhood and then added a few more to the pile with the invention of eBay. Raj would have been so jealous. He loved game night and was exceptionally good at it, considering his penchant for wise moves. But he and Theo and Elaine had been in Santa Barbara for the better half of the week, so they were out of luck.

Operation was my personal favorite, so Adalia and I played on the coffee table while Mom looked on, fascinated by the movements of our hands.

"I guess I can deal with losing to you," Adalia told me. "It's Gilford that needs a smack down once in a while. He wins too much."

I giggled. "Since when do you call him Gilford?"

"Since I found out it annoys him so much."

"Aah."

"Your turn."

I grabbed hold of my tongs and picked up a fake leg bone. Then, squinting, I attempted to place it in its proper place without setting off the buzzer. I missed. And the resulting sound hit my mother's nerves in just the right way to send her jumping from the adjacent seat. She covered her ears and shrieked incoherently about monsters, and though I was at her side immediately, she was no more comforted by my presence than she would have been a stranger's. There was a good reason for this. Lately, she had no idea who I was.

"Mom, I need you to calm down. You have to stop screaming. Rita, please." I tried calling her by her first name, hoping it would jog her memory.

Soon, everyone had assembled in the living room, Laura at my side, the rest of the house looking on with concern but knowing better than to interfere. My father watched us from the stairs.

"Mom, please," I said, wrapping my arms around her. She reacted badly, slapping my arm and then my face. "No. Mom, stop it." I grabbed her hand. "You can't do that."

"Why do you keep touching me?" She sobbed. "I don't know you!"

I ignored her, trying still to offer her a comforting touch.

"Get away from me!" she wailed. "You brought the monster!"

"I didn't bring a monster, Mom. It was just a game. Look…it's just a game. Adalia." I motioned for the girl to bring the offending object for examination. Adalia approached cautiously, offering my mother the board.

"No!" Rita knocked it out of her hands, and it crashed to the floor loudly.

"Okay, okay. You don't want it. You don't have to have it. Okay? It's all right."

"Stop touching me! Stop touching me! Stop touching me!" she shouted again and again, but I fought to hold her still. I knew that she'd lash out if I let her go, possibly get hurt, possibly hurt someone else.

"It's worse with so many people here. Please, guys…" I begged everyone.

"They can go, but let me help you," Laura said.

"Okay."

The room emptied, and for over an hour Laura and I remained with Mother, literally restraining her on the couch until she'd tired of fighting. By the end of it, my body was crying to move, every muscle throbbing and half my limbs asleep, but with the help of Laura's energy, Mom had finally calmed enough that her screaming had turned to hiccupping breaths.

It almost felt like a betrayal, doing this to her—like I had to break her spirit just to ease the miserable episode. But the sooner I got things under control, the better, because Duncan had witnessed this little incident, and when Mom had her worst moments, he always brought up a certain topic that angered me to even think about. Drugs.

I examined my poor mother, lying bunched in my arms, her face stained with tears and mucous, and wanted badly to clean her up, to deliver her some dignity after what had happened. But if I moved too fast or spoke too loudly, I could set her off again. So I said in the quietest voice, "Mom, you want to go upstairs? I'll wash your face and then you can go to sleep. Your bed is nice and warm and safe. Would you like to hide under your covers and be all comfy?"

A few more hiccupping sighs later, she nodded faintly.

"Okay. Let's go upstairs, then, okay? I'll help you."

Laura moved away from us and let me stand. It was only four in the afternoon, but this was the best option for her until I could decide what to do next. Very carefully, I held out my arms, and Mom took hold, letting me lead her upstairs. Everyone else had disappeared, knowing to maintain absolute silence until I'd gotten things under control.

She let me wash her face and even blew her nose when I handed her a tissue. As I cared for her, it really hit me that, at some point, my mother had become my child. The idea broke my heart.

After she fell asleep, I crept back downstairs and found Wendell, Raj, Christian, and Laura convened in the kitchen. They stared at me as I collapsed in a chair beside Laura.

"She's out," I said.

Wendell crossed the kitchen to lay a hand on my shoulder. "This was a bad one, Nick."

"Yeah."

"You okay?"

I thought about that. And the answer was no. I wasn't. I wasn't any manner of okay. Quite the opposite, actually. I wanted to scream and cry and ball up and throw a huge fit—pretty much exactly like my mom had done. But between the two of us, somebody had to keep it together.

"I'm fine. She'll be okay."

"No, she won't," came my father's voice from the doorway. "I'm calling a doctor tomorrow. She needs to be on something. She's out of control."

"Dad, no. We don't have to go that far. I can handle this."

"I'll make that call. And from what I've seen—you can't."

Where normally I'd be inclined to back off and let my dad have his way, this subject left me fighting the urge to jump up and smack him hard, instead. So I compromised and looked to Wendell, mouthing a "please."

Duncan caught this and glared at me. "You think you can go above my head? This decision is mine to make, not his. She's *my* wife."

This didn't sit well with Laura, and she stood up immediately. "Stop acting like a tyrant, Duncan. Rita's a human being, not an acre of land! And all of a sudden you're going to be her husband, huh? That's touching, but I'd like to know where the hell you've been for the last three years!"

That bulging vein in his neck was back with a vengeance. He was going to burst.

"Dad," I said, trying to diffuse things, "she's just scared. But I swear, I can handle her."

"You can't handle her, Nicole. Not anymore."

"That's not true."

"She doesn't even know who the hell you are! She doesn't even know who the hell *she* is!"

"But she comes around. She has good days!"

"She gets worse all the time. It's hopeless."

"Listen," Wendell said, "until Rita actually proves that she's a danger to herself or anyone else, why not hold off on the medication thing? Nothing is hopeless. And frankly, there's a possible solution that you're not examining here."

"Wendell, if you're about to suggest what I think—"

"William might be able to help her!" Wendell blurted. "Duncan, he helped Theo. He saved Christian!"

Duncan backed away from us as if we had the plague and lowered his voice to nearly a growl. "This is over. Don't you *ever* suggest that I allow one of those filthy, bloodsucking fuckers to lay a hand on my wife again or—"

"He's not like them," Christian broke in. "I owe him my life, Duncan. He's not one—"

"Oh, no, no, no. Not you, too. Am I hearing this right? Are you out of your mind?"

"Christian has every right to his opinion as you do," Wendell interceded.

"Screw you, Wendell! I've been putting up with your pussy-assed brand of leadership for years, and I'm sick and tired of it. You and Abram Saru ought to go buy a private island and take all the monsters with you. You can grant them forgiveness while they suck you dry!"

"Goddamn it," Laura said. "Show some respect!"

"To hell with that! If he ever brings this up again, so help me, I will leave this group so fast your heads will spin. I don't give a *shit* what the Society says about Seer fealty."

He stomped off before any of us could react further, but that was probably for the best. My father had shamelessly and unjustifiably insulted his Seer in front of everyone, and I couldn't think of a more disastrous karmic mistake. If he kept going like this, he'd be lucky if he kept an Endowment the next time his soul was born.

Christian shook his head, plainly troubled. "Why do you tolerate that, Wendell? Why didn't you just put him in his place?"

Wendell shrugged. "His flattery doesn't bother me. He's a deeply troubled man, and my refusal to argue only makes him think more, which is a good thing."

"Well, I don't know how you stand it. If he'd talked to me like that, let's just say things wouldn't have ended so civilly."

"Oh, I know that, Christian." Wendell smirked, chuckling to himself, and I stared at him, trying to figure out what the heck was so funny. Then I realized it was pointless to wonder. I'd seen that look on Wendell's face before—it was the expression of someone enjoying an inside joke. And being a Seer, Wendell had plenty of them.

True to his word, my father called a doctor to set up an appointment for Mom first thing in the morning. When they explained that the next opening would not be for a matter of weeks, he flew off the handle, demanding to speak with a supervisor, and I'm sure, making an obnoxious nuisance out of himself. Dad's reputation as an asshole was not exclusive to Sentient circles.

Naturally, he managed to harass them into working her into their clinic schedule, and as a reward, I was expected to take her to said appointment and see that she was prescribed a drug that I hated to make her take. God forbid that my father should have attended.

"I'll come," Christian offered, grabbing his keys and opening the door. "I'll go with you—in case, you know."

I'd been all but avoiding Christian for days after the incident at the theater. While Laura had sworn up and down that there was no guarantee of what he'd heard on his walkie-talkie, I didn't believe her. It was just exactly like her to pull a stunt like that.

I very desperately wanted to rebuff Christian's offer to escort us to the doctor, but that would have been a foolish act of pride because he was right. Taking Mom to a crowded clinic without some backup was probably a mistake, considering her touchy state. And for all I knew, maybe he hadn't heard any of the confessions I'd made to Laura. I mean, he hadn't said a word afterwards, and his behavior hadn't changed that I could tell. I was probably just overreacting.

"Thank you." I forced myself to smile. "That would help."

"It's no problem. I'll drive; that way you can sit with her," he said.

I stared at him for a second, still amazed by his kindness. It was a gift, that sort of compassion. It had nothing to do with being a Sentient and everything to do with being good. And there it was…the ache again, the pain that tugged at my heart and my center, the same one that I felt anytime he smiled too warmly, anytime he spoke in that particularly gentle way.

Picking my heart up from the floor, I locked it securely in a box marked "Broken, return to sender" and then proceeded to gather our things to leave.

The clinic was far more packed than I'd ever imagined it would be. People were actually seated outside of the main waiting area, mulling around the doors, snacking on takeout and looking absolutely bored off their skulls.

"This is a bad sign," I muttered to Christian as we neared the entrance.

"Why do you expect that?"

"Well, this kind of crowd means a backed up clinic for sure."

Just as predicted, the sign above the check-in desk read "1 hour behind." I sighed, and Christian smiled sympathetically. "It won't be that bad, will it? Look, they have a television." He pointed at the wall-mounted TV, currently playing an episode of *SpongeBob SquarePants*. I frowned, stepping up to sign my name to a clip board, all the while keeping an eye on Mom. She looked harassed, her eyes darting everywhere, clearly overwhelmed by the abundance of sensory stimuli.

"I think we'd better sit out in the hall," I told Christian, "just in case the noise scares her too much."

The chairs that lined the wall outside the clinic were well broken in. I was tempted to run to the restroom and grab some paper towels to line them with, but I pushed my germophobia aside and cringed as we sat down.

The first twenty minutes were fine. Mom asked me repeatedly where we were, who "this handsome boy" was, but other than her loss of memory, things had been fairly easy. That is, until an elderly man showed up, wielding a walker and an angry agenda. He'd been billed wrong, he told the front desk. He was sure he'd been overcharged, and it was all their fault. And it didn't matter how the receptionist tried to soothe him, to explain that it was, in fact, his insurance that had made the decision not to cover his treatments, the old man was irate beyond reasoning, slamming his walker on the floor, upsetting nearly everyone around him, including my mother. Her hands shot instinctively to her ears as they had the night before, and I dreaded what was coming.

Christian did, too.

Immediately, he was out of his seat and urging me to switch places with him. I complied, reluctantly, moving aside to let him sit beside Mom.

"Rita," he said quietly, wrapping an arm around her shoulder and dropping his head close to hers. "Shall I tell you a story?" he whispered.

Mom ignored him, hands still clasped to her ears, but Christian went on. "It's about a little boy."

Rita looked up at him, lowering her hands slowly. "Okay," she whispered. "About a boy?"

"Yes."

I watched, sad and fascinated, as he seemed to calm her with words alone. Of course, I knew that he must have been using some potent energy—maybe the kind he used with Samantha—but the rest was all him. He whispered in a tone so quiet I could hardly make out what he was saying, and it drove me crazy not being able to hear his story. The tale seemed to go on and on, only interrupted when my mother would ask him questions like, "Was he very young?"…"Did it scare him badly?"…"Did he save her?"

Then, to my relief, she started giggling. "Serves her right!" she said, and I sighed heavily.

"I'm kind of jealous right now," I admitted. "I'm missing a great story."

"It's interesting," Christian said, smiling.

"Does it have a happy ending?"

"Not yet."

"Oh, then go ahead and finish."

"I did," he said.

"But…"

"Abbot!" called a nurse from inside the clinic room, and Christian and I stood, almost simultaneously.

"Rita, let's go visit the doctor, all right?" Christian smiled at her. "You can hold my hand," he said, offering it to her.

She took it, standing up without hesitation. "You should tell the doctor your story, Carter."

"Rita, it's Christian, remember?"

"Oh! Sorry. You should tell the doctor your story, Christian."

"I should," he chuckled.

My God. Did they even make guys like this anymore? With manners and chivalry and consideration and stuff? Wendell had once said that you could tell a lot about a guy by the way he treated his mother, and if he was this kind to mine, I could only imagine how good he was to Clara Wright.

Sighing deeply, I watched in awe as Christian led Mom toward the nurse. He was, quite literally, the perfect man for me. So why the hell couldn't I have been the same for him?

I was definitely flipping the universe a flying, shitting, squawking bird right now.

Chapter Nineteen

It's not that I was against medication, per se. I mean, I'd seen the benefit it had on some people with very specific, very severe psychological disorders. But my mom—she'd been traumatized, she'd been messed with by a spirit, and meds could stifle the symptoms a bit, but her ailment had no medicinal cure. I was convinced that a supernatural malady required a supernatural tonic. Unfortunately, my father's limitations were uncompromising on that front.

At least Mom's doctor seemed like a practical guy, and I was especially glad when he'd suggested the very lowest dose of anxiety medication. He seemed to understand my concerns about dulling her senses too much, even if he had no way of knowing the truth behind her condition. So we'd left with a small victory in hand via a mild prescription. I could show Duncan the medication, and he'd be happy, and I wouldn't feel quite so horrible about giving it to Mom.

"This will make you feel better," I told her, setting the pill beside her bowl of oatmeal.

She made a face. "Medicine tastes awful."

"Oh, I get it. You forget my name, but you remember how medicine tastes," I said, smirking at her.

"What?"

"Nothing, Mom. And it won't taste so bad if you swallow your orange juice right after. Go ahead and see."

She looked at me skeptically, but placed the pill on her tongue, making a dramatic sour face before sipping her orange juice loudly. I couldn't help giggling at her noisiness. I mean, in the middle of all this pain and confusion you had to laugh at the little things, right? Otherwise, you might as well just dig a grave and lay there 'til you stopped breathing.

The phone rang and I jumped, ready to do damage control should the sound freak Mom out. But someone else had beaten me to it.

"Nicole!" Gil shouted from the top of the stairs.

"Coming."

I left the kitchen and made it to the bottom step, just managing a, "Gil, do *not* toss that phone down the—" But it was too late. I had to lunge like a maniac to catch the phone and then delivered him a dirty look before answering, "Hello?"

"Nicole? It's Carol Fitzpatrick."

"Oh, hey!" I said, winded and half-laying across the steps.

"I was wondering if I could take you up on that offer to come over here for Samantha's session? My nine o'clock is going to be late, and I don't want to cancel. She's my best customer."

"Of course! Yeah. Nine-thirty?"

"You got it."

This was exactly what I'd wanted, anyway—to watch Samantha's reactions in her home environment, in her own space, in a place that felt comfortable and familiar.

After I hung up the phone, I rolled onto my back to find Christian standing above me and grinning. "Are you so tired that you couldn't make it all the way up here before collapsing?"

I laughed. "I was rescuing the phone…long story. Anyway, that was Samantha's mom. She wants me to come over to their house for today's session."

"Ah ha," he said, nodding. "Shall I come along?"

Yes, please! "That would be fine, if you can."

"I'm there. Shall I drive?"

"Sure," I said. I'd discovered that Christian's driving was akin to an old woman's most days, which was highly unique for a Combatant. My father was a lead foot, as was Elaine. Something in the aggression of their nature seemed to demand a disregard for speed limits. But Mr. Wright was the ultimate in responsibility. If he went five miles an hour over the posted allowance it was something, and I supposed it all came back to the sense of uber conscientiousness he had about everything and everyone. Anally observing traffic laws was just another way of protecting people, it seemed. And Christian obviously trusted himself more than anyone else behind the wheel, so I let him drive when he asked. It was the least I could do to thank him for all the work he'd put in with Samantha.

The Fitzpatrick's house was completely charming, if a bit out of the norm. But then, the Fitzpatricks were out of the norm themselves, so it fit. The front lawn was decorated with shiny copper balls, gnomes, wind-chimes, and pinwheels. The landscaping was obviously done professionally, but it had an eccentric touch, with bushes growing taller and somewhat wilder than those of the surrounding homes. Above the front door was a hand painted sign that read "Raiki Massage Therapy."

Carol and her husband had split their ranch style home in half. On the right were several massage and aroma therapy rooms and on the right, the family's home.

"Hm. Massage?" Christian noted, raising an eyebrow. "And *why* haven't you brought me here before?"

I sighed on his behalf. "Sorry. All business, no pleasure."

"Slave driver."

I smiled. "Come on."

Carol had the door opened before we'd reached the grass, standing with her hand on Samantha's shoulder. She and Laura would have gotten along so well. Carol was practically a younger snapshot of my favorite Sentient, straight out of some Woodstock footage, with long, blond hair that looked like she'd spent hours at the beach and a denim jumper with a smiling cloud across the front. "Hi!" She waved at us enthusiastically.

"Good morning," Christian said. "Hi, Samantha," he added, kneeling with his arms out. She only hesitated a moment before coming right to him, taking a seat on his bended knee.

Carol grinned happily, shaking her head. "Gosh, that just amazes me. She never does that with anyone else."

"Not even me," I added with a twinge of annoyance.

"She can't help it." Christian wrapped his arms around Samantha's waist. "It's the accent."

Carol smirked. "Oh, it completely is. And why are you single again?"

Christian's bravado turned to a shy smile as he rubbed the back of his neck.

I blushed. "So, shall we get started?" I asked, redirecting.

"Sure!" Carol said. "My client will be here in a minute, anyway." She stepped inside, letting us pass. "You remember where her room is?"

I nodded. "I'm sure we'll find it."

"Fabulous! I'll see you guys later. Be good, Samantha." She kissed her little girl on both cheeks and then headed in the direction of her therapy rooms.

The house looked smaller from the street, mainly because half its girth was hidden by overgrown plants. But once you were inside, you realized just how much room there was. This was an affluent neighborhood, after all, and Phillip Fitzpatrick was a well-established doctor of osteopathy. They simply chose not to flaunt their means to the world. It was one of the reasons I liked them so much.

We headed left, and once we'd passed the great room, I recognized the bedroom hallway. Christian followed me, holding Samantha's hand.

"Here we go," I said.

"Which one is hers?"

"It's on the left. Right in the middle. But let's come back to it. I'd actually like to let Samantha wander around for now. I want to observe her a little."

"Oh. All right then," he said, and Samantha's hand had barely slipped from his grasp before she was sprinting toward the front of the house again.

I laughed. "Well. I don't think I've ever seen her move that fast."

"Me either. We should follow." But finding the girl proved to be a tougher job than we'd thought. After searching the western half of their home to no avail, I started to get a little worried.

"Maybe she's run into a massage room?" I said.

"Uh oh."

"Well, let's look around back before we interrupt Carol."

Christian nodded, following me to the front of the house and outside again. There was a gray foot path made of large single stones, and it led around the side of the house. We followed it, and when I saw the back yard gate hanging wide open, I figured we were on the right track.

Sure enough, there was Samantha, sitting at a picnic table under their lovely old cedar tree, staring at her knees.

"Sam, you sneaky little girl. There you are," I said, joining her at the table. "You don't even have a coat on, honey." I frowned, but Christian was already sliding out of his jacket and wrapping Samantha inside. The little girl was dwarfed in its bulk, but the sight was adorable.

Christian rested his face in his hand, smiling amusedly at her. "You're rather dodgy all of a sudden," he teased. She didn't respond, just looked up at him with lovely violet eyes and blinked against the sun. "Oh, now, that's not fair," he added. "You shouldn't use those on people without warning."

He was one to talk, sitting there with the sunlight in his hair, looking and sounding like some kind of commercial for British sex gods with impeccable manners. It seemed like the harder I tried not to want him, the more I did. It was exhausting.

"So?" Christian started.

"Hm?"

"What do we do from here?" he asked. "Or shall we have a picnic?"

"Oh. No." I laughed. "Well, since the wandering didn't work so well, maybe we should go to her room after all, huh?"

"Sure." Christian stood. "Come on, darling," he said to Samantha, lifting her up.

She laid her head on his shoulder, and I smiled. "Do you realize what an incredibly good father you would make?" I said. Then, of course, I mentally shoved a gag in my mouth. I was getting too comfortable with him. Things were more natural between us, and I was just liable to say something completely stupid.

Christian's face turned thoughtful. "I don't let myself consider things like that too deeply," he said, "unless I fancy a foul mood."

Huh? "A foul mood?"

He smiled weakly. "Not much opportunity for family planning as a Combatant, is there?"

Ah. Yes. Now I was *really* jamming my foot in my mouth. That made sense, didn't it? Here was one of the glaring pitfalls of being gifted that I'd always seemed to forget about in my haze of self-pity. What if you wanted a normal life? What if you wanted things that had nothing to do with sentience? What about that suburban paradise? The two car garage and plasma TV and manicured lawn and Sunday dinner with the family? Hell, what about the family, period? Didn't Sentients deserve the most simple satisfactions of life, too? Especially after risking their necks so often to make things safer for the rest of us? Suddenly, I felt kind of bad for him.

He'd never spoken of his own dad, but the bits I'd gathered from everyone else told me that Daniel Wright had been a wonderful family man. It was no surprise that Christian would be as well, even if he had no clue of it. I'd encountered all kinds of parents, and I certainly intimately knew the variations on bad fathers. There was a certain detachment that some of these men carried from a young age. They'd become emotionally closed, desensitized, for whatever reason, and I feared the coldness of their hearts more than the opposite—the explosive personalities, the passionate emotions.

Gil and Katrina seemed to think that Christian had a lot of shit boiling under the surface of his collectedness—and maybe that was true. But while some of that was likely latent anger, I wondered if a lot of it was an unmet desire to be loved, as well. Looking at his interactions with Samantha, it seemed obvious that his capacity for love was immense.

Christian carried Samantha all the way back into the house, and she remained content the whole way, relaxed on his shoulder. But once we reached the bedroom hallway her little head shot up, and by the time we'd made it to the door, she was fidgeting in his arms.

"Hey, you want down?" he asked, releasing her. She immediately headed for the hills, but Christian was ready for her this time. "Hold on there, Samantha," he said, speeding after her and picking her up again. "You're going the wrong way." He chuckled. I watched her, her eyes wide, unusually alert. Even her breathing had picked up.

"Perhaps she equates the bed with bed time," Christian suggested. "And no child likes that."

"Very true," I said, opening the door to her room. Samantha laid her head on his shoulder again.

Christian chuckled as we entered. "She's squeezing the air right out of me. Relax, Samantha. We're going to play. It's not bed time yet."

There were no windows in Samantha's bedroom, and it was surprisingly free of clutter. Only a pinkish-orange nightlight in the form of a miniature lamp sat on her dresser. Christian turned on the light and then put Samantha down on her bed, taking a seat beside her.

"You'd better close that door behind us, just in case she gets restless," he cautioned.

"Was just thinking that," I said, doing as he'd suggested. Then I joined them on the bed. "Okay," I began, "so let's just watch her play for…oh…" My plans were thwarted as Samantha climbed back into Christian's arms and settled there with no apparent intention of moving. "Uhm, Christian, try extricating the kid and standing up, eh?"

He snickered, prying the little girl off him, and then he stood up quickly. Samantha examined him from the bed for a moment before proceeding to stand up, raising her arms in the air. Christian frowned at me.

"Huh. It appears she's especially clingy with you today," I said.

"It looks like it. Shall I pick her up?"

"No. Walk over to the other side of the room and see what happens."

Christian did as I asked, proceeding to the opposite side of the bedroom to stand next to a giant teddy bear. Without changing her facial expression, Samantha shuffled across the room and wordlessly repeated her prior request, arms out and ready to be held.

I shook my head. "Okay, this is interesting."

"Yes. And rather depressing. Can I pick her up now? She looks so very pitiful," he said, pouting.

"Of course. Tell you what, you two play while I go and grab my instruments from the hall."

I opened the door briefly, heading out into the brighter space to get my things. As soon as I reached for them, I heard an exclamation of dismay from Christian before a tiny form jetted out of the bedroom toward the den. "Are you serious?" I said, sighing heavily.

"I'm sorry!" Christian apologized, rushing out of the room. "She jumped when she realized that the door was opened."

"Ugh. Come on," I said, heading into the living room to find that Samantha had skipped right through it to the kitchen. With my hands on my hips, I stared down at her, watching as she fingered the metal rim of the island counter blankly. "Child, you're giving me an ulcer," I said.

"And me a hernia," Christian added, reaching behind him to rub his lower back.

"Though it seems she's had her fill of being held for now."

Christian huffed. "Your fickle affections are wearing on my heart, Samantha."

"Aaw," I giggled.

"I think it's necessary that this be rectified," he started, "before I do something drastic."

"And how's that?" I smirked.

He held his arms out to me. "I am an equal opportunity embracer," he said.

I stared at him, raising an eyebrow.

"What? I'm being friendly," he said.

I shook my head, turning to Samantha, and Christian lowered his arms, moping. "Am I that unlovable?" he asked, sighing dramatically.

Why did he have to be so pathetic about it? Someone like him had no excuse to be love-starved. "Christian, really?"

He sighed again, his shoulders slumping.

"Oh, for the love of God, come here," I said, opening my arms.

"No, no, don't worry about me," he said, looking around the room for effect. "No, I'm quite fine over here…rejected…cold and alone…"

"Well, in that case, okay then."

His lower lip jutted out even more, and my heart melted. Son of a bitch, he was doing this on purpose! "Ugh," I said, stomping over to him. I'd intended to make the hug quick and brusque, but as soon as I'd made contact his arms came securely around me, and I was immediately overwhelmed by the way he smelled and the warmth of his body. I relaxed into him, laying my head against his shoulder.

"This isn't so hard, is it?" he whispered. I tensed, trying not to shudder, but I couldn't help it. This wasn't fair. I went to pull away but he held on tight, and in a voice that sounded horribly uncertain, I said, "Christian, please let me go."

"I'm just hugging you."

"We've got work to do," I reminded him, but even as I said this, my hands, having a mind of their own, clasped tightly to the back of his shirt. I didn't really want to let go, so the whole thing was completely unfair. He was stronger than me in more ways than one, and this little stunt was only torturing me when I just wanted to do the right thing.

He turned his head to whisper, "You smell nice," and the sensation of his breath against my ear sent me jumping backwards.

"We…work," I stammered. Work. Work, work, work, work, work.

He narrowed his eyes at me, his expression stiff for a moment, and then he relaxed, smiling cheekily. "Of course. Work."

I grabbed my bag of tricks and started pulling out every instrument I owned. Suddenly, it was extremely important that Samantha and I play the maracas and the tambourines and the castanets, and if we had to, we'd compose an entire symphony with the triangle. And while we worked, I decided there were a few rules that needed following. Rule number one had just been written—do not hug Christian Wright. He was cagier than he looked.

Still, regardless of the hugging incident, this session had been interesting, and when Carol emerged I was relieved to tell her that we'd gotten an interesting response from her daughter. "Is she always so clingy when you take her to her room?" I asked. "We assume she's not a fan of bedtime."

"No, she hates it," Carol admitted. "It's the hardest point in the day for us. We think she's afraid of the dark, so we usually stay with her until she falls asleep."

"What does she do if you don't?"

"She throws an awful tantrum. Screams and cries. She doesn't cling to us, though. That behavior seems strictly reserved for you, Christian. Sorry about that," she said.

"It's no problem," he assured her.

"Well, I think we'll have to repeat this experiment again," I said.

"Definitely," Carol agreed. "You don't mind coming all the way out here, though? I mean, I'm happy to compensate for gas."

"No, no. That's not necessary, Carol. This is my job."

"Okay." She smiled. "Thank you so much, Nicole. I just don't know what I'd do without you. You're the only hope we have that…" She trailed off as her eyes misted. "Well, we just don't know where else to turn. She's been to so many people and we've tried so many things. You're the only one who's ever given us any hope."

I sighed. "And we're working on it, Carol," I said. "I won't give up, okay? We'll find a way."

The second I'd made the promise, I was sorry I'd done it. What would compel me to say something like that? Autism wasn't a broken bone, and assuming that Samantha had the condition, it would take some kind of miracle to fix it. The very thought made me grumble at the universe. I was surrounded by miracle workers, so where the hell were the magic tricks when you really needed them?

<h1 style="text-align:center">Chapter Twenty</h1>

I had to admit, things were definitely easier since we'd started giving Mom medication. She still couldn't recognize her own life, but instead of panicking about this, she was somehow calm in her lack of knowledge. Should she have a brief moment of awareness, all I had to do was explain the topic at hand, remind her that she was Rita Abbot and I was her daughter, Nicole, and that she lived in this house with her family and friends, and she was happy. She'd smile contentedly and say, "Oh. I see." And then she was fine for a few hours until I had to do it all over again. Sometimes she'd ask a question like "What state is this?" or "How old am I?" or "Did you say I lived here?" And I would tell her what she needed to hear, over and over, with all the patience I possessed.

I missed the days when she remembered some things on her own, since fate had allowed her a semblance of belonging then. But that Rita had faded and faded until every little thing confused and frightened her. And even though life was an amnesiac cloud for my mother now, at least I could keep her content. At least she wouldn't have to fear a world full of monsters, real or otherwise.

Things were quiet on the home front today—rather uneventful for a Saturday, and everyone but my mom, Adalia, Elaine, and Theo had gone away for the weekend. Elaine had stayed home as a favor to an ailing Theo, but she wasn't thrilled with the idea. Our Sentients hadn't left for some run-of-the-mill spook fest. No, things were a bit more ominous this time. They were investigating some towns just south of us where a few missing person reports had erupted in the last few weeks.

Wendell's red flag was raised. It wasn't out of the norm for someone to go missing through human acts of treachery, but vampires left a footprint.

You could almost pinpoint where a coven had been and when they had fed, simply by keeping an eye on the larger picture—the scope of disappearances across a whole state, a certain region of the country. Should a speckling of abductions occur around the same time, vampires were likely involved. They liked to spread out during feeding time—a tactic to help them avoid Sentient interference. And they cleaned up after themselves, too. Vampires were smart enough to dispose of their victims well, carrying them into hiding and burning them to ashes.

Considering the possibilities, Elaine was a little nervous about staying behind, but unlike his wife, Theo wasn't in the best physical shape, so illnesses seemed to hit him especially hard. He had been feverish and miserable for days, and now that our Sentients had Christian as a Combatant, they would be all right without her for a simple stake out.

Left behind or not, we'd really been enjoying ourselves this weekend, with the exception of Theo, of course. Between the night before and this morning, we had watched nearly twelve hours' worth of *Twilight Zone* episodes. Apparently, Adalia was a huge fan of the classic black and white program, quoting Rod Serling's famous lines expertly. The only damper on the marathon was Theo's loud nose blowing and rather frequent pleas for juice.

"Elaide," he groaned from the couch for the sixth time in twenty minutes. "I'b out of tissue. Do you mide grabbig a dew box?"

She rolled her eyes and left to get her husband some Kleenex while Adalia giggled at his Rudolph impression. His face fell. "Dote laugh, Adalia. This is very serious. I'b got the plague…I thik I'b dying."

"Poor Theo." I smiled at him. "You're having a really tough year, aren't you?"

"Yes," he agreed. "That's right." He blew his nose again. "But, at least I hab a beautiful wife," he finished, just in time for Elaine's return. She traded his empty tissue box for a new one.

"Better?" she asked, smirking at him.

"Yes. But…" He sighed.

"What?" Elaine asked, her hands on her hips.

"I cat reach by throw blaket." He eyed the crumpled fleece cover longingly.

"Here, dear." She appeased him, pulling the blanket up to his chin.

"Thak you. That's buch better," he said.

"Of course, sweetheart. And while you're so comfortable and settled in, I don't suppose you'd mind if the rest of us took a little nature trek, would you?"

I raised an eyebrow while Theo questioned, "Eh, dature? What kida dature trek?"

"Well, I don't know if any of you have grasped through your boob tube stupor" —she turned to us— "but it's a beautiful March day. Looks like spring wants to come early. I was hoping we could go and see the trees?"

"The redwoods?" I smiled. "Hey, Mom, you feel like seeing the redwoods today?"

Rita looked at me thoughtfully. "Me? You called me Mom?"

"Yes." I nodded. "That would be you. You're my mom."

"Oh. I see."

"Right. So, would you like to see the redwood trees?"

"Redwood trees? That's fine."

I glanced at Elaine and shrugged. Mom's old enthusiasm for the forest seemed to be gone with the rest of her former self, but who could say for sure if a trip to the redwoods wouldn't jog her memory just a little. "Sounds good to me," I said. "Adalia?"

"Yeah, sure," she answered distractedly, still glued to the television.

Elaine wore a wry smile. "So, Addy, you're saying that you'd like to go and get your eyeball pierced?"

"Yeah, sure," Adalia repeated. "Wait…what?" She finally turned from her program.

Elaine snorted a laugh. "Get moving, ladies. We're goin' out!"

"Wait," Adalia jumped up. "What did she say?" She looked at me, a hand rising to her eye reflexively.

"Your eyes are safe," I chuckled. "She was just kidding."

"Oh. Man," she whispered to me as Elaine reentered the room with an armful of clothes. "Combatants are sadistic."

"Not all of them," Elaine started, "just me. Outerwear, anyone?" She offered us jackets.

Elaine was right. It was beautiful outside and unseasonably warm, in the low sixties. We weren't the only ones who had caught on to this, either. Lots of people were visiting the trees today, so we took our time, avoiding the tangle of larger groups in case they bothered Mom.

Adalia was thoroughly enjoying herself. Apparently, she'd only really visited the redwood park once or twice when she was a very little girl, and then it was only thanks to a class field trip. This drove me nuts, considering how important these trees were in the region's history, but it was just like what Katrina had said about tourism. When you grew up with something, when you were close enough to see it anytime you chose, I suppose it didn't seem so impressive as say, the great pyramids or the Empire State Building. But these trees were more than all the wonders of the world, in my opinion. They were around before the great pyramids were ever built and ages before such a thing as skyscrapers had dawned on our species. They had witnessed in solemn silence the evolving societies of mankind; they had withstood the test and the wear of time; they had lived and lived and lived. So how could any of us here, amongst these giant immortals, not feel the humility of our station?

"Can I look for pine cones?" Adalia asked, veering off to the right.

"There won't be any good ones, Addy. They're only fresh in the fall," I said.

"Oh, but I wanted to collect something to take home."

"Sorry, chickie," Elaine informed her. "The park doesn't let you to take anything but pictures. How about if we stop by the gift shop when we're done?"

"Aw," she complained. "Well, are we at least allowed to leave the trail?"

"I guess, but why would you want to?" Elaine asked.

"To be adventurous!" Adalia said.

Elaine laughed. "Sentient, through and through. All right, trouble-maker, but don't go far in. Stay at the edge so we know you haven't been eaten by a bear."

"No problem!" Adalia said, weaving into the trees at the path's perimeter.

"Teenagers." Elaine shook her head. "Always trying for freedom."

"I guess we're just not cool enough to hang out with her anymore," I said.

"It was only a matter of time. Oh, that reminds me, Mateo is picking her up tomorrow. He wants to take her out for the day, poor guy."

Poor Mr. Lopez, indeed. He'd been restricted to evenings and week-ends—and there were ground rules even then. Without a Sentient around, Adalia was really only safe in a public place, like the mall or an amusement park. She couldn't spend the night away from the house without a Sentient present either. Sentient or not, Adalia was only a kid, and she had no idea how to properly protect herself.

"Hey, Addy?" Elaine said after a little while. "Show thyself."

I peered into the woods, which weren't terribly dense, but couldn't spot her. "The little snot has gone farther in than she was supposed to," I said.

"It appears that she has. Paging Adalia!" Elaine called again. No answer.

"You might want to go fetch her," I suggested. "She might be climbing a tree or something."

"Yep. I'm on it," Elaine said. "You stay with Rita, please."

I nodded, taking my mother's hand. "Hey, Mom? Let's rest here for a second while Elaine gets Adalia, okay?"

"Okay. But why are we stopping?"

"Because Elaine needs to get Adalia," I repeated.

"Oh. Who?"

"Adalia?"

"What about her?" Mom asked.

I sighed, chuckling. "Never mind, Mom. Just stay with me."

"Okay."

People passed once in a while, and I glanced at my watch every few minutes, sighing anxiously. Finally, I took Mom's hand and pulled her over to the edge of the trees. "Elaine…Guys?" I tried not to shout too loudly, since I felt stupid enough yelling at the redwoods as it was, with all the trail-goers around. "Adalia?"

At first I thought I'd imagined the faint sound of Adalia calling, so I listened even harder, and again I heard her, though her voice was so muffled that she had to be at least forty or fifty feet in.

"Honey? What are you doing?!"

"Nicole!" This time she screamed.

"Mom…stay here," I said. "Just stay here, okay? Don't move!"

I left her on the trail and ran in among the redwood trunks, my heart beating against my chest. "Elaine!" I shouted. "Adalia! Somebody…"

The second I glimpsed Adalia, I stopped. She was standing not ten feet from Elaine, mesmerized, and it took me a moment to register what I was seeing.

Elaine's head was tilted oddly to the side, and something…*someone* seemed to be whispering in her ear. Closing the distance between Adalia and myself, I was granted a more accurate view. As a few stray trickles of blood dripped down the skin of Elaine's neck, I realized what was happening.

"Adalia, go to the trail!" I ordered. "And *don't* come back here, no matter what!"

She looked at me, wide-eyed with panic. "What's he doing to her?"

"Just go!" I demanded. "Oh, wait, here…" I tossed her my cell phone. "Call Laura. Hurry, Adalia!"

Adalia snapped out of her astonishment, running back toward where I'd left Mom, and I swallowed hard, breathing in sync with the intense rhythm of my heart. The vampire was impossibly thin, just skin over bone, and dressed in what looked like a filthy, torn pillowcase. Even under all the grime I could tell that his hair was almost translucent, but I couldn't see his face, buried in Elaine's neck. How much had he already taken from her? I had no idea. But I did know that I couldn't fight a vampire. All I could do was distract it. So bending to pick up the nearest stone, I threw it at the thing with as much force as I could, missing it by a few feet.

"Hey!" I yelled, picking up another stone. "Hey!" I said, throwing it at him again. This time the rock grazed his shoulder, and he jerked his head away to look at me. The sight of his mouth, covered in Elaine's blood, was nowhere near as horrible as his eyes. Black as night, absolutely hollow. I couldn't imagine how he even saw me there.

To my alarm, he decided that I wasn't a threat worth his time, and he returned to Elaine, studying her neck. I watched as the wound seemed to widen under his gaze, the blood pooling there for him to drink. It was disgusting, but the phenomenon didn't surprise me. We all knew how they fed. Enthralling a victim, rendering them helpless in a trancelike state, was effortless to vampires. It took little more than a touch of their hand. But the act of feeding wasn't so easy. It took more energy, more purpose than that. Vampires didn't need silly things like fangs, they didn't need to tear through flesh when they could simply focus their minds hard enough to divide cells, cause the blood to flow on its own. The task took a lot out of them—which is why the enthralling adaptation probably evolved to begin with; it was a hindrance to struggle with your prey when you needed all your concentration elsewhere.

God knows it was a foolish notion on my part, but since rocks weren't working I had few other options. Steeling my nerves, I ran for the vampire, kicking it in the side with all my might, hoping it would let her go, even for a moment. I only needed his enthrallment to be broken for an instant so that Elaine could fight back.

At the feel of my assault, the vampire hissed and whipped its head around to snarl at me.

"Come and get me," I said. "Come on…leave her alone and come and get me." But he was smarter than that. He could sense that I wasn't equal to his present victim. "Come *on*!" I screamed again. He sneered at me, growling and momentarily irritated, but then he returned to Elaine, his focus singular.

I had no choice. If I hoped to save her, there was only one option, and it could very well end up getting us both killed. Ah well. My life was shit, anyway. Here was my chance to go out trying.

With all the momentum I could gather, I ran at him again, this time from behind and jumped on his filthy back, holding on like a maniac, all the while assuming that he'd either enthrall me, too, or break me in half. To my surprise, he staggered backwards and away from Elaine, and before I could fathom what had happened, I was on my back in the cool dirt with the vampire hovering over me.

"You're a terrible pest!" he screeched, spit and blood flying out of his mouth and into my face. His breath stank like rotten meat.

For a second I thought about escaping, but that changed as my entire mind drew a blank. There was no sound, only a vacuum, and everything felt like a dizzying dream. The air grew heavy and lethargic, and all I really cared about was closing my eyes and going to sleep. I couldn't see where I was, but I assumed it must be heaven, because I'd never known a feeling of peace so powerful before.

Then, just as I was about to drift off into the best sleep of my life, I was ripped awake to find myself staring at the tops of redwood trees and gasping for air. I heard a loud, disgusting crack, and rolled my head to the side to see the vampire fall to the forest floor beside me, quite dead. His eyes were still open.

I gasped, and then shot up. "Elaine!"

The Combatant trudged over to me and held out a hand.

"Save your strength." I pushed myself up, and then stared at the vampire. "Thank God."

"Yeah," Elaine said.

"You've lost a lot of blood?"

"I'm all right, Nick."

"Are you able to walk?"

"Yes. He couldn't have taken much," she said. "They drink slowly, otherwise it passes through their system too fast. Shit, where's Adalia?" she asked.

"I sent her back when I found you with him. What in the hell *happened*?"

"I didn't sense him!" Elaine said. "I would have, but the fucker dropped onto me from the canopy top! Instant enthrallment. Let's get the hell out of here in case there's another one," she said, glancing upward.

"Elaine, your neck," I said, wincing at the deep opening in her flesh.

She touched a hand to her skin and pulled it away, cursing when she noted the blood. Then she tugged her collar up, buttoning it completely to cover the wound. "Let's go."

We made a dash for the trail, and I was relieved to find that both my mother and Adalia were there, huddled together on the ground looking horrified. Adalia was crying, holding my cell in her hand.

"They're here, Laura!" she spoke into the phone before handing it to Elaine.

"We're on our way." I overheard Laura's worried announcement, along with another garbled line about getting, "the hell out of there."

"No shit," Elaine said in a lowered voice. "Those little assholes are getting trickier, Laura. I'm telling you. And what was he doing out there all by himself? What the hell is going on?"

As they spoke further, Laura informed us that Wendell and Duncan had found evidence of the coven in question, the one that was responsible for the disappearances south of Eureka. She said that their cell had finished feeding and were making a hasty upward sweep toward the northern border. Our little pal here was likely a greedy straggler.

There was no way that Wendell or Laura would have wanted to break the vampire stuff to Adalia in such a dramatic way, but certain truths were unavoidable. After what the girl had witnessed this afternoon, we had a lot of explaining to do, and Adalia knew it. She'd been nagging us for more information ever since we'd left the redwoods, but Elaine refused to budge. Understandably, she didn't want to trump Wendell's station, so she told Adalia to wait a few hours until the group returned home. Unfortunately, Adalia was intent on bringing the topic up at every turn.

"Why can't you tell me now?" Adalia asked. "This is not fair, Elaine. I deserve to know what happened! I mean, not that I couldn't guess. I've seen enough horror movies, you know."

"Adalia, Wendell should talk to you about this first. He'll be home any minute, so relax," Elaine said.

"Seriously annoying," Adalia grumbled, leaning back in her chair and crossing her arms.

"You'll live."

"Well, I'm not sure now!" Adalia spouted, glaring at our Combatant. "Seriously…*vampires?*"

"Adalia…"

"Please, just tell me. Yes or no. Was that a vampire or not?"

Elaine sighed, resigned. "Yes, okay?"

Adalia's jaw dropped. "Shut *up!* Are you—"

"Topic closed 'til Wendell gets back," Elaine cut her off.

"So mean," Adalia frowned, re-crossing her arms. "You could at least let me see your neck again."

Elaine smirked at me. None of us really minded the teenage mood swings. We all liked having Adalia around. Our group hadn't experienced any youth, any new blood, for years, and the addition of Addy was a welcome breath of fresh air. Of course, no way in hell were we going to tell her that.

Elaine was nearing the point of bribes or extortion to get Adalia off her back when heaven intervened, and we heard a car—clearly not my father's noisy pickup—pulling into the driveway. The mudroom door opened and Elaine said, "Hey, see? They're back."

Adalia got up, barely making it past the end of the table before Chris, Laura, and Gil rushed into the kitchen, clearly upset. Laura went straight for Elaine, grabbing her by the shoulders. "What did that bastard do to you?" she asked, reaching for Elaine's collar to appraise the damage for herself.

"I'm fine," Elaine brushed it off. "Considering what could have happened."

Gil drew back at the sight of the wound. "God, that looks painful."

"It is," Elaine agreed. "But again, I'll take painful over…" She stopped, her eyes flitting quickly to Adalia. The girl was glued to every word coming out of their mouths, and Elaine didn't want to scare the poor kid with talk of changing. Nevertheless, *someone* was going to have to break the ugly truth to Adalia. I supposed that's where Wendell would come in.

"Where's Wendell and Raj?" I asked.

"They left after we did," Gil said. "So did your dad. It's just me and Laura and—hey!"

Christian nearly knocked Gil over, his eyes intense and determined as he made a beeline for me. "God," he said, grabbing me into a huge hug. "You're all right?" he asked, holding me at arm's length. "You're all in one piece?" he repeated, and then he kissed my forehead before pulling back to look at me again. I flushed.

"Yeah. I'm okay, Christian," I muttered.

He nodded, bringing a hand up to touch my face. "If I had been there, I would have smashed his head in."

I smiled. "Appreciate that."

"By the way, Elaine said you tried to attack him!" Christian said, looking every bit as angry with me as he was with the vampire. "Are you absolutely mad?"

"Well, what was I supposed to do? Let him make a meal out of her?"

"But you had no way of fighting, Nicole!"

"Apparently, I did."

"Oh?" His eyes narrowed. "So, piggybacking vampires is a martial arts maneuver now, is it?"

I gawked, glaring darts at Laura. "You *told* them?"

She threw her hands up. "Of course I did! That was the best part! Nicole tackles a vampire. Come on, babe. It'll be legend."

"Well," Elaine started, "I, for one, am really glad you didn't just leave me there to die, Nick."

Christian frowned. "I'm glad of it, too."

"Huh. I don't know how convinced I am of that," Elaine said.

Laura laughed. "Don't worry, Elaine. We're all relieved that you're alive, even Christian."

"Thanks," Elaine said. "And on a positive note, Theo hasn't asked me for anything since we got back. He's upstairs sleeping, thank God. Haven't heard a peep out of him."

"There you go," Laura said.

Adalia sighed amidst the chatter, becoming really put out with all the chitchat. "Guys? How long 'til Wendell gets back?" she asked.

"I don't know," Christian answered. "Maybe half an hour?"

"Argh!" Adalia moaned, stomping off to the living room and throwing herself on the couch.

Christian looked confused. "Eh, was it something I said?"

"No, it was something you *didn't* say," I explained. "Namely, everything you've ever learned about vampires."

"Oh. I see, then. Well, she can't really handle that yet, can she?"

"She's already seen them in action, Christian," Laura told him. "The luxury of holding things back is gone. Might as well get her acclimated to the rest."

"I suppose," he said, but the disapproval was written all over his face.

I had to smirk at his attitude. More and more I realized how protective Christian was of not just me, not just his family, but anyone who seemed even remotely at risk. It was just his absolute gut instinct to shield them, not only from physical but emotional harm, as well. I wondered if this was some component of a Combatant's DNA, but then again, someone like my father didn't seem to care about anyone but himself, and he was a Combatant. So maybe it was just Christian who behaved this way. Maybe it was the consequence of all the painful stuff he carried around.

I knew how he felt, and I couldn't fault him for reacting so sternly sometimes. It was close to home for me, as well. Where matters of my mom were concerned, I had always been extremely protective—possessive even. She came first, period, and I would do anything to keep her safe. So Christian's was a viewpoint I appreciated, even though some might find it tedious. In my opinion, his behavior wasn't merely the result of a worrisome nature. It stemmed from an overflow of consideration for the well-being of others.

Adalia was going to pull her hair out before Wendell came home. *Twilight Zone* or no *Twilight Zone*, she was far too distracted to watch TV now, for logical reasons. She'td witnessed a vampire feeding, for God's sake. How many fifteen-year-olds could claim this? And the experience wasn't exactly everyday fare for me, either. This was only the second time I'd laid eyes on a vampire myself, let alone wrestled with one. The first time had been in junior high, the morning after one of our famous camping trips, and my mother and I were cleaning out tin pots in the creek when I noticed someone—gangly and seemingly without pigment—peering through the nearby trees, its white face a stark contrast to the gaping midnight of its eyes. I hadn't known what vampires looked like back then. In fact, I feared he was a ghost, so I called for my father, who then led a rather involved chase through the campgrounds in search of the thing. Sadly, Dad never did find his vampire, but I remembered the sight of it. It wasn't something you forgot easily.

Chapter Twenty-One

I swear Adalia was ready to wet herself in anticipation by the time Raj and Wendell arrived. The girl was antsy beyond reason, fidgeting and pacing around in her best attempt at allowing our poor Seer a moment to recoup from his travels before bombarding him with questions. The moment he'd finished assessing Elaine's injury and catching up on events though, Adalia pounced.

"So, Wendell? Can you tell me about them? About vampires? Elaine and Laura said you would."

The two women looked at each other and then at Adalia. "Snitch," Elaine said.

"What? You did!" Adalia argued.

Wendell laughed. "Don't worry, Addy. I can see why'd you be eager to know what happened today. Why don't we go in the living room and have a chat? Come on, everybody. Time for a powwow."

Adalia hurried ahead of us, sitting down expectantly, and Wendell grabbed the remote to switch off the television.

My mom looked up. "Oh, you turned off Rod Serling. I was watching that," she said.

Wendell chuckled. "Sorry, Rita. We'll turn it back on soon, if that's all right. I just need to talk to Adalia for a bit."

"With who?"

"With me, Rita," Adalia reminded her. "I'm Adalia."

"Oh," Mom said and sat back again, satisfied with the answer.

Wendell liked to wear socks with sandals, that way it was an easy fix should your feet get too hot. He slipped off his shoes, leaving his socks on, and sat Indian style on the couch beside Adalia. "So, Vampires 101," he said. "I forgot to bring my syllabus, so I'm winging the class. Actually, what if we make it a question and answer session? Go ahead. Ask me anything."

"Anything?" Adalia seemed skeptical after Elaine's evasive maneuvers.

"Anything. I mean it. Try me."

"Okay. Well, first of all, if vampires are real, why are they here? I mean, did God make them?"

Wendell cocked his head to the side, staring off into nowhere thoughtfully. "Well, God—if that's what you want to call the mastermind of this universe—didn't make vampires. But God allowed them to be. Even vampires have a purpose, Adalia."

"What? And how are they born? And where did they come from?"

He snickered. "Deep breaths, Addy," he said. "See, there are a lot of imperfections in this universe. And those dark things are just as important as the good things, because without them we wouldn't appreciate the light. We couldn't understand who we are, what we're made of. You see what I mean?"

"So, like, they're the opposite of us?"

"Well, yes. They are. We're born of light, they're not. They help us remember who we are."

"If we come from light, where do they come from?"

"They're born from the last spark of a dying soul, Adalia. After that, all that's left is an empty shell that's capable of existing but incapable of aging."

"So, you mean they don't get old?"

"Well, they stick around a long time, but they don't age, they don't die unless you kill them."

"Why not?"

"Because they have no soul, and the soul is what progresses us forward, gathering new knowledge of itself, always moving in a loop of enlightened existence. Humans are born in absolute communion with living energy, but vampires are lightless vessels with exceptionally clever minds, and in the absence of wisdom, their intellect has evolved and evolved. Now, intellect alone, fueled by flesh and hunger is a terrible thing, because it means that your concentration is on one thing and one thing only for all your existence."

"What?"

"Thirst," Wendell said.

"For blood?" Adalia concluded.

"Yep, essentially…on the surface, anyway."

"On the surface?"

"Yes. Blood sustains their physical bodies, it's true, but it does something else, too, something that makes them want it even more desperately. Can you guess?"

"Me?"

"Mhm."

"Uh…no."

"Well, just think about it, Adalia. That vampire you saw back there, he wasn't some normal Joe off the side of the road, was he?"

"No way. Definitely not."

"Explain what you mean."

"Well, he had like…like hypnotic mind powers or something."

"Ah ha, there's the word I was looking for. It makes them powerful. For a short time, it grants them some light energy, and though it's nowhere near the same as having a soul, it's still a kind of high. They crave the feeling of power that our energy gives them. And this is so dangerous, Adalia, because their minds are fine-tuned, they're incredibly advanced, and they use that bit of energy with great skill."

"So, that's why they can do things like hypnotize people? And what about Elaine's neck? I mean, he didn't even bite her like they do in the movies! He just looked at it! It was *nasty*," she said, grimacing.

"That's right. They don't need to bite or cut a human at all, Adalia. And some of them don't even need to touch you to make sure that you can't fight back."

Adalia sighed in a way that was already beyond her years. "You know, all this makes me really wonder something else."

"Oh, yeah? What's that?"

"Just, isn't it kind of mean for the universe to torture them with something they can never have? I mean, don't they just want to be human like us?"

Huh.

The room had become intensely quiet all of a sudden. Adalia had laid out a tough question, and I had no idea what the answer was. Hopefully Wendell did.

"You know," Wendell began, contemplating his answer carefully, "most of them don't. They simply want the perks of our energy minus the conscience that goes with it. But—and this is where things get amazing, kid—sometimes, they *do* want to be human again. Sometimes, whatever blood they've consumed sparks a memory of good—a memory of love, I think. And you can't imagine how very, *very* rare this phenomenon is. But it's happened."

"Really?"

"It has."

"When?"

"Well, personally, I've only seen one vampire go through that kind of change in being. He was a Sentient before he was ever turned into a vampire though, and I think that's what guided his decision to ask for help."

"He asked for help? From who?"

"From a Seer."

"Woah. And the Seer said yes?"

"Of course. He was a very good Seer, and he helped the vampire get his soul back."

"Are you serious? He got his soul back?"

"Yes. He did."

"Holy crap. So vampires don't have to stay that way?"

Wendell sighed. "Honestly, that's where it get tricky and confusing, even for me. See, there are all these conditions that have to be met just right in order for that to work, and they rarely are. This is the only one instance I know of, personally, where the stars aligned perfectly."

"Oh. Okay. And he's like, a normal person now?"

At this, Christian snickered a little, and we all turned to look at him. "I don't know that I'd call Maddox *normal*," Christian said, smirking. "He's a bit on the gangly side, really. But otherwise, he's an all right guy."

Adalia gasped. "You know him?"

"Yes," Christian said, nodding. "He's a member of the group I came from. He…he's a good man. He saved my life, in fact."

"Wow. Really?"

"Really."

She processed this for a moment and then looked back to Wendell, obviously contemplating her next words. "So, basically, it sounds like, in all the scariness and stuff, there's still hope, right? Even for vampires?"

Wendell smiled. "You know, I really do like that assessment, Addy. I truly do."

"Thanks. And besides, I think everybody deserves to be happy, so long as they're good," she said.

"Absolutely, Addy," Wendell agreed. "Absolutely."

Adalia turned to Elaine, studying the Combatant with new eyes. "It's really crazy, you know? I mean, when you'd said you were a Combatant, I guess I never imagined that you, like, fought monsters. That's really scary, Elaine. You must be so brave."

Elaine considered this. "Brave? I guess—if courage means caring about something enough to fight for it."

"Fight for it? I know what we're fighting against, but what are you fighting for?"

"Each other," Elaine told her. "What else?"

"Right," Adalia said. Then she grinned broadly, as if she was only now realizing that she fit into this whole crazy world. "You know, one day when I'm older and I have—" She stopped talking as the front door swung wide open.

My father stalked inside, tossing his bags to the floor and slamming the door shut behind him. He stared at the group of us, and I shrank back a little. From the look on his face, I knew this would be bad. "What in the hell were you idiots thinking?" he roared, barging into the room.

Wendell ignored him and spoke to Adalia calmly. "Addy, why don't you take Rita upstairs for a little while, huh? Put on a movie?"

I shook my head. "No, Wendell, I can take her—"

"I need you here for this," Wendell interrupted calmly. "Adalia?"

Adalia dared a frightened glance at my father and then nodded quickly, taking my mother by the hand and leading her away from a guaranteed unpleasant experience.

"So, let me get this straight," Duncan said to me and Elaine. "You two decide to take a little stroll in middle of the woods with *my* addled wife, is that right?"

"Dad, I never took Mom into the woods. She stayed on the path with Adalia."

"You mean you left her with a child?"

"Yes. I mean, I had to! Elaine and Adalia—"

"Are Sentients!" He slammed a hand against the door frame. "They're Sentients, Nicole! You should have let them sort it out for themselves! You could have gotten them killed!"

"She's the reason we're alive!" Elaine interjected, standing up. "If it wasn't for her, I'd be dead by now, and quite possibly Adalia, too. She saved our lives, Duncan! She fought a damned vampire!"

My dad opened his mouth to speak, and then looked at me, then at Elaine and back at me again. "You fought a vampire?"

Well, yeah, damn it. "I guess I did," I said.

His eyes narrowed in concentrated thought, as if the idea was too much to comprehend, as if gray matter would leak out his ears at any moment. I could have sworn he smiled, and then his expression hardened again, and he said, "Well, this has still got to be the *dumbest* thing you've ever done, Nicole!"

"I think it's brilliant," Christian said from the couch.

"Keep out of this."

"Don't tell me to keep out of it," Christian said, getting up to stand next to Elaine. "I've kept out of it long enough. So has everyone else here. Somebody needs to call a spade a spade."

"Oh, I see. And you're gonna do that, huh?" Duncan mocked.

"Definitely!" Christian said. "Duncan, you're a bastard. And more than that, you're an angry, hateful coward who resents anyone you can't protect!"

Duncan swallowed hard, his neck and face splotching with scarlet and purple. "Is that right? Well, aren't you just a fucking hero, you pansy ass little twit. And I'm supposed to take this bullshit from a stupid little boy who doesn't know squat about shit? Who doesn't have the guts to live up to his own combatance anymore?"

"What the hell is that supposed to mean?"

"Come on, Christian. You're defending vampires and making excuses for stupidity now? And what's with your little rebound via my daughter? It's a good thing Gil told me about you two when he did. And thank God Nicole had the rare common sense to cut things off when I asked her to."

Wait a *fuck*ing minute. Gil? *Gil* had told my father about me and Christian? Why in the hell would he have done that? I glared at him, but he refused to return the gesture and for good reason. If he'd seen the look on my face, he'd have fled the house immediately.

In the meantime, Christian had reached teeth-grinding status. "Don't you ever call her a rebound again, you hateful, horrible man. Have you made it your mission in life to make people as miserable as you are?"

"Say what you want," Duncan dismissed him. "But I'm just doing my job, making the hard decisions. And it's high time you started doing the same. All that guilt about offing your daddy has really fucked with your head, you know that? I'm sure Daniel would be proud to know he'd raised a son just as weak as he was."

Christian stopped breathing, his whole demeanor changing from angry to lethal. "I will tell you once, but that's my final warning—don't you *ever* speak that way about my father again, do you hear me?"

Duncan snorted. "Or what, boy?"

Christian grabbed my father by the collar, slamming him against the wall, and I stood up quickly. "Christian…"

"Let them go, Nick," Wendell told me. I held still.

Christian gripped my father's collar with renewed vigor and said, "You don't even deserve to say his name."

Dad shook his head, even while Christian held him there. "If your father was half the man he could have been, he'd still be alive, boy, and you wouldn't have turned into such a pussy. Hell, I'm shocked you had the guts to put the bullet through his chest before—"

Christian squashed my father's insults by releasing his collar and punching him hard enough to send him toppling over. "*Stop*…" Christian shouted, punching him again, "*calling*," and again, "*me*," and again, "*boy!*"

Duncan shielded his face, growling, "Get off me!" But I was already jumping between them, pushing on Christian's chest and pleading with him to remember his sanity.

"Christian," I said, my eyes locked with his. "Christian, you need to stop. You need to stop this," I repeated. "You can't do this."

The contact seemed to bring Christian back, and his muscles relaxed under my hand, his eyes softened. He dropped my father to the floor and backed away from us in a daze, and I steeled myself, glancing down at Duncan. Both of his eyes were swollen almost shut, and his mouth and nose were dripping blood.

I held out a hand to help him up, but he pushed it away. "Save your pity, Nicole," he said through blood and broken teeth.

"I think we need to get you to the hospital," Elaine suggested quietly. "You'll need stitches on that lip, at least."

"I'm fine!" Duncan snapped, pushing himself up. "I don't need any stinking hospital."

"Don't be foolish," Wendell started.

"Oh, save it," Dad said. "You want to help me? Get this menace out of the house!" he ordered, pointing to Christian. "Get him the hell out of here."

"If you say another word, *you'll* be out of the house, do you hear me?" Wendell threatened. "And if you presume to tell me how to handle my Sentients again, I'll repel you to San Francisco."

Laura raised an eyebrow, smirking shamelessly. In fact, we were all stunned by Wendell's sudden severity, but I seemed to be the only one who kept this reaction to myself. I'd known Wendell Russettman all my life, and he had never threatened anyone, which was probably why my father was sufficiently intimidated and shuffled out of the room, cursing all the way.

Christian took a deep breath and looked around at everyone. "I understand if you want me to leave."

Wendell shook his head, saying, "Christian, you don't have to go anywhere, but I will ask that you refrain from beating anyone else to a pulp, much as Duncan may have deserved it."

"Wait," Gil finally spoke up. "You're just going to let this slide?"

"Gil," I began, balling up my fists, "you say another word and I'll beat the shit out of you myself. Now go away. I'll deal with you later." Gil shut his mouth, hung his head and obeyed, slinking out of the room like a weasel.

Christian turned to me. "Nick, I'm…I don't even know what to say. I'm so sorry."

To be honest, I didn't know how to feel about Christian at the moment. He'd completely lost it, just like Gil had warned, just as Trina had feared. But it's not like my father hadn't been asking for it. What was the right thing to say? Whose side was I on, anyway?

"Nicole, please speak to me. Or slap me or punch me or anything," he pleaded.

I glanced at everyone, and Wendell caught on to my discomfort. "All right. Come on, people," he said, sweeping his hand to indicate that they should clear the room. Once we were alone, Christian approached me carefully, and I stood, confused and torn, wondering whether I was supposed to be angry with him.

"Please talk to me?" he asked in a quiet, wary voice. It was the opposite of the Christian I'd witnessed just moments ago—the one who might have killed my father had I not intervened.

"Christian," I said, sighing. "What happened?"

He stared at his feet. "I don't…God," he said, shaking his head in frustration.

"You really lost control. That was kind of scary, you know that?"

Again he looked at me, but this time his eyes were glassy moist. "I have no excuse. I don't know what that was about, Nicole."

"Yeah, you do."

"I do?"

"Christian, I've been a therapist long enough to know that this was more about your father than mine."

He stared at me blankly, and then his expression turned pained, and he contemplated the couch for a moment before walking over to sit down. I deliberated, not knowing whether this was an invitation to join him or a rejection of the subject. Then he said, "My father was the best man I've ever known."

I walked to his side, sitting on the arm of the couch.

"You know, if karma functions right, he should have lived a long life," Christian continued. "He should have grown old and had grandbabies and been happy. He made everyone else happy. And you can't even imagine how well he deserved that. There was never a more generous man than my dad. He would've given a stranger the shirt off his back or the food from his table," he said, his voice wavering. "And he was always smiling, always happy. He laughed all the time, Nicole. He just enjoyed life so much, and the one thing that made him happiest was his family." He smiled. "You know, if I sneezed he was proud of it?"

I sat in silence, listening to him as I'd been trained to do—with an unbiased ear, without judgment, without agenda. And I knew he'd go on, if I just remained this way.

"We were all supposed to stay together," he went on. "Not just when we fought in Vancouver, but any job we were on. We always stayed together…that was the rule. No one was allowed to fly off on a hero's fancy, you know? So when he told us to leave him alone in those sewers, I just knew it was the wrong thing to do. I *knew* it. But he insisted on finding the rest of our group to make sure they were okay. He couldn't bear the idea of leaving them behind. It's just, we'd been fighting in the sewers for the better part of a day, and we were all exhausted and confused and scared. There were scattered Sentients around from other groups, so we reasoned that he'd be okay, that he'd have backup." Christian stopped, swallowing hard. "We were wrong. We left the sewers, went back to our hotel, and the whole time I couldn't shake this sick feeling that we'd made a horrible mistake. And when everyone else returned but him, we knew. We just knew," he said, finally breaking down.

Leaving the arm of the couch, I sat beside him and pulled him into a hug. He buried his face in my neck and spoke through his tears. "By the time we found him, he'd already been drained and made to drink from the coven's blood. It was too late. It was too late," he repeated. "We were wrong to leave him. I should have said something. I should have argued with him, but I didn't, and fate showed me just how stupid I'd been. It gave me a gift I'd never forget," he said. "I got to kill him. I got to shoot him and watch the life go out of him," he sobbed, bitterly. "I killed him, Nicole. I murdered my father."

"Stop it." I shook him. "You just *stop* saying that, Christian, do you hear me?" I ordered. "The universe isn't some sadistic bitch that gets her jollies out of screwing with people's hearts."

He shook his head against my shoulder in silent argument, but I ignored him. "Sometimes things just have to happen so that you'll end up where you're supposed to be. You're born into bad circumstances or you miss the boat or the anvil falls on your head, and if we believe any of the stuff we've been taught since infancy, then it's all supposed to mean something bigger than what we can understand, right?" He sniffled, lifting his head to look at me. "And you *can't* obsess over things for the rest of your life. You can't blame yourself for everything bad that ever happens to anyone. You can't protect everybody."

"Nicole…"

"Will it always be your fault because you weren't obsessive enough, weren't fast enough, wise enough, strong enough? Just *stop*. Stop thinking that you need to be any more than what you already are."

He leaned back, peering at me. "I will when you do."

"You'll…" *Wait.* "What?"

Christian shook his head slowly and said, "Physician, heal thyself."

"What's that supposed to mean?"

"I think you can figure it out, Nicole. Everything you're saying to me applies to you, too."

"This isn't about me, Christian! And it's not the same thing."

"Oh, it's definitely the same thing!" he said. "You've got this huge complex, you know that? You don't trust anyone, and it's glaringly obvious that you think you're somehow unworthy compared to the rest of these people when, in reality, you're this strong, loyal, enduring, beautiful, gifted human being who's made it her life's work to help people in the most impossible circumstances! Do you think all Sentients can do something like that? I can promise you—they can't."

I stared at him, too baffled to compose a counter, and he added, "You're not any less than they are, just because your soul hasn't run as many laps around life's gymnasium. Am I right?"

Was he right? "Well…"

"Good. Then you agree."

"I didn't say that."

"You didn't *not* say it."

"That doesn't even make sense. And are we really going to argue like a couple of six year olds?"

Christian chuckled. "What? That's not an approved psychoanalytical method?"

"Don't make fun."

"Why? Should I worry that you'll jump on my back?"

I frowned. "You're really fond of beating a dead horse, Christian."

"I apologize," he said, grinning warmly. "And that was the last time, I swear. And Nicole…"

"What?"

"I'm really glad you forgive me for beating your father up and all."

I allowed him a smile.

"And you know what else?" he went on.

"What's that?" I said.

"You were never a rebound," he stated seriously. "That was never the case. In fact, and I know this will sound awful, but, if anyone was—it was Lily."

Narrowing my eyes, I said, "Lily?"

"Yes. You see, she came into the picture and kind of cleared the air for everyone, and I think somewhere along the way, I'd confused hope with love. But she was right. I only wanted her because I thought I should have her—it was so easy, really. And completely wrong of me."

"So you don't love her?"

He smiled. "Oh, I love her very much. But not in the way you're thinking."

"I see."

He smiled again. "By the way, regarding your little trick today with the vampire…"

"Christian, don't start."

"I'm actually quite proud of you for it," he said.

Oh. Well, then. "You are?"

"Yes. Just, don't do it again, please."

"I'll sure try my best."

"That's all I ask," he said, and then, for the second time that day, he kissed my forehead, and I held my breath. He was too close again, and he was looking at me in that way, in that intimate, deeply personal *way* of his, with so much kindness. It almost felt like a magnet was pulling me in, like I had to fight against gravity or something. It was frustrating. And most frustrating of all was this inkling in the back of my head that maybe, just maybe, I shouldn't be fighting at all.

Christian seemed to catch on to my moment of weakness, and he bent in a fraction of an inch, and a fraction more, until I felt his breath against my face and knew that I was seconds away from throwing in the towel. So I took a shaky inhale and sat back, earning an aggravated sigh from Mr. Wright.

"I need to check on Adalia," I said.

"Nicole, would you stop—"

I spoke over him. "She's got to be freaking out. I mean, she's just a kid. And after today, right? So, I'll see you at dinner," I rambled, backing out of the living room. Okay, more like running out of the living room while a chorus that sounded something like *Don't go back there. Don't go back there. Don't go back there. Why am I not going back there? Go back there!* screamed in my head.

When I'd reached my bedroom, I shut the door and locked it behind me, my heart pounding, my stomach leaping and turning, and worst of all, my body begging me to unlock the damned door and call him upstairs and give him anything in the entire world he ever wanted for as long as I lived. I mean, what if I did have something to offer? What if I could make him happy? What if…but…

Who the hell was I kidding? Look at who I was talking about here. Circumstance and birthright had seen to it that Christian's main motivation in life was shielding people from harm, so wouldn't it be a disastrous plan for him to pair up with someone who didn't have supernatural crime-fighting super powers? He'd be worried night and day! He'd have a stroke by forty. He'd be white-haired by fifty.

God. What was I going to do?

Chapter Twenty-Two

Oh, he could run, but he couldn't hide. Gilford Boyd had a lot of explaining to do, and the little snot had done everything in his power to avoid exactly that. He'd effectively ducked out, hidden out, and otherwise run out as many times as I was willing to stand for, all in hopes of avoiding the inevitable confrontation. But I had moles in place, and Laura had tipped me off that Gil was in the greenhouse today. It seemed that he'd taken a sudden interest in seedlings, the weasel.

Storming off the deck and along the side of the house, I heard Raj's voice behind me. "Nicole," he said, tailing me across the beach. "Nicole, don't do anything too drastic."

"Drastic like kicking him in the stomach? Or drastic like feeding him to a shark?

"Well, could you settle for a good old-fashioned telling off, eh?"

I stopped immediately, sand kicking up around my feet. "Raj, he screwed with my head and my life! He had no right to go to my father about Christian. My *father*, for God's sake!" I said, storming along the beach again. "What the hell was his motivation?"

"Nicole, hang on!" He grabbed my sleeve. "Nothing's ever what it seems. Remember that, okay?"

"What do you mean?"

"Just promise me something, since Gil is my friend, too, and I'd hate to see him suffer a coma from head injuries."

I exhaled, calming myself. "What, Raj?"

"Promise that you won't kill him…"

"What? Of course I won't. Are you serious?"

He smirked to demonstrate otherwise, but added, "Nicole, please?"

"Raj, sure. I'll try to be reasonable. Just let me go now, please."

He released my arm. "Okay. Sorry."

As I neared the glass greenhouse, I slowed down, catching my breath before opening the door. Gil's back was to me, but he knew my energy by now, and he froze like a statue. Chris glanced up at me, his gloved hands cupping the roots of a small plant as he nodded in greeting.

"Chris, do you mind if I hijack your greenhouse for a few?" I asked.

He smiled subtly, setting his plant back in its pot, and brushed his hands together. "Not a problem," he said.

"Thanks."

As Chris headed for the door, Gil made a move to follow. "Hold it," I said, and he winced, standing still while Chris kept going, smirking as he left the building. I shut the door behind him, then standing in front of it, I said, "Have a seat," and pointed to one of the benches against the wall. Gil gulped and sat down, staring at his knees.

Walking over to sit beside him, I watched out the window as slate blue waves broke over the shore, and I set my breathing to match their ebb and flow until my mind and body were calm. I'd promised Raj that I'd be reasonable, after all.

As soon as I felt like I could honor Raj's request not to shove a trowel up Gil's ass, I said, "Since when do you have a green thumb?"

Gil didn't answer.

Okay, so he was going to play the quiet game. "Fine. So we're skipping the small talk and moving straight onto the good stuff. How about you tell me why? Why'd you do it, Gil?"

"Why?"

"Yeah, why, you know? It's a one word question. It's not rocket science, and even if it was, you're a fucking genius, so explain to me…*why?*"

"You *know* why. Because he was dangerous. Because he's wrong for you!"

"So, laboring under that belief, you were compelled to go to my *father*, of all people, and use him to manipulate my personal life and screw with my heart? Do you know how that feels? Like a slap in the face, Gil…no, like a stab in the back."

"I'm sorry, Nicole, okay?"

"You know, you really don't sound sorry."

"Well, I am! I'm just…I think…"

"Think what?"

"I just think…God…" He ran his hand through his hair, tapping his fingers on his knee.

"Gil…?"

"I don't know, okay?!" He stood up, pacing. "I mean, you'll like, disown me or something."

"Is that right?"

"Yeah, it is."

"And when have I ever disowned anyone for bad behavior, Gil?"

"I…guess…never."

"Right."

He stopped pacing and pushed some flower pots across a table so he could sit on the edge in front of me. "You're…I've been lying to myself for a long time, Nicole. I've told myself that I was keeping you safe, that I was being valiant, but I don't know that I deserve to harbor that delusion anymore."

"Delusion? What the hell does that mean?"

"Well, you've always been this person that I could defend, you know? You've always been 'poor Nicole,' the one that Duncan picked on, the odd man out, the one who didn't belong. And somewhere deep down, maybe I thought that as long as you were here to play the part of the black sheep, then I wasn't the square peg. No matter how lame my endowment was, I'd still be a head above you. I wouldn't just be this really smart guy who felt like a fake living with all these gifted people who can talk to the dead or reach out and touch someone with their mind. I was a Sentient and you weren't, and maybe that was my comfort zone. And then Christian came along, and he didn't even seem to notice the difference between you and everyone else. He…he was going to close that gap that made me feel superior."

I stared at him and waited, waited for his words to sink in, waited for my mind to wrap itself around the idea that my best friend had somehow been sabotaging me all along. Even if he didn't realize he'd been doing it, he'd put his chicken shit ego before me. He'd hurt me in the worst way, and at this point, I couldn't decide who was worse—him or my father.

Shaking my head, my first thought was to get as far away from him as possible before my hands were on his scrawny, two-faced, weasely little neck, strangling the life right out of him. So, in a rush to avoid a homicide charge,

I took off for the beach, blind with rage and hurt, and headed toward the giant yellow blur that was our house. Nothing could have prepared me for this. Nothing could have been worse. Nothing, of course, but the feel of his traitorous arms grabbing me from behind and pulling me backwards.

"Please don't hate me," he said.

I tried to yank myself away, but he held on tight. "Let me *go*, you son of a bitch! Don't you touch me!"

"I'm not letting go, Nicky. I won't let go 'til you forgive me!"

I twisted around in his arms, and my knee met his groin. "*Screw* you, Gilford Boyd!"

Naturally, this sent him dropping to the sand in a groaning, wincing heap, and I turned again to leave him but he grabbed my ankle, and I fell down beside him.

"No!" he said, still doubled over and puffing in pain. "No. I won't let you hate me. You're my family, and I know I'm a fucking schmuck. I know I don't deserve your forgiveness, but I need it! I need you to forgive me."

"*Why?* So that you can go back to using me?! Fuck you!"

"No!" he shouted, and then his voice cracked. "No, Nicky." He shook his head and began to cry. "No. Never, ever again. I promise. I just want you to be happy. I'm so sorry. I love you, Nick. I'm so sorry. I'm so sorry, Nicky," he said, crying pathetically.

He was right. He *was* a schmuck, but as I took in his wretched state, I understood that all along, while I'd thought that I was the pitiable one, while I'd believed I was pathetic, certain people were feeling the same way about themselves. We were all just playing into the same illusion for our own personal reasons.

"I tried to keep you down, Nicky," Gil said, whimpering now. "Every time you've gone on those stupid diets, every time you've mentioned leaving…it just freaked me out, because I wanted to keep you here, just as you were. And I know it was wrong. I know I've been selfish, but I was scared. I was a loser. I *am* a loser!"

Damn it. I didn't *want* to forgive him! I *wanted* to bury his face in the sand. But Raj had asked me not to kill him, so I'd have to reign myself in. And now I wondered, had Raj known all along how insecure Gil was? That he'd used me to make himself feel better? It occurred to me that, in his own way, my father had been using me to mask his insecurities, as well. Like Christian had said, anything Dad couldn't protect, he resented. Maybe he didn't hate me. Maybe he was afraid of me…afraid *for* me. Maybe he couldn't let himself get too attached because, unlike Christian, my father wasn't strong enough to feel love in the face of his fear. He wasn't brave enough to take that risk.

At least Gil had exceeded my dad in one respect. He'd had the courage to tell me the truth.

"Gil," I sighed. "You're not a loser. You're a complete asshole, but you're not a loser."

If I was being honest with myself, I'd probably always kind of sensed all this, but instead of calling Gil on it, I had just let myself die here because it was convenient for me, too. It eased some of my guilt for what had happened to Mom, for disappointing my dad. But it was time for me to start standing up for myself. I didn't want to hide in anyone else's shadow anymore.

"Say you forgive me," Gil pleaded again, "and that you won't cap my ass while I'm sleeping…"

As much as I didn't want to, I laughed anyway. "Fine, you jerk. I forgive you," I said, proving my point by laying my hand over his. "But I need you to be my friend, please. Just support my decisions. Let me do what I need to do and stop standing in my way. Can you handle that?"

He nodded. "Yeah. Anything, Nicole."

"Even if it somehow involved Christian?"

He stiffened a little, and then grumbled, "Yeah, fine."

Now that I had more accurate information, it was obvious that Christian's presence had worsened Gil's inferiority complex from the beginning. "I admire the fact that you were honest with me," I said. "That takes a lot of strength, you know that?"

Gil perked up. "Strength? You think?"

"Yeah. I really do."

He nodded, a grin washing over his face.

"Come on in!" Carol Fitzpatrick's voice sounded from inside her house, and Christian opened the door letting me go first. In a moment, she emerged with half a bagel in her mouth, a wedge-shaped piece of Styrofoam under her arm and Samantha at her side.

Christian laughed. "Would you like some help, Carol?"

"I would," she said, nearly dropping the bagel from her mouth. Christian picked up Samantha, freeing one of Carol's hands. She took the bagel out of her mouth and said, "That's better. Thanks."

"My pleasure," Christian said.

"I hate to make a quick exit, but my client's already in there. Oh, by the way, I bought bagels!" she announced, holding up her breakfast. "Please, help yourselves."

"Why, thank you!" Christian said, already heading toward the bagels with Samantha. There was a counter dividing the kitchen from the living room, and he sat the little girl there while he picked out some breakfast.

I smirked at Carol. "Christian doesn't believe in passing up food."

"That's right," Christian responded over the counter. "I cannot function on an empty stomach."

"Or play," I added. "Or do pretty much anything that involves being alive."

"Of course not," Carol agreed, and then she lowered her voice. "I swear he gets more handsome every time I see him."

Christian nodded as he scooped some cream cheese onto a butter knife. "It's true, you know," he said. "*And,* if that weren't intimidating enough, I have exceptional hearing. It's overwhelming, I know."

Carol laughed. "Uh oh. I think I need to cut out before I create a monster. See you in a bit, folks."

Carol left me to watch Christian chewing happily on his bagel, licking his fingers occasionally—an act that drove me to drink when most people did it, and yet somehow, I didn't mind when Christian did. Actually, I found myself wishing that he'd let me do it *for* him.

I'd been having a lot of thoughts like these lately…specifically since he'd delivered a fistful of just desserts to my father. Where I'd initially expected to be angry with him for hitting Duncan, it turned out the whole episode had been kind of therapeutic for all of us.

Christian broke off a piece of bagel and offered it to Samantha. "Bite?" he asked.

She blinked at him.

"Hm. I guess not, huh?"

I frowned deeply. We'd have to start fresh today, like always, and it was reaching the six month mark now. I hadn't been able to help her, and at this rate it would probably take years to figure out her reactions and non-reactions.

I'd promised Carol I would find a solution, but I feared that my promise had been empty. The universe hadn't granted me my miracle for Samantha.

"You finished in there?" I said.

"I think so," Christian said.

"'Kay. You want to play in the yard, Sam?" I said, walking around the counter to address her closer. "Outside, honey?" I repeated, and she took a quick little breath, lifting her head to look out the kitchen window. "That's right!" I smiled. "Come on. Let's go."

I pulled her from the counter, took her hand, and waited as Christian contemplated, with a sheepish grin, the idea of grabbing another bagel to take with him. I laughed at him. "Just take it, Christian. You know you want to."

"Right." He eagerly obeyed, and then we headed outside to enjoy the day.

The sky was the color of corn flowers, with wispy feather clouds that brushed across its canopy at random, and maybe it was the sweet, green-smelling air that did it, or maybe it was simply chance, but Samantha was more aware than I'd anticipated. Between the pair of squirrels fighting over tossed bits of Christian's bagel and the constant motion of the tree branches, newly budding, Samantha seemed to take notice, though she didn't say a thing, and her attention was hard to hold.

As usual, I made note of the things that captured her eye, but there was never a pattern to them. And I hummed to her, hoping to take advantage of her heightened state. Christian applauded uproariously when she mimicked my singing, though it was only one note and the sound only lasted for a few seconds, at most.

It was the same thing—just another slight improvement on a day like countless others, and my heart was heavy with the thought that this was as good as it would get for Samantha. This was the only life she'd ever know, this limited, profoundly entrapped way of seeing the world.

I closed my eyes and turned my face to the sky, breathing in the energy of the sun, and prayed. *God. Please. If there's a way to fix this…if it's meant to be fixed…show me how.*

"Nicole?"

I kept still, answering Christian with my eyes shut. "Yeah?"

"If you could be anything in the whole world that you wanted in your next life, what would it be?"

What would I want to be? I opened my eyes and considered his question carefully, taking in my surroundings. The breeze was constant but gentle, and I followed its path as it rustled branches in a line across the tops of the neighboring trees.

"I think I'd want to be a tree," I told him, finally.

"A tree? Why's that?"

"Because. Everyone loves a tree."

"Ah." He nodded. "I see."

"So, what about you? What would you want to be?"

"Well, considering your answer, I suppose I'd want to be a boy, sitting on park bench somewhere beside a tree named Nicole."

As soon as his words registered, I looked at him, only to turn away quickly as my eyes welled with tears. I could think of a hundred conflicts, a hundred arguments as to why I should ignore my own happiness, but as my heart came to a pounding stop, I knew that I was seconds away from telling him that I didn't want to do that anymore. But Christian spoke first.

"There was something I wanted to talk to you about," he said. "Something I needed to tell you."

"There is?"

"Yes. I've been thinking that…oh. Well, it appears we're off again," Christian chuckled as Samantha surprised us both, hopping from the picnic table to wander off toward the house.

Christian followed her, and I furrowed my brow in silent protest of the ill-timed interruption but went along anyway, catching up with them in the bedroom hall. I was surprised to see Samantha standing in the doorway of her room, looking inside.

"Sam?" I said. "You want to play with some toys?"

She ignored me, turning to Christian instead, and said, "Toys."

"Yes," Christian said. "All right. Go in, then."

The little girl glanced into the dark room again, then turned back to Christian and held out her arms. I smiled, and ever compliant, Christian picked Samantha up and turned on the light. We sat on her bed, just as we had before.

"They really need to turn the A/C down," I said, my teeth chattering. "It's way too cold in here."

"It is," Christian said.

In keeping with her practice for the day, Samantha was distracted. She held to Christian tight but fidgeted in his lap, looking back and forth, back and forth between her dresser and her favorite Combatant.

"You want to look at yourself in the mirror, Samantha?" he asked her—a logical conclusion considering that the mirror was the only real point of interest aside from the lamp and a brown, wooden jewelry box.

Christian got up, nearing the dresser with Samantha, and she wrapped her arms around his neck, hiding her face in his shoulder. "What? No? Then it's no to the mirror. Did you want the lamp on, then? Here." He turned the knob on the little orange lamp, but she didn't lift her face from his collar.

"Maybe she wants the jewelry box?" I suggested, noting that it hadn't been there when last we'd visited. Perhaps it was the "toy" she'd been so interested in.

"Hm." Christian lifted the lid of the tiny box, and to my delight, a lovely tune began to play.

"Oh! It's a music box," I said, and then I recognized its song. Twinkle, Twinkle, Little Star.

I wasn't at all surprised when Samantha began to scream, clawing her little fingers into Christian's body, her whole form shaking violently, and I stood up to stand behind them, speaking calmly. "Sweetheart…Samantha…calm down. Shh. It's okay."

"I'm coming!" Carol's voice sounded from down the hall before she rushed into the room, looking mortified. "I'm so sorry, guys," she shouted over the sound of Sam's screaming. "You want me to take her?" Carol offered, holding her arms out to Christian, but Samantha wasn't going anywhere.

"Here, Sam," I said, closing the lid to the music box. She calmed immediately.

"She really hates that bloody song, doesn't she?" Christian said.

"I don't know," Carol said. "I honestly don't think she can make up her mind, since she plays hide and seek with it all the time."

"Hide and seek?" I asked.

"Mhm. It's crazy. I mean, she hates to play with it, so I tried putting it away in her closet a few times, but it's always back on the shelf again the next morning. So she obviously wants it out."

Christian stopped rubbing Samantha's back and peered at the box. "Where in the closet did you put it? Just out of curiosity."

"On the top shelf!" she laughed. "Which is the craziest part. Somehow she managed to climb up there in the middle of the night and get it."

"I see," he said.

I peered at him, questioning everything without words. I was familiar enough with Christian's mannerisms now to realize that he was mulling something over very seriously.

"So, the box must be special to her," Christian continued.

"Oh, it was a gift from an old man we met in Louisiana. A funny old guy—really into Voodoo and stuff. Though he called it Hoodoo, I think."

"And *he* gave Samantha this box?"

"Actually, he gave me the box, and I gave it to Samantha," she said.

"I see. That was very nice of him. Was that long ago?"

"Oh, maybe three years ago."

Three years ago. As I recalled, that was when Samantha's behavior began to change.

"By the way," Christian added, "it's quite cold in here. Any chance your A/C is broken?"

"No. We've had a repairman look into it, but there's nothing wrong with the system. It's just cold sometimes."

That was it. I needed to talk to Christian alone. *Now.*

"Carol, why don't you go back and finish your session," I suggested. "She's fine now."

"Oh, are you sure? I don't mind cutting it short."

Christian shook his head. "No, no. Don't worry. We're good."

"Okay," Carol said reluctantly. "But I'm just across the house if you change your mind."

"Thank you."

Once Mrs. Fitzpatrick was out of ear shot, I said, "Okay, *what* is going on here?"

Christian examined the box with an evil eye. "I suspect this thing is very much haunted," he said. "And if I had to guess by what…well…I'd rather not, frankly."

"And you think it's been hurting her?"

"It's probably been terrorizing her for a long time now," he said, instinctively wrapping his arms around Samantha tightly.

"So what do we do?"

"We destroy the damn thing and hope that's enough. In fact, I'd like to get it out of the house all together."

"How? I mean, how do we explain that to Carol? We can't just say, 'Oh, darn, look at that. We've somehow splintered your rare Cajun collectible to bits, so here, let us take it off your hands.' Should we tell Carol the truth about all this?"

Christian considered my question. "No, I don't think we should. There's no guarantee that destroying the box will destroy the entity, and I think the Fitzpatricks have been through enough. If I could just get it out of here, away from Samantha, maybe Laura could exorcise it properly."

I nodded. "Agreed. So how the hell do we do it?"

"Huh. I wonder…"

"Wonder?"

"I wonder how much it's worth to her?"

"Are you serious? You're going to *buy* it from her?"

"If I have to."

"But what if it's like, a thousand dollars or something?"

"So be it," he said.

"Christian," I sighed, reaching up to touch his face. "You are amazing, you know that?"

He raised an eyebrow. "Took you long enough to admit it."

Christian and I stared at the nasty little brown box in the backseat of his car. So far, we'd made it home without event, but neither of us was thrilled about the prospect of touching the cursed object again, let alone bringing it into the house.

"I can't believe she *gave* it to you," I said, chuckling nervously.

"My lucky day, I guess," Christian said dryly.

"Well, that and the fact that Carol Fitzpatrick has a giant crush on you."

He smirked. "Yes, that bit helped, too."

"So you're going to bring it in, right?"

"Can't wait," he said, grabbing the box and heading toward the house. "Laura!" he called once we were inside. "Are you 'round?"

The Pathcrosser stuck her head out of the laundry room at the sound of her name. "What's up?"

"We need you," I said.

"Okay." She left her chores behind, joining us in the mudroom. "Whatcha got there, kiddies?"

"It's a box, a rather dodgy one," Christian said, holding it out to her.

Laura reached for the box, and we all jumped back a pace as it shot out of her hand, smacking against the wall and sliding under the coat stand.

"Uhm…haunted much?" Laura said.

"Definitely. It's Hoodoo," Christian explained.

"And most likely the root of Samantha's problems," I added.

"Oh, my God. That poor baby," she said, kneeling down in an attempt to retrieve the box again.

"Laura…" I started. "Is it just me, or did that box just growl at you?"

"It's not just you," Laura said. "It—" She jumped back as the object let out an ungodly roar, which naturally attracted the whole house's attention.

Gil and Raj hunched in close, and Gil arched his head down to stare at whatever Laura was so engrossed in. "It's a box," Gil said.

"Thank you," Laura remarked.

"And it's pissed," I told them. "So stay back."

"A box is pissed?" Adalia questioned, stooping down to join the group.

"It's possessed," Christian corrected her.

"A box is possessed?" she asked.

"Yes," Laura laughed. "And it seems to know exactly what I am, too. Now, Addy, Gil, everyone, can I get some air here?"

The group took several steps back, and Laura stood up. "Christian? Can you help me out?"

"Certainly. What shall I do?"

"I'm hoping you can hold the slippery little bastard for me."

"All right. Let's see." He bent to grab the box with both hands, and it didn't make a peep.

Laura moped. "Well, way to make it look easy, Mr. Combatant."

"Sorry," Christian muttered.

"Let's just get this over with," she said, rubbing her hands together. "Now. Come on out, you pain in the ass."

She was using all her energy to draw the astral forward, I could see that. It must have really, *really* liked its box, because Laura never had such a hard time pulling a possessing spirit from its host.

"Are you serious?" she huffed at the box. "What kind of shit did they use to mix you together?"

As if answering her, the object growled again, even more menacingly, and I fixated on the very bottom corner, where a waft of shadowy black was pouring out of a crack in the wood.

"Christian…once this…jackass is…out…" Laura strained, trying not to lose her focus, "smash the…box and then…grab him…for me…please!"

Christian nodded, and after a few more exhaustive moments, the last bit of shadow seeped out of the wood, and Laura said, "Now!"

With that, Christian dropped the object and stomped on it hard, splintering the thing into pieces, and then threw his arm out, grabbing hold of the shapeless shadow. "There now," he said. "Much better."

"Yup," Laura said, once again pushing her energy forward, and thankfully, she hardly had to try at all this time. The astral lit up at once in a raging white ball, and Christian dropped his hand, shaking it.

"Sorry about the heat," Laura apologized.

"Think nothing of it," Christian said, his eyes on the burning white blast. In no time at all, the flaming entity burned itself out and its ashes fell to the floor.

Laura cracked her knuckles. "Phew, that was a doozy," she said. "I swear, when the wrong people try to manipulate energy, bad things happen."

"I second that," Christian agreed.

"So tell me the back story, guys. How the hell did the Fitzpatricks get a hold of a Hoodoo box?"

"Carol said an old man gave it to her when they visited New Orleans," I said. "But why would someone be so sadistic as to give an innocent person a possessed box?"

"Well, it's possible that the old man was possessed himself. Or maybe he was scared of it, and just wanted it off his hands, you know? People do crazy things when they're desperate."

"I guess. So now that we know about all this, Christian thinks the entity could have been messing with Samantha. What do you think?"

"I lmph. Definitely. Where'd they keep it?"

"In her bedroom."

"What?! Why?"

"Carol thought Sam liked it, so she gave it to her."

"Holy shit. That poor little girl. Well, God, it probably gave her horrible nightmares, maybe it kept her up at night, and who *knows* what it did to her energy. But…what made you guys think to bring it here? What clued you in?"

"A few reasons," Christian said. "For one, Samantha clung to me any time we were in her bedroom, so something clearly bothered her in there. And then she was oddly fascinated with it, but didn't want to go near it at the same time. Then when we opened the box and it started playing some music, she went bonkers."

I nodded, adding, "The song. Remember, Laura? I told you how she hated it when I played Mozart? Well, that's why."

Laura took a dramatic inhale. "Son of a gun. So, the answer was there all along, huh?"

"I guess. But I wouldn't have known without Christian's expertise."

Christian turned to me. "Nicole…*no* one would have known if it wasn't for you."

"That's right, honey," Laura said.

"Then it was a team effort," I said.

"All right. That's a fair compromise," Christian concurred.

Chapter Twenty-Three

I couldn't sleep. All I could do was think. Think about Samantha, about how much better her life would likely become. Maybe she'd talk again. Maybe she'd use full sentences or laugh or any number of normal, childish things. But as much as I wanted to sound the trumpets, I knew I should wait a few weeks and make sure that the astral hadn't somehow done irreparable damage. Wendell suspected that things would improve quickly now, that her parents would be able to continue her therapy at home until she'd recovered, but I was still going to hold off the celebration until I'd seen the signs for myself. The idea was too wonderful to count on quite yet.

And then there was Christian.

It always seemed to come back to him, somehow, even in spite of all my efforts to deny it. The whole situation was beyond my meager will now. From day one, Christian had latched onto my heart and wouldn't let go, and no matter how I'd tried to push him away, he simply wouldn't have it. So why was I fighting him anymore? Why was I being such a fool? And why was I lying here thinking, thinking…always *thinking*, when he was just down the hall, a few meaningless feet from me?

Throwing off the covers, I sat up quickly. I could do this. I wanted this.

My knees shook as I left my bedroom, crossing the hall to his door. Well…this was déjà vu. I'd been here before, but it was all wrong then. I swallowed hard and felt my heart beating like crazy. With all that blood pumping around, you'd have thought I'd be hot, but the feeling I had at the moment was more akin to cold sweats. I was truly afraid. I'd never initiated anything I'd ever wanted in my entire life. This was the scariest thing I'd ever do.

Leaning forward, I rested my forehead on the door, breathing out and laughing quietly. "Don't puke, Nicole," I whispered. "You can faint, but don't puke."

Swallowing again, I tried to slow down my breathing, and then I did something completely insane. I knocked on the door…and then cringed like crazy.

Why the hell did you knock on his door? You idiot! It's eleven o'clock! He's probably sleeping. And what if you wake someone else! Idiot, idiot, idiot, idi—

The door opened and I jumped back, somehow shocked to see him there.

"Hello," he said, chuckling at me. "Are you selling cookies, little girl?"

"I…" Don't vomit. Don't vomit.

"Are you all right? You look as if you might vomit."

Don't vomit!

I held my breath, but quickly realized this was a bad idea when my head began to swim. "Chr…istian. Can I come in?"

He raised an eyebrow, then composed himself, stepping to the side and saying, "Yes, by all means. Please, come in."

With the door closed behind us, I wasn't certain if I felt better or worse. I only knew that my knees were ready to give out at any minute. I needed to sit down, but his bed was the only place for that. Oh God. *Don't vomit!*

"Nicky, would you like to sit down?" he asked.

I nodded, and he laid a hand on my back, ushering me to the bed.

"So, as long as you're here," he began, taking a seat beside me. "Shall we play a game of Scrabble?"

I pursed my lips and then gave up, giggling. "I came to talk to you," I said at last. "Obviously. Though I'm doing a really awful job of it."

"Hm." He nodded, hinting at a smile. "Well, try again, then. We'll just call that other business a rehearsal."

"Okay. Well…I've…I've been thinking."

He eyed me with that restrained grin still playing at his lips and nodded in encouragement.

I swallowed another lump in my throat and pressed on. "Just…about, I mean, not to presume that there's…I mean…that it's not too late for…" I stared at my lap, locking my fingers together. "For…"

He chuckled and knocked his shoulder into mine. "For?"

"I…I'm…" I shook my head, finally looking at him with an exasperated expression. "I don't know how to do this."

"Do what?" he asked, leaning in close. "Would it help if you whispered?"

I laughed again. "It would help if I was someone else."

"Ah. But I don't think so, because I wouldn't have let you in then."

I smiled, hit with a sudden sense of release. It wouldn't matter what he said. I had to tell him how I felt for my own sake. I'd deal with the consequences after. "Christian, I don't know if I have any right in the world to say this. I don't know if I deserve to say this, and it may backfire in my face, but I can't live my life knowing that I didn't at least tell the truth."

"Nicole," he chimed in, his expression turning serious. "Before you go on, I never got to talk to you this afternoon, remember? At Sam's?"

"Oh, yeah, I forgot about that."

"Yes, and, depending on what you're about to tell me, well, it's probably best if I talk first."

My heart fell. "Okay." I forced a smile. "Go ahead."

He nodded. "Well, your father was right about something."

I was sure an amoeba living on Mars could read the skepticism on my face.

"Er, indirectly, anyway," he corrected. "You see, at first I was angry after my run-in with your father, after he asked Wendell to kick me out, but then it occurred to me that he was right. I *should* leave."

"What?" I whispered.

"Nicole, I've been running away from things for too long. If it was hard to see, hard to understand, I just took off. And when I think of my sister and my mum, they've been so patient. And Abram. I left him with only one Combatant. That was so selfish of me. I mean, all my life they've let me run off and do whatever I had to without a single complaint. They've supported everything, no matter how wrong or right I was. And if I leave here, Wendell can easily replace me, not that he'd need to, with Elaine and your father. But, poor Abram doesn't have the cooperation of the Society, and you'll notice, he hasn't been able to fill my post yet." He shook his head. "My father's memory deserves better than what I've done. He wanted me to live my own life, to be happy, but he also wanted me to do the right thing for those who deserve it. And I have to go back."

While he spoke, I'd been wiping away tears. If he felt like he did, if this would put his mind at ease, who was I to hold him back? But one thing was sickeningly certain. When he left, he'd take the air with him. In fact, I already felt like I was suffocating.

I sniffled. "When will you leave?"

"The end of the month."

"That's next week."

"Yes."

I nodded, clenching every muscle to hold back the onslaught. "Well, thank you for telling me," I said, my voice wavering and breaking.

"Nicole…"

"No, yeah, I mean, yeah. This is good. This will be good for you."

"Nicky, listen…"

"Samantha will miss you," I said, standing up quickly. "I can record some videos so you'll see if she talks…when…when she…" And then I lost it, weeping silently as I lumbered toward the door.

"No!" Christian practically leaped for the exit, blocking me from leaving. "Nicole…" He reached for me, taking my face in his hands. "Come with me."

I shook my head. "What do you mean?"

"I mean *come with me*. Leave all this behind and come with me to Abram's."

"Leave? Christian, I can't leave! My mom is here. She needs me!"

"Then bring her!"

"I can't! My dad would never agree to that. And besides, Christian, this is all she knows. This is safety to her."

"To her? Or to you?" he asked, dropping his hands from my face.

"I'm sorry?"

"Tell me something. How many able-bodied adults live in this house? What is it, eight, not counting you and me? So when did everyone get together and vote you primary caregiver of your own mother?"

"They…they didn't have to. It was just…"

"What? Expected? Because fuck them if that's the case. And shame on you for buying into it."

"Christian—"

"*You're* the one obsessed with being safe, Nicole. You're my absolute, polar opposite in that regard. You've tied yourself down, you've kept yourself here and unhappy because you didn't believe you deserved to be anything else. And now you have the chance to be happy and you're going to throw it away?"

"Throw what away?"

"Bloody Christ, I *love* you, Nicole! I fucking adore you, and you love me, too! You said it to Laura!"

"Laura…" Son of a bitch. *The walky-talkies!* "So, you *were* listening in? You had no right—"

"Oh, stop it. It wasn't on purpose—at least, not on my part, anyway. But I'm glad I heard it. God knows you weren't going to tell me the truth otherwise."

"Well, there's a reason for that, Christian. I was trying to do the right thing. I was trying to keep from weighing you down. Just because you want something, that doesn't mean it's what's best for you. It doesn't mean it's what you need."

Christian seethed, towering over me and looking me right in the eye. "Listen, Nicole, I've had all I can take of you telling me what I need. Have you ever stopped to think that maybe you're exactly what I need? That maybe, in the middle of all this miserable neck-snapping and repelling and crossing the bloody hell over, all I really want is *someone*…someone good who will let me be a fucking man? Just a fucking human being with flaws and unenlightened days? Is that too much to ask? That you let me fucking love you, Nicole? Because *that's* what I need! That's all I'd ever need from you. Just to love you. Can you deny me that?"

I was overwhelmed, and it felt like every tear I'd ever held back wanted to pour its way out of me tonight. "I…can't leave her," I said. "I can't."

"Please." Christian grabbed my shoulders. "Just say you love me. Say it out loud."

I shook my head. I couldn't say it now. His news had changed everything, and my resolve was set in a much bleaker way. I opened my mouth to speak when Christian dropped all reserve. Without warning, I was pressed firmly against the wall behind me, with his lips on me, his body pressed into mine, and everything in my head just blew away. It was unfair. It was cruel to do this before I could take my stand, before I could make up my mind, but it was impossible to do anything but feel him now, warm and wet, pliant and eager, so powerfully sure that I could shut the consequence of tomorrow away. The way his tongue found mine, melding our mouths together, one moment angry, one moment slow and deep, shredded my judgment. I couldn't bring myself to stop him. A blink of happiness was still happiness, after all. It was still more than I had ever known.

There wasn't a cell in my body that didn't want him on me. There wasn't a thing I could refuse him in this moment, and as he turned and pressed me into the bed, I melted beneath him, absolutely overcome.

Gripping my shorts, he slipped them down to my knees and then hooked his finger into my underwear. "Up, Nicole," he ordered.

I complied at once, only wondering at my own boldness for an instant as he pulled them down to my ankles, alternating between their removal and fumbling to unzip his jeans. A few botched efforts later, he'd tugged his pants off and pulled the blanket over us.

Burying his mouth in my neck, he took the flesh between his teeth, and then parted my thighs with the back of his hand, pressing his thumb into my skin. "Nick…Nicole…I want you to look at me."

I made myself do as he asked, though my cheeks blazed in a blend of embarrassment and arousal. He positioned himself at my entrance and kissed me again, then, with his lips still on me, he entered me quickly, sucking my tongue into his mouth to muffle our moans.

There was no way to wrap my head around this miracle, this beautiful man moving insistently inside of me. But he was so very warm and so close, and I wanted him here. I could try to convince myself otherwise, but my body gave me away. I wrapped my arms around his shoulders and he picked up speed, thrusting deeply.

Lifting his head, he locked eyes with me. "Say you love me."

As if I had a choice. As if I could lie to him now—like this.

"I love you. Always."

He smiled, lowering his face so that our foreheads rested together. "I want to touch you," he whispered, ceasing the motions of his body. Then his palm spread across my stomach and he slipped it between us. His fingertips explored my center, feeling for the swell there, and as he made contact, I moaned.

"God, you're so wet." The movement of his hips turned erratic, his body trembling. He was close. *I could give him this.* The very idea had me clawing at his back, crazed with the need to see it, to feel it. But Christian's hand was unrelenting, his resolve obviously set on seeing me peak first, and the feeling rose and rose and screamed out of me in a blast of moisture and clenched muscles. I gasped and cried out, whimpering against his cheek.

"Ugh…*beautiful*," he moaned, panting, and his muscles tensed, then rippled. "Nick…I'm…"

"*Yes, please,*" I urged him. "*Please.*"

He gritted his teeth, his jaw set tightly, and dropped his head, kissing me and cursing indistinctly. Entering me fully, he held firm there, at the deepest part of me, shuddering against my body, and I wrapped my legs around him, clinging with all my strength, waiting for the vibrations in his body to still.

When he'd finally come down, he gazed at me through hooded eyes and said, "I haven't" —he paused to kiss me languidly— "felt this good in a long time." He shuddered again. "A long time, Nicole."

❧

I'd never woken up with anyone before, and as I felt Christian's arms around my waist, his breath on my back, it seemed that there had never been a place so sheltered, so peaceful as this, with the smell of him all over me—it was beyond reason. How could I refuse this? How could I say no to this?

But the inevitable decision wasn't as simple as what felt good versus what didn't. Christian had said that he needed to find a balance between his own happiness and doing the right thing. Well, wasn't that my situation, too? How could I possibly trust anyone else to care for my mother? Was it wrong of me to consider the possibility of leaving? Was it wrong of me not to? Or was there no right and wrong in any of this?

I slid as softly as possible from Christian's arms, praying that he was a deep sleeper, and pulled my clothes on, creeping across the room to the door.

"You aren't sneaking out on me, are you?" Christian muttered groggily. "I didn't take you for the love 'em and leave 'em type."

Sighing, I turned around to see Christian leaning on one arm, smirking through tired eyes.

"Well, I kind of wanted to get presentable before anyone woke up."

"Oh, piss it. We have plenty of time. Look, the sun's not finished rising yet. Come back here."

Wanting to keep the peace, I wandered over to his side of the bed to sit down, and Christian lay back, pulling me on top of him so that I faced the ceiling. "Here we are," he said.

"This is an odd position, Christian."

He wrapped his arms around my waist like a seatbelt. "I don't know, it feels just fine to me."

"Yeah, but I can't move."

"That's the idea," he said, brushing his lips against my ear.

"Oh," I chuckled, shivering.

"So, I was thinking about Pennsylvania, and we'd probably want a place of our own, you know? I mean, it's completely crowded around Abram's, and surely we could find a flat with a monthly lease."

"Christian…"

"Or at the very least, maybe we could talk Abram—"

"Christian, *hang on*."

He went silent, and I pulled from his grasp, searching for something to say. In the meantime, tired of waiting, Christian sat up to look at me, narrowing his eyes before he spoke. "You don't honestly mean that you're still considering staying here? Even after last night?"

"I just need to think about it. I just need to think."

"Nick, for the love of God—"

"Let's not ruin this, please."

"Ruin it? How would we ruin it?"

"Because I don't have an answer for you, Christian!" I admitted, standing up. "I need some time. I'm sorry."

For a horribly awkward moment, everything was silent as Christian glared at me. Then he exhaled an aggravated laugh, shaking his head and lifting his hands to rub his face. "Fine."

"Listen, I'm not—"

"I said fine."

☙

He loved me.

The phrase rang through my head all morning. As I showered, as I dressed, as I brushed my teeth, and set up music books for my eight o'clock student. It didn't matter if I'd made him angry. It didn't matter if I'd left his room on questionable terms. He loved me, and that had me flying—that is, until my mother woke, shuffling down the stairs to the couch and sitting down to a blank TV. Right about now, I would normally have breakfast waiting for her to eat while she watched *Good Morning America*. This had become her new routine, one of many rituals that held her together. But I'd forgotten all about her breakfast today, and suddenly I felt terribly ashamed.

Who else would make her oatmeal? Who else would protect her from the dishwasher? Who else would explain to her a hundred times a day who in the hell all these people were?

But he loves me, I told the universe. And of course, as predicted, the son of a bitch didn't answer. It just kept its mouth shut like it always did, laughing at my maddening state of cluelessness and non-sentience.

What was *my* fate? What was *my* destiny? Where was my road map? Everybody else in this damned house had their paint line drawn for them, but not me. And yeah, yeah, I knew they'd had their fair share of confusing past lives, enough of them to warrant a clearer present one, but I was still so tired of knowing their secrets, of keeping them, but not benefiting from them.

Stomping into the kitchen, I pulled out a packet of instant oatmeal and microwaved it, and then I carried the bowl into the living room to my mom, setting it on the coffee table and turning on her TV show. "Here, Mom," I said, charging out of the room and into the kitchen again.

I was angry now, which was easier than scared and easier than sad, so I could see how my father preferred the emotion. Oddly, Dad did seem to be choosing the cowardly approach lately, avoiding Christian, never looking me in the eye. Was he really afraid of us? Or was he just pissed off that Christian had wounded his ego in front of everyone? Of course, anger came with its own price. For the first time ever, I felt myself resenting my mother, something I never imagined possible, and the emotion confused me even more. If I stayed here with her, what kind of person would I become? What kind of a daughter? Didn't stagnant things rot?

Considering my present state of mind, I nearly broke the phone when it rang. But as soon as I heard Carol Fitzpatrick's shaking voice on the other end, I pulled it together.

"Carol? What's the matter?" I said. "What's wrong?"

"Nothing's wrong! I know it's a Saturday, Nicole, and I'm sorry to call so early, but oh my God! You have to come over as soon as possible!"

"So everything's okay?"

"She's talking! She's talking, Nicole. She's talking!"

"Talking? You mean…like how?"

"I mean talking! I don't know how, but you guys finally broke through to her. She's hungry! She woke up asking for bagels!"

"She…what?" I laughed into the phone.

"Bagels! My baby wanted bagels!"

"And did you give her some?"

"Are you kidding?! I got her bagels and donuts and scones and I bought half the bakery!" Carol said, half-laughing, half-crying.

"Oh, Carol," I beamed. "This is amazing."

"I know! God, I know. When can you come over?"

"Well, I have students this morning, and Christian is still asleep, but after lunch?"

"Okay. Yes! And Phillip is here. Oh, God, Nicky, I'm freaking out!"

"Understandable," I said, grinning so hard my cheeks hurt. Stupid Hoodoo spirit got exactly what it deserved. And now, it looked like the Fitzpatricks would, as well.

❧

After Christian woke up, I wasted no time in telling him about Samantha. He was so excited that he'd nearly jumped in his car and driven over there himself, but he refrained considering that *I* was her therapist. And between my morning full of students and everyone's very clear knowledge of what Christian and I had done the night before (if the noise didn't tell them, our auras surely did), he and I hadn't had a moment alone to discuss our little morning-after debacle.

Now, here we were in a car together, and it was kind of unavoidable. Knowing Christian, he'd want an answer. And he deserved one—if only I had one to give. Finally, Christian pulled the car into park in front of Samantha's house. Then he turned to me with a very sober look on his face, and I knew to brace for the real deal.

"I just want you to know that I realize you have a life out here," he said. "That you've built a career and that you're a remarkable woman, and I didn't intend to belittle what you have in any way. I respect your dedication to your mother, Nicole. I can relate to it well. Plus, I didn't mean to press you for a decision on the spot, either. It was…it was impetuous of me, but you need to know that my feelings still stand. I want you with me. I love you, and if you don't come back to Philadelphia I'll be a complete wreck. But regardless" —he frowned, sighing in the most pathetic way— "I won't drive you insane about it. I promise."

He had no idea how grateful I was for the reprieve. "Thank you."

"You're welcome."

"Now let's go meet the real Samantha, shall we?"

Christian smiled. "I can't wait," he said, and we headed for the house.

This time, Phillip Fitzpatrick opened the door, looking frazzled and disheveled with wild hair and oversized glasses. "You're here!"

"Where is she?" I asked, grinning excitedly.

"They're in the yard," Phillip practically giggled, and Christian and I followed him around to the back of the house to find Carol sitting in the grass with Samantha in her lap, the two of them concentrated on a feather in Carol's hand.

Mrs. Fitzpatrick kissed her daughter's cheek and said, "Wanna touch it?"

Samantha nodded, reaching out to take the feather. She lifted it up and held it out so the light would shine through.

"Do you like it?" Carol asked. "It's soft, isn't it?"

The little girl nodded again, twirling the feather around between her fingers. Then Carol noticed we had joined them. "Oh, hey, we have guests," she grinned, pointing toward us. "See?"

Samantha lowered her face to look at us, her tiny forehead creased in thought. Then, very slowly, she climbed out of her mother's lap and wandered in our direction. I held my breath—the anticipation nearly killing me—and then knelt down in front of her. "Samantha?" I looked her deeply in the eye, and she responded by reaching out to touch my face.

"Hi, Nicole," she said.

I nearly came undone, grabbing her up in a monumental hug and kissing her face repeatedly. "You know me!" I exclaimed, pulling away to look at her again. "Hi!" I said, laughing. "Your mom says you've been eating bagels."

Samantha smiled. "They're good."

"They are!" Christian spoke, and Samantha's eyes went wide. From the look on her face, she'd just now recognized who he was. It was intense, the way she examined him, the way her smile had changed into an expression much older, much more profound. "Can I get a hug, too?" Christian requested, holding his arms out gingerly.

With that, Samantha's little lip quivered, her eyes moistened, and she flew into his arms, weeping silently. Phillip Fitzpatrick moved to intercede, but Carol grabbed her husband's pant leg and held him back, shaking her head.

Christian wrapped Samantha fully in his arms, whispering, "Don't cry, Sam. It's okay now."

She lifted her head, and Christian offered her his sleeve, which she made use of, drying her eyes clumsily between hiccupping breaths. "Is your magic gone?" she asked him.

Christian cocked his head to the side. "Magic?" he chuckled.

"Where did the light go?"

The light…she had seen his light?

Christian leaned in, whispering, "It's still here, Samantha, but I guess you don't need it now."

She stared at him thoughtfully. "Did you make the bad dreams go away?"

Christian nodded. "I helped," he said, "but Nicole did most of the work."

This was a marvel. Somehow, Samantha had been seeing Christian's aura, and she'd recognized its particular strength, though she wouldn't have known why. As a Combatant, Christian's energy must have felt more protective than most of the other Sentients Samantha had unwittingly met, but she'd never reacted the same way to Elaine or my father, so it wasn't just the combatance that attracted her. Christian deserved more credit than that. It was his heart, his soul that she was feeling. I'd asked the universe for an answer, and it had been standing right there beside me all the while.

But *how* had she seen what she did? How could she have recognized his energy? It had to be some kind of adaptation. Just as the blind develop a keen sense of hearing, maybe Samantha's spirit had illuminated what her mind could not. In the absence of distraction from normal human knowledge, Samantha had been granted a broader view. She may not have comprehended, but she understood.

Chapter Twenty-Four

The salty surf mingled with sand and fizzled between my toes, and I buried them deeper, sitting back with my weight on my hands so I could take the sight in properly. I was freezing. I'd been out here for who knows how long, just staring, just thinking, but the soothing pulse of the water, the inhale and exhale of the waves, was ideal for luring me into a trance. So, even if I could only feel my uppermost appendages anymore, it was worth it. The end of the day was just now reaching its pinnacle—the sun a giant orange globe, sealed to the horizon with blue streaks and a pinkish glow, and the water beneath it splattered in pastel ink.

"Want some company?" Wendell's voice startled me half to death.

"Wendell! Shit…sorry," I said, laughing as I caught my breath.

"No, *I'm* sorry," he said, plopping down beside me. "I'll make more noise next time."

"It's okay. I'm recovered."

"This is good," he said, and then he wrapped an arm around my shoulder and gave me a squeeze. "Talked to Carol again today," he said. "She can't stop thanking me for the referral."

I sighed happily. "You know, she called me five days in a row with updates? Twice yesterday. It's like she's watching Samantha grow up in high speed."

"Well, essentially, she is."

"Yep. Sam's got a few years' worth of backed-up development to make up for, and she's not wasting any time."

"Evidently," he agreed. "So…what from here?"

"From here?"

"Yeah. What's the plan?"

Plan?

Oh, yeah. That.

Christian was leaving tomorrow, and I still hadn't acknowledged it to myself, let alone given him a definitive answer. I was an absolute ostrich. And in turn, Christian had been distant with me the last few days. True, it was probably a device of self-protection, but he was also keeping his promise. No pressure. So here I was, countdown practically over, and I would have to make a choice.

"I guess I still have an in-box full of people that a certain Seer has convinced of my brilliance," I said to Wendell.

"Hm. That's true," he said. "You could go that route."

"Yes."

He nodded, smiling a little. "Or not."

"Or not?"

"Exactly."

Or not? Just as simple as that? "There are lots of 'buts' attached to that latter option, Wendell."

"Nah."

I peered at him. "'Nah'? Are you serious, Wendell? Where's the sage advice? The wise counsel?"

He laughed at me. "Since when do I give out sage advice, Nick? My sage advice is not to give out sage advice."

"Ugh, but I could use some right now!"

"So, let me get this straight, you want *me*…to tell *you*…how to live your life."

"No. I mean, no, of course not." Did I?

He continued on, smirking all the while. "You want me to say, 'Nicole, it's okay for you to go to Pennsylvania. It'll all be easy after that. Your mom won't miss you, your dad won't be angry.' Or were you hoping that I'd ask you to stay?"

Well…what did I want him to tell me? "I don't know. I just wanted an opinion."

"Exactly. So have one."

"What?"

"A soul evolves from making choices, right? Some are healthy ones, some aren't. But most are completely benign in the grand scheme of things. Choices move us forward, you know? Like dots on a triptych. There's no judgment, and you're allowed to draw your own map any way you like. So, why do you keep working off everyone else's?"

"What?"

Wendell sighed and stood up, wiping sand off his khakis. "You want an opinion? What shouts with joy from the deepest part of your heart?" he asked in an excited voice. "What ignites your spirit? Make your *own* choices, Nicole," he said, walking back toward the house. "And then be happy with them!"

❧

Christian was the most organized male I'd ever met. As long as he'd been with us, his room was always immaculate, he was on time for everything, and, not surprisingly, his bags were already neatly packed, ready by the mudroom door the night before he was to leave for Pennsylvania.

Now that the morning had come, everyone was saying their goodbyes, helping Christian with his luggage, exchanging hugs and handshakes at his car while I stayed out of their way, waiting for each one to have their moment so that I could have mine.

After Wendell's pronouncement, I had hidden in my room, thinking through a conclusion that I could live with. I'd felt around the recesses of my heart and made a choice. And now, I'd just have to be strong enough to deal with it.

It wasn't like he didn't know. There were giveaways—like my lack of bags, or the fact that I hadn't cancelled any of my students. But I was still dreading the goodbye. I didn't know if my heart could take it.

Standing in front of him, I pleaded without words, searching his face for understanding. "If things were different…if my dad was different," I started, absolutely ordering myself not to cry, "then nothing could have stopped me from coming with you."

Christian's eyes narrowed and watered, and he nodded curtly.

"She has to come first," I said more quietly as my father passed us, garbage bag in hand, on his way to the dumpster.

Christian glanced at my father for a second before speaking louder than necessary. "You have to do what you have to do. I understand that. But I love you, Nicole, so before I leave, I just need to ask you a favor. You've got to promise me that you won't shrivel up and die, that you won't bear the weight of your *father's* inadequacies until you have no heart left to give."

"That wouldn't happen."

"Don't be so sure," he said. "We're a botched up pair of opposites, you and me. I've spent a good bit of my life running away, while you've lived yours in hiding. That's not what your mother would have wanted for you, and God knows I don't want to hurt you, but if anyone's in danger of turning into your father, *you* are." I shook my head, but he pressed on. "And for what? Shame? Guilt? Don't double your tragedies, Nicole. No one knows how that works better than me."

By now, my whole body was shaking, and after croaking, "Have a safe trip," I fled for the house, banging into a snooping crowd on my way to the first secluded place I could reach.

Locking myself in the bathroom, I buried my face in my hands and shouted in frustration. There was no way in hell I would *ever* become my father. The notion was insulting! I mean, my father was terrified of anything he didn't understand. My father was set in his ways. My father was unreasonable and uncompromising. He was alone.

Then, like a cannonball to the stomach, I knew that Christian was right.

I was terrified of what I didn't understand. I was set in my ways. I was unreasonable and uncompromising. I was alone.

I was alone.

Jolting up, I pulled the bathroom door opened and rushed into the kitchen, only to hear Christian's car peeling out of the driveway.

"Miss Abbot?"

When I was twelve years old I'd had my tonsils taken out, and I couldn't remember much from the experience, other than an abundance of lime sherbet and the struggle to wake up after the anesthesia started wearing off. It was an odd feeling—like you were swimming up through a sea full of fog, trying to remember yourself.

I hadn't been able to break the surface since Christian left.

"Miss Abbot?"

But I'd made up my mind, in spite of Laura's consternation, in spite of my own uncertainty, I'd made a decision, by damn it. And I'd stuck to it.

"Uhm, excuse me?" My most anal retentive piano student tugged at the end of my sleeve.

"Huh? Oh, Peter, I'm sorry. Kind of zoned out there, didn't I?"

"Yeah. That's okay, Miss Abbot."

I'd been "zoning out there" for a week, and my students probably thought I was losing my mind. Hell, maybe I was. I felt heavy and numb, like my heart had stopped. But I wasn't dead; that couldn't be it. Laura would definitely have told me if *that* had happened.

"I can't find my second lesson." Peter frowned, rifling through a stack of starter books.

"Book two? It's in the bench," I said, and he stood up to let me have access.

I opened the lid and grabbed the books, with several slipping from the bottom of the pile and onto the floor. Bending to retrieve them, something caught my eye, glinting red and gold from beside the foot of the piano.

"Hey," I said, picking up the worry stone that Ginny had given me in Philadelphia.

Try not to lose it, she'd said. Right. I'd failed at that one.

"What's that?" Peter asked.

"It's a worry stone," I told him.

"What's a worry stone?"

"Well, it's this rock that's been worn until it's smooth to the touch, and then they make an indent in it, like this." I pointed out the nook in its center. "You're supposed to rub it when you get worried."

"Hm. That's kinda dumb," Peter said, ever a downer.

I raised an eyebrow. If anyone needed a worry stone, it was Peter. "I don't know…I like it," I said, replaying Ginny's words in my head.

And water ran over it and over it, and it used to be all rough and sharp, but now it's not.

Kind of like people, I guess. Maybe even my father would soften at the edges someday…or maybe Duncan Abbot was one rock that would never smooth out naturally. Maybe fate would have to take a sandblaster to him or something.

Peter had been my last in a long afternoon of students, and after dinner, I sorted through e-mails, reviewing my list of disordered children, desperate parents, all of them hoping that I could somehow repair their lives. But that seemed laughable now, since I was pretty sure one of the qualifications for therapy work was giving a shit. Unfortunately, all I could find the energy to do was read the messages anymore, just like I'd done the night before and the night before that. I didn't have the heart to e-mail anyone back. I couldn't bring myself to choose a new Samantha, and that scared the living shit out of me.

I needed comfort, and for once, I was going downstairs to fix *myself* some tea.

Standing over a steeping kettle of Chai, I let the rising steam warm my cheeks, inhaling the sweet, spicy scent. I would take my mug up to my room and hide. Maybe I'd even go to bed early.

"Can you take this to your dad?" Laura dropped a wrench on the kitchen counter in a rush. "He's working on his car."

I scowled at the tool. "Do I have to?"

"Sorry! Running late!"

Grumbling, I grabbed the stupid wrench and headed outside. The hood of my dad's truck was up, and his head was hidden behind it. He'd always insisted on fixing his own car, of course. Why waste money on a mechanic when he could handle the upkeep of his vehicles just fine all by himself?

Damn diesel engines grated on my last nerve. Besides the fact that his truck was a gas-guzzling monster, it was loud as hell. In retrospect, the roaring clatter did kind of make for a fitting heads up to his arrival.

Clonking the wrench down on the hot engine beside him, I spun around, crunching gravel noisily underfoot in my haste to leave.

"You shoulda gone with him."

I paused. "What?"

"You shoulda left," he muttered gruffly. "There's nothing for you here."

I turned back around, unable to process what I'd just heard, and watched as he worked the wrench into a tizzy. "I don't understand."

"After everything that's happened, you *should!* Obviously Christian's not what I thought he was. He's soft. You two are more compatible than I thought. And while I'm at it, did I ask you to be a martyr? No. You did that yourself!" he launched angrily. "And don't look at me like that, Nicole. You know what the hell I mean."

"I wasn't trying to be a martyr, but *someone* has to take care of Mom," I said. "And you never tried, so what am I supposed to think?"

He dropped the wrench on the car and it clattered to the ground. "So this is *my* fault?"

"What's your fault?"

"The fact that you're weak?"

"I'm not weak, Dad."

"Well, that's how it looks to me."

"And, as usual, you're wrong." I raised my voice, welling with a very powerful, very foreign emotion that strangely resembled anger. *Was I really going to do this?*

Yes. Yes, I was!

"You think everyone should be loud and demanding and angry or they're not worth a damn. But that's bullshit, Dad! There's courage in peace, too, and there's strength in having the willpower to shut the hell up!"

Duncan stared at me, his mouth gaping, and then he bent to grab his wrench and return to the car engine. "Fine. Then I can take care of my own wife. Go to Pennsylvania, Nicole."

"Pennsylvania? But you said Christian—"

"I *changed* my damn mind!" he roared, slamming the wrench down again. "Shit," he mumbled, shaking his head. "I should have known that vampire thing was a fluke. Laura doesn't know what the fuck she's talking about."

Son of a…"You know what, Dad? The hell with you! If I choose to go to Pennsylvania, I will. And if I want to stay here, I'll stay here! This is *my* life, not yours, so keep out of it!" I shouted, resisting the urge to stomp my foot as I left him outside.

What the hell was he doing? And what made him think I'd just up and leave my mother in his care? The jackass. All of a sudden he was going to try to be valiant? All of a sudden he was going to start making sacrifices? And how ironic, considering the present condition of my father's face, that he'd have the nerve to call Christian soft.

Barging into the kitchen, I cursed under my breath, opening the fridge to stare blankly and then slamming it closed again.

"I take it your dad talked to you," Laura said, entering the room.

"Yes," I snapped at her. "And why are you still here?"

"I lied."

"What?"

"I lied, Nick. I didn't have to leave yet. I just wanted to get you out there to talk to Duncan."

"Then…you know what he said?"

"Yes. We all had a nice little chat with your father last night, and we came to a conclusion. Elaine! Show time," she called, and like clockwork, everyone but my father piled into the kitchen, shuffling around in various states of unease. Only Wendell and Laura looked me in the eye.

"So, now that we're all here," Laura started, "we have something to say, so hear us out, all right?"

I nodded. "Okay."

"Good. Well, it's simple, babe. We've unanimously concluded that there's been a serious mix-up in communication around here for quite some time. And in the name of clarification, we'd like to point a few things out."

"Uh huh," I said, eyebrow raised. "Such as?"

"For one, we happen to be quite competent. We can cook breakfast, we can make tea, we can walk without tripping, we can turn the dial on the television. In fact, most of us are pretty fine huggers, as well."

"Uhm…congrats?"

"And for another thing, not one of us here—not *one*—has ever held you responsible for what happened to your mother. That's a myth that needs busting right now, Nicole."

Blushing, I countered, "I never said—"

"You didn't have to!" Elaine interjected. "The guilt is stamped all over your face in red ink, hon. It's decided every move you've made since your mom got hurt."

"She's right," Laura said. "And frankly, it's kind of insulting that you won't trust us with Rita. I mean, I know she's your mother and all, but come on, kid. She's still my best friend. She's my family. We can take care of her. We *want* to take care of her, Nicky. And we want you to start living your life now."

"Laura, I'm—"

"Look, we can't make your decisions for you…mainly because Wendell won't let us." She gave our Seer the stink eye. "But we can make your life a living hell in the meantime."

"That's right," Gil added. "I'll spike all your drinks with espresso. You'll never sleep again."

"And I'll start burning all the *naan*," Raj said.

I gasped. "Rajeep. That's sacrilege!"

"I'll do what I have to."

Slack-jawed and flustered, I stuttered, "I…I don't know what to say."

Laura responded by pulling her cell phone off its charger cord and punching some buttons on the QWERTY. "We're not the ones you need to talk to," she said, handing it to me. "Now, I really do have to leave this time, so I'll catch you later, baby cakes. People? *Vamanos.*"

At once, the room erupted into a round of goodbyes, and then they left me alone with phone in hand. I sighed at it, examining the screen where Laura had pulled up "Abram Saru" from her list of contacts.

I bit my lip, a mounting smile twisting at the corner of my mouth. What was it that Wendell had said? I think it was something about joy. *What ignites your spirit? That's how you know it's right.*

Epilogue

I'd lost track of how many students I taught. There'd been no point in being so precise until now, and it was crazy how much I was going to miss them—perverted old men and neurotic children alike. But I would have new students now, and I'd just have to find a way to do my job from a new place, under different circumstances.

As goodbye tokens, I'd received various thoughtful items from my students: a songbook collection from Peter, for instance. And when the Fitzpatricks learned I was leaving, they'd surprised me with a year's worth of concert tickets to the best classical music venue in Philadelphia.

I was incredibly attached to Samantha, and it was so hard to leave her—almost as hard as it was to leave my mom, but that's what trains, planes, and automobiles were for.

Presently, only Abram, Katrina, and Anna Wright knew of my plan, and they'd promised to keep it a secret from Christian until I got there. Abram was especially happy about this idea, mentioning something about how much he loved surprises.

Maybe it was just me, but the trip to Pennsylvania took an eternity. I'd had to stop at a few motels along the way, updating my secret informants of my whereabouts, and now, after days on the road, I was finally nearing my destination.

"You seriously need to be here like yesterday, because he's dying to go out," Trina complained over the phone. "You have no idea what sort of shameful lies we had to tell him so he'd stick around for the weekend. But we had no choice. He's kept so busy since he came back that I don't think he takes time to breathe anymore."

"Well, I'm just down the road. I can see the house from here."

"Good. I'm going, then."

I parked several cars down from the familiar Victorian, smiling as my stomach fluttered around like mad. For once, this was a welcome feeling. It meant I was close to him.

The porch was empty, though I'd half-expected the girls to be there. They were obviously taking their job seriously, keeping up the façade. So I climbed the steps alone, trembling pathetically. This was a huge decision for me. I, Nicole Abbot, had waved goodbye to California so that I could move to a city on the complete opposite side of the country. I'd abandoned my security blankets and guilt complexes, and I was about to jump, heart first, into something I needed more than anything else. My own life.

The younger crowd still inhabited their own half of the house, so I approached the left side door. It had a lovely old knocker in the shape of a lion's head right in the middle, but I passed up the *Scrooge* prop and rang the bell instead.

With a wooden creak, the door opened, and I was met by a devastatingly handsome British man wearing a bewildered stare. Christian didn't seem to comprehend what he was seeing.

"Any chance you're still interested in buying some cookies?" I asked him.

He gave no warning—not a word uttered or even the smallest sound—before he attacked, before the world was nothing but arms and hands, desperate lips and kisses that could never be deep enough, never be long enough. But we would try to keep up.

ACKNOWLEDGMENTS

To my friends and family, who I hold dear and value more than words can say. Thank you for the unconditional love.

To my editor, who knows the spirit of this series as well as I do. Your kindness and patience is a gift.

And to Elizabeth, because of your vision and your faith.

ABOUT THE AUTHOR

Jennifer DeLucy is the author of Seers of Light, the first book in The Light Series, as well as a freelance editor. Jennifer grew up in the valley city of Scranton, Pennsylvania, where she developed an obsession with all things literary and musical thanks to the influence of an extroverted and creative family. Currently living in the Midwest, Jennifer continues to pursue opportunities as an author, editor and musician. She is determined to put her love of the arts, nature and spirit to good use, broadening minds and opening hearts in every way she can.